Clare Connelly was raised in small-town Australia among a family of avid readers. She spent much of her childhood up a tree, Mills & Boon book in hand. Clare is married to her own real-life hero, and they live in a bungalow near the sea with their two children. She is frequently found staring into space—a surefire sign that she's in the world of her characters. She has a penchant for French food and ice-cold champagne, and Mills & Boon novels continue to be her favourite ever books. Writing for Modern is a long-held dream. Clare can be contacted via clareconnelly.com or at her Facebook page.

Kim Lawrence lives on a farm in Anglesey, with her university lecturer husband, assorted pets who arrived as strays and never left, and sometimes one or both of her boomerang sons. When she's not writing she loves to be outdoors gardening, or walking on one of the beaches for which the island is famous—along with being the place where Prince William and Catherine made their first home!

THE SECRET
SHE MUST TELL
THE SPANIARD

CLARE CONNELLY

THE PRINCE'S
FORBIDDEN
CINDERELLA

KIM LAWRENCE

MILLS & BOON

First published in Great Britain 2023
by Mills & Boon, an imprint of HarperCollins*Publishers* Ltd,
1 London Bridge Street, London, SE1 9GF

www.harpercollins.co.uk

HarperCollins*Publishers*
Macken House, 39/40 Mayor Street Upper,
Dublin 1, D01 C9W8, Ireland

The Secret She Must Tell the Spaniard © 2023 Clare Connelly

The Prince's Forbidden Cinderella © 2023 Kim Lawrence

ISBN: 978-0-263-30665-1

02/23

MIX
Paper | Supporting
responsible forestry
FSC™ C007454

This book is produced from independently certified FSC™ paper
to ensure responsible forest management.
For more information visit: www.harpercollins.co.uk/green.

Printed and Bound in Spain using 100% Renewable Electricity
at CPI Black Print, Barcelona

THE SECRET
SHE MUST TELL
THE SPANIARD

CLARE CONNELLY

MILLS & BOON

CHAPTER ONE

'I'M SO SORRY, I…' The apology died on Alicia Griffiths' lips as she looked up, and up, past a broad chest, wide shoulders and tanned neck, into a face that was not only familiar to her but burned into her retinas.

Despite the fact ten years had passed, there was no mistaking the man before her.

Graciano Cortéz.

The ground beneath her feet seemed to give way. She lifted a hand to the fine necklace she wore, looping her finger through the chain and pulling it from side to side, her throat constricted, making speech almost impossible.

'Alicia.' His surprise was evident, but he recovered far quicker than she did, his obsidian eyes narrowing, regarding her slowly, scanning her face first—from the tip of her pale hair to her wide-set green eyes, to her curving pink lips—and then lower, to the décolletage that was exposed by the silk evening gown she wore. She'd already been a bundle of nerves—the night was the biggest charity gala she'd organised and she'd put a lot of pressure on herself to raise a small fortune. But seeing Graciano tipped her completely off balance.

'What are you doing here?' she blurted out. True, she hadn't seen a guest list for two days—once all the tickets were sold, she hadn't been particularly interested in who was coming, only that the usual high-flying donors were registered to bid in the charity auction. But she would have noticed Graciano's name on the list, which meant he was a late addition.

'Last I checked, it's a free country,' he drawled, his voice rich with authority and mockery, his accent so familiar to her that her toes curled inside her shoes. Everything inside her pinched together. This man— he was a sinkhole. He always had been. But it was so much worse than that, now. He was also the father to her daughter. Their daughter—a child he knew nothing about, because he'd made it impossible for Alicia to contact him after that one awful, heart-destroying morning in Seville.

'Did you come here to see me?' she asked, confused by his appearance after ten years. Good Lord, was it possible he knew about Annie? Had he come to confront Alicia? To take Annie away? All the heat drained from her face as the possibility of that scored deep into her heart.

'What reason could I possibly have for wanting to see you, Alicia?'

Her eyes widened at his obvious scorn, and even when she knew she should be *glad*, because it meant he didn't know the truth, it only made her more on edge.

The last time she'd seen this man, he'd been eighteen years old—still a teenager, but with more determination in his little finger than most people had in their whole bodies. There had to be a reason for him being at the auction.

'You tell me,' she suggested, casting a quick glance over his shoulder. She needed to get towards the stage, but her feet felt almost glued to the ground.

'No reason,' he said firmly, lips compressed. 'Ten years ago, I swore you were the last person I wanted to see, and my opinion has not changed.'

She flinched at the coldness in his tone. That morning in Seville, her father's words, what he'd accused Graciano of—it was burned into her mind. How many nights had she dreamed of that, had she wished she'd done something, said something? Instead, she'd taken her father's side and watched this man be eviscerated, bullied and then sent packing. Never mind that she'd tried to apologise, to explain. That she'd tried to tell him about the child they'd conceived.

He'd removed Alicia from his life completely, and she couldn't fault him for that.

'It was a long time ago,' she said quietly, even when that wasn't really true. Annie made their past very, very relevant.

'Yes,' he agreed with a shrug. 'If you'll excuse me, my date is waiting.'

Before she could stop herself, she glanced over her shoulder to see a leggy redhead emerge from the ladies' room and swish her curling hair over one shoulder, then strut towards Graciano as though she were on a catwalk and not in a hotel ballroom corridor.

'Graciano—' Alicia said his name with a frown. What could she add? Annie was at the forefront of her mind. She'd tried to tell him, but as he'd become more and more successful, it had become impossible to contact him. Eventually, she'd given up trying and come to terms with the fact that even if she'd told him, he wouldn't have wanted anything to do with a child of Alicia's. But now? He was right in front of her. Alicia surely had an obligation to find a way to break the news to him?

And then what?

Risk a custody dispute if she'd been wrong?

With someone this rich and powerful?

'I—'

His glare was withering, his hands in his pockets a casual stance that was belied by the taut lines of his muscular frame.

'Could you meet me for a drink later?' she said softly, knowing that no matter how terrified she was of telling him, it was the right thing to do. She certainly needed to at least get to know him again now she had this opportunity, to work out what her next step should be. After all, Annie had to be her number one priority. Whatever debt she owed Graciano had been watered down by his refusal to take her calls, and then by him changing his number to be sure she got the message, loud and clear.

'No.'

His bald refusal made her stomach drop to the ground. She hadn't anticipated that.

'Give me ten minutes.'

'It is a long time since I've felt I needed to "give" you anything,' he ground out, and she knew then that the passage of time hadn't watered down his feelings at all. He was as angry with his treatment now as he had been then.

And little wonder. Her father had berated the man for nearly thirty minutes, hurling every insult in the book at him, and Alicia had stood there, silent, by her father's side, complicit in the abuse because she'd stood there and said nothing. She could still remember the look on Graciano's face as he'd turned to her. She'd known he'd been waiting for her to defend him, to explain that it hadn't been sexual assault at all, but a relationship.

And Alicia hadn't been able to bring herself to incur

her father's anger. She'd put self-preservation above everything else, even Graciano.

For anyone, that would have been a deal breaker, but for a man like Graciano, who was as proud as the sun was hot, who'd been mistreated and abandoned almost all his life, her rejection had been unforgivable.

'Please.'

His eyes narrowed at the softly voiced word, and her spine tingled from the base of her head to the curve of her bottom. The redhead was almost level with them now; Alicia knew the window was closing. But if he'd come to the ball, then her assistant would have his contact information. She didn't have to do *anything* tonight.

'Never mind,' she said after a beat, shaking her head a little so a clump of smooth blond hair fell over her eyes. She lifted a hand to move it, and her skin lifted in goosebumps as his gaze followed the gesture. 'It doesn't matter.'

He dipped his head in silent agreement, and before she could say another word, he turned, placed an arm around the redhead's waist and led her deeper into the ballroom, where the festive scene was completely at odds with the churning sensation deep in Alicia's gut.

The door to her past had just cracked open, and she had no choice but to step through it.

There was not a lot that held the power to surprise Graciano Cortéz. But the truth was, ten years after being thrown out of Alicia Griffiths' home, he'd truly believed he'd never seen her again. He believed she no longer held power over him, that he was beyond her reach. He believed she was dead to him.

As she stood on the stage before him, the bolt of recognition spiking in his spine belied that—the same bolt that had almost sheared him in half in the corridor twenty minutes earlier.

A decade ago, in that brief, halcyon time of his life, he'd thought for a moment that he'd found his feet, that someone had accepted him just as he was—loved him, even. Someone had made him smile, and laugh, and trust, and all of the things he thought were dead inside of him she'd brought back to life. Not effortlessly. He'd built his protective shielding brick by brick, and he'd tried to hold on to it in the face of her attention, but little by little, she'd drawn down his guard.

Which was why that morning had been so powerfully awful.

Bitterness washed over him, as memories of his foolish mistake hammered through his brain.

You're worthless, boy, pure street scum through and through, and you always will be. Always. You're dead to me. Now get the hell off my land before I call the police.

Even now, ten years later, the ugliness of that morning had the ability to tighten the nerves in Graciano's body, to flood his body with adrenaline and fill his mouth with a metallic taste.

At the first test of his true sentiment, Edward had thrown Graciano out, back onto the streets, with no care for how that rejection might impact him. And Alicia had watched, silent, choosing to lie to her father rather than admit that the sex had been consensual, that they were in—no, not love. It hadn't been that. At the time, he'd thought it was, but he'd been a stupid, foolish teenager, looking for something that didn't exist.

It had been hormones, lust, desire, the pleasure and temptation of the forbidden fruit, one of the oldest seduction tools of all time. He'd wanted her because he couldn't have her. Love wasn't a part of it. As for Alicia, she'd thrown him under a bus, letting her father accuse him of rape and throw him back onto the streets. She'd moved closer to Edward, slid her hand into the crook of the minister's arm, making it clear that she had no intention of speaking the truth.

She'd betrayed Graciano. He'd learned a lot from her and her father, and ever since, he'd kept people at arm's length as though his life depended on it.

He ground his teeth together, watching intently as she strode onto the stage, replaying their brief interaction. Her smile was self-conscious. Because of him?

Graciano tightened his grip on his knee, sitting as still as a piece of stone as she moved to the lectern.

'Good evening.' Her eyes swept the crowd. Looking for him?

That she was older was obvious. She was more sophisticated and womanly, her bearing far less mischievous than that of the sixteen-year-old he'd followed around like a puppy dog when he was, himself, only eighteen. Her hair, rather than being a tumble of coarse blonde curls that flopped wildly down her back, was still fair, but far sleeker, pulled back into an elegant ponytail that glistened as she moved her head. Her makeup was impeccable—the Alicia he'd known had never worn anything cosmetic. Her father would have never allowed it for his little girl.

Objectively, she was beautiful, but she always had been. Despite his hatred of her, Graciano had felt old feelings of desire stir in his gut that had made him want to lean forward and brush her loose hair from her face, to let his fingers drift over her cheeks. He'd wanted to touch her soft lips with his hand, then his mouth—beneath his breath, he uttered a curse.

Ten years had passed since they'd touched one another, and he'd been with enough women since then to know how to indulge his body's wants. But this was different.

He didn't simply desire Alicia.

It was darker than that.

He felt a compulsion to be with her, to remind her of what they'd shared before her father had ruined it. To make her admit it had meant something. Until that moment, he hadn't realised how much he needed that.

Her father had hurt him, yes, but it had been Alicia's rejection that had irrevocably broken something inside of him. She'd acted as though he meant nothing to her. She'd acted as though he didn't matter, and suddenly, it was the most important thing in Graciano's life to make her admit that hadn't been the case.

'Thank you all for coming.' Her voice trembled a little and he leaned forward, wondering if it was the effect of seeing him again that had unnerved her. 'This is the fourth year I've had the privilege of organising the annual McGiven House charity auction, and the first in which I'll be taking part,' she added with a wry grimace, finding her confidence as she went on. The crowd cheered loudly. She lifted her hands placatingly, effortlessly charming and modest in a way he took to be studied. After all, the rapturous response spoke of an established acceptance of the fact that she was in high demand.

He leaned ever so slightly forward in his seat, oblivious to the people at his table, including his date—who, in that moment, he couldn't even remember the name of.

'Never fear, I will *not* be your MC for the evening,' she said with a soft laugh that sent a thousand arrows firing through his skin. That laugh had brushed over him, breathing across his body, teasing him, promising him, taunting him, demanding of him, just as it always had.

Could you meet me for a drink later?

He pressed his fingers into his thigh with more strength. The invitation had blurted out of her mouth, and he'd been so tempted to agree—which was why he'd immediately, harshly, responded in the negative.

He dropped his head forward, his breath strained, and he felt his date cast him a curious look. It sobered Graciano, and he remembered an important lesson he'd learned many years ago: never reveal your feelings. Keep your cards close to your chest. Never show them how you feel.

Never let them know you're hurting.

Never let anyone see your pain.

He straightened, renewed determination in his eyes as he focused with laser-like intensity on the stage, waiting with the appearance of calm as the charity auction proceeded, many valuable items being offered to the delighted audience. The sums attained by each lot were truly eye watering, reflecting both the value of the listings as well as the worthiness of the cause: McGiven House offered respite accommodation to those fleeing domestic violence. It was a cause close to Graciano's heart—he had personally donated millions of euros to charities such as this, and yet it never felt like enough.

Until he could forget what it was like to go to bed starving and afraid, he would never feel that he'd done what was necessary.

Graciano went through the motions for the evening, making conversation where necessary, even as every cell in his body was focused on the last lot of the night—Alicia herself—and an idea began to take hold.

A foolish idea, one he knew he shouldn't credit, yet couldn't ignore.

As he watched her, so effortlessly graceful and charming, convincing everyone that her heart was made of pure gold, all he could think of was her actions towards him, of how easy she found it to see him cast out onto the street once more, of how that rejection had stung him to the core.

Graciano didn't make decisions based on emotional impulses; it wasn't wise. But in that moment, it was a thirst for revenge, a need for retaliation, that had his insides firing to life with determination. Ten years ago, she'd destroyed his trust, and even though he'd moved on and built a hell of a life for himself, the effects of her treatment had spread through his life like poisoned tentacles, and he sought—needed—an exorcism of sorts.

He wouldn't have sought her out, but given that they'd crossed paths once more, he refused to look a gift horse in the mouth.

Alicia Griffiths would be his, and he'd make her admit how wrong she'd been to discard him as though he were trash.

'Remind me why I let you talk me into this?' Alicia muttered to her assistant, casting her a pleading look as the second-to-last auction item entered a frenzied bidding war. It had been nerve-racking enough *before* she'd known Graciano was in the audience.

'Because you are altruism itself,' Connie said with a wink.

'Yes, yes, but I'm *behind-the-scenes* altruism. Auctioning myself off is madness.'

'Firstly, you're auctioning your considerable experience as an events planner, not yourself. Secondly, it's far too late to back out. I happen to know Maude Peterson is desperate to secure you for her granddaughter's wedding and has her chequebook at the ready.'

Alicia raised a single brow, but she was distracted. 'A wedding, hmm?' That would require her to put aside her innate disbelief in the idea of *happily ever after*— or at least, pretend to.

'A very expensive English country wedding with a list of well-heeled guests who would all be excellent donors to our charity,' Connie pointed out, bringing Alicia's attention back to the current scenario.

'I don't think I can tout for donations at a wedding.'

'No, but Maude is a gossip and she's bound to tell everyone about the charity.'

'Yes, that's true.' Alicia pulled her lips to one side, eyes skimming the audience as her stomach flipped and flopped. Just the idea that Graciano was there, that he'd be watching her, made her feel a thousand kinds of strange.

Butterflies filled her belly as the auctioneer raised his gavel. Her eyes flitted to the screen behind him, blinking with surprise at the huge amount the first-class trip to New York—donated by a footballer—had achieved. Well above the ticket price, but of course, it wasn't just flights and premier accommodation: the internationally famous sports star had offered to cook dinner for the winners and host them in his home—a truly generous donation. Everyone was doing their bit, and now it was Alicia's turn.

Besides, taking a week of annual leave and using it to plan an event for some rich socialite was hardly arduous. She could plan any event in her sleep, and it would be nice to turn her skills to something other than charity dinners, fun runs and auctions.

The auctioneer began to introduce Alicia, reading the bio Connie had provided:

'Alicia Griffiths is a name known to all of us for her tireless work at McGiven House. Since joining the organisation four years ago, she's more than trebled the charity's income and raised the profile, enabling us to expand our offerings fourfold. In practical terms, that means we help a lot more people because she's put us in a position to do so. Prior to joining McGiven House, Alicia worked for the Royal Family as a protocol and events officer, and now, her pedigree and skills as an event planner are available to you. Alicia is generously offering one week of her time to arrange whatever event you have in mind. Be it corporate or personal, her work will be limited only by your imagination.'

The auctioneer turned to the side of the ballroom, where Alicia continued to wait in the wings. 'Alicia? Join me on stage.'

Her stomach was in a thousand knots and her knees were shaking. He was out there somewhere; that derisive curl of his lips haunted her as she walked on stage.

'You're sure I can't back out?' she muttered to Connie, only half joking as she took a step onto the stage.

'I'm sure.' Connie gave her a gentle nudge, pushing her the rest of the way. Alicia crossed to the auctioneer's side, glad that it was impossible to see out into the crowd because her nerves wouldn't have stood the idea of all those eyes staring back at her.

'Shall we start the bidding at ten thousand pounds?'

What if no one bid on her? And Graciano was there to witness her embarrassment.

'Ten thousand pounds!' She recognised Maude's voice and dipped her head forward in a smile. The wedding was clearly very special to the older woman. For a moment, Alicia felt a familiar pang, the same aching sense of longing whenever she was confronted with the love one family member had for another. How nice it must be to have someone prepared to fight your fights! But Alicia, in the end, had fought her own—was still fighting them, in fact. Being a single mother, even to a wonderful little girl, wasn't a walk in the park.

'Ten thousand pounds,' the auctioneer said after a brief pause that denoted surprise. He leaned forward on the lectern. 'Do I have fifteen?'

'Fifteen!' Another voice—a woman, but not instantly familiar to Alicia—entered the fray.

Before the auctioneer could respond, Maude chimed in. 'Twenty!'

Then another voice, male this time, and older. 'Twenty-five.'

Alicia turned towards Connie, her face a study in surprise. This had not been anticipated.

'Thirty!' Maude again. She really was determined.

'Thirty-five.' The other female voice.

'Fifty!' Maude shouted, and Alicia could just imagine the woman's determined expression.

'I have fifty thousand pounds for one week of Alicia's time.'

Alicia dug her fingernails into her palm. She was going to have to pull out all the stops for this bloody wedding: doves, rainbows, magic. It would have to be perfect.

Keeping a smile plastered on her face, with her heart beating so loud it filled her ears, she scanned the room. The lights were too bright to see clearly, but she knew he was out there, and it set fire to every nerve ending in her body.

'Fifty thousand pounds going once.' The auctioneer

paused dramatically—and without any real need. No way would anyone spend more than that for an events planner. 'Going twice.'

Alicia held her breath with the rest of the crowd. There was total silence. She waited for the gavel to drop, desperate for this to be over so she could scurry offstage, but in the seconds before, as the auctioneer lifted it, a voice rang out, clear and gruff, accented and immediately impactful, sending something inside Alicia rioting on a tumble of uncertainty.

'Five hundred thousand pounds.'

The silence gave way to murmurs of shock and Alicia lifted a hand to her lips. She recognised the voice instantly. Her heart leaped into her throat and she turned to the auctioneer, who was beaming with pleasure.

'Just to be sure I didn't mishear…was that five hundred thousand pounds?'

'Yes.'

Alicia stood there, in the middle of a world that had begun to spin far too fast on its axis. 'A generous offer indeed! Are you a registered bidder, sir?'

Alicia leaned closer once more and spoke automatically, her voice heavy with emotion. 'All ticket holders are pre-registered to bid.'

The auctioneer covered the microphone. 'Then it's binding.'

Alicia turned to face the crowd, her lips parted with shock. Silently, she pleaded with Graciano, wherever he was, to rethink this. But it was too late. Such a generous offer was going to be snapped up by the auctioneer, who rushed to drop the gavel. Alicia flinched, eyes huge as she stared out at the crowd.

'Ladies and gentlemen, what a truly exceptional evening. Those of you lucky enough to secure an item, or person—' he turned to Alicia and grinned '—please leave your details and payment at the administration booth near the door within the hour. Collection will be arranged Monday morning.'

Alicia waited by the administration desk with nerves that wouldn't calm down. Five hundred thousand pounds? What on earth had he been thinking?

She paced behind the desk as other winners came and signed contracts, obligating them to make payment for their items, or left cheques, all of which Connie would oversee in the office Monday morning. She waited and her eyes skimmed the crowd—more visible now the lights had softened—looking for Graciano. Maybe she could get him to change his mind?

But the idea of losing that money for the charity tightened around her throat like a noose. She couldn't do that.

'This is a mistake,' she said to Connie as she stalked behind the table. 'I can't... This is... We should approach Maude and see if she's still happy to pay—'

'That will not be necessary.'

With her back to the room, Alicia froze, all the colour and warmth draining from her face as his voice wrapped around her, strangling her, shocking her, so her heart felt as though it had been electrocuted.

'Connie.' It was a strangled plea, but for what? What did she want her assistant to say or do?

'Good evening, sir. Are you the lucky winner of Miss Griffiths' services?'

She barely heard Connie's question. Her ears were ringing and her mind was in free fall at the realisation that not only Graciano was here, but that he'd *bid* on her.

'Yes.'

'Wonderful. And what was your name, sir?'

Alicia turned slowly, bracing herself to come face to face with him again, this time with the knowledge he'd just pledged an exorbitant amount for a week of her time.

'This is Graciano Cortéz, Connie,' Alicia said quietly.

A thousand billion feelings slammed into her like an out-of-control train.

Her face was ashen, her eyes haunted when they met his, but only for a moment. She rallied quickly, imposing a cool mask to her features, but oh, how it cost her. What was he thinking? He'd swiftly declined even the idea of a drink, of ten minutes of shared airspace, and yet he'd bid an outrageous amount on her event-organising skills?

'Someone you know?' Connie asked.

She was quick to dispute that. 'Just someone I spent time with many years ago.' It felt important to delineate the past from their present. She ignored the mockery that shifted on his face, a mockery she immediately understood, because she understood *everything* about Graciano Cortéz, and probably always would.

'I see.' Connie frowned.

Alicia infused a note of disdain into her voice; after all, what more did he deserve? 'I take it you have an event you'd like me to organise?'

His eyes narrowed almost imperceptibly. 'Correct.'

'I see. Well, if you leave your details with my assistant, Connie, I'll be in touch once the payment has cleared.'

'I'll require you to start Monday.'

'Monday?' Alicia stared at him, momentarily forgetting she was supposed to be unflappable. 'Why so soon?'

'The event is at the end of the month.'

'How come you haven't arranged it already?'

'I wasn't aware my five hundred thousand pounds also bought me an inquisition. Can you do it, or not?'

Alicia shot Connie a look of disbelief and Connie's own features reflected bemusement. 'You have two meetings, but I can move them back a week...'

It was not the answer Alicia wanted.

'What is your name?' Graciano's attention shifted to Alicia's right.

'Connie.'

'My assistant will send an itinerary to you tomorrow morning, Connie. I will require Ms Griffiths' services for five nights. Her flight will leave first thing Monday morning.'

'Hold on a second.' Alicia needed to draw breath. For a moment, she was sixteen again, all her hopes and wants and dreams centred around this man, and the reality of how far life had taken her from him, of how far from one another they were now, almost made her physically ill. Would her sixteen-year-old self ever have understood that they could speak so coldly to one another? For a time, he'd truly felt like the other part of her. But it had just been a childish dream, nothing more. 'A week of my time means a week of my time, not... I can't... You're not seriously expecting me to go to Spain with you?'

'I presume my five hundred thousand pounds buys me your undivided attention?'

'Well, yes, but I can give you that from my office at home—'

'No.' He responded coldly, but with obvious determination. 'The event is to take place on my island, and so, too, should the planning. You cannot possibly arrange what is necessary without seeing the place for yourself. If you want my money, accept these terms.'

Her jaw dropped.

'Mr Cortéz.' Connie tried to imbue a little formality back into the conversation. 'That is not the way these things usually—'

'My donation is not usual,' he said with the confidence of a man who was completely right. 'This is the deal. Take it or leave it.'

Every fibre of Alicia's body willed her to reject it—to tell him to go to hell. A week on Graciano's island? She wasn't crazy. She wasn't stupid. But she'd already tabulated what his half a million pounds could do—how many families it could help. There was no way she'd be the reason the charity lost his donation. Bitterness crept through her as she mentally moved the pieces of her life around. Diane would have Annie. Her schedule was hectic, even though she was only working part-time now—she volunteered extensively, and had a wide social circle. But Alicia knew she only had to ask and Diane would help. The older woman had become like a mother or grandmother to Alicia, the one person in her life she had been able to rely on since Annie was still growing inside of her.

It would be a wrench to be away from her daughter for five nights—they'd never been separated for more than a night, and even then only rarely and when necessary—but Annie was no longer a baby. At nine years old, she felt on the cusp of becoming a teenager already, her legs growing impossibly long and slim, her hair falling all the way to her waist, wild like Alicia's always had been, but chestnut brown rather than sunlight blonde.

Annie no longer pined for Alicia, calling for her in the middle of the night. She was a confident, well-liked girl who adored school and spoke with the maturity of a much older child. She would cope without Alicia for a week.

A pang of hurt resonated in Alicia's heart, even when she knew that independence was a good thing, really. It still felt like a betrayal of sorts.

She watched as Graciano reached into his pocket and withdrew his phone. 'I'll wire the money now, if I have your agreement.'

How on earth did he become so ridiculously wealthy?

An image of him on that last day formed in her mind, as clear as if it were a photograph: scruffy running shoes, old jeans, a loose T-shirt. Her throat ached. Even with his second-hand clothes, he'd always carried himself with confidence and class. He'd always been destined for more than the life he'd found himself living. The question wasn't how he'd made his fortune, but why she'd ever doubted him.

'Alicia?' Connie frowned at her boss, obviously picking up on Alicia's ambivalence and hesitating in response.

Alicia stared at Graciano, wishing she understood him as well now as she had then. What was he thinking? What did he want?

'It's a very generous donation, Mr Cortéz.' She deliberately kept them on a more businesslike footing, but his lip curled with a hint of derision—lips that had dragged over her body, tasted her most intimate flesh, teased her breasts, left purple circles on her skin from where he'd sucked her until she'd cried out. Heat flushed her face and she looked away quickly. 'Connie will handle the formalities. If you'll excuse me, there's someone I have to speak to.'

'You're really going to Spain? For a week?'

It was impossible to meet Annie's intelligent, inquisitive eyes. A new kind of guilt, most unsavoury, flooded Alicia, to look at the little girl who was so like the father she'd never met—the father who'd made it clear he didn't want to hear from Alicia ever again.

Until last night.

She was baffled and she was terrified in equal measure as choices she'd made as a scared, abandoned sixteen-year-old were suddenly raised to the light, making her question everything she'd once chosen.

She'd *tried* to tell him, she reminded herself. She hadn't wanted this. She hadn't chosen this. Nonetheless, the fact she had borne Graciano's baby and raised her for nine years suddenly felt like a crime.

'Mummy?'

Mummy. Alicia's heart clutched. Not such a pre-teen yet, then.

Tears lodged in her throat as she made herself look into her beloved daughter's eyes directly. She was all tucked up in her still very childish bed, in the small pale pink room at the top of the stairs.

'Well, darling, it's supposed to be five nights, but I'm going to try my hardest to get home sooner. Do you think you'll be okay?'

Annie wrinkled her nose, snuggling deeper into the pillows. 'You do know Didee lets me eat ice cream *before* dinner when you're not here.'

Alicia laughed. 'Is that why we never seem to have any left in the freezer when I go looking?'

'No, that's because Didee has two huge bowls all to herself,' Annie corrected, and Alicia's heart panged. 'What's Spain like?'

Visions of sunshine flooded her thoughts, of oranges picked straight from the tree and eaten while still warm, crystal clear water, rolling hills, clay buildings, music that breathed life into your soul, the kindest people in the world… Graciano when he'd first arrived, all skin and bone with angry, dark eyes and fascinating, capable hands, so silent at first, so cold, that she couldn't help but want to make him smile.

'It's beautiful.' Her voice was croaky.

'How long did you live there?'

'Five years.' She cleared her throat. 'We moved right after your grandmother—my mother—passed away.'

'Where exactly?'

'Your grandfather had a property outside of Seville, and a church on the edge of the city.' The mission had been attached to the church, caring for homeless kids, of which there'd been a large number.

'Will you go to Seville?'

'Not on this trip.'

'Will you see your father?'

Anger flattened Alicia's lips but she avoided expressing it to her daughter. 'No, darling. I don't think so.' She'd been careful not to colour Annie's opinions of the minister, but as the little girl grew older, she had naturally shown more curiosity. One day, Alicia would have to be honest about the rift that had formed between them, about the way her father had thrown her away, so disappointed in her for becoming pregnant at sixteen that he hadn't been able to continue living with her.

You are my greatest failure, Alicia.

One day, she'd tell her daughter that Edward

Griffiths, admired and respected man of faith, had threatened to press charges against Graciano if Alicia ever spoke to him again. That threat had hung over her head for years. As a girl, she'd believed it unfailingly, and even now, as an adult, she credited the cynical likelihood of Edward's words.

That boy from the streets, with no family and no one to speak for him, took advantage of you in my *home. No police officer or judge is going to believe him. He will rot in jail for this. Just give me the excuse to do it and I will. He deserves it.*

'Why not?'

She was dragged back to the present, her palms sweaty, her heart quickening.

'I'm going for work, and I'm not going to waste a moment doing anything other than work, because I'll be so desperate to come home to you.' She leaned forward and pressed a kiss to Annie's forehead. 'Di will pick you up from school tomorrow,' she said. 'And I'll see you Saturday morning for football, okay?'

'We're playing Ridgehaven.'

'I know.' Alicia smiled, standing, doing her best to hide the distracting direction of her thoughts.

'They're really good.'

'Yes, but so are you.' She tousled her little girl's vanilla-scented hair. 'Go to sleep, darling. I'll see you in the morning.'

Graciano's eyes chased the rolling waves as though he could find meaning in their rhythm, as though the depths of the sea might help him gain clarity, but there was none. He stared at the sea, all the questions that usually plagued him swirling and churning—and central to those questions was where was his brother? He thought again of yet another thwarted lead, of hopes raised then dashed, of the compounding certainty that he was all alone on this earth, his entire family lost to him forever.

He'd come to accept that reality.

But seeing Alicia again had stirred everything up, had made him remember a time when he'd hoped for a new family, when his heart had begun to crack open, just a little.

Only for it to slam shut in spectacular fashion, never to be opened again.

The decision to invent a function for her to organise had been spontaneous and immediate, yet he didn't regret it. Graciano trusted his instincts, and the moment he saw her again, he'd known it was long past time for her to reckon with how she'd treated him.

Lately, he'd been thinking of his brother again. Of his parents. Of a childhood that shimmered on his horizon like blades of sunshine— ephemeral and striking, warm and impossible to grab hold of. His mother's laugh, his father's voice, his brother's little body, his hand slipping into Graciano's to hold as they crossed the road, walking to school.

He'd been loved, and he had loved deeply, and then he'd lost, in the most horrific of circumstances. He could vividly recall the sound of metal on metal as their car was hit and pushed into the railing on the side of the road.

He closed his eyes, pushing those thoughts away, ignoring the throbbing feeling deep in his gut, a yearning for something he'd lost long ago that could never be replaced.

Graciano was a pragmatist. He couldn't get his brother back, he couldn't save his parents and he couldn't find his way back to his family, but he had all the money in the world, and on this one occasion, he could use it to right at least one wrong of his past: he could make Alicia eat crow, and that was a delight he intended to savour…

CHAPTER TWO

IT WAS A RELIEF, Alicia told herself, that Graciano hadn't appeared at London City Airport to meet her on Monday morning. It was also a relief that he hadn't been onboard the extremely luxurious private jet that had carried her from London to an airstrip in Valencia, and from there to a sleek, white helicopter that had lifted up over the Balearic Sea, conveying Alicia the short distance from mainland Spain to a cluster of islands a little to the east of the city.

The helicopter circled the cluster before moving closer to one, the largest of six, something that from the air, at first glance, looked like a place that time had forgotten. The forest was so verdant and sprawling it seemed almost prehistoric, but as the helicopter came in lower and offered a different vantage point, she saw that the western side of the island was more developed. A golf course was unmistakable, as well as a large, white-walled mansion with a central courtyard bursting with colourful vines, and several smaller buildings dotted away from the main house but joined to it via paved roads. Lower still they came, and she saw a fleet of golf buggies, some parked at the smaller cottages, others lined up on the side of the mansion. The beach was immaculate, all white sand and clear sea, and there were two swimming pools—one beside the house, and a smaller one surrounded by colourful trees and vines, but most inviting of all on a warm day like this was the ocean that glittered with the force of diamonds, making her ache to wade out to hip height, then dive beneath the surface.

How long had it been since she'd had a holiday?

Any kind of holiday?

She'd taken Annie to Cornwall when she was four, just for a weekend, but it had been perfect. They'd eaten ice cream and bought fish and chips, which they'd shared with dozens of hungry—or plain greedy— seagulls, and walked through narrow, cobbled lanes while smiling at locals. But it had been short, and hardly exotic. This, though, was not a holiday, despite the picturesque location.

Not only was this a work trip, but she couldn't afford to forget that fact for even one moment. She had no idea why Graciano had done this, but there was no forgetting their past, and she couldn't ever relax around him.

The issue of their daughter was an ever-present nightmare, a ticking time bomb she knew she would have to face head-on, but had no idea how to.

The helicopter touched down on a paved circular area joined to the house by a path lined on either side with espaliered fruit trees. Graciano stood in the centre of the path, feet planted wide and arms crossed over his chest, his body language anything but welcoming. In fact, if he hadn't paid so much money for her expertise, and insisted on her coming to this island, she'd have said he was resenting her presence.

Well, that made two of them.

From the confines of the helicopter, she took a moment to observe him without being observed. Time had changed both of them, though she feared it had been much kinder to him. As an eighteen-year-old, Graciano had been slender—far too slender, courtesy of his life on the streets and too many skipped meals. He'd always been hypermasculine despite that, with a raw virility and confidence, but this was something else. His six-and-a-half-foot frame had filled out, so he stood muscular and strong, every inch of him conveying pure alpha male dominance. She knew enough about men's clothes to know that those he wore were the very best, though they weren't visibly branded. Their quality was obvious. He didn't go to any effort with his appearance; he was too much of a man's man for that, too focused on other things, but that didn't matter. Effort or not, he was, without a doubt, the most beautiful person she'd ever seen.

His face was remarkable.

It always had been.

Her heart leaped into her throat as she remembered the first day they'd met. A summer storm had crossed Seville. She'd been terrified of the lightning, and from her reading spot in the conservatory, it was louder and brighter than anywhere else in the house, only she couldn't get inside without crossing through the garden. Graciano had been working, pruning fruit trees, when he'd heard her scream. He'd told her later that it had chilled his blood. He'd thrown open the door and lightning had crashed behind him, but she was no longer afraid. She hadn't even seen it.

All of her had become focused on all of him.

He'd worn a singlet top and shorts that sat low on his hips, and his shoes had been old and saturated. But none of that had mattered. She was transfixed by him. His jaw was square, as if chiselled from stone, his cheekbones angular and sharp. Stubble covered his chin, and his eyes were the darkest brown she'd ever seen, rimmed in thick, black lashes that were made even more dramatic by the falling rain. His hair had become drenched, but he'd driven his hands through it, pushing it back from his face, which had only served to draw attention to his high, fascinating brow.

'Who are you?' she'd gasped, lifting a hand to her chest.

'Graciano. Are you hurt?'

It was so like him. He'd brushed aside the fact they didn't know one another and had concentrated only on the information he'd wanted. He'd taken control, even then, as a street kid with nothing and no one.

He was Graciano. All hail Graciano.

As he stood there now, she felt the same power emanating off him, the same unfaltering command of a situation, and she knew she had to do a better job of guarding against those feelings this time, or she'd be as fully under his spell as she had been back then.

The thought terrified her into action.

She unclipped her seatbelt and moved to the central door of the cabin, so that the moment it was opened and the stairs brought down she could disembark, in control and ready for business. To prove that point, she pulled her handbag over one shoulder, taking comfort from the weight of her laptop and notebook. Only at that exact moment, her eyes sought, of their own accord, Graciano, and the manoeuvre of pulling her strap threw her off balance, so that as she took the second step, her ankle twisted and rolled. She extended an arm on autopilot, her hand curling around the railing for a vital second before slipping, her knees crumbling. She righted herself, somehow, for another excruciating second, but the momentum was too great.

She tumbled to the ground and lay, splayed like roadkill, on the elegant herringbone red brick pavers.

'Great,' she muttered under her breath, the sting in her scraped knees nothing to the monumental hole in her pride. 'Just bloody great.'

To Alicia, it felt like a lifetime, but in reality, it took Graciano mere seconds to reach her. First, she heard his feet, not running, but walking with speed, and stopping right by her head, so she was greeted with obviously hand-stitched leather boots right in front of her face.

'Alicia.' He drawled her name with that awful cynicism of his.

Ignoring his proffered hand, cheeks flaming, she pushed up gingerly, her knees complaining as she moved, so she curled one hand around the railing and dragged herself halfway to standing before her ankle gave an almighty shot of pain and she let out a groaning sound, angry eyes piercing Graciano, as though he had somehow manipulated these circumstances.

'What is it?' he demanded again, and now, to her absolute chagrin, he put a hand around her back, steadying her, or at least, intending to steady her, but in reality it had the opposite effect, as a thousand blades shot through her body at his simple, light touch. His fingers splayed wide, forming a barrier over her hip. The movement somehow so intimate and familiar, and she was far too aware of him.

'Don't,' she hissed, pulling away from him, then yelping again when her ankle almost rolled once more. 'I've twisted my ankle,' she snapped, as though it were his fault.

'Evidently.'

'I saw a heap of golf carts when we were flying over. Maybe one of those could help me to the house?'

'That's not necessary.' Before she could intuit his meaning, he caught her around the waist and lifted her, cradling her against his chest as though she weighed nothing. It was an overwhelming moment. Ten years ago, they'd been lovers, but only once, only one night, and since then, they hadn't seen each other. She hadn't been touched by anyone. She'd been flirted with, asked out on dates, but no one had elicited a single frisson of warmth from her, let alone a full-blown fire.

Why the hell was it like this with them? Why did his touch send her nerves skittling all over the place?

She startled against his body, aware of every movement of his muscles, aware of his masculine fragrance, the stubble on his jaw.

'I'm sure I can walk,' she lied, earning a look of cynical mockery from him.

'Do you want me to put you down so you can try?'

He'd called her bluff, and damn it, they both knew the answer to that. Even if she hadn't found being in his arms powerfully addictive, her ankle couldn't possibly support her weight in that moment.

She didn't answer, focusing her gaze on the house in front of them instead. There was plenty to look at, and even more as they drew nearer to it. From the sky, it had been beautiful, but on the ground level, she could observe and appreciate many more features, like the windows that were carved into the walls, each boasting a terracotta window box overflowing with geraniums and sweet peas.

'It's stunning,' she said, before she could stop herself.

He walked slowly, each step long and confident, but the house felt like it was miles away. Each step bumped her against his chest, so her body was aware of him on a cellular level. She wanted this to end, she told herself forcefully, even when a part of her—a very small part—was transfixed by the power of this moment, by the strangest sense in the world that being in his arms was like…coming home.

As she'd noticed from the air, the house was square in shape, with a large central courtyard. When Graciano stepped through the double-width blue wooden door into a tiled hallway, she caught glimpses of the courtyard and almost swooned. She put it at the top of her list for further investigation, once her ankle permitted. The rooms were large with high ceilings. He carried her through the entrance way and into a living room with Moroccan-style tiles on the floor, a tapestry on the wall and mid-century lounges. It was an eclectic, stylish mix of furniture that she put down to an interior designer's eye rather than Graciano's.

When he reached the sofa, he placed her down onto it, releasing her immediately so she wanted to cry out at the desertion of his touch, but she tamped down on that instinct forcefully.

She'd fallen for this man once before; no way would she let their physical chemistry tempt her again. Things between them were too complicated to allow for any personal desire. Annie had to be her priority—working out how to deal with the fact they shared a daughter he knew nothing about.

With a mutinous expression, she nodded stiffly. 'Thank you.'

Surprisingly, he laughed, a sound that made her blood simmer. 'You sound as though you'd rather tell me to go to hell than thank me.'

She ground her teeth together. 'Can't they both be true?'

'Touché.'

'Why have you brought me here?' she asked, cutting to the chase. It was hard to have the high ground she'd sought from where she lay on the sofa, but it wasn't going to stop her from seeking to take control.

'You need to rest your ankle,' he pointed out, either accidentally or purposely mistaking her question. 'Stay here while I get some ice.'

'I'm fine,' she lied, waiting until he'd strode from the room before pulling up the hem of her trouser. She was relieved to see her ankle looked normal size, with no swelling that might indicate a sprain or a break. But when she thrust it over the edge of the sofa and tested her weight on it, the joint gave a sharp burst of pain.

Damn.

She lay back and stared at the ceiling before turning her head towards the windows that framed a picture-perfect view of the Mediterranean garden in the foreground and the glistening ocean just behind. It was a perfect day, sunny and warm, summer's pleasure all around her—except there was no pleasure here, just bitterness and danger, as the secret she'd held close to her chest for ten years was now something she was being forced to grapple with.

She'd had the luxury of pretending for the past decade. Pretending he didn't exist, pretending he'd forgotten all about her, pretending this was for the best. Pretending Annie didn't need to know about her father, that she was better off without him.

It was far easier to accept those sentiments when Graciano was an absent, abstract concept, rather than a flesh-and-blood man occupying the same space as her.

Given what had happened between them, and how it had ended, she knew she'd made the only decisions she could at the time, that she'd done what was necessary to give Annie a stable, steady home. She'd always done her best for Annie.

But that didn't negate Graciano's rights.

It didn't absolve her of guilt.

And being here with him threw all that in her face, so she wanted to close her eyes and weep.

He entered the room quickly, a linen tea towel in his hand. She half expected him to hand it to her, but instead he came to her side, bending to one knee as he moved a hand over the affected ankle. Only then did he pause, a moment, before touching her, before lifting the fabric of her trouser just as she'd done—only this time, a thousand sparks ignited in her bloodstream.

'It looks fine,' he said gruffly.

'Well, it doesn't feel it,' she said with a tilt of her chin.

His eyes shifted to hers and then returned to her ankle, his hand resting there, his fingers pressing against her skin. Slowly, he pressed his fingers deeper, his inspection clinical and swift, checking for breaks, but that didn't stop Alicia's pulse from exploding in her veins.

Her mouth was dry, making speech almost impossible.

'It does not seem broken.'

'No.' The word emerged as a husky plea.

'You must rest it.'

So much for taking control. Graciano issued the command and she felt her body immediately obeying. The touch of ice against her skin was an unwelcome

change—she wanted Graciano's hands back. The realisation terrified her.

She had to get a grip.

'Why don't you tell me about the event you want me
to organise?'

He stood, turning his back to her, walking towards
the window, silent for several beats of time, so she
asked, quietly, 'Graciano?'

'It's business,' he said, quickly. 'To mark a merger.
Nothing too big—around one hundred people. Food,
drinks, music. You know the sort of thing.'

She frowned. The details were a little scant for an
event that was only a month away. 'Are you imagining
people will stay on the island?'

'I haven't imagined anything.' He turned to face
her, his eyes hooded, revealing nothing. 'That's why
I bought you.'

'My services,' she corrected, mouth parched.

He dipped his head once in what she took as a nod.
'I'd like to see some concepts from you by Wednes-
day. I'll let you know which I like, and then you can
get organising.'

'You have a lot of confidence in my abilities.'

'Why do you say that?'

'To be able to organise something suitable for your
purposes in two days…'

'I do have confidence in your abilities,' he said after
a moment. 'Your reputation precedes you.'

Pleasure zinged across her spine. 'How do you know
about my reputation?'

'The charity auction,' he said with a casual shrug.
'The guests at my table spoke highly of you.'

'I see.' So he hadn't kept tabs on her.

Of *course* he hadn't, and for that, she should have

been immeasurably glad. If he'd done *any* looking into her over the years, he'd have known about Annie. And knowing about Annie would have led to him seeing a picture of her, and then it would have been impossible to ignore the connection.

A frown marred her beautiful face at the thought of that. She'd *wanted* him to know about Annie, at first. But then, years had passed and it had been impossible to imagine Annie as anyone's but hers, to imagine her life expanding to include Graciano. He deserved to be in Annie's life, but he'd made that impossible. This was his fault, not Alicia's. But that didn't mean the situation wasn't fraught. It didn't mean she could continue to ignore their connection now that they were here, on his beautiful island, and the opportunity to confide in him was ever present.

But what if that was the wrong choice for Annie? After all, what did she know about the man Graciano had become? Not enough to embroil him in Annie's life without a little thought and planning, without doing some…research. She owed her daughter that much. The thought of spending a week with Graciano had terrified her, but maybe it was an opportunity. To get to know the man he'd grown into, and ascertain what role he could play in Annie's life. As for the buzzing she felt whenever he came close to touching her, she'd simply have to ignore it.

Alicia stared at the window, eyes intent on a single tree while she forced her breathing back to slow and rhythmic.

'You are renowned for the events you manage.'

For ten years, she'd been almost able to push the thought of Graciano's paternity from her mind, but now, it was staring her in the face, an obligation she could

no longer outrun. Her reply emerged a little strained.
'Thank you.'

'I was not flattering you, so much as stating a fact. I
grew my business by capitalising on people's strengths.
I need an event organised in a hurry. You're capable of
making it brilliant.'

'And so you paid five hundred thousand pounds,'
she said with a shake of her head. 'That doesn't make
sense. Any number of event companies would have—'

'None were available on short notice.'

So he'd tried booking elsewhere? That deflated her
contentment a little.

'Why is it short notice?'

'The merger talks are moving more quickly than anticipated. The contracts will be signed this week and
the legalities should complete within a fortnight or so.'

'And why a party?' she prompted. 'Is that something you do every time you acquire a company? If
so, I should imagine you'd have an events coordina-
tor on staff.'

'Meaning?'

'Only that you buy so many businesses, it would
make sense.'

'And how do you know what businesses I acquire?'

Heat flamed her cheeks as her guilty secret—how
often she googled him—flooded her. 'You think you're
the only one whose reputation precedes them? Or do
you believe I'd come to a meeting in the middle of nowhere with a man I barely know without doing at least
a hint of research?'

'With a man you barely know? That's not how I
would categorise our relationship.'

'No?' She responded breathlessly, leaning forward
a little until her ankle gave a dull throb of pain and she

was forced to stay exactly where she was. 'Then how would you describe this?'

'Not having seen each other for many years does not change how well we know each other. How well we understand each other.'

She bit down on her lip. 'It was a long time ago.'

'And a lot has happened since,' he agreed, moving closer, eyes boring into hers, probing her, reading her. 'But have you ever forgotten?'

She gasped, the question lancing her with its directness, with its importance. 'Graciano—'

How could she answer? Danger surrounded her.

Think of Annie!

She had to do what was right for their daughter.

'You taught me so many lessons, Alicia, I have found it impossible to forget you.'

Her heart was beating so hard and fast it was all she could hear in her ears. 'What lessons?'

'How self-serving people can be, for starters. Even the beautiful, sweet-seeming ones.' He brushed his thumb over her jaw. 'Perhaps them most of all.'

She shivered, wrenching her face away, angered that even then, when his manner was derisive, his touch remained incendiary. 'What about me was self-serving?'

'Your silence, for one thing.'

She squeezed her eyes shut, because he was right. She'd listened to her father turn on Graciano and eviscerate him, to threaten to call the police and press charges for sexual assault, listened to her father ripping shreds off the man she'd loved, and she'd said nothing. She'd been mute, struck silent by the awful, mortifying position she'd found herself in. But then, when her father had threatened to go to the police if she ever contacted Graciano again, she'd closed off her heart, knowing she had to protect the man from the awful crime her father wanted to hang around his neck. Only when it had been imperative to speak to him had she taken that risk—not for herself, not because she'd missed him with all of herself, but because he'd had a right to know they'd made a baby. And deep down, because she'd believed he would be able to fix everything. Her heart strangled to remember the confused, terrified teenager she'd been then.

'Not everyone is as strong as you,' she said after a long, pained pause. 'My father was all I had—'

If anything, that seemed to make Graciano angrier. He made a dark sound of frustration and moved closer, crouching down beside her so their eyes were level.

'Your father accused me of raping you,' he reminded her, and the anguish in the depths of his eyes took her breath away. The accusation still had the power to hurt him. And little wonder! 'You said nothing to correct him. You let him think that of me.'

Shame sucked all the life from her cheeks. 'I told him the truth later. Afterwards.'

His eyes narrowed. Sceptically? 'Not that morning—not when it mattered.'

She shook her head slowly. 'He was so angry.'

'He had no right. We knew what we were doing.'

'We were little more than children.'

'So? What does that mean? Do you believe we made a mistake?'

How could she agree to that when Annie was the result? And even if there'd been no Annie, Alicia couldn't bring herself to regret anything about that night; it was only the morning she had wished, many times, to change.

He didn't wait for her to answer. Good, because she couldn't, anyway.

'I know you never thought I was good enough.'

She shook her head angrily. 'That's *not* true.'

'Just like your father, you were looking for a project.'

'Stop it,' she ground out, conscious of the hurt of his insults but also the closeness of his face. Of their own volition, her eyes dropped to his mouth, glorying in the outline of his lips even as she wanted to shove him backwards. How satisfying it would be to send him straight onto his butt.

'You are someone who looks to feel worthy by "helping" those less fortunate.'

'Is there something wrong?'

He ignored her interjection. 'That's what you were doing that summer, wasn't it?'

'It was ten years ago,' she said quietly, her heart splintering. She tried to stay focused on Annie, to remain calm in the face of his anger. 'Why does it matter?'

But it did matter. A decade might have passed but the pain of their parting was as much a part of her now as it had been then. She tried to blink away from him but her eyes felt trapped.

'True. And so much has happened since.' He lifted a finger, pressing it to her cheek, and she trembled, desire making her pulse frantic. 'We're different people now.'

They were. Ten years, nine of them spent sole parenting, almost completely on her own. Alicia was not the impressionable teenager who'd fallen in love with this man the moment she'd laid eyes on him.

'But that night, the pleasure you felt, that was real, wasn't it, Alicia?' He said her name how he used to, heavy with his Spanish accent, loaded with desire. Her skin lifted in goosebumps and she shuddered, desire making it impossible to think of or feel anything else.

He leaned closer, his mouth just an inch from hers.

'Do you remember when we first kissed?'

Her heart kicked up a notch. 'No,' she muttered.

His lips showed he saw that for the lie it was. 'It was in the library. You told me you needed help fetching a book that was on the top shelf. I retrieved it, and when I handed it to you, our fingers touched and you made a soft little gasp, before lifting up and looking at me, just as you are now, silently begging me to kiss you. Do you remember that?'

She shook her head, but to which question, to which assertion?

'You snapped your fingers and I came running.'

She frowned. He wasn't wrong. Graciano had always been there for her. Anytime she'd needed him, she'd only had to ask and he'd done whatever she required. But he was mischaracterising it, taking what she'd believed to be loyalty and…friendship…and turning it into something sinister and manipulative.

'You're acting as though what happened between us was a big deal,' she said, when she could trust herself to speak again. 'But *you* were the one who left without a backwards glance. You were the one who told me, in no uncertain terms, that you'd moved on with your life, to never call you again. You were the one who changed your number.'

'I did not change my number to avoid you,' he said.

'No, I'm sure by then you'd forgotten all about me.'

'Yes. But not the lessons you taught me.'

It stung as though she'd been whipped. 'If you'd truly forgotten about me, then why does it seem as though you hate me?'

A muscle throbbed at the base of his jaw, drawing her attention to it. 'I hate people like you, like your father—'

She flinched at that. 'You don't know me.'

'I know all I need to know.'

She swept her eyes shut, fighting a tsunami of pain that was unexpectedly strong. 'Then why hire me? And don't lie to me. This isn't because you need an event planned in a hurry.'

'Why can't it be both?' He lifted a hand slowly, as though trying to fight himself, to her ear, cradling it lightly. Sparks ignited. She swallowed hard, but moved closer, even when that brought them nose to nose.

'Both what?' She could barely speak, much less think.

'A way to kill two birds with one stone.'

'I don't understand.'

'I always told myself that if I ever saw you again, I'd cross to the other side of the street. Once was enough. I had moved beyond you, beyond your father, beyond that morning.'

Her heart twisted at the raw emotion in his words. 'Then why—'

'I was wrong.'

The admission seemed dragged from him.

'I still want you.'

She gasped, his words landing hard in her chest. 'Graciano—'

He moved his hand lower, pressing a finger to her lips. She tried to remember, to remember sense and logic and the fact they were parents to a daughter, that their situation was complicated, but in that moment, everything felt simple. A strong chemical urge was pushing her forward; to hell with their past.

'And you were there, offering yourself to the highest bidder. How could I not act on that opportunity?'

She swallowed, eyes huge when they met his. 'It's not… I'm not—'

'You're here to plan an event,' he said, moving his mouth to the pulse point at the base of her throat and pressing his lips there. 'But I have you here, in my home, for five nights, and I intend to make the most of them.'

CHAPTER THREE

'WHAT EXACTLY DOES that mean?'

Great question. Graciano had gone back and forth on this plan since it rammed itself into his damned head at the charity auction. Seducing Alicia for revenge appealed to him on so many levels, but it also disgusted him. It infuriated him that she still had any kind of power over him, even as he recognised he wanted to exert his own power right back over her.

To prove he was different to the lovesick eighteen-year-old she'd used and discarded. To show her that he'd grown into the kind of man she'd never thought he could be.

To make her want him as though he were her universe.

To walk away, as he had then, only this time memories of Alicia wouldn't torment his sleep, wouldn't make him want to weaken and return to her side because he'd be leaving her by *choice*.

This was his chance to show how far he'd come, how strong he now was. How completely in control. Revenge wasn't a particularly worthy emotion, but there was no other way to describe how Graciano felt, nor what he wanted. Was it petty, after ten years, to seek vengeance on a woman who'd moved on with her life, as he had his?

Something twisted in his gut, something dark and angry, something that made him face the truth of his character, something he hadn't known about himself. Yes, he would go to these lengths. Yes, he wanted revenge just this badly. Yes, he wanted to destroy her the way she'd destroyed him.

Because she had.

When her father had stood over Graciano and accused him of raping Alicia, Graciano had felt as though he'd been stabbed. He'd looked to her to speak some sense, to set her father straight, and she had only cowered, pinning herself to her father's side, the beautiful woman he'd made love to hours earlier someone he no longer recognised. She was a coward. She was a traitor. She had let Edward berate Graciano, calling him the worst names in the world, and she'd said nothing. Done nothing. When Edward had thrown Graciano off the property, telling him he'd call the police if he ever saw the eighteen-year-old again, she still hadn't said anything.

She'd chosen peace and her 'nice' life over truth, passion and Graciano, and he'd never forgotten that betrayal, nor forgiven her for it.

He hadn't thought of her consciously these past ten years, but the speed with which he'd sought his revenge made him wonder if he hadn't always wanted this, if he hadn't been looking for an opportunity to right the wrongs of the past.

It was petty, it was cruel, it was almost certainly something he'd regret, but Graciano was, as always, following his instincts. Heaven help him—levelling the score had never been so tempting.

Ten years ago, he'd been slow. Gentle. Cautious. He'd thought her fragile, and had been so wary of breaking her. They were both older and wiser now. He knew better.

'Graciano? What do you mean?' she repeated, with urgency, but her body remained where it was, close to him, so close he could breathe her in—so close he would have been in danger of losing himself, if such a thing were possible. Her sharp intake of breath and rapid exhalation brushed against his cheek. 'Graciano…'

There was so much he wanted to know and understand about this woman, so much he needed to comprehend in order to have closure. 'Why did you call me after I'd left?'

Her eyes fluttered closed, and he leaned in. One shift from either of them and their lips would brush. Her eyes opened and she started, but didn't move away from him. Her hand lifted, fingers pressed to his chest, and sensations rushed through Graciano. It was a worrying tilt away from control. He had to manage his needs, to master his wants. He wouldn't lose himself to her again.

'Why do you think?' Her eyes were pleading with his. 'I was mortified. I couldn't believe the things he'd said to you.' To his surprise, tears filmed her eyes. 'I couldn't believe I'd *let* him speak to you that way. But you have to understand—'

Sympathy was a danger he hadn't expected. He couldn't soften to her. 'I understand that you chose to let him think me a rapist rather than tell him the truth.'

'I did tell him the truth,' she said urgently, swallowing, her fingers curling in the fabric of his shirt. Surprise flashed through him, then swiftly, disbelief. He couldn't believe her—he didn't want to. 'I did. I just couldn't do it right then. I was too…shocked. Scared.'

Her breath smelled like vanilla. He inhaled it, his arousal jerking against the fabric of his boxers.

Hell, he hadn't wanted a woman this badly in a long time. Possibly not for ten years.

He ignored her claims. He couldn't process them. His body was in sensory overload. 'And did you think I'd come back to you?'

'No,' she whispered, shuddering. 'I knew it wasn't possible. He'd have never allowed it.'

'And you always do what your father wants.'

She blinked down, away from him, shielding her thoughts from his gaze. 'I was sixteen.'

'Old enough to give yourself to me,' he reminded her firmly.

'And so what? Did you think I'd run away from home to live on the streets with you because we slept together? Is that what you wanted?'

It was like being doused with ice-cold water, reminding him of where her true priorities had lain. She'd chosen her 'nice' life of comfort rather than to stand by him. She'd wanted material security instead of the loyalty and love he'd thought they shared.

'After that morning, I didn't want a thing to do with you,' he corrected without any emotion in his voice. 'I don't believe in second chances.'

She pulled back a little, but kept her hand in his shirt. 'I just…needed to speak to you.'

'And yet, your actions were the making of me, *querida*. I left Seville, I grew up, I changed. I forgot all about you.'

Her eyes barely met his. 'Good for you.'

'Yet here we are, ten years later, and I can't help but wonder…'

'What do you wonder?' she asked, unable to keep the husky note from her voice.

'What it would feel like to kiss you,' he said simply, eyes skimming hers, seeing the awakening there, the desire, unmistakable. 'Not as we were then—teenagers—but here, now, two adults, with experience behind us...'

'Graciano...' His name was a plea. For sanity, or seduction?

'Do you wonder the same?'

Her lips parted, and it was Alicia who moved closer now, her eyes hooked to his, uncertainty and fear in their depths, and a strange, angry mix of emotions in his gut that he would be ashamed to analyse later.

'I can't,' she said, so close to him he felt the words rather than heard them.

'You don't want to?'

She shook her head. 'It's complicated.'

'Is it? Why?'

Her lips quirked downwards. 'Because you're you,' she responded softly.

'We are completely alone here,' he said gruffly. 'Neither of us has to be ourselves for the next week.'

Her eyes widened.

'Besides, a kiss is just a kiss.'

She made a throaty sound, her fingers in his shirt twisting, holding on to him as if for dear life. 'I don't know if that's true.'

He'd never wanted to kiss a woman more. Not even Alicia, not even back then. There was a force at his back, a steel-like drive pushing him to her, and yet he held his ground, determined to triumph over even his own desire.

'I will not kiss you unless you ask it of me.'

She bit down into her lip. 'I can't do that.' Her eyes showed confusion. 'I won't. Graciano, our past—'

'The past is irrelevant to this,' he interrupted angrily, even when he knew the past had defined him in every way that mattered.

'Graciano…' Now his name was unmistakably a plea, and she leaned in, surrendering to him, so he exulted in the victory as he crushed his lips to hers, claiming her with all the need, anger and resentment that had stitched their way into his soul a long time ago.

Alicia almost jumped with the electrical current that arced inside of her when their lips touched. This was not a gentle kiss. It was not a kiss of two people reconnecting after years apart. It was a kiss of total dominance and, yes, of anger. She felt it in the bruising way he commanded her, demanded of her, and yet she didn't—couldn't—mind. She was angry, too, angry in a way she'd never allowed herself to be because of how futile that anger was. But how could she not feel it now? The waste of it all. The devastation wrought by her father's behaviour, by Graciano's disappearance.

She'd had their child, and kept her a secret from him.

He'd said the past was irrelevant. He'd said they weren't themselves this week. And if that were true, then anger wouldn't matter, but they couldn't really step out of the past.

Anger was a natural way to feel, for both of them.

Her hand in his shirt moved to his shoulder and she was pulling him harshly down on top of her, fury swirling with hunger and need and fear, because Graciano had awakened something inside of Alicia she'd thought long dead.

A voice in her head screamed at her to stop this madness, to see sense, but she'd done the sensible and right thing for ten long years and Lord if she didn't want to give in to desire just once, now. To satiate a hunger that had overtaken her, not bit by bit, but rather as an avalanche, all at once.

'Please,' she groaned against his neck as he moved his mouth to the flesh beneath her ear, then dragged it lower, to the pulse point at the base of her throat. He flicked his tongue against her skin and she whimpered, squirming, because her body was alive with flames and only he had the power to douse them. But first, he stirred them, fanning them, making her too hot, too desperately hungry for him. He lifted up a little, staring down at her with an expression she couldn't understand, and then his hands pulled at her shirt, popping the top two buttons to reveal the delicate lace of her bra.

She panted as his hand moved to cup the underside of one breast, as if appraising it, evaluating it. She lifted her pelvis, no longer in control of her body, totally overcome by needs that were beyond her ability to temper.

His fingers brushed her nipple and she cried out, the touch electric and intimate, and so unfamiliar. Not since Graciano had anyone done this to her.

Always, he'd had this power over her.

Always, she'd been his.

But he'd never been hers. Not really.

Where she had loved him completely, and carried that love inside her, along with their child, he'd moved on as soon as he'd left Seville. The broken pieces of her life had been hard to order. How she'd needed him in that first year. How she'd pined for him.

Her grief flooded her, reminding her of the catastrophic after-effects of what had happened between them, and it was enough to kill her libido, to douse the fever pitch of need he'd stirred so ruthlessly.

'Stop.' She pressed a hand to his chest now, her breathing uneven, panic making her skin pale and clammy. 'We have to stop this.'

Oh, God. What had she been thinking? She couldn't be kissing this man! She shouldn't even have agreed to come here. Everything was far too complicated. They shared a daughter, a daughter he knew nothing about. She'd kept Annie from him and at first that had made sense. But now? What justification did she have for lying to him about their daughter? How could she explain it?

It was so complicated and tangled, and terrifying, because Annie was *her* daughter. Graciano had given up his claim on her a long time ago. At least, that's what Alicia had been telling herself. But could a parent ever really give up on their own child, without being informed of the child's existence?

Panic set in, pummelling her lungs so the air left them completely and she couldn't reinflate them no matter how hard she tried. Her eyes filled with stars and her skin drained of all colour.

She wasn't conscious of much, except for Graciano's steady, confident hands lifting her into a seated position, then bringing her head forward, dropping it lower, his hand on her back rubbing rhythmically, his voice, Spanish words, low and soft, musical, reminding her of the way he'd spoken to her in Spanish back then, teaching her phrases, helping her learn his dialect.

Tears filled her eyes, but at least she could breathe again.

He evidently felt the steadiness return because he pushed to standing and moved away from her, staring out of the window for several long seconds, which she used to pull her shirt back together as best she could when the buttons were missing.

'That was a mistake,' she whispered, quivering fingers lifting to her lips and pressing against them. She closed her eyes and saw Annie's face and felt as though she'd been felled at the knees. She was a mother first. Her personal wishes were a lot less important than what she owed to Annie.

He turned to face her slowly, hands on hips, expression impossible to read—only there was darkness in the set of his features, a danger that made her tremble.

Whatever love there'd been between them, even if it was just from her, had turned to something else. Something dark and angry. Hate.

'You don't want me to kiss you again?'

Her eyes lowered. What she wanted? It was better not to explore that. 'It can't happen again,' she repeated instead.

'There is unfinished business between us, with only one way to resolve it.'

Promise hummed between them, a fierce, undeniable pull into temptation and desire. She bit down on her lip to stop herself from agreeing with him verbally, but in her heart, she knew he was right.

All the reasons she had to keep him at bay paled in comparison to the fact that she wanted him, desperately—that she needed him with all of herself. Maybe here, on this little island, she truly was in an oasis, away from Annie and her duties to their daughter, away from the life she'd carefully built for herself. Maybe, just maybe, she could be reckless and no harm would come from that, this time. Or *maybe*, she should run like hell rather than give into temptation for the second time in her life.

Alicia had been strong this past decade: strong when she'd stood up to her father; strong when he'd exiled her from Spain and stranded her in England with a grandmother she hardly knew; strong when she'd become a single mother at sixteen; strong as she'd raised Annie single-handedly…and she needed to be strong now.

'You're wrong, Graciano.' She spoke quietly, but with a hint of steel. 'There is nothing unfinished between us. You finished it, when you disappeared into thin air—when you refused to return my calls, when you ceased to exist in my life.' She stood, knees shaking a little. 'I know that my father treated you like dirt—worse than dirt—but you left without a backwards glance. You left without—'

'Without what, *querida*?' The term of endearment caused her to flinch. 'Your father was not the only one who treated me like dirt. True, he spoke the words, but you echoed them with your silence.' His eyes narrowed. 'What was I supposed to do? Stay and be arrested for a crime I never committed? For a crime so heinous—' He let the words hang there, his pride obviously wounded. His nostrils flared and he crossed his arms over his broad chest, staring down at her with darkly intense emotions swirling in his eyes.

Alicia couldn't bring herself to respond to that. The idea of Graciano being charged with rape after what they'd shared turned her blood to ice. But she couldn't be derailed from the point she needed to hammer home. 'All those years ago, that was the time to explore our unfinished business. Not now.' She pulled herself up to her full height. 'Now if you'll excuse me, I have work to do, and the sooner I finish, and can get off this island, the better.'

CHAPTER FOUR

ALICIA STARED AT her laptop without seeing any of the information on the screen. She'd spent the afternoon researching—previous events Graciano had hosted, the companies he'd bought, the events his enormous corporation had thrown, anything that would give her an insight into what he wanted without actually having to talk to him about it.

Which was childish and stupid.

Despite what had happened between them, she'd come here to do a job, and she wasn't about to ignore her obligations on that front.

Her ankle was still tender, but far better than it had been, courtesy of the painkillers he'd provided her with hours earlier before helping her to a guest room where she'd changed into a shirt with all the buttons in place.

But as she looked out at the glistening sea beyond her window, she couldn't help but regret that she'd only packed business clothes.

It had been an act of defiance at the time, a demarcation of her purpose at Graciano's. A statement of intent.

She'd planned to wear her suits and heels, to provide a starkly visible reminder to both of them, at all times, that she was there to work.

Had she anticipated, even then, that desire would

overcome them? Probably, but she'd expected to make it through at least one hour without wanting to rip his clothes off.

She looked across at her bed ruefully, to the discarded shirt there, and grimaced, then turned her attention back to the screen.

It was hard work—not because it was difficult to pull together a profile on what Graciano's events were like. She had a clear idea of that. But because events hosted by Graciano featured a lot of Graciano, and by necessity, she'd spent most of the afternoon staring at photographs of him dressed in custom tuxedos surrounded by stunning guests, many of whom were glamorous women looking at Graciano as though…as though they wanted everything Alicia did.

She moaned, dropping her head into her hands, mortified and made alive in equal measure by memories of what they'd done that afternoon. Her heart raced faster with adrenaline as she contemplated how wonderful it had felt to be kissed by him.

Except he wasn't just a handsome man with whom she shared a past. The matter of Annie was a sharp knife pressing into her side, something she was struggling to make sense of.

Contacting Graciano once he was worth all the money in the world, just about, hadn't been easy. There was a wall around him. His phone number was unattainable, his location unknown, security tight. Even when she'd woken in the middle of the night, body coated in the perspiration of the panicked, and she'd realised she couldn't keep Annie a secret from her father, she'd had no idea *how* to tell him.

Until he'd turned up at the charity auction, he'd been

as out of reach to Alicia as any other billionaire or ce-
lebrity.

But they were here together now. The conversation
could be had. And then what?

She groaned softly, closed the laptop and jerked to
standing, a frown on her face that was a copy of the
ache in her heart.

If Graciano had intentionally planned to seduce Alicia
with his lifestyle, he couldn't have chosen a better location. She'd expected to grab a piece of fruit for dinner, but when she walked slowly out of her room on an
ankle that was feeling much better and went in search
of the kitchen, she found a table for two had been set
in the middle of the courtyard. She stopped walking,
staring first at it—the white cloth, the wine bottle, the
candles and crystal glasses—and then looked around,
taking in the broader aspect automatically. It was her
first opportunity to regard the courtyard properly, and
now she saw details she couldn't possibly have appreciated from the air.

A large staircase led up one side of the courtyard to
a balcony that wrapped around the internal walls, and it
was these walls that vines tumbled over, cascading like
floral waterfalls towards the ground, creating a feast
for the eyes and a heavenly fragrance. Bees hummed
around the blooms and birds twittered overhead. Terracotta pots marked the base of each pillar, and fruit
trees, perfectly topiarised and large, broke up the effect
of the wall. The sky overhead was turning to dusky colours, and lights had come on around the walls, creating
a warmth and ambience that made Alicia feel she was
in a five-star resort—but even better, because it wasn't
so pristine and manicured.

There was whimsy and charm here, and so much history. She looked around once more, right as Graciano emerged into the courtyard, head bent as though deep in thought, so she had a moment to study him, and pull herself together, before he saw her.

He wore beige shorts and a loose white linen shirt, the quintessential image of relaxed charm—only Graciano, she suspected, never truly relaxed. It wasn't in his nature. Even as an eighteen-year-old, there'd been a drive about him. It was why his father had employed Graciano at the homestead, rather than just the mission home.

'That boy never stops,' Edward had marvelled, again and again. 'Just look at him go.'

And Alicia *had* looked. She'd looked until her tummy had been in knots and she'd wanted things that made no sense to her. Her mouth went dry as memories flooded her, memories that left her flushed with warm, moist heat between her legs as Graciano approached, his uniquely masculine fragrance reaching her nostrils and sending her pulse tripping.

'Hungry?'

'Yes,' she said truthfully.

His eyes met hers and something sparked in her bloodstream. She swallowed hard, looking away.

'Please, have a seat.' Such civility, but she felt the hum between them, the intensity of his words. As she moved to a seat, he pulled it back for her. She sat, and his hands glanced her shoulders briefly—the softest caress, but enough to lift her flesh with goosebumps.

'Thank you,' she murmured, as he came to sit opposite her.

She opened her mouth to say something, but a moment later, footsteps heralded the arrival of a slender woman with greying hair and a crinkled face.

'Isabella.' Graciano dipped his head in acknowledgement. The older woman's grin was one of easy affection.

'It is nice to see you back, sir.'

'It's nice to be back. Isabella, this is a colleague of mine. Miss Griffiths.'

Alicia's skin prickled for a different reason now: dislike. She heard it in the way he rumbled the syllables of her surname—her father's surname—and felt all his enmity barrelling towards her.

'Alicia,' she responded with a taut smile of her own.

'Alicia,' Isabella repeated. 'It is a pleasure to welcome you here. Would you like some wine to start?'

Terrible idea. Wine would only loosen her already non-existent inhibitions. 'I—' But at the same time, her nerves were frayed beyond bearing. One glass might help her get through the night without dissolving into a jumble of anxiety at Graciano's feet. 'Yes, wine would be lovely, thank you.'

'A bottle of the Rioja,' he said, smiling, and her heart tripped over itself, so pleased—so surprised—to see that on his features.

Isabella nodded and disappeared through a pair of timber doors.

'I thought you said we were completely alone.'

His eyes zeroed in on hers, and she shivered as their connection sparked inside her bloodstream, his smile shifting into an appraising expression. 'Disappointed?'

She couldn't admit that, even to herself. 'Relieved, in fact.'

The quirk of his lips showed he didn't believe her. 'There is a skeleton crew on the island. Isabella is my housekeeper.'

'Does she live here?' Alicia gestured to the mansion that surrounded them.

'You might have noticed cabins across the island as you flew over?'

'I presumed they were for guests.'

'Some are. Some are for my permanent staff.'

'How many are there?'

'Eighteen cabins.'

'I meant staff.'

'Four. Isabella, my chef Juanita, a gardener, Rodrigo, and Luis, who runs security.'

The same security who'd made it impossible to contact him all those years ago, when she'd wanted to tell him about the daughter they shared.

Isabella returned at that moment, and beside her stood a young woman, perhaps nineteen or twenty. She blushed when she looked at Graciano, and Alicia pitied her. She knew the power of the man opposite her. What woman would be able to resist his charms?

Alicia looked away as Isabella poured two glasses of wine and the young girl placed a platter of tapas before them—chorizo, breads, olives, cheese, fruit and little tartlets with anchovies and garlic.

When they were alone, she couldn't resist asking, 'Your chef?'

'One of Isabella's projects,' he said with an air of affection that ripped Alicia's own heart out. For a moment, she caught a glimpse of the boy Graciano had been, the boy who'd had all the time in the world for her—who, despite his awful upbringing, had always smiled for her.

The sense of loss was dazzling.

That boy no longer existed for Alicia, but he did for others.

'Projects?' she queried, reaching for her wine and

taking a gulp, so glad for the relief she didn't notice the delicious flavour until her second sip.

'She recruits people from the streets,' he said, eyes focused straight ahead. He was looking at Alicia without really seeing her. 'She cares only that they work hard and don't do drugs—her two rules.'

Alicia's heart shifted in her chest. 'Does she know about your time living rough?'

'It's something she and I have in common.'

Alicia leaned forward a little. 'Isabella, too?'

'She was one of the first I hired.'

'All your staff come from that background?'

'What's the point of employing people if not to give them a second chance? Here, they have a roof over their heads, a good job. Like Isabella, I have very few rules.'

She sipped her wine again. 'What are your rules?'

'Honesty and loyalty.'

Alicia flicked her gaze down to the table. From Graciano's perspective, Alicia had failed him on that front.

'And qualifications?'

'In my opinion, people can become qualified in anything if they're motivated enough, and nothing motivates like having lived on the streets.'

'When you left Seville—'

'When your father threw me out?'

Parched throat, she nodded. 'I worried about you.'

His eyes narrowed.

'I hated the thought of you going back to the streets. Some of the things you'd told me—the things you'd done, the things that happened to you… I couldn't sleep for fear of how you were living.'

Silence crackled between them, broken occasionally by the tweeting of an evening bird drifting overhead.

'Your worry was redundant. As you can see, I was fine.'

'But how?' she asked, urgently, leaning forward, then reaching for her wine and forcing herself to relax. 'How did you do all this?'

'Do you suspect a crime? That I somehow stole my fortune, Alicia?'

Her pulse kicked up a gear at the sound of her name in his mouth.

'Of course not.'

'Or that I became a gigolo to some wealthy woman and swindled her of her fortune?'

'That hadn't even occurred to me,' she muttered. 'Though if it had, you'd have only yourself to blame. Do you remember what you said to me the second time I called? The last time we spoke?'

His face gave nothing away; his features remained set in an iron-like mask.

'You told me you'd found someone else to have sex with. That's how you described it. I sacrificed everything for you and you—'

'What did you sacrifice for me?' he demanded.

'Did you think my life was a bed of roses after I told my father the truth?' she demanded fiercely. 'How do you think he reacted? What do you think he did?'

It was obvious that Graciano hadn't contemplated that. 'I had no idea that you would tell him the truth after I'd left. You certainly showed no intention of it that morning.'

'Of course I did,' she spat. 'That morning, I was in shock. I was terrified, and ashamed—a lifetime's conditioning is hard to shake. My father's messages of purity and innocence were pressed deep into my soul. But I did tell him later, and my world fell apart. I called you because I needed you, Graciano. I needed you.' It was impossible to keep her bitter resentment from her voice. 'And you turned what we were, what we'd been, into something so sordid, into an irrelevancy. You'd replaced me. That was that.'

A muscle jerked in his jaw; otherwise, he didn't react.

'Is that really how you felt?'

He took a sip of his own wine—his first. 'What do you want from me?' he asked after a moment, replacing the glass with deliberate care. 'After all this time, do you want me to say I lied? That I hadn't moved on? That I missed you? That I needed you, too?'

'Only if it's true.'

He stared at her long and hard and she held her breath, but a moment later, the young woman reappeared, carrying more food—steaks and potatoes and a salad.

When they were alone again, the fight had left Alicia. She felt stunned and numb, too devastated by their conversation to pick it up again.

Evidently, Graciano had the same lack of appetite for continuing that train of thought.

'There are two options for the party,' he said, taking a pair of tongs and using them to move food onto her plate first—far more than she could possibly eat, but she sat silently as he heaped steak and potatoes and beans and rocket, then olives and flans in front of her. She finished her wine, then replaced the empty glass.

'This courtyard makes sense. It's close to the kitchens, and the ground is steady, which is saying something, as much of this side of the island is mountainous.'

She wondered at the ease with which he'd pivoted to business; then again, none of this really mattered to Graciano. He'd moved on, as he'd been at pains to point out.

'However, there is a spot down near the beach, also nice and flat, and the drama of the cliffs and the ocean would make a spectacular backdrop as the sun goes down.'

Alicia tried to kick her brain into gear, but she was spinning wildly out of control so one plus one wouldn't equal two, no matter how hard she tried to make it.

'I'll need some more information on the kind of party,' she said eventually, the words coming out far flatter than she'd realised.

'Now is your chance. Ask whatever you want.'

The problem was that what she wanted to know had nothing to do with the party. She toyed with her napkin in her lap as Graciano refilled her glass. 'You said around one hundred people?'

'Yes. Intimate. The directors of the company I'm buying, the directors of my own company. Some valued staff.'

'Friends?' she prompted, curious about the life he was leading.

His brow lifted. He knew what she was asking.

'Do you mean girlfriends of mine, specifically, Alicia?'

Her cheeks flamed, caught out before she'd even realised what she was asking. 'Well, you do date.'

'That's one way to describe it.'

Heat infused her cheeks. 'Really? It's always just about sex for you?'

'It's rarely about more,' he said with a lift of his shoulders.

She pounced on that, wondering what kind of glutton for punishment she was. 'But sometimes it is?'

'Does it make any difference to your plans if I have a lover here with me or not?'

A lover. So sensual. So intimate. So difficult to contemplate. She dug her fingernails into her palms and stared straight ahead.

'A party is a party, no?'

'Yes,' she said, her voice husky. She took a gulp of wine to massage her vocal cords back into submission.

'So this is personal interest alone?'

She dropped her gaze to the mountain of food in front of her and lifted her fork, spearing an olive. 'Yes.' There was no point in lying. As she'd explained, her curiosity was not only natural, it was reciprocal.

'I'm not seeing any one particular woman at the moment.'

'Are you seeing more than one woman?'

'I am always "dating".'

'Like the redhead from the charity ball? I wonder what she would think of you bringing me here like this?'

'She wouldn't care. Caroline is under no illusions about my monogamy.'

The jealousy was unmistakable. It almost sheared her in two. She lifted her eyes to him, shocked by the visceral reaction—angry with it, too. It had been ten damned years. Of course he'd been with many, many other women since her. She knew that to be fact, so why did this hurt so much?

Because they were face to face, and time was no longer a linear constant but a vortex into which she could be sucked backwards. Sitting across from Graciano, they could be a decade younger, two hearts beating in unison, their futures unmapped, hope still a credible notion.

'Good for you,' she muttered to fill the silence and kill the hopeful sentiment.

His laugh was low and soft. It drifted across the table towards her, wrapping around her like a vice, as beneath the table, his leg kicked forward, his ankle brushing hers so she was trapped and stunned, stuck like a bug in a spider's web.

'Careful, Alicia. You sound jealous.'

'I'm not,' she spat. 'Believe me.'

He lifted a brow, that same mocking smile tilting his lips.

She drove her fork into a piece of meat with anger. 'Why would I be jealous?' she demanded, the question one she was trying to answer herself. 'What happened between us was over years ago. We've both moved on.'

'Yes,' he agreed easily, quickly, but his eyes narrowed slightly and he watched her intently, so her throat was parched. 'And yet, when I kissed you—'

'I already told you, that was a mistake. It won't happen again.' Something clutched in her chest, but she had to be strong. There was too much at stake to be drawn into conversations about their past, their chemistry. 'Just…drop it, Graciano. I'm here to work.' She blurted the reminder into the air between them, as if she could verbally raise a shield. She really just hoped it would hold out for the week.

CHAPTER FIVE

ALICIA TOLD HERSELF she was delighted that she didn't see Graciano the next morning. She dressed in a suit, for lack of other options, and worked for several hours in her bedroom before hunger drove her out in search of some fruit or something light to eat. Isabella was dusting in the lounge room and intercepted Alicia, all too willing to help her with a far more substantial breakfast than Alicia had envisaged. Nonetheless, it was nice to be fussed over, and the savoury omelette, fresh-baked bread and butter, and coffee was a delicious way to start the day.

As she cooked, Isabella chatted, and every third word was 'Graciano'. Graciano is so kind, so thoughtful, Graciano works too hard, Graciano is very generous, so Alicia found herself nodding and barely listening until, eventually, she said, 'And where is Graciano today?'

Isabella had smiled apologetically, perhaps mistaking Alicia's question for a desire to see the man, rather than avoid him. 'He has flown to Barcelona, for work. I told you, he's always working.' She shook her head, but smiled as she placed another coffee in front of Alicia.

Alicia doubted he was *always* working. After all, he'd been at pains to point out how active his love life was.

For Alicia, Graciano's absence meant opportunity.

It also meant she could breathe freely. 'Do you think he'd mind if I had a look around?' She gestured to her laptop. 'It's for *my* work.'

'He would not have brought you here if he did not trust you. Just let me know if you need my help with anything.'

Alicia didn't express her scepticism of that to the housekeeper. 'Thank you.'

'What time would you like to eat lunch?'

'Lunch? I don't think I'll need it after that delicious breakfast.'

'You must eat! This is Spain—the food is too good to refuse. I have some marinated octopus and rice. I'll put together something light. Say one o'clock?'

Alicia could see it was pointless to argue so she nodded.

'In the courtyard.' Isabella nodded with satisfaction, pleased with having won Alicia over.

That gave Alicia a few hours in which to properly tour the house and surrounds, and she didn't intend to waste a moment of it. Pausing only to fill up her water bottle, she started with the house, peering into rooms with open doors, avoiding those that were closed or locked, not wanting to stumble upon Graciano's bedroom or anything else too personal.

The house itself was quite fascinating, obviously old, but beautifully preserved, as though someone had spent a fortune renovating it at some point—as evidenced by the new wiring and air conditioning—while preserving the original features. Parquetry floors, mosaic tiles, elaborate murals and wall carvings... It was ornate and beautiful.

It was also the last place she could ever have imagined Graciano.

But then, as she walked, she remembered snatches of conversations—when he'd admired the sconces of her father's home, or explained the history of the building to her from the arches to the windows.

Where had she imagined he might live?

Had she thought he would always be homeless and penniless?

No. She simply hadn't thought that far ahead. She had imagined, in some strange way, that they would be always together, and at sixteen, hadn't been able to foresee a life distinct from her father.

Bitterness flooded her mouth and she wilfully pushed those thoughts from her mind.

The upper story of the mansion could easily be re-purposed. A large dining hall could be used to house a band. With the doors open, four musicians could be on the balcony itself, and the rest would add depth to the songs. The magnificent staircase would have flowers wound around the railings, and party lights could be strung over the whole courtyard to create the feeling of a carnival.

Tables and chairs would be in the centre, with floaty white cloths and flower arrangements to play up the colours of the vines. It would easily accommodate the number of tables required, she thought, imagining round tables at first before changing her mind and envisaging two lengths, a classic banquet setting, to capture the drama of the perfectly square courtyard.

Ideas came to her as she walked, so when Isabella appeared in the courtyard at one, she was startled out of her reverie.

'Lunch time already? My goodness, that went fast.'

'Graciano has asked you to join him on the terrace.'

'Graciano?' She went from relaxed to anxious in the flash of an eye. 'I thought he was in Barcelona?'

Isabella shrugged, nonplussed. 'His meetings must have finished early, eh? Do you know the way?'

She was tempted to ignore his request, but she was a professional and this was, first and foremost, a job. She was being paid to be here—or the charity was—and her personal code of ethics refused to allow her to give anything less than her best.

'No.' She flattened her lips. 'Would you mind showing me?'

Graciano seemed to be deep in thought when she walked through a set of wrought iron gates framed with bougainvillea and onto a delightful terrace that overlooked the ocean. The view was so breathtaking she had to pause a moment to appreciate it, to inhale the fragrance of sea salt and tropical flowers, before turning back to him and then, immediately, wishing she hadn't. He wore another suit, navy blue this time, but he'd discarded the jacket and tie over the back of a chair and undone the shirt at his throat so her eyes immediately dropped to the thick column there and the sprinkling of hair that was revealed. Her mouth went dry and her legs felt hollow.

Graciano stood, and the action broke the effect of her concentration. She wrenched her gaze away, drawing in a breath, trying to calm her scattered nerves.

'I've been exploring the house,' she blurted out, willing him not to make one of his sarcastic remarks about the way she was staring at him like a lovesick teenager.

'Isabella mentioned.'

'Is she spying on me?' Alicia asked with surprise,

moving to the seat opposite Graciano but pausing before easing herself into it.

'Not at all. She likes to talk. Perhaps you noticed? She mentioned you've been poking around in all the rooms.'

'Not all of them,' Alicia was quick to refute. 'I've been careful not to open any doors.'

'There is nothing you cannot see,' he dismissed with a shrug.

'I didn't want to invade your privacy.'

'By stepping into my bedroom? I'll live.'

But she might not have. She was already finding it hard to breathe. The thought of seeing his private space, of being surrounded by its masculinity, made her head spin. When he'd stayed with them all those years ago, he'd slept in a dormitory her father had repurposed for runaways in need of safe haven—at least, that's what her father had said. Now, she saw it more as exploitative. Free labour. There had frequently been two or three hand-picked teens staying with them at any one time. Graciano hadn't had a bedroom of his own. Nor had he had any possessions, so Alicia hadn't ever seen his room, nor could she imagine what it would be like. But she was better not knowing.

'How long have you lived here?' she asked after a moment.

'I don't live here.' Isabella appeared with an elaborate tray—octopus, rice salad, fruit, cheese and bread. When they were alone again, he continued. 'I split my time between the island, Barcelona and London.'

Her heart went into overdrive far too fast for her to cope with. She pretended interest with the glass of mineral water he was pouring, her eyes tracing the bubbles, all the while her pulse frantically moving into dangerous territory. 'London?' she murmured, hoping for nonchalance but aware the word came out strained.

'I have an office there.'

She swallowed, but her throat was thick, nerves all bunched together.

'Do you go often?'

'For about a week every month. Why?'

She bit down on her lip, toying with her fingers in her lap. She lived in a sleepy little part of zone three, in a hook on the river. It wasn't as though they were likely to run into each other. But the idea of Graciano having been within a tube ride of Alicia—and Annie—all these years, and Alicia having not known, made her head spin, and her heart ache. It was all so impossible.

'I'm just trying to get a picture of your life now.'

'Does it help you plan the event?'

'It doesn't hurt,' she said honestly, then sighed, deciding honesty was the best policy—at least with this. 'But more so, I'm just curious. You've come so far. I'm interested in how you live. In how you did it.'

'I worked hard.'

'But doing what?' she pushed. 'Within six months of leaving Seville, you were a high-end realtor. That's not something you had experience with.'

'Real estate is about people, and I had a lot of experience with them.'

It was casually said, but she felt the sting in the words. She thought of the experience her father—and Alicia—had given him, and fought an urge to wince.

He took a drink of water. 'I found it easy,' he said after a moment. 'I was good at understanding what people wanted, how to give it to them. I'd spent years on the streets—I had an innate understanding of property, values, the quality of one neighbourhood versus another, and I was strongly motivated to succeed. I didn't sleep for at least three months. I chased down every lead, sold every house, met every vendor, drove buyers from the airport all around Madrid. By the end of the first year, I was earning more than a million euros in commissions.'

Her lips parted on a rush. 'You must have been so… thrilled.'

'Thrilled? No, Alicia.' She shivered as he caressed her name. 'I was hungry. I wanted *more*. You couldn't possibly understand. You've never felt that way—to worry about when you will eat again, where you will sleep. To me, it wasn't possible to *ever* earn enough. It's still not.'

She shook her head sadly. 'But you're worth a fortune.'

'Yes.'

'And this place?'

She gestured around them.

His smile set her blood on fire. It was so intimate, so natural. So genuine. It made her crave the connection they had once shared.

'I wanted it the minute I saw it.'

She nodded slowly. 'It's beautiful.'

'Yes.' He leaned back in his chair, looking around them. 'The history is unique.'

'What is the history?'

'Ferdinand the seventh built it for his mistress.'

She frowned. 'Is he the guy with a penchant for marrying his nieces?'

Graciano grinned and bubbles formed in her blood as she was plunged back into the past, when he'd smiled at her so readily. 'This was not built for a niece, but for a woman he apparently loved very deeply. Perhaps you saw the turret while you were exploring this morning?'

She shook her head. 'No, I didn't. Where is it?'

'I'll show you later. It's not important. But it was built as a lookout, so that she could watch for his arrival. He came by boat, of course. He was jealous and guarded her fiercely—he was the only visitor she ever had.'

'That's...' She searched for the right word. 'Kind of sad.'

He lifted a brow, silently prompting her to continue.

'As time went on, he visited less and less, but she watched for him always.'

'What happened to her?'

'She went mad.'

'Mad?'

'Completely crazy, yes.'

'How awful.'

'Yes.' He lifted his shoulders. 'But interesting.'

She looked around, seeing the place through new eyes now. 'It's very grand, for one person.'

'There was an army of staff as well.'

'Naturally,' Alicia agreed with a hint of a smile. 'Perhaps she found happiness with one of them. A secret affair that history forgot, by virtue of how well they guarded their transgression.'

'You'd prefer to think she fell out of love than stayed loyal?'

'To the point of insanity? While he went about his business, marrying woman after woman? Yes, I'd infinitely prefer to think she found some level of happiness independent of him.'

'Is the idea of loyalty in the face of adversity so hard to imagine?'

'This isn't about loyalty,' she said after a beat. 'He hid her away here for his pleasure, but only when he saw fit to visit. Meanwhile, she lost her youth, her life and finally her mind. What of his loyalty? His obligations?'

'She had a choice in the matter, I presume.'

'That's presuming a lot,' she muttered, well aware that agency was a matter of perspective.

'You think he kept her against her will?'

'A gilded cage is still a cage.'

'It's a leap to suggest she wanted to leave but couldn't.'

'Loneliness literally drove her mad. I don't think it's that great a leap.'

'And what would you have done?'

She didn't hesitate. 'I'd have swum to shore.'

'Even if you loved him?'

'That's not love.'

'How can you be so sure?'

'You disagree?'

'I asked first.'

She pulled a face. 'Love isn't selfish,' she said finally, and with authority. 'What he did was. Ergo, it wasn't love.'

'So black and white,' he murmured. 'You don't make any allowance for nuance?'

'You make way too many allowances,' she corrected carefully. 'You're predisposed to identify with him. Rich, powerful man.'

'Capturing a woman for the purpose of sex? Really, Alicia?'

'Well, I mean…' Heat flushed her cheeks. 'If I hadn't stopped us yesterday…' She couldn't complete the sentence.

'Then let me be clear. You are free to leave at any point, and I will not even make you swim to shore. My helicopter is at your disposal.'

She tilted her face away, breathing forced and wretched as she tried to get to grips with how their conversation had reached this point. Whenever she tried to focus on the job she'd come to do, they got carried away and she lost command of things.

Sucking in a deep breath, she turned back to him resolutely. 'I'm not a quitter, Graciano.' The words were husky. 'I'll stay until I've finished organising your event.'

'Four more nights,' he said, and she shivered, because there was a challenge in his statement, and oh, so much promise.

Graciano read the message carefully, once more.

Hi, handsome. I'm in Barcelona for the night. Join me?

With a devil emoji, then a flame emoji.

Anastasia was one of the world's most renowned lingerie models, and he'd always enjoyed their time together. She was intelligent, interesting, beautiful and, most importantly of all, completely casual. She hated the idea of commitment, so catching up with her was always a pleasure.

His finger hovered over the screen and he paused, uncharacteristically indecisive. His office was on the top floor of the home and had windows on both sides. From one, he could see the ocean, sparkling all the way to mainland Spain. From the other, he looked down on the courtyard and across it, towards the turret.

Quite by chance, he moved to the back windows, with the vantage point of the internal walls, right as Alicia moved across the courtyard, a notepad in her hands. She was writing furiously, looking around, squinting, eyes chasing the windows, so he moved back a little. But there was no need to hide. She was looking at the windows without really seeing. Her mind was busy imagining, planning, preparing for the event he'd created out of thin air, simply to justify bringing her here. He watched, fascinated by this side of her.

More fascinated by her than he wanted to be—certainly more than he'd anticipated he'd feel. This week was supposed to be about showing her how different he was to the young, impressionable eighteen-year-old she'd used and discarded. It was supposed to be about making her want him, to enjoy the chemistry they shared and then walk away on *his* terms.

But since she'd arrived on the island, they'd sparred and sparked. Time spent with her was a unique agony of desire and desperation, anger and anticipation. For two days, she'd been right here, within arm's reach, and yet he knew nothing more about her than he had a week ago.

And suddenly, that wasn't good enough.

They had a finite amount of time together—there was nothing on earth that would convince him to pursue her beyond this week—and it was slipping through his fingers.

He wanted to bed her, undoubtedly. But he also wanted to understand her. To answer questions that were lingering in his mind. To put the whole matter to rest, once and for all.

She lifted a hand, rubbing the back of her neck, then closing her eyes and stretching as if in pain. He was frozen to the spot, unable to tear his eyes from her. Her fingers moved delicately lower, needling the tops of her shoulder so his own fingers began to tingle with a desire to replace hers.

Abruptly, she dropped her hands to her sides. Her phone was ringing.

He watched her scan the screen and smile, then lift it to her ear. The look on her face made his gut fall to his feet with the force of a rock boulder. Happiness. Pleasure. Contentment.

Whoever she was talking to made her look so damned joyous. He'd never known that feeling. Or not for ten years, at least.

'You brought me coffee?' She stared at the outstretched mug with scepticism, feelings she couldn't decipher fluttering in her chest. 'Why?'

'A peace offering,' he said, with a lift of his shoulders. Her eyes dropped to the impressive breadth there, to the strength of his frame, and her mouth went dry, so she reached for the coffee and took a quick, grateful sip. It wasn't hot enough to burn her mouth, thankfully.

'You look surprised.'

'You aren't someone to make peace.'

He laughed, the sound melodious and warm and, oh, so dangerous. 'How do you know, Alicia?' Her name on his lips rolled over her, so she pulled her lips to the side, fighting a smile of her own.

'Because you're stubborn and—'

'And what?'

'—angry,' she said quietly, honestly, peeping at him from beneath her lashes. 'Like you used to be before—'

Their eyes met and held. She didn't need to finish the sentence. He'd been angry, with a huge chip on his shoulder, when he'd arrived at the mission, but over the summer, as they'd got to know one another, he'd changed, morphing into a different man altogether.

'I am not angry, in fact,' he said with a lift of his shoulders. 'At least, not often.'

'Not with anyone but me?' She couldn't resist asking.

His smile almost felled her at the knees. 'You are more direct than you used to be.'

'I've had to be.'

'Why?' He was studying her, his body a study in nonchalance, but she knew him better than that.

She hesitated, sipping her coffee again, the feeling of the afternoon sun warming her back. The ocean air, salty and mysterious, called to her, and again, she rued her decision to only bring corporate clothing.

'I suppose we all become more confident over time. I was just a girl back then.'

'*Si,*' he agreed, and her heart stammered because understanding that brought them one step closer to forgiveness; until that moment, she hadn't understood how much she wanted him to forgive her.

Silence fell, but it wasn't uncomfortable. They stood only a metre or so apart, the sun warming them both, neither speaking, until after a minute, he said, 'Tell me about your life.'

It was a command, and it made her laugh, despite the inherent danger in the question. After all, Annie was the biggest part of her life. How could she discuss her day-to-day existence without mentioning their daughter? And how could she bring up Annie until she understood him better? Until she knew how he'd react?

'My life is busy,' she said. 'I work long hours.'

'You never married?'

Her heart stammered. 'I'm only twenty-six,' she pointed out.

'Are you seeing anyone?'

She bit into her lower lip. 'After the way we kissed yesterday?'

He lifted his shoulders. 'We didn't have sex. It would hardly have been a massive betrayal.'

Her lips parted in surprise. 'No,' she said quickly, not meeting his eyes. 'I'm not seeing anyone. And if I was, I wouldn't have kissed you like that. I'm not quite so cavalier with my feelings are you are.'

His smile prickled at her heart. 'Peace offering, remember.'

'Maybe there's too much in our past to ever achieve peace?' she said softly, hoping that it wasn't true. They shared a daughter; for Annie's sake they needed to resolve their past.

'Perhaps peace is overrated,' he said, eyes boring into hers, warming her, teasing her, tempting her. She stared at him, every nerve ending in her body reverberating in recognition of what he was suggesting, of the truth in his words. She took an involuntary step backwards, gripping her cup more tightly.

'Thank you for the coffee,' she mumbled. 'I should— I need to go.'

'Coward,' he taunted softly, his smile sending her nerves into overdrive.

As she hurried across the courtyard, she heard his soft, mocking laugh and her insides squirmed with unmistakable desire—a desire she knew she had to conquer.

CHAPTER SIX

'COME WITH ME.'

She lifted her face to his as if awakening from a dream. 'What time is it?'

'Eight o'clock.'

'Eight o'clock at night?' She flicked a glance back to her computer screen. 'Wow. I didn't realise. I've been working.' She stood up with unconscious grace, rolling her head from side to side to ease the pressure in her neck. His eyes followed the gesture so she stopped abruptly. She'd been hiding in her room since their earlier exchange in the courtyard, terrified of how quickly he could wind her up and turn her insides to mush. She had to focus on the business side of things. 'Would you like to hear what I've come up with?'

'Not particularly.' His eyes held hers and desire sparked in her bloodstream.

Business, business, business.

'What can I do for you?'

His eyes bore into hers, slicing her with the heat of his gaze, and she shivered as a frisson of awareness travelled the length of her spine.

'I want to show you something.'

'What is it?'

He expelled a sigh. 'I did not say I want to *tell* you something. Come with me.'

His authority was compelling. 'Do I need shoes?'

'No.' And to her surprise, he held out his hand, staring at her impatiently.

She froze, the offered hand so much more than just a gesture. Her heart leaped into her throat and she looked down at his wrist, his fingers, with a sense that putting her own in his would be like sealing her fate—a fate she might not want to exist with, a fate she couldn't outrun.

Slowly, she moved closer, and then, of its own volition, her hand lifted, meeting his halfway. The moment they touched, an electrical current fizzed through her, so, startled, she turned to him.

'This won't take long.'

Did he feel it at all? Did he realise how even the air around them seemed to change when they touched?

He led her out of the house through yet another set of doors. 'I swear, after two days' exploring, I still can't get my bearings.'

'I'll give you a tour tomorrow.'

Her heart thundered.

Careful, Alicia. Once bitten, twice shy...

'Another peace offering?'

He flicked her a grin and her insides knotted together.

The grass was dewy underfoot, the evening air still sultry and warm, the day's heat refusing to budge despite the setting sun. She moved closer to him on autopilot, despite the warmth, and he held the line, so their bodies brushed as they walked. Each light brush of skin sent her pulse into overdrive and sparked a tangle of need in the pit of her stomach, so she was breathless by the time they reached the sand of the shoreline.

'There.' He pointed to a large stretch of grass that ran beside the sand.

'Your second option,' she said breathlessly, because it was perfect. But so, too, was the courtyard! 'Both stunning,' she said honestly. 'You'll have to choose which you like best.'

'Do you have a preference?'

'I won't be here,' she said, and she wasn't imagining the wistful tone to her voice. She covered it by plastering an overbright smile to her face. 'I suppose the house has more practical advantages, but there's no reason not to have sunset drinks here, at the water's edge. This could have a whole other theme. Whereas the dinner at the house could be more formal, with a classical band, this could be relaxed—a beachy, tropical party, with a percussion band to dance to.'

'Dancing?'

'What's a party without dancing?' she responded archly.

'I'll take your word for it.'

'Don't tell me you don't dance?'

'That surprises you? Did we ever dance back then?'

'No. There wasn't the opportunity.'

And then his other hand lifted to her cheek, cupping it, holding her still so he could inspect her better in the fading light of the day. His eyes trapped hers and it felt as though she were tipping off the edge of the earth. She was in a void with nothing and no one else—just Graciano and herself.

'I dance rarely.'

'I bet you're good at it.' She could have sewn her lips together!

'How much?'

'An actual wager?'

'Sure. Unless you're scared to lose?'

'I won't lose. I know you've got rhythm.'

His features showed scepticism. 'We'll see.'

'Okay. A hundred euros?'

'I was thinking more like a non-monetary wager.'

Her heart crashed into her ribs with the force of a jet engine. 'Such as?' The words were barely audible.

'If I win, you'll answer any question I have.'

Danger lurked. Annie was, as always, in the back of her mind. 'No.'

His eyes narrowed. 'Keeping secrets?'

She blinked down at the grass between them. 'I'll give you three questions,' she said unevenly. 'And I get to veto one of them.'

'You drive a hard bargain.'

'What do I get if I win?'

'What do you want?'

She felt heat stain her cheeks and looked away, embarrassed by how easy she was to read. 'The same deal. Three questions.'

'And a veto.'

'Fair enough.'

He dropped his hand to her other, capturing both. 'Are you ready?'

'What for?'

'To dance.'

'*With* me?' she squeaked.

'Did you think I was going to torture myself solo?'

But she was trembling from top to toe. How could she possibly dance with him? Alarm sirens blared but she couldn't heed them. He drew her into his body and she let him, his large frame wrapping around her, one hand in the small of her back, the other holding her hand close to their shoulders.

'There's no music,' she said as he began to move with, as she'd guessed, impeccable timing.

'There is the beat of the waves hitting the coast. The birds overhead. Listen, and you'll hear it.'

She turned her head, pressing her cheek to his chest so the fast beating of his heart added to the background song nature was weaving around them. He was right; there was music everywhere. She closed her eyes, breathing in, tasting his masculine, spiced scent, letting it flood her body with strength and need.

Time ceased to exist. They danced—for how long, she couldn't have said. For a long time, and not enough, their bodies enmeshed, their steps in perfect unison. The sun set and the stars shimmered, the night sky a perfect inky black overhead. Alicia felt the illicit pleasure of this moment, of being held by him as though it were normal, their bodies brushing together in the seemingly innocuous task of dancing, when really, magic was weaving around them, making them both want—need—so much more.

That need terrified her, and despite the nirvana of the moment, Alicia forced herself to stiffen in his arms, to stop swaying in time to the magical music he'd made her aware of and look up at him. All her futures, all her hopes, distilled into that one single look. She was standing on a precipice, a terrifying drop before her, and yet she moved closer to the edge, lifting a hand to his chest, fingers splayed against the fabric of his shirt.

'I win.' The words were husky, and the sting of tears made her throat hurt.

At sixteen, she'd wanted him with her whole heart. She'd never really recovered from that.

But he'd walked away, she reminded herself quickly. True, she'd failed to defend him the morning after her birthday, when Edward Griffiths had found them asleep in a field, limbs entwined, only a flimsy blanket for cover. But he'd disappeared, and when she'd tried to explain, to apologise, he'd refused to let her explain. He'd been so brutal in his rejection.

It had broken her heart.

It was still broken.

What other explanation was there for her celibacy since? She had told herself it was because of Annie, that being a single mother took all her focus, but that didn't explain her disgust at the idea of dating any other man. Graciano's rejection had left her terrified of experiencing that same pain again.

Yet here she was, dangerously close to him in every sense, her heart beating a frantic, desperate tattoo, all for him. She knew she had to stay away, or at least harden her heart before it could hurt anew, but closeness was addictive, and suddenly, Alicia was tired of fighting herself.

'I think we should call it a draw.'

She lifted a brow, her pulse tripping over itself. 'I'm not sure that's fair.'

'Dancing is subjective.'

'So you entrapped me in a bet I could never truly win?'

His smile was sheer arrogant masculinity. 'I don't like to lose.'

Her stomach squeezed. Conscious of how she stood, in the circle of his arms, she pulled back, the walls of her world splintering, but she was determined not to let them shatter completely. There was a secret she held deep inside her, a secret she'd sworn she'd keep. But the longer she spent with Graciano, the more at risk that secret became—the more she wanted to tell him everything.

Fear sliced through her. She couldn't even imagine how Graciano would react to the news that he was the father to a nine-year-old girl. Just the idea of having that conversation drained all the colour from her face and she had to turn away from him abruptly, to face the ocean, to hide the response from him.

She alone had borne the consequences of the night they'd shared, and that had seemed right. After all, it had never been 'just sex' for her, which meant their baby was not a burden, despite what it had cost Alicia—despite the way a bomb had blown up in her life.

Her decision-making had been sound, but standing beside him now, it felt like a grenade with the ring pulled. She didn't know how to stave off the devastating explosion.

'Okay. You go first,' she said, to buy for time, needing to distract him from the way the past was rushing at her, haunting her, terrorising her.

'Tell me about your life.'

'That's not a question.'

'No. I suppose it's not.'

A small smile lifted her lips. 'Want to try again?'

He considered that a moment. 'Have you always wanted to work in events?'

Alicia's lips pulled to the side. 'I've always been organised—'

'I remember.'

His interruption did something funny to her tummy, making it twist and tighten. 'As for events, it was a... friend...who suggested I pursue this career.'

'A friend?'

She nodded softly. 'Diane's sister worked in events,

and got me a job at the palace. It was a baptism by fire, but so rewarding. I learned so much.'

'You left, though.'

'Yes.' She nodded. Annie had been in nursery school, and Alicia had needed something with more flexibility. 'The hours were incredibly long, and a job came up in the charity. The work environment is very flexible, and incredibly rewarding. It was a good fit.'

'And you've done very well for the charity.'

'Is that another question?'

'An observation. Your services were hotly contested.'

'Well, yes, but no one had quite the deep pockets you do.'

He shrugged.

'Why did you bid on me, Graciano?'

'To organise—'

'No.' She bit down on her lip. 'You have people to organise events. You have whole departments. Why me? Why now?' Her voice shook a little on the last question.

His nostrils flared as he exhaled, eyes roaming her face, and then he moved closer, so they stood toe to toe, staring at each other. 'It was a spontaneous decision.'

'A very expensive one.'

He dipped his head in agreement.

It didn't make any sense.

'Have you thought about me?'

'What do you mean?'

'Since you left my father's. Have you thought about me?'

'Yes.' The tone of his voice left her in little doubt: those thoughts were not good.

'I have another question.'

'I've lost count of how many you've asked.'

'Does it matter?'

The air around them crackled. She wondered if he was going to argue with her, but he stayed silent, waiting.

'Have you ever been in love?' The question was out of her mouth before she could think it through, before she analysed how much it revealed about her. Before she debated whether she even wanted to hear the answer. But she held her breath, waiting, staring up at him, analysing his response.

He dropped his hand away and turned to face the ocean. His dark eyes scanned the frothy waves, the stars. 'Veto.'

She sucked in a shaky breath and mirrored his posture, turning to face the sea. Far across the rolling water, mainland Spain stood sentinel, its rich history and tapestry the place Alicia had felt most at home. She closed her eyes against the pain of that, against the devastating body blow of loss.

'It's not a hard question.'

'The ability to use a veto isn't dependent on the difficulty of answering.'

She ground her teeth together. 'You're not playing the game properly.'

'You're right. Let me answer your earlier question better, then. You asked why I brought you here.'

She held her breath, staring at him.

He studied her right back, appraising, and she felt a rush of emotions swamping her, drowning her, so she struggled to stay standing. Perhaps he realised, because a moment later his hand came around her back, supporting her, pressing her forward, no longer in an invitation to dance but in an embrace that made the nerve endings in her body vibrate furiously.

'And?' she whispered, glad for his support.

'I was curious about you.'

'Angry with me?' She pushed, because she'd felt it humming off him in waves that night at the charity ball.

'It was ten years ago,' he pointed out with a voice that was all reason and calm.

'You said you'd be honest.'

Silence whipped the air between them, followed by a sharp hiss of breath between his teeth. 'I was angry,' he agreed after a beat. '*Si.* I was made to feel worthless for a long time, by many people. Until I met you, no one had ever seen value in me. No one had ever wanted me.'

Her heart twisted painfully in her chest.

'But *you* wanted me. I didn't realise how much I cared for your good opinion until it was wrenched away. Do you remember what he said? What he accused me of? The threats he made? And I turned to you, looking for support, sure that you would help me make him understand. You were silent. Worse, you moved to him, put your hand on his arm. I was so angry with myself. I had let down my guard with you. I'd let myself need someone for the first time in my life. I'd let myself believe...'

'You were right to believe,' she whispered, the words tortured, her throat heavy with emotion. 'My father made the situation untenable, but that didn't change how I felt. I was only sixteen, Graciano. Just a girl.'

'Not when you were with me.'

'No.' A wistful smile twisted her lips. There was so much water under the bridge. 'With you, I felt like a woman.'

'I left Seville and swore I would never let another person have the kind of power over me that you did that summer. I lost myself in you, *querida*, and it's a mistake I've never since repeated.'

Her heart soared even when a rock dropped through

her body, landing low in her gut. 'But when I called to apologise—'

'I'd learned my lesson,' he said with a lift of his shoulders. 'You were dangerous. Quicksand. When I was around you, I wanted only you. I forgot about my brother, my plans for my future, my desire to succeed. There was only you.' His lips tightened into a grimace. 'I was too selfish to allow for that.'

Her eyes swept shut at his admission. Was that it? Would their relationship have been doomed to fail anyway? He was an ambitious man—his success proved that—so perhaps he would have moved on anyway, rather than risk his ambitions failing.

'So you told me you'd moved on—'

'Oh, no, Alicia. I didn't lie to you.'

Her chest panged.

'I wanted to put you from my mind, to erase you from my body. Sex seemed like the most expedient way.'

'Did it work?' she challenged, tilting her chin defiantly to cover the shattering of her heart.

'Yes.' His eyes glittered with a challenge when they locked to hers. Her skin flushed hot and cold.

'That still doesn't explain why you brought me here,' she said unevenly. 'If you were angry, why not ignore me? Leave without speaking to me?'

'Where's the fun in that?'

She flinched but didn't back down, didn't move away. 'Where's the fun in this?'

'Are you not enjoying yourself?'

Her stomach somersaulted through her. She felt as though she were on a medieval torture device; at the same time, she couldn't imagine walking away from

Graciano at the end of this week and never seeing him again. It would be like losing a limb.

'I'm here to work,' she said quietly.

'And did you come here thinking it would all be about work? Or were you hoping...?' He let the question dangle in the air between them.

'I didn't even know if you'd be here,' she said, truthfully. 'I had no idea what to expect.'

He paused. 'Nor did I.'

Frustration zipped through her—frustration with him, their past, their circumstances, with how much she wanted him and how strongly she knew she should fight that. 'Are you playing games with me?'

She saw the response in his eyes, his expression, the minute changes before he quickly resumed a mask of total control.

'To what end?'

'I don't know. To punish me?'

'Revenge?' he prompted.

'Yes.'

'It did occur to me.'

She shivered at the bald acknowledgement. 'That's why I'm here? So you can sleep with me and make me... what? Love you?'

'I don't want your love,' he dismissed quickly.

'But you do want me to want you,' she said after a heavy pause. 'You know what you do to me, how you make me feel. You brought me here to capitalise on that, to seduce me. And then what?'

He was silent, but his jaw was locked, and she felt his emotions, dark and...ashamed? Angry?

'I intended to, yes. I wanted to make you mine, for this week, to make you forget about any other man you've been with, to make you admit you wanted me like you want air. There is unfinished business between us, Alicia.' He took a step backwards from her then, and the moon pierced her with a fine, silver blade. 'But the truth is, that one night we were together was a lifetime ago. Just like you said—ancient history. Let's leave it where it belongs—in the past.' And with that, he spun on his heel and began to walk back towards the house.

CHAPTER SEVEN

'DON'T YOU WALK away from me,' she shouted, with far more command than she felt. 'You're the one who brought me to this island, who paid a fortune to secure my time. Don't turn your back when you don't like the way the conversation's going.'

'That's not it,' he snapped over his shoulder.

'Isn't it?' She scrambled after him, propelled by frustration.

'What do you want from me?' he muttered, the words only barely audible. She moved faster, until she was almost level with him, then reached out and caught his wrist.

'Damn you!'

The sound of their breathing, each as frantic as the other, filled the air, and then he made a gruff, growling sound and freed his wrist, only so he could wrap his arms around her and yank her body to his, pulling her to him. 'Your father robbed us both of a chance to explore this,' he said, but his voice was quiet, as though he was speaking to himself more than her. 'That's why it feels as though there's something unfinished between us. That's why there's this compulsion. We need to get it out of our system, to let it burn out, and then we can move on.'

Move on. It all made sense, but his words had a brutal resonance that made her heart feel bruised and heavy, and she didn't know why.

The question formed in her mind—a barbed, painful thought she couldn't contemplate—because she knew now, beyond a shadow of a doubt, that her daughter deserved better than this.

'Graciano,' she said, with urgency. She wasn't ready to tell him about Annie, but she did need some kind of absolution. 'I was angry, too. So angry. I was only sixteen, and you were the best friend I'd ever had.'

He made a noise of disbelief. She ignored it.

'If I let you down, then you did the same to me. I needed you. I needed you…'

He kissed her then, the kiss angry and gentle, a kiss of mastery and promise, a kiss designed to silence her sad pleas. He pulled her to the ground, the grass beneath them cool and dewy in the evening air, his weight on her a drugging delight. His hands moved over her quickly, discarding her clothes with impatience while he kissed her, crushing her lips, moving his hips, promising her, silently, always, of the pleasures to come.

Naked beneath him, she arched her back, then lifted up, seeking him once more, but he stayed where he was, still clothed, staring down at her. His eyes held hers until her heart exploded and she had to close the distance between them and kiss him to stop from saying three words that were pulsing around her mind without any anchor point in reality. She didn't *love* him. She'd *loved* him, once, a long, long time ago, as a teenager who'd had no inkling about life and people and loyalty and what love really even meant.

Kissing him was simple, though. When they kissed, and touched, no explanation was necessary. She needed no time to analyse what any of it meant; it was written in the stars. She said his name over again, the syllables husky and exotic beneath the Mediterranean moonlight, the taste in her mouth building like an incantation, a spell over both, over this glorious bay and all that was here on this island.

He ripped off his shirt, discarding it at their sides, his chest moving powerfully with each breath. The moonlight landed like a shaft across his torso, catching words that ran in cursive script just beneath his heart. She lifted a finger, chasing them, saying them aloud so they washed through the air, adding weight to the incantation of his name.

'*Que cada palo aguante su vela.*' They were beautiful words, though she didn't understand their literal meaning.

'*Si,*' he agreed, though, and then he was moving over her, kicking out of his shoes as her hands found the button of his trousers and unfastened it, then pushed them down, hungry for him, terrified of her need, but unwilling—unable—to stop.

Ten years ago, their coming together had been tentative and gentle—an exploration, an awakening—but now, a decade's worth of need pulsed through them like a live wire, driving her hands so she stripped him naked as he pushed out of his trousers, working together to liberate him, needing him with the power of a thousand suns.

'Please,' she groaned to underscore her desperation and he laughed, a low, growling sound that pulsed in her belly, but then he stopped, moving over her, his face just an inch from hers.

'We can't do this.'

Something dropped inside of her. A weight. A loss. An ache spread. 'What do you mean?'

'I don't have a condom.'

'Oh, my God.' She lifted a hand to his chest, shocked that she could have been so caught up in the moment she'd forgotten the simple precaution. Even that night, he'd used one—though it hadn't stopped her from falling pregnant.

'I never don't use protection,' he said through ground teeth, lips clenched, and then he cursed, the word vibrating around them, and she flinched, not from the word itself but from the force of his disappointment—a perfect echo of her own.

'No,' she groaned, squeezing her eyes shut, trembling with her need. In that moment, she would almost have risked another child simply for the exquisite pleasure of knowing his possession once more. 'I can't believe it.'

'I'm not—I'm sure—' But what could she say? That she was sure they wouldn't fall pregnant? When the impossible had already happened despite them using protection?

'I won't take the risk.'

Her heart skipped, because his protestations showed how devoutly he wanted to avoid the complication of a pregnancy.

'Are you on the pill?'

Oh, she wished she was, but why would she have been? Slowly, she shook her head. 'I'm not in the habit of this kind of thing.' She dropped her gaze between them, hating how much that revealed to him, hating how unsophisticated and inexperienced she was. But he moved quickly, his mouth finding hers and kissing her until she wasn't thinking straight and her hips were moving, silently inviting him to take her, to become one with her. His hand moved between her legs while he kissed her with his own desperate hunger, his fingers finding the sensitive cluster of nerve endings and brushing over them so she cried out into his mouth, the noise harsh and afraid. Pleasures almost unknown to Alicia began to cut through her like blades of lightning, arcing from the centre of her womanhood through every cell in her body until she was a trembling mess beneath him.

He struck a finger inside of her and she jolted off the ground at the invasion, surprising and welcoming, and he laughed again, but there was restraint to it, as if he was just holding on to his own sanity. With no experience to guide her, only instincts, her hands moved across his body, feeling the sculptured lines of his abdomen before running lower, to the hardness of his arousal. He swore as she gripped him in the palms of her hands, as he throbbed and swore again. Then he moved his own hand faster, and she was no longer capable of moving or hearing or speaking. She was on fire, burning from the inside out, every part of her aflame. She whimpered into his mouth, against his cheek, and then, as the heat of her orgasm detonated all through her, she cried his name into the night sky and arched her back, utterly, totally overcome by the strength of her pleasure, but also, regardless, by her need for him.

He watched her come back to earth, his control considerably frayed at the edges given the way her hands were spasmodically clutching his length, her grip animalistic and primal, desperate and possessive, her face scrunched up in pleasure and his body desperate to feel her, to be inside her. He moved his hands to her hips, then higher to cup her breasts, so she released her grip on him and lay back on the grass, staring at his face, frowning, as though she'd never seen him before.

Something hummed in the air between them—words unspoken, a confession—and he wondered. He felt a weight inside of her, felt an ache he couldn't fathom, and so he kissed her slowly, wanting to erase the frown, wanting to taste her, to feel her.

Ten years ago, when he'd made love to her—taken her innocence in a field not dissimilar to this one, their backs then on a picnic rug rather than the grass—he'd felt a connection unlike anything he'd ever known. Before that, he'd had sex. But with Alicia, it had been a connection of their souls, a frighteningly intimate experience that had changed him.

He'd never known a feeling like it since, and he couldn't help but wonder... Would it be like that again now? Even watching as she came had pulled at a piece of him, unravelling bonds he'd formed many years earlier, a tightness in his chest that had served him well.

But this was just an itch he needed to scratch, like he'd said. They had unfinished business. The sooner they finished it and could move on, the better.

He lifted her just as he had the first day she'd arrived and twisted her ankle, holding her naked body against his chest as they approached the house, and she was too alive with nerves and anticipation to think clearly. Only as he shouldered the doors in, she startled, putting a hand on his shoulder. 'Isabella,' she reminded him anxiously, looking around.

'Is nowhere to be seen.' But he moved faster, and rather than entering the courtyard, he turned right and took a set of stairs that led to a part of the house she hadn't explored. When he shouldered in the door to his bedroom, her heart splintered apart, just as she'd known it would, to be crossing this threshold of intimacy, to be entering his private sanctuary.

Her senses were overloaded. The room was large, with a huge bed against one wall, darkly wooded side tables and a leather sofa across the space. A television hung above a fireplace, and two narrow doors marked the edge of the room—one leading to a wardrobe, she guessed, the other, a bathroom, going from the tiles she could see on the floor. The artwork on the walls was bold and modern, and the curtains that hung were dark navy. Everything in here was overtly masculine, including a lingering aroma of cologne that made her groan softly.

He placed her on the edge of the bed and stood back, regarding her slowly. 'Are you sure you want this?' he demanded, watching her, his face terse, his eyes showing impatience.

She was tempted to toy with him, to tease him, but her desire was too oversized, and their shared past and pain too mighty to be treated frivolously.

'Yes.' A simple answer that had him moving quickly to his bedside table and opening a drawer, removing a line of condoms and perforating one from the rest before slicing it across the top. She watched, riveted, as he unfurled it over his length, then came back to her, standing over her, chest heaving so her eyes fell first to his tattoo then lower, to his arousal. She gasped, because he was so very large and tantalising that her skin lifted in goosebumps and she felt a strange heat spool between her legs.

'I want you,' she insisted again, lifting a hand to reach for him, but that wasn't necessary. Graciano was already moving, his body nudging her backwards on the bed. She wriggled up into the centre and he chased her, his mouth finding hers and claiming it as his knee nudged her legs apart, and his body pressed down on hers, every soft curve of her against all his hard planes.

She trembled with the promise of what was to come, with the force of her need. His hands caught hers, lacing their fingers together, holding them to the side, and she squirmed beneath him, trying, needing, to feel him inside.

His throaty laugh sent goosebumps all over her.

She arched her back and he moved a hand to her thigh, lifting it this time, pushing it aside, before nudging his tip at her entrance, teasing her so she moaned and tried to take him deeper, but Graciano was in complete control. Or was he? When she peeked at his face, she saw the effort that control was taking, his features carved from steel, his skin ashen.

'I want you,' she repeated, like a prayer, then bit down on her lip as finally he thrust into her, once, hard, fast, and she exploded, his possession unique and perfect, barriers that only he had breached in the past, only once, broken again, her muscles so tight around him, squeezing him so she cried out as the beginning of an orgasm began to froth in her fingertips, to spread through every cell in her body.

'*Cristo*, you're so tight,' he ground out, moving his mouth to her neck and sucking her flesh there, his stubble a delightful pleasure-pain offset by the sweetness of his lips and tongue, the warmth of his breath. Then he was dragging across her décolletage, moving harder, deeper, until she couldn't see straight and thought she might pass out from pleasure.

She tilted off the edge of the earth, no longer human, no longer recognisable, grabbing hold of his shoulders as she spun away from any form of reality, and he whispered words in her ears, Spanish words that she couldn't understand properly but adored nonetheless. A moment later, while she was still grappling with the waves of her pleasure, the turbulence rocking her, he began to move once more, and she realised how much of himself he'd been holding back the first time, because this was *all* of him, everything, so much so that she bucked and twisted and cried out in delirium as new pleasures spread through her and she was barely human.

Again she felt the world slip away from her, mania driving her to the edge of reason and sense, and this time he was with her, his guttural cry as he exploded only adding to the intensity of her pleasure, the perfection of that moment.

She sobbed as he lay on top of her, their hearts racing, his arousal jerking inside of her as he rode his own wave of euphoria, his breath brushing her cheek.

A single tear rolled down her cheek, landing between them, so Graciano shifted, frowning as he lifted up to look at her. His eyes scanned hers, worry in their depths, but then he smiled, a smile that creased the corners of his eyes and made her heart do a strange twisty looping. *This* was her Graciano as he'd been then, without all the cynicism and anger, without the boundaries he'd been forced to build around himself except when they were together.

He rolled away from her onto his back, separating them so her body reacted with a violent protest, not wanting him to be apart from her even when she knew, with every fibre of her being, that they would be together again. There was no way they could fight that. Not for the rest of this week. Beyond that, their futures were apart, but here, now, being together was imperative.

They lay side by side for a long time, rushed breathing eventually slowing, her eyes drying, sense returning. There were no regrets.

'That was…' She couldn't think of an appropriate word.

'Nice?' he interjected, teasing a little.

'I suppose it was,' she agreed, grinning.

'Nice?' he repeated, with mock outrage. 'I really hope not.'

'Is there something wrong with *nice*?'

'It's a little bland for what we just did.'

She laughed softly, then turned to face him. It was a mistake. Her heart lurched and the world tipped off its axis completely. Fresh tears filmed her eyes. She flipped onto her back once more, staring at the ceiling; it was far safer.

'What is it?'

How could she answer that? How could she tell him how sad she felt for what they'd lost? The chance to be together, to be a family, the chance to know one another properly, beyond that night they'd shared?

She'd been bullied into giving him up. Her love for him had been manipulated by a father who couldn't bear to lose control of his 'good' little daughter.

She ground her teeth together, the past a prickly patch to contemplate. 'What does this mean?' she asked, changing the subject as she ran her finger over the tattoo on his chest.

He hesitated, as though he wasn't going to answer. 'It means, "May every mast hold its own sail."'

She pulled her lips to one side. 'I don't get it.'

'On a ship, each mast holds a sail of its own. That sail fills with wind, and the wind directs it. We make choices, those choices have consequences.'

Her heart skipped a beat. 'Every mast has its own

sail,' she repeated, thinking of her own choices, thinking of Annie, a lump in her throat.

'When did you get it?'

'Years ago.'

She rolled her eyes. 'Two years ago, five years ago, ten years ago?' Her throat went dry as she offered the last suggestion.

'About eight, I think. I can't quite remember.'

'Why did you choose it?'

'I like the expression,' he said with a shrug, as though it barely mattered. 'It's something my father used to say.'

That pricked her attention. Only once, back then, had he referred to his real family, referencing deceased parents and a younger brother. She knew he didn't like to talk of them, so hearing the casual reference to his father had her pushing up onto her elbow, looking at him with more care. 'Tell me about him.'

His eyes shuttered. She'd pushed it too far. He wouldn't speak.

Her sigh was soft—an acceptance of his boundaries, of his desire to keep that part of his life locked up. 'My own father is still in Seville, you know,' she said after a pause, lifting a finger and absentmindedly tracing the tattoo.

'I wasn't aware.' There was a coldness in his tone, but she understood it.

'He's no longer involved in the church, but his life is there now.'

'Not with you?'

'I haven't seen him in a long time.'

She felt his chest still, as though he were holding his breath.

'A month after you left, he sent me to England.'

'Sent you? Without him?'

She nodded.

Graciano's eyes flicked to hers, a thousand questions in them. 'How did you feel about that?'

She frowned. 'Better not to ask how I felt then. Now, I'm glad he sent me away,' she said firmly, with defiance. 'It was the right decision.'

'You were sixteen. He was your only family.'

'Not quite. I lived with my grandmother—his mother.'

'Even then, you didn't see him?'

The colour had drained from her face. 'He wouldn't see me,' she said quietly.

Graciano caught her hand, holding it still on his chest. 'Because of me?'

'Because of us,' she said softly, on a gentle sob. 'Because of what we did.'

He swore under his breath. 'You were a teenager. You made a mistake.'

'He didn't raise me to make mistakes. He didn't raise me to sin,' she corrected with vehemence. 'What we did was a crime in the eyes of the Lord. His words, not mine.'

'And so he threw you out?'

'Not onto the streets, as he did you,' she said angrily.

'It was just one night,' he said with a shake of his head, clearly not realising how that evaluation cut her. 'What about forgiveness?'

'I have come to understand that my father talked the talk but didn't walk the walk. His faith is skin-deep.'

'I have had the same reflection.'

Their eyes met and something hummed between them—a shared understanding.

'Why did you bother telling him the truth about us? I had already left, with no intention of coming back.'

She bit down on her lip. Even now, ten years later, it still stung. 'I…'

'Be honest,' he insisted, after she hesitated.

Alicia nodded. 'I couldn't bear for him to think what he did of you. I couldn't bear the thought of him…telling anyone…what he believed you'd done. I didn't want what we'd shared to be sullied in that way. You deserved so much better.'

He lifted a hand to her cheek, stroking it gently. 'I was wrong about you. All these years, I thought you a coward.'

Her heart soared, but she didn't deserve his praise. Annie was always there, in the back of her mind, a secret she'd kept to protect Graciano, but now, as an adult, she realised how greatly she'd deprived him.

'My own father was an excellent man,' he said into the silence so her stomach twisted and she moved closer unconsciously. 'I was only seven when he died, but my memories of him—and my parents—are strong. Perhaps loss sharpened them?'

She stayed quiet, waiting, knowing that her silence would encourage more confidences than probing questions.

'He was a lawyer. As a child, I knew only that he worked hard and always carried a heavy briefcase. Now, I have more information. He was a family lawyer, a working legal aid for children. My mother was a doctor.' His smile was regretful. 'She didn't work when we were young, but she'd just started talking about going back. They sometimes fought about it.'

'He didn't want her to work?'

'I suppose not. My memories of the details there aren't clear. She was very beautiful,' he said, distracted. 'She had long, dark hair that she would loop into a bun high on her head every day. Then each night, she would sit crosslegged on the sofa and pull out the pins, one by one, until it unfurled like a waterfall over one shoulder. My father would comb it with his fingers, and she'd purr like a cat.'

His smile was, strangely for Graciano, almost self-conscious. 'It's odd, the things we remember. Some memories like that are locked in my brain. I can replay them on cue, like a TV show. Others are grainier.'

She weaved their fingers together, dragging his hand to her lips and pressing a kiss against it.

'I know she used to read to my brother and me every night, but I cannot ever remember which books—only the sensation of my brother's little body being curled up at my side and my mother perched beside us, my eyes growing heavy even when I was determined to stay awake, her hand brushing my forehead as I fell asleep. Fragments of memories, impressions of feelings.'

'It sounds like you were very loved.'

'They were good parents,' he said with a small nod. 'They taught me the importance of family.'

'Your brother… Did he…?' She let the question hang in the air.

'No. He survived the crash, but afterwards, we were separated.'

Her brow was quizzical. 'What do you mean?'

'He was badly injured. I was not. I had to be put into foster placement immediately. I saw him in hospital once, but not again—he was too ill. I thought I'd see him when he was better, but days turned into weeks and weeks into months. My foster parents couldn't afford to care for another child. A different home was found for him.'

Alicia gasped. 'That's awful. Could you see him at least?'

'No.' He squeezed her hand. 'Perhaps if a lawyer like my father had been involved, but neither foster parent welcomed the contact. After three months, I was moved to a different home, and then another.' He stood abruptly, striding naked across the room to a tall chest of drawers. He hesitated a moment, then opened a small drawer at the top and removed a piece of paper, crossed the room and handed it to her. 'This is all I had.'

She sat up, taking the photo from him and cradling it in her palm. It was aged, and had obviously been well loved. Her eyes roamed the faces staring back at her: a man who was slender and smiling, wearing a buttoned shirt with jeans and dark hair shoulder length, and two little boys—Graciano with his knees up under his chin, a look of concentration on his face, and his baby brother, with chubby cheeks and a silly grin.

So he'd been serious even before the accident, before the foster care system, before life on the streets?

The photo made her smile, even as it formed a heavy notch in her belly, because how could she ignore the woman in the photo? A woman just as Graciano had described: very beautiful, with silky dark hair and soulful eyes, a woman who was so familiar to her, so achingly known and loved. This was Annie's grandmother—but it could have been Annie. Their eyes, their smiles, their hair. This was Annie's family.

She lifted her spare hand to her mouth and pressed her fingertips there, the heaviness of her betrayal landing like a thud in the centre of her chest.

'As a child in the foster system, you are somewhat powerless. I could do nothing to find Diego. But I remembered my father's voice. Again and again, when we were boys, he would say to me, "He's your brother. It's your job to take care of him." I never forgot that.'

Emotion weighed down on her. She nodded, not trusting herself to speak.

'When I was older, one of my social workers took the time to look into it for me. I was told he'd been adopted by Americans. I don't know if it's true or not. Adoption records are sealed, but perhaps.'

'That's devastating for you. Surely now there must be something—'

'I hired an investigator, some years ago,' he said, closing down on her, the conversation growing too heavy, too frustrating for him. 'I have learned a little more about his life after the accident, before his adoption, but nothing after.'

'Hire a different investigator,' she advised swiftly. 'There *must* be something.'

'Believe me, I've tried. It's as though he's been erased. I do not know where he went, and for years, I lived with the guilt of having let down my father.'

'Your father wouldn't blame you for this,' she assured him quickly. 'None of it is your fault. It seems barbaric to me that any foster agency would split two brothers…'

'Yes,' he said after a beat. 'It is barbaric. You're right.'

But wasn't she just as bad? After all, she'd split Graciano from his daughter. It was hard to look at him without feeling that monumental burden of guilt.

'Why did you leave foster care?'

Again, she felt him closing down. 'I had several bad placements in a row. I was fourteen by then. Life on the streets seemed more appealing.'

'And was it?'

He contemplated that. 'I was my own man.'

'But surely in foster care you at least had a bed, a roof, some food…'

'Everything has a price, Alicia. I preferred to pay mine on the streets.'

It was all so sad. She ached for the life he'd experienced, for what he'd gone through.

'What about an estate?' she murmured, the idea occurring to her out of nowhere. 'Surely your parents had a home, savings, things that could have saved you from living rough.'

'In fact, they did,' he said quietly. 'Unfortunately, I didn't know about it until after I'd made enough money of my own to pay someone to look into it for me.'

She gasped with indignation. 'But surely that should have gone to you.'

'Probably. By the time I learned of the inheritance, which was held in trust for us jointly, I didn't need it. I have saved it for my brother. I don't know how he's living, whether life has been kind to him, but if he wants it, it's his.'

'I'm sure you'll find him,' she said, her words ringing with confidence. 'People don't just disappear into thin air.'

'I would simply like to know he's happy,' Graciano said, moving so that he could see the photo. 'As boys, we were very close. I adored him. It's strange that we're not in each other's lives now.'

She handed the photo back, feeling stung and uncertain. Nothing made sense. The words he'd just used were exactly how she felt about Graciano. She'd loved him so much ten years ago. How often had she thought of him since? Every day. Every damned day. And she'd thought that was because of Annie, but looking at him now, she was no longer convinced. It was Graciano she'd missed. Graciano she'd wanted.

The feeling that she was adrift in a churning sea only seemed to be getting worse, and she had no idea if there was an anchor or life vest to save her.

He thought she was asleep, but then she moved, pinning him with those assessing, intelligent eyes and something stirred in his gut—something long forgotten.

'Graciano.' She pressed a hand to his chest, then yawned, her eyes heavy. 'Before, when we were—'

'Having sex,' he provided, amused that even after sleeping together again and again, she couldn't form the words.

'No, before that. Outside.'

He waited, watching.

She seemed to be wading through sleep and thought, concentrating hard. 'We didn't have protection. Is that— are you—'

He frowned, not following; Alicia's expression showed frustration. 'You don't...'

'What are you trying to ask?' he asked, but with a soft laugh, lifting her hand and pressing it to his lips, a sinking feeling forming in the pit of his gut.

'Children,' she said quickly, not meeting his eyes. 'You don't want children?'

His brows shot up. 'Do *you* want children?'

She focused on the tattoo scrawled across his chest. 'You seemed disgusted by the idea.'

'No. Not disgusted,' he corrected, searching for a better way to describe how he felt. 'Adamantly opposed,' he settled on eventually.

Alicia's face was impossible to read, her eyes shielded from him by her determined focus on his chest. On the one hand, he was flattered. On the other, he wanted to see, to understand—to know what she was feeling. Danger perforated his lungs, making breathing difficult. He knew he should get out of bed, but he wasn't strong enough. Not then.

He'd been in the wilderness a long time; for now, he just wanted to enjoy the strange sensation that he'd come home, without analysing why that was problematic.

'Why?'

Her small-voiced question took a moment to understand. He'd forgotten what they were talking about. But
how to answer? How to explain the hole that opened
up inside his chest when he'd lost his family so many
years ago? As a teenager, he'd known he'd never have
a family. He was a loner, through and through. In fact,
the only time he'd doubted that decision, that deeply
held knowledge, was that one summer, what felt like a
lifetime ago, in Seville.

'They're disgusting,' he said, flippantly. 'Tiny hands,
sticky fingers.'

'I'm serious,' she said, blinking up at him so something jolted in his chest.

'So am I. Snotty noses. Do I really need to elaborate?'

'But your own children,' she said after a beat. 'Surely
you've thought about it?'

'No,' he said firmly. 'That's one decision I've never
doubted.' He didn't know why, but he couldn't admit the
truth to Alicia—that as a boy of eighteen, when they'd
met and he'd felt like maybe he wasn't a loner after all,
he'd imagined a future rich with all the things so many
people aspired to. That Alicia had made him doubt his
desire to be solitary and truly independent.

But he'd been wrong then—there was no sense owning those feelings now.

'My family died when I was just a boy—I have never
wanted another family. I have never wanted that for myself.'

He waited for her to say something else, but her eyes
were closed, her body still, and he let her sleep, or feign
sleep, because the silence suited him, too.

CHAPTER EIGHT

IT TOOK A MOMENT, and considerable skill, to coax his arm out from under Alicia without waking her, to slide from the bed slowly, gently, then stand, taking a few beats to stare down at her and reassure himself she was still asleep. After all, they'd had a disturbed night, punctuated by passion when their chemistry had sparked between them and demanded indulgence. He'd reached for her, or she'd reached for him, and the next moment, they'd been kissing, exploring one another, making love as though it were their lifeblood.

Her body was now as familiar to him as his own, and yet, she was still a mystery.

He stiffened, remember the words she'd spoken the night before describing her father's rejection of her, and a dark anger consumed him completely, forcing him away from the edge of the bed and away from Alicia, lest he make some kind of noise in response to the emotions rolling through him.

The truth was, minister Edward Griffiths was a total *bastardo*.

But why hadn't Graciano anticipated there would be consequences for Alicia? He grabbed some boxer shorts, then strode from the room, shutting the door gently before moving down the hallway towards the central stairs, while deep in thought.

The unpalatable truth was that he'd been so focused on himself he hadn't thought about Alicia, beyond how disappointed he'd been in her—how angry, how all his hopes and feelings and barely acknowledged future aspirations had been destroyed. That anger had prevented him from predicting the likelihood that she would go to her father with the truth. He hadn't foreseen that.

Now he wondered how that was possible. He'd spent months that summer watching her, admiring her, understanding her. She wasn't like anyone he'd ever met. She didn't judge him; she didn't care about his background. She was the first person in his life who really saw *him*, and wanted *him*. It was those very traits that had made her rejection sting all the worse. She'd brought him out into the light and then turned it off, and he'd been determined not to forgive her for that—but even when, as it turned out, she hadn't deserved a decade of his scorn?

He stopped in the kitchen, pressing his palms to the bench in a physical response to that. Snatches of that morning came into his mind, memories he'd spent a decade trying to ignore.

Edward Griffiths shouting. *You took advantage of my daughter! You raped her!*

And Alicia, silent, eyes to the floor, face ashen. He'd waited for her to interject. To say *anything*.

Get the hell off my property. If I ever see you again, I'll call the police. Hell, I'll call them right now.

And then Edward had put his arm around Alicia and led her away. They'd walked off, side by side, a team, Alicia's loyalty made oh so obvious by her choice to stay silent, to walk with Edward.

Graciano wasn't an idiot, though. His experiences

had made him particularly demanding of fidelity, unable to forgive disloyalty. It was possible he'd expected more than any sixteen-year-old girl, who was alone in the world besides her father, could deliver. But he was sure she'd looked at him with coldness that morning. He'd felt her rejection—it had turned his blood to ice—but what if he'd been wrong? What if that had been fear of her father? His gut twisted at that new idea.

He made a coffee, then slipped out of the kitchen before anyone could appear and interrupt. He needed to be alone to reflect on the fact that last night had shifted something inside of him—something he'd held on to for a long time. Parameters that had defined his existence, that had been established for his safety and protection, were moving without his consent.

He took a long drink of his coffee, the first sip of the morning always a balm, then moved out into the garden, his eyes instinctively gravitating to the flat piece of land down by the sea. Without any forethought he moved there, legs long, carrying him with ease over the ground he knew so well, mind running over the predicament he found himself in.

He wasn't a foolish eighteen-year-old any more, under her spell for the first time, but nor was he blind to the problems that would arise if he let them become more entangled. His life was predicated on being alone, on being able to walk away from anyone and anything at any time. It was easy to exist in a world with tragedy and unfairness if one didn't develop attachments. If one didn't love.

The accident would not have destroyed him the way it did if he'd loved his parents and brother less. If his heart had been more under his control, he wouldn't have known that deep, gaping pain.

And again, as an eighteen-year-old, when Alicia's father had thrown him out…

Being alone was now his preferred mode of living, and Alicia was a grave threat to that. Or she would be, if he didn't continue to exercise total control in all their interactions—if he let himself forget that she would be leaving in a matter of days, if he let himself dream, for even a moment, that there could be a future for them… The whole point of having her here was to prove—to himself and her—that he could control his desire for her, that he could walk away on his own terms.

He finished his coffee, then bent down to retrieve her clothes from the night before, his hand fisting around the soft, dewy fabric before breathing in deeply and smelling her scent, sweet like vanilla. His gut rolled. There would be no future. Even though she'd explained her version of what had happened back then, it didn't change Graciano's reality.

Twice in his life, Graciano had known the god-awful pain of having had the rug pulled out from under him, the discombobulating certainty that his life was altered for ever and that he was powerless to contain that—once, when the car accident had taken his parents and brother from him, and again, when he'd known he'd lost Alicia. It was a pain he'd never open himself up to again. He would never allow himself to be destroyed like that again; he wasn't sure he'd recover a third time. He had to get away from her, from this, from their past, and the suddenly compelling lure of a future with the woman he'd sworn he'd always hate.

Alicia blinked away from the startlingly beautiful view of the ocean awash with the sun's morning light. At the sound of a glass door sliding open, her heart gave a now familiar lurch at the sight of Graciano. He was fully dressed, in a pair of dark trousers and a white button-up shirt with the sleeves pushed to his elbows, and something inside of her tipped totally off balance.

'I didn't realise you were out here.'

Her heart flip-flopped.

'I was just having a coffee.' She pushed a smile to her lips, telling herself she was imagining the coldness to his tone. 'Want to join me?'

His response was immediate: a swift shake of his head. Her heart dropped to her toes.

Graciano didn't leave, so that was something. But the longer he stood there without speaking, just frowning, the more she felt the ground beneath her shift.

Did he regret what had happened? Was he angry with her again? If so, what on earth for? She racked her memory for their conversation the night before, but couldn't find a single point over which they'd argued.

Her stomach knotted and she turned away, her eyes chasing the lines of the ocean instead.

'I have meetings in Barcelona today.'

He was leaving. Running away?

She pursed her lips. 'I see.'

'I'll be back for dinner.'

She angled her face towards him, pride demanding she keep her feelings concealed. She wouldn't let him see that she was hurt by that—that she was worried. 'You don't have to report your movements to me.' She softened the acidity of the words with a tight smile.

'I thought you might notice my absence,' he said after a pause, a small shrug shifting his shoulders. 'It's a courtesy.'

'Noted.' She tapped the papers beside her—notes

she'd been making about his event. 'I have plenty to keep me busy, don't worry.'

'I'm not worried. I'm just letting you know that I'll be gone for the day.'

'And I'm saying, I don't care.' Hurt made her words more acerbic, the stinging tone designed to hide the way he'd upset her so easily. 'What happened last night doesn't change anything, Graciano. You didn't tell me the first time you went away for work. You don't have to tell me this time. It's fine.' Bitterness flooded her body as she spoke words she didn't feel, as she picked a fight she didn't want, and for no reason other than that she was disappointed—disappointed that he'd come out here frowning and cool, rather than wrapping her in his arms and kissing her, disappointed that he'd immediately delineated a line between the passion they'd indulged the night before and how he wanted things to be outside the bedroom.

Disappointed that she'd let herself hope, even without realising she was doing it, for more—for something different in her life. For Graciano.

For a family.

The thought was so strong, so achingly searing, that she almost gasped. Had she really let herself fantasise about that? About the last ten years evaporating into thin air, and them becoming parents to their daughter, one happy family after all this time?

What a fool!

'Isabella has my contact information. If you should need anything, just call.'

She forced an over-bright smile to her face. 'I'm sure that won't be necessary.'

His eyes bore into hers for several long seconds and then he turned and left, without so much as a goodbye.

And she was glad. Glad he'd left, because suddenly her eyes stung with tears and she desperately didn't want him to see them, to know he'd done that, to know how he could affect her.

A moment later, she heard the helicopter whir to life and expelled a soft, shaking sigh.

It was a blessing that Graciano was so busy. The takeover was in the final stages of negotiations, an occupation he generally relished, for it was at the end that the advantage was all his. By then, he understood his opponent—and he always regarded the company he was buying as the opposition—and he knew which buttons to push to achieve his aims.

He usually relished focusing with a laser-like intensity on the final meetings, but today he was distracted—not enough to negatively impact his work, but enough to drag him down to the level of being a mere mortal, so he was angry with himself as the day wore on, and his mind felt more scattered than he could remember it feeling.

Graciano closed the door gratefully after his meeting, and paced to the windows overlooking Barcelona. The unique city with its striking architecture always filled his heart with satisfaction. It was here that he'd come when he had nothing, here that he'd built a fortune. This was his home—his place in the world, his land of opportunities. It was here that he was king of his castle. But his eyes gravitated south, in the direction of the sea just beyond Valencia, and in his mind, he was approaching the island and Alicia was in the turret, waiting for him, watching for him—needing and wanting him.

He swore under his breath, dragging a hand through

his hair. This was messier than he'd appreciated. Harder than he'd thought. She was taking him over on a cellular level and he had no idea how to stop it, but he knew that he must. He knew that he couldn't let her become his sun and moon ever again—no one could be trusted to wield that kind of power. The whole point of this exercise was to prove he was stronger than the power she wielded over him—that he'd changed, grown, beyond Alicia and the way she made him feel.

It was here, in the office, in the corporate world, that he was at his best. Here, life was simple. He could control everything. He didn't care what people thought of him. He didn't care what enemies he made. There was an objective measure for success—financial achievement—and it was the only benchmark he cared about.

Alicia's place in his life and mind had to be as tightly controlled as any other facet of his life. Determination fired inside of him, and without skipping a beat, he moved to his desk and lifted his phone from the cradle.

'Book me a dinner somewhere. And call Isabella to let her know I'll be in the city tonight, rather than returning to the island.'

He hung up, wondering why having made that firm decision didn't feel better—why the expected weight, instead of lifting from his shoulders, seemed to have thudded deep inside his gut.

Alicia stared, frowning, at the empty chair, the nerves that had been fraying all day now jolting through her.

He wasn't coming back tonight.

The message had been relayed by Isabella with a casual air. After all, the housekeeper could have no idea how much Alicia was looking forward to seeing Graciano, how she'd been building up to asking him why he'd been in such a strange mood that morning.

Isabella couldn't have known what kind of rejection there was in those simple words.

But Alicia did.

She felt it deep in her soul.

There was no more effective way of telling her he regretted what had happened between them than by showing her, and that was exactly what he was doing. Could he put any more distance between them than he already was?

She stabbed her fork into the piece of fish, lifting it to her mouth and forcing herself to chew when she was no longer hungry. She'd skipped lunch, though, and she knew she should eat, but every time she went through the motions of putting food in her mouth, it became harder and harder to swallow.

Sleeping together had been a mistake. She'd let herself believe things could be different for them, but that had been a fool's paradise. Even if Graciano were capable of change, even if she were able to put her heart on the line again, nothing would change the fact that she'd kept their daughter from him, that he'd made it impossible to tell him, and then she'd accepted that. They both had a right for far too much resentment. There could be no coming back from that. There was no hope here.

She had to tell him about Annie. Not because of what had happened between them, but because it was the right thing to do. Annie was his daughter. He needed to know.

But…was that selfish? He'd made it clear he didn't want children. His answers on that score were unequivocal. Telling him might feel right to her—it might even feel good—but what if he chose to have nothing to do with Annie? What if Annie's existence ruined his life in some way?

She groaned softly, dropping her head forward with the sheer weight of worry that was pounding her from either side. She had no idea what to do, but sitting here pining for him wasn't an option.

Que cada palo aguante su vela. Every mast has its own sail.

She was her own person, more so now than she'd been at sixteen, when she'd had to submit to the strings of her life being pulled without her say so. Now she could pull back.

And there was no way in hell she was going to stay on this island, as much a prisoner as the original occupant of this house, desperately waiting for the scattered attentions of a man who didn't, or couldn't, be everything she wanted.

She had to leave.

CHAPTER NINE

HE'D PUSHED HIMSELF to remain away most of the following day, too. He told himself the emotion coursing through him was that of satisfaction, that he was glad he'd been able to resist her, to continue with his normal life. He refused to acknowledge the powerful zipping in his veins, the almost superhuman strength bursting inside of him that was the result of knowing he'd see her again soon—that his abstinence would be rewarded. They could share a meal; he could watch her and listen to her and admire her, then draw her to his room and make love to her all night long, safe in the knowledge his willpower was stronger than his need for her. Control. It was everything.

His body hardened as the helicopter came down low over the island, exulting in the prospect of the night ahead.

Until he looked out of the window and saw Alicia standing in the middle of the path that approached the helipad, just as he'd stood when she'd arrived days earlier. There was nothing untoward about that. He might even have found it exciting, except for the suitcase at her side and the impenetrable mask of steel her features bore.

'Alicia.' He practically growled her name as he drew close, and every single treacherous cell in her body went into high alert at his nearness, heat spooling between her legs, breasts aching for his touch. She ground her teeth and kept her eyes focused on a point just beyond his shoulder, on the helicopter that would soon—she hoped—take her part of the way home.

'Graciano,' she responded in kind, but without a hint of warmth in her voice.

'Going somewhere?'

'Yes.' Now she forced her eyes to meet his and her stomach dropped to her toes. 'Home.' The word quivered a little. She swallowed, tamping down on her emotions as she'd had to do for so many years. 'I've got everything I need, including your assistant's information. We had a long chat today. I know exactly how to proceed. There's no reason for me to remain here.'

'Isn't there?' he asked, moving dangerously close, his voice silky. Her throat hurt. She stood her ground.

'No.'

Perhaps he wasn't expecting the resistance. His eyes widened for the briefest moment. Then a scowl settled on his brow.

'However, we had an arrangement. Five nights.'

Her spine tingled. 'Our arrangement's changed.'

'Not from where I'm standing.'

'You'd seriously want to keep me here against my will?'

'Is that what I would be doing?'

She swallowed hard, ignoring the swirling desire moving through her, the desire that would wreak havoc with her life if she allowed it—not to mention her self-respect. As if he could read her thoughts, he moved forward, closer, dangerously close so her pulse fired into high frequency and her heart twisted.

'Stay,' he murmured, bringing his lips to the base of

her throat, kissing her slowly. God, how she wanted to listen to him. Her bones felt as though they were made of molten lava.

'I've told you what I want,' she said, trying to be firm. 'I'd like to leave now.'

'That doesn't suit me.'

She glared at him. 'Why not?'

'Because we had a deal.'

'Oh, for crying out loud. Is that the sum total of your argument? Because if so, it just underscores *why* I'm right to leave.'

His eyes skimmed hers and she knew she'd said too much. She'd shown how hurt she'd been when she'd intended to keep that pain wrapped up inside herself.

'You're angry that I went away.'

There was no sense fighting that. 'I'm angry I let you use me. I'm angry I didn't see through you. And yes, I'm angry that you went away, but I suppose there was no point in staying. You got what you wanted. So now, just let me go.'

He swore softly, then caught her at the elbow and turned her away. 'I didn't use you, Alicia. What happened between us was very mutual, very satisfying. Do not rewrite it.'

'I'm not coming back to the house with you,' she said, her voice rising, approaching hysteria. She'd already mentally torn herself from the beautiful place. She couldn't go back. 'I want to go home.'

'I'm not going to have this conversation here,' he said, gesturing to the helicopter pilot and the open air around them. 'Come inside and we'll talk.'

'There's no point.' She wrenched her arm free. 'Nothing you can say will change my mind. I want to go. I have to go.'

'Why?'

Because I'm one more sensual night away from falling in love with you and I can't allow that to happen. Because we have a daughter and I need to tell you about her but I can't work out how or when, when I'm on your island and in your bed. But I will when I have finally found the courage and the words. She almost shouted her response, so awash was she with feelings. 'Isn't it obvious?'

'What did you expect me to say and do the next morning? How did you want me to act?'

Her insides were bruised; his questions hurt. 'Like a decent human being?' she muttered, before she could think through her reply.

His face blanched visibly and all too late she remembered her father throwing those words at him back then. But the charge was deserved now. He'd treated her like dirt.

'You wanted flowers? Perhaps a string quartet to play to you from beneath my window?'

'Don't speak to me like that,' she ground out. 'You started pushing me away the second you woke up. I don't care that you've been in Barcelona, that you had to work. It's the *way* you told me. The way you spoke to me. The way you stayed silent while you were gone. What we shared—'

But she was moving into dangerous territory now, as truths she hadn't even acknowledged to herself seemed to be thrusting forward, demanding to be spoken.

'Was sex. As inevitable now as it was back then. We both agreed to that.'

Tears filmed her eyes and she blinked furiously, trying to stem their progress. 'If that's so, why are you fighting me about leaving? Why would you want to keep me here?'

A muscle jerked in his jaw as her question exploded between them. 'I'm a man of my word,' he said finally. 'I presumed you would also have a personal code of honour. Having agreed to stay for five days—'

'That's a load of crap,' she contradicted forcefully. 'You know better than anyone that circumstances change. I'm not staying here after what happened with us. I can't. And I know you're too good a person to make me.' Her voice cracked; her heart splintered. 'So stop arguing and tell your damned pilot to take me to Valencia.'

He dragged a hand through his hair and she waited, her nerves stretching tight, waiting, hoping he'd have something to say that would unlock the pain in her heart, setting it free, high above them, flying out over the ocean and dispersing for good.

There'd been so much pain in her life, and much of it was linked to this man.

Bitterness washed through her, and panic, too, because nothing would be the same after this. The question of Annie could no longer sit in abeyance. Alicia had to work out how to proceed. She knew she couldn't continue to abide by the decisions she'd made as a scared, lonely sixteen-year-old. Everything was so complicated, and the weight of that complexity pressed down on her now, making breathing almost impossible.

'Why do you want me to stay?' she asked when he didn't speak, and she could feel the situation slipping away from her. 'And don't say it's because we had a deal. The deal was for me to organise your event and that's well underway.'

'I want you to stay for the same reason we slept to-gether.'

She held her breath.

'There's unfinished business between us.'

'I think it's finished now.'

'Do you?' He lifted a single brow, mockery in his face. 'So you'll fly away and never think of me again?'

Her eyes dropped to the ground between them, everything shifting wildly out of focus. She'd thought of him every day for the last ten years. She knew that wouldn't change. 'We'll never finish this,' she said after a beat. 'From the moment my father reacted the way he did, from the moment he made those threats, he set our lives on courses that could never come back together. There's nothing to be gained by this.'

He moved closer again, so close she caught a hint of his masculine, spiced fragrance, and her pulse went into overdrive, desire lurching through her. 'I want you out of my head,' he said finally, the admission wrenched from him, and she closed her eyes on the welling of grief, because she understood how he felt. They were each a torment to the other.

'So much so you're willing to keep me here, even when I've asked to leave?' she whispered, knowing the answer, knowing she was moments away from his acceptance.

They were both trapped by the past, by another man's choices, but one of them had to be strong enough to break free. Staying here wasn't the answer. Alicia needed to get back to her real life; she needed space to breathe and think, neither of which she could do here, where Graciano filled every single one of her senses—even with his absence.

'No,' he said, finally, the word shattering inside of

her. 'I want you to stay, but the choice is yours.' He took a step back, crossing his arms over his chest and looking at her dispassionately, no emotion visible in his handsome face. His extreme control only underscored her reasons for needing to leave.

He might think she was under his skin, but he didn't understand what it was to feel, to love, to need, with an all-consuming passion. He couldn't fathom the torture she'd experienced because of her feelings for this man. She'd triumphed over those feelings once—she'd been strong and resilient and had made a life for herself—but being around him threatened that completely.

'Staying isn't an option.' In the end, it was that simple.

Only then did a flicker of feeling seep into his features, a look in his eyes that she'd seen once before, the morning after they'd slept together, when her father had berated him and thrown him off his property. Betrayal.

She sucked in a breath and spun away from him, blinking rapidly as her attention landed on the helicopter.

'Come with me,' he commanded, striding past her, picking up her suitcase, then moving to the helicopter.

It was a done deal; she was leaving. She'd gotten what she wanted and didn't feel a hint of satisfaction in that. Disappointment jarred her with every step she took, but she knew this was the right course of action. It was as it had to be.

The helicopter was barely in the air before he knew he'd made a rare mistake. Graciano, who was no expert at reading people, at manoeuvring them to do his bidding, had erred. His own feelings had been coursing through him, making it impossible to understand hers, to know how to respond to them, how to give her what she wanted.

He planted his hands on his hips and watched, grim-faced, as the helicopter lifted up, wondering if she was looking down at him, wondering if she was regretting her decision, too.

He knew one thing for certain: this wasn't the end for them. After ten years, he'd had enough. He wanted closure, and watching her walk away from him wasn't how he'd achieve it. There would be a better way. He just needed time to consider that, and come up with a plan.

'You're home!' Annie pushed back her chair, a huge grin on her face as she zipped around the table and towards Alicia. Alicia could only stand there, stricken by the sight of her daughter, and all the similarities to Graciano she'd been able to blot out for the past nine years that were now forcing themselves to be acknowledged—similarities not only to Graciano, but to his family. Annie's family.

She bent down so she could wrap her arms around Annie, hugging her little body tight, tears filming her eyes as she nuzzled into the curve of her neck and her silky dark hair. She inhaled, eyes closed, and then blinked open, so her gaze landed across the room on Diane, who was watching with a small frown.

'You're early!' Annie remarked, moving to pull back, except Alicia held her tight, as though her life depended on it—as though she knew that the world they'd built, of being just the two of them, could no longer go on.

'I finished ahead of schedule,' she said unevenly. 'And I wanted to come home.'

'Yay! How was it?'

'Lovely,' she lied.

'Did you take a billion photos? Diane showed me the one of the beach, but that's all. Did you go shopping? What was it like?'

Alicia laughed softly. 'I was working. I didn't get many photos.'

'But you took some?'

She thought of the beautiful beach, the gardens, and nodded. 'I'll show you in the morning. It's late now.' The only flight she could get out of Valencia had been an evening one, and it had been held up on the tarmac.

'Diane let me stay up watching a movie.'

'She did, did she?' Alicia tried to relax into the normalcy of this, the domestic contentment of her normal life, but she knew she no longer belonged quite the same way. She was different. Everything had changed.

'And eating ice cream.'

'Dibber dobber,' Diane responded, moving closer with a wink.

'Well, it's bedtime now.' Alicia pressed another kiss to her daughter's forehead, then straightened, heart heavy with the weight of her responsibilities.

Once Annie had padded upstairs, Diane propped a hip against the door, her silvering hair shimmering in the soft lamplight. 'You're upset.'

It was a correct guess, but Alicia shook her head, pushing a bright smile to her face. Diane was one of the few people who knew all of Alicia's secrets. She'd been there from the beginning, when Alicia had come to hospital appointments on her own and Diane, the paediatrician on call, had taken a special interest in the teenage mother. She'd held Alicia's hand when she'd tried to speak to Graciano and had seen her heartbreak when he'd rejected her.

'Yes,' she said, pulling her lips to one side. 'But I probably deserve to be.'

'Pish, what happened?'

Alicia sighed softly, then began to talk, to explain everything to Diane, who listened with a sympathetic, loving expression, nodding from time to time.

'Do you still love him, darling?' Diane asked, after a beat.

Alicia startled. 'Love him? Of course not. How can I?'

'Because you have the biggest heart of anyone I know. You've been single ever since him. And you look as though you've left a part of yourself behind in Spain.'

Alicia opened her mouth to deny it again, but found her mind too swamped. 'It doesn't matter how I feel. We've both made too many mistakes, Di. You must see that? What future can there be for us, after all that's come before?'

The following day, Graciano flicked through the document, scowling.

There was no denying: it was excellent. With very little input from Graciano, Alicia had somehow planned the perfect evening—for his non-existent event. It was a shame he wasn't planning to host any such party, as it would have been exceptional. The plans were comprehensive and professional, detailing guest transportation, staffing needs as well as accommodation, dietary requirements, menu suggestions, marquee placement and dance floor. She'd suggested two music options: a DJ for by the beach, and more of a lowkey acoustic band for the dinner. She'd arranged for fireworks, scheduled interviews with several high-profile magazines... Everything had been thought of.

He got to the bottom, then quit the document, re-turning to the email she'd sent, rereading it for the tenth time.

Graciano,
Please see attached event plan. I've gone through the details with your assistant, who's happy to run point on the night. You shouldn't need anything more from me.
    Best wishes,
    Alicia

It was not unlike any number of emails he received on a daily basis, and that in and of itself was a problem.

She wasn't just some colleague…someone he'd em-ployed for a job. She was Alicia.

Unfinished business, indeed.

With a grim expression on his features, he hit Reply.

Alicia,
I have some questions. Can we meet to discuss?

Graciano hesitated before he remembered he didn't second-guess himself and hit Send.

The ball was in her court, but he already knew what she'd say. No one who took such obvious pride in their professional abilities would disappoint a client.

He leaned back and waited, every cell in his body stretching taut for no reason he could think of.

She swore as she read the email. It wasn't completely unexpected, but it sent a thousand feelings rioting through her. She knew she'd need to see him again, to finally tell him about Annie, but it still felt almost impossible.

I can speak now.

She waited, and sure enough, the reply came through within a minute.

No, in person. I'll send a car.

Her heart leaped into her throat.

Are you in London?

Yes. What's your address?

Everything began to tremble.

I can't come right away. I have an appointment at four p.m.

She had Annie's parent-teacher interview scheduled for that afternoon.

The response was immediate.

Tonight?

Everything shifted. She wanted to tell him no and she wanted to tell him 'Hell, yes.' But at the end of the day, this was just business, the last of her obligation to him. He'd paid five hundred thousand pounds for the privilege, after all.

I can give you an hour. Six o'clock?

What's your address?

She shook her head. She wasn't going to let him send a car. She couldn't live in a world where Graciano knew where her house was.

I'll come to you.

If you prefer.

He included an address in Knightsbridge at the bottom of the email and she pushed her phone away like it was poison, before reaching for it once more to see if Diane—her saviour—was available to help with Annie.

She was.

Seeing Graciano again, then, was only a matter of time. And this time, she couldn't squander the opportunity.

She had to tell him about Annie. She'd gone to the island knowing she must, but wanting to learn more about him first. While he'd always be a form of poison to her, he was also the father of her child.

Nothing else mattered.

Not their past, not their future, not her heart, her wishes, their desire. They shared a daughter, and working out how to deal with that reality had to be their sole focus. It would take every single bit of nerve she possessed, but Alicia could wait no longer. Tonight would be the night.

CHAPTER TEN

SHE'D PRESUMED THE address would be for an office, but the moment she approached the front of the building, she realised the error of her ways. This was residential, plain and simple. She double-checked the email, seeing that the address included an entry code. She keyed it in and waited as the glass doors swished to let her pass.

The foyer was stately and impressive, with shiny tiles and a double-height ceiling, the wall-to-wall windows showing a view straight through to Hyde Park. It was spectacular. She moved to the bank of lifts and waited for one to arrive, then moved inside, again consulting her phone for instructions. She pressed the button that corresponded with the floor number he'd given her, then stepped back and waited. It whooshed up quickly, leaving her tummy back in the foyer.

When the doors opened, it was into a small room, with a leather bench seat and an impressively ornate mirror. She caught a glimpse of herself, pale and nervous, and pinched her cheeks, sucking in a deep breath before pressing the doorbell for the only door in the place.

Her nerves stretched tight and she discreetly observed the time—just before six. Maybe he wasn't home? Maybe he'd forgotten? Her heart trembled and she tried to work out how she felt about either possibility, and then, the door pulled inwards.

Graciano stood on the other side, and all she could do was stare, as Diane's question went round and round in her head. *Do you love him?*

She'd denied it to Diane, and to herself, but now, she had to face reality: yes, she loved him. Still. As much as ever. She'd never stopped.

'Alicia.' Apparently oblivious to her emotion turmoil, he stepped back and waved an arm into the apartment. She hesitated on the threshold, aware that crossing it was a metaphorical hurdle as well as a physical one.

'I don't bite,' he growled, so she startled, moving past him quickly and putting as much distance between them as she could, but his eyes held hers for several beats and then dropped lower, his appraisal swift but fiercely hot, burning her with the intensity of his scrutiny. His gaze scraped hungrily over her frame, over the business suit and two-inch spike heels she wore—a confidence boost, usually. She trembled and turned away from him a little.

Had it really only been ten days since they'd seen each other? It felt like so much longer, and at the same time, it felt like no time had passed at all.

The reality of their situation, of all she had to tell him, burst and suddenly her stomach was in knots. This was terrifying.

'Thank you for coming,' he responded, gesturing deeper into the apartment before taking some steps towards the spectacular windows framing a view of the busy street and Harrods just down a little way.

She lifted her shoulders. 'I'm a professional.'

'So I gather. I was impressed by your proposal.'

Her heart fired. 'But you have questions?'

'I'll come to that. Would you like a drink?' He moved to the back wall, into a large, open-plan kitchen that would have been at home in a five-star restaurant.

She shook her head. 'I'd prefer to get this over with.'

His eyes hummed across her face. 'Still adamant you don't want anything to do with me?'

Her nerves jumbled faster. 'I'm not here to discuss what happened between us.'

'Why not?'

'For all the reasons we discussed on the island. Primarily—' she sighed '—there's no point.'

'I disagree.'

She hesitated, then moved closer to the kitchen, staying on the opposite side of the bench, glad for the physical barrier between them.

'I made a mistake.'

She watched as he pulled a bottle of sparkling water from the fridge, then poured two glasses. Alicia pretended fascination with the bubbles.

'Oh?'

'I didn't handle things well.'

Her heart slammed into her ribs. 'I don't want to talk about events of a decade ago.'

He frowned reflexively. 'I mean last week. When I went to Barcelona, the day after we slept together, I was running, but it was insensitive and hurtful. I'm sorry.'

It was the very last thing she'd expected. Her lips parted on a soft exhalation and the knots in her tummy grew bigger. 'Graciano,' she said after a beat, looking down at the countertop.

'Let me say this,' he asked urgently, leaning across and putting a hand on hers.

She swallowed past a knot in her throat, then nodded once.

He came around to her side of the bench, moving so close to her that her treacherous body trembled in immediate response.

'Twice in my life I have been without an anchor—the first time, when my parents died and my brother disappeared.' She dug her nails into her palms, knowing what was coming. 'And the second time was when I left you.'

Her heart twisted.

'I was almost destroyed, twice.'

She closed her eyes, the emotions too, too real.

'I refuse to let it happen a third time.'

Her heart broke for him, then, and it broke for her, too. Her father had destroyed so much, but they'd been complicit. He'd been complicit by letting that rejection destroy him instead of fighting for what he must have known was the truth.

'You were wrong to leave,' she said after a beat.

'You think I should have let the police throw me in prison?'

'I would have defended you.'

'You see everything through your eyes, through your privilege. I was a street kid. There was no one who'd believe me over your father. Besides, you couldn't even defend me to him.'

Sadness welled inside of her.

'Why not tell me that?' she asked quietly. 'Why not tell me that you'd left for self-preservation?'

'I was too angry,' he said with a shift of his shoulders.

'We're going in circles here,' she said throatily. 'And I'm not convinced any of it matters anymore.' Sadness engulfed her. She loved him, and she'd have put money on him having loved her at one time, but that didn't mean they'd be able to make it work.

'It matters,' he responded gruffly, closing the distance between them, putting his hands on her hips to hold her steady. 'I knew I'd made a mistake as soon as your helicopter left. I want more time with you.'

It should have delighted her, but she heard the restrictions in his statement. 'How much time?'

He lifted his shoulders. 'More.'

'Until you're over me?' She pushed, mercilessly, because she needed his absolute honesty. This wasn't love. It wasn't everlasting, for all eternity, happily-ever-after love. His offer was limited, driven by sex and ego.

'Until we're *both* ready to move on,' he corrected carefully. 'Tell me you don't want that.'

'God,' she laughed unevenly, sadly. 'What I want? You have no idea of the gulf that exists between what I want and what I can have. You have no bloody idea.'

'Then tell me,' he demanded, moving closer so their bodies were touching and his lips were an inch from hers. 'Show me.'

And he kissed her, a slow, searching kiss that curled her toes and made everything shimmer like gold dust.

'Does anything matter when there's this?'

She was on the edge of a cliff, her feet nudging farther and farther into open air, a fall imminent. She clung to him—her saviour and danger. He stared down at her, his eyes inscrutable, desire zipping through her, other feelings, more dangerous, more cloying, tightening around her. But in the back of her mind there was Annie and the past, her father, their lost opportunities and the reality she had to face: they hadn't loved each other enough to make this work. If that had been the case back then, it would definitely condemn their relationship now.

'This can't happen,' she mumbled, but even as she

said it, she was lifting up, seeking his lips, knowing it was impossible but wanting him anyway. 'I can't—'

'Don't overthink it,' he said into her mouth and she bit back a sob, knowing there was wisdom in that—or was it self-interest? She wanted him enough to almost mute all sense and logic. But not quite.

'I need to talk to you.'

'About the event? Later.'

'No, not that. I need—'

He pulled back, pressing a finger to her lips. 'Later.' The word was laced with the same fierce need burning her alive. Defiance, though, had her staying where she was, separated from him by an inch.

'Are you sure you're not going to disappear into thin air again?'

His response was to kiss her, slowly at first, then with the need that was building inside of them so their bodies were moving deeper into the penthouse, away from the kitchen, to the plush leather sofas and back onto them, a tangle of limbs and clothes as they discarded them, shucking desperately, needing nakedness and to be together.

She held her breath as he paused to sheathe himself and then drove into her, the relief immediate and complete, so she barely heard the low rumbling of her phone. All she was conscious of was Graciano, his movements, his body, so powerful and strong, and she tilted her head back, sweat beading her forehead as she bit down on her lip and surrendered to this completely, knowing then that she could never have enough of him, knowing that she would go anywhere and do anything to be with him, for the chance to be like this.

It was a terrifying realisation and even more so because she could no longer deny what fuelled her—the love that ran though her. It was a love she'd felt the moment they'd met, a love that had grown as they'd spent time together, that had exploded the night they'd made love, and that she'd clung to all these years, an oasis in the midst of the desert of difficulties that had been her life for so long.

Tears filled her eyes as an orgasm built inside of her and then she was tilting over the edge, nails scoring marks down his back, and he was right there with her, his voice rising, his hands holding her hips steady, his face over hers clenched, his eyes squeezed shut. She stared at him as she tipped over the edge, fascinated, overwhelmed and so full of love that she almost couldn't bear it.

She was conscious of their bodies all tangled together, their loud breathing, his breath warm against her forehead, the feeling that they'd burst an oversized balloon, the sense of relief even as his proximity was stirring new feelings to life —and then, finally, she was conscious of a buzzing noise, faraway seeming at first and then, not so far away. Just across the room.

'Your phone?' he asked, pushing up onto his palms and looking down at her.

She almost wanted to tell him it didn't matter. It was hard to muster any interest in the outside world, but maternal instincts weren't easy to switch off, and despite the fact Annie was with Diane, a premonition of disaster that was always easy to reach for had Alicia putting a hand on Graciano's chest.

'I'd better check it.'

He cocked a brow but moved to release her, pulling out of her body so she bit back a groan of complaint, and he stood, pacing across the room to retrieve her handbag. He carried it to Alicia, allowing her to marvel at his frame, his masculinity, his strength and power.

'Thank you,' she murmured, a smile whispering at the corners of her lips. She lifted her phone from her bag and saw Di's name, and a hint of guilt coloured her cheeks pink. Somehow, she'd still managed to fail at telling Graciano about his daughter! 'I have to take this.'

And then the truth, she promised herself, swiping the phone to answer.

'Hi, Di.'

Graciano turned and strode to the kitchen, then pulled out a beer and popped the top off it.

'Don't panic.'

'Oh, God.' Her heart sunk and she was standing, looking around for her underwear. Graciano had frozen in response to the tone, beer midway to lips, and now he replaced it on the counter. 'What's happened?'

'I said don't panic.'

'"Don't panic" is what people say when there's something to panic about. Is it Annie? Di? What's happened?'

She stretched her knickers on, then her trousers, breath rushed.

'She's okay, but we're on our way to hospital.'

'Hospital? Oh, my God. Why? Where? Which hospital?'

She named one in Hammersmith, just across the Thames from her flat. She knew Diane consulted from there sometimes. 'There was an accident at football training.'

Alicia squeezed her eyes shut. 'Please stop being so vague and tell me exactly what's happened. I can handle it.'

Guilt was a dagger in her stomach. She kept the phone pressed to her ear as she hooked her bra into place. Out of the corner of her eye, she saw Graciano matching her, dressing, without the sense of panic but with all the efficiency.

'She collided with another player and got knocked into the goal. Her arm is broken.'

Alicia swore, all the colour draining from her face. 'Is she in pain?'

'Yes, darling, she is.'

It was so like Di—a doctor—not to sugar-coat it.

'But she'll live. She needs to get it set and at this time of night, a hospital's the best place.' Di paused. 'While I'm there, I want to get her head checked out. She hit it pretty hard as well.'

Alicia's stomach was in knots. 'I'm coming right away. I can be in Hammersmith within fifteen, twenty minutes at the most.' She cursed the fact it was peak hour, that the roads between Knightsbridge and Hammersmith would be at their busiest.

'Tell her Mummy's coming. Tell her I love her.'

'She's going to be okay. This is just a precaution. You don't mess around with head injuries is all. Try not to worry.'

'Just tell her, okay?'

She disconnected the call, turning to Graciano without really seeing him. 'I have to go.' This was a God-awful mess, but her situation with the Spaniard had been bumped lower on her priority list—so, too, the conversation she knew they had to have. This wasn't the time.

'To Hammersmith, I heard. I'll drive you.'

It should have raised alarm bells—she should have known to fight it—but in that moment, anything or anyone who could make this journey easier earned her gratitude.

'Come on. My car's downstairs.'

She was strangely calm as they rode the elevator in silence, but once she was in Graciano's black four-wheel drive with the engine throbbing beneath her, an over-whelm of hysteria bubbled inside of her so she had to look out of the window to muffle her soft sob.

For several minutes neither spoke, but then, as they crossed through South Kensington, he pulled up at the lights and turned to face her.

'You have a child.'

It was like the dropping of a blade, right against the side of her neck.

She swallowed hard and nodded, eyes stinging. 'Annie.' She whispered their daughter's name.

'Why didn't you tell me?' His features showed surprise, shock that she'd kept this from him.

She groaned, pressing her head back against the headrest. 'It just…wasn't that simple.'

'Why not? It seems like a very easy sentence to form. "I have a daughter."'

It wasn't how she'd wanted to tell him, but there was no way she could carry on without being honest. 'Annie's nine,' Alicia said, the words trembling in the car.

The light turned green and Graciano took off, but his knuckles were white against the wheel as her revelation sunk in. Silence met that statement, but it was a silence that was heavy with the turning of his brain as he analysed that from all angles.

South Kensington morphed into Earl's Court and then West Ken, all more familiar to Alicia now.

'Nine,' he said, pulling up at another set of lights, turning to face her. 'So you had her soon after we were together.'

Alicia nodded, her throat thick. 'About eight months later, actually.'

His eyes flared wide and she could see the genuine surprise in his features. This was the last thing he'd been expecting. Her knees trembled.

'I wanted to tell you.'

He swore, then accelerated as the lights changed, his gaze focused straight ahead.

'I came over tonight to tell you—'

'That I have a daughter?' he roared, gripping the steering wheel again, an obvious attempt to regain control. 'She is *nine*,' he said, the words dragged from him. 'And this is the first I am hearing of her?'

Alicia squeezed her eyes shut. 'I tried to tell you.'

'When? When did you goddamned try to tell me about my daughter? She is *nine*,' he repeated, in shock.

His anger was understandable—she'd expected it—but that didn't mean it hurt any less.

'I tried to tell you,' she said again, sucking in a deep breath. 'Back then, when I found out. You made it impossible.'

He snorted. 'Come on, how can that be?'

'You told me you didn't want to hear from me—'

'So you blurt out that you're pregnant!' he roared. 'You *find a way*.'

She shook her head. 'You think that's easy? I was sixteen, completely alone, living in a foreign country, terrified, hurt, rejected and ashamed.' She twisted her face away from him. 'You were awful when I *did* call.'

'So your pride was hurt, and therefore you kept my child from me?'

'You don't even want children!' she snapped.

'Don't.' His lips pressed together, and she knew that was a mistake. How he felt about a hypothetical child was completely different to how he might feel about a daughter already in the world.

'Fine.' She lifted a hand appealingly. 'But you have to see this my way—'

'No,' he refuted swiftly, driving through Hammersmith without so much as a glance at Alicia. 'I don't. I need only see the facts.' He pulled up on a double yellow line outside the hospital. 'You have had nine years to tell me about her—'

'You're not exactly an easy person to speak to!' she said quickly. 'After you changed your number, I had literally no way to find you.'

'Through my office?'

'I tried. But short of telling the receptionist who answered our personal business—'

'Why not do that?' he demanded fiercely. 'Why not do whatever it took to get this information to me? Do you think I would *ever* have chosen to be absent from her life if I'd known?'

A huge lump formed in Alicia's throat. 'I don't know,' she said with a shake of her head. 'I just know that I wanted to tell you, and then I rationalised that it was better this way.'

He swore in Spanish. 'That's convenient for you.'

'Don't,' she spat, putting her hand on the car door. 'Don't you dare imply that I took the easy way out. If you had *any* idea how hard this has been for me, how much I struggled raising our daughter on my own...'

'Because of a choice you made,' he said, unrelenting. Her heart hurt. She loved him, but she hated him, and she could see more clearly than ever that any future was impossible for them. There was too much water under the bridge, far too much resentment.

He opened his car door, stepping out into the evening, hands on hips. She did the same, staring at him over the bonnet of the car.

'Graciano, I'm—'

'Which way?' he interrupted, eyes boring into hers.

She blinked away, staring up at the hospital, then sucking in a deep breath. 'You can't mean to come in with me?'

'She's my daughter, too, isn't she?'

Alicia bit into her lip. 'Yes, but this isn't the time to meet her. This is a little girl we're talking about, and she deserves better than to have this kind of drama. Especially when she's hurting. Just—go home. I'll call you when I know what's happening.'

'This is my daughter.' He ground the words out.

'I know.' She shivered, but not from the cool evening air. 'I get that. But this isn't about us right now.'

'No, it's about her. It's about the fact she has a father she knows—*Cristo,* I have no idea what you've told her about me.'

Tears welled in Alicia's eyes as she stalked towards him, needing him to understand.

'She's my family,' he said firmly, and her heart squished, because she understood, better than anyone, what that meant to him. He'd been robbed of his family already, and now Alicia had done the same thing. Guilt was an unavoidable wave, crashing over her.

'I must see her.'

'I… I'm worried it will upset her.'

'You think I can't control myself?' His nostrils flared angrily.

She knew the opposite was likely true, but that didn't change a thing.

'I can't…stand here and argue with you. I need to go to her.' She lifted a hand to his chest but he flinched, pulling away from her. 'Just, please,' she whispered.

'Don't do anything to upset her. She has to be our priority.'

The look of anger in his eyes turned her heart to ice, but she couldn't stay there and dwell, nor could she try to fix this. Annie needed her.

She checked her phone as she swept into the hospital, approaching the triage nurse's desk.

'My daughter's here, with Dr Wallace.'

'Ah, yes. They've just gone up to orthopaedics. Third floor, turn left at the elevators.'

'Thank you.' She didn't wait for Graciano but knew he was right there with her, and even though she'd fought this, even though she could feel his fury, she was glad he was there. There was strength in his presence, and she needed that strength in that moment, more than ever.

'Di?' A tear slid down her cheek at the familiar sight of her dearest friend. Alicia sped up, moving down the corridor to where Di was waiting, glasses around her neck, clipboard in hand.

'There you are, darling,' Di reached in for a hug, eyes flicking to the handsome stranger in Alicia's wake. 'Now, there's nothing to worry about.'

'Her arm's not broken?' Alicia pulled away to look in Di's face.

'Oh, it sure is, in two places. She did a real good job of it.' Di tsked. 'Then again, that's our Annie. Doesn't do anything by halves.'

'Can I see her?'

'Sure. She's just with Dr Wallace, but you can go in.'

Diane's gaze lingered on Graciano, but Alicia couldn't worry about anything besides Annie. She slipped into the hospital room, pushing past all of her tangled emotions to offer Annie a smile.

He was moving slowly, dread and disbelief half paralysing his limbs, but eventually, short of stopping completely, it was no longer possible to push this moment back, even for a second.

He stepped to the open door and hovered on the edge of it, eyes flicking into the room, ignoring the silver haired woman who'd just been locked in conversation with Alicia.

A young girl sat propped in bed, head bent forward so her dark, silky hair formed a curtain around her features. Music was playing from a nearby iPhone. She wore a shiny blue-and-yellow football shirt and her nails were painted fluorescent green. When she moved slightly, he saw that her cheek was bruised, and then she lifted her head, looking around the room idly, as if bored, until her eyes landed on him.

It was like being punched, hard, in the solar plexus.

This was his daughter.

Fierce, out-of-control paternal pride burst to life. She was a part of him, a part of his brother and mother and father—a part of his family, unmistakably. She was a dead ringer for his mother, except her eyes, which reminded Graciano of his brother. Her skin was brown like his, but then she smiled a little curiously and he saw Alicia, and felt his heart buckle. Every idea of not wanting children burst into flames at the sight of this little person who was, unmistakably, of him.

'Hi.'

He couldn't look at Alicia, standing beside the bed. Anger was rushing through him, a tsunami of blame and recrimination meaning he wanted to exclude her from this moment. This was about Graciano and his daughter, about the connection he deserved to have felt from this child's birth—not now, nine years later.

'Hello.' He knew enough to fill the silence, to take control of the conversation.

The doctor flicked her gaze up, then returned to her work of setting the cast.

'It looks as though you've done an excellent job on that.' He nodded towards her arm.

'Broken in two places.' Annie nodded. His heart lurched. She was so utterly familiar to him—it was like discovering a piece of him he hadn't even realised was missing. 'Have you ever broken a bone?'

'My nose.' He pointed to the bump halfway down. 'And my wrist.'

She pulled her lips to the side in a gesture that was pure Alicia. It was like being stabbed.

'Are you family?' the doctor asked, her tone casual, he imagined, to a child, but Graciano heard the undertone. She was sounding him out.

'He's with me.' Alicia's voice was weak and watery, but it was enough. Rather than hold back and stay silent, she was speaking up now, not like ten years earlier. But it was hardly a ringing endorsement of her courage: she was speaking to keep him secret from Annie. That was all.

'And you are?'

'That's my mum,' Annie said, conspiratorially. 'Don't worry, I'm okay,' Annie reassured her, a lopsided smile on her lips.

He felt excluded. He felt lost. He felt fascinated by this daughter of his, by this beautiful, interesting girl he knew nothing about.

'Oh, darling.' He watched as Alicia quickly stepped

to the edge of the bed and pressed a kiss to Annie's forehead. 'What happened?'

'It was just a collision, Mum.'

Alicia frowned, obviously not convinced.

'How do you know my mum?' She returned her attention back to Graciano, apparently far more interested in him than debriefing a football accident.

Alicia spoke first again, desperate to conceal the truth. It was the right thing to do, but in that moment, all he could see was her cowardice and shame, the lies she'd been telling for ten years that tripped off her tongue without premeditation now.

'I was doing some work for Graciano,' she said.

'In Spain?'

He interrupted before Alicia could answer. 'Yes, that's right. Have you ever been to Spain, Annie?'

'No, but I'm learning the language.'

Something shifted in his chest. 'Are you?'

'Mummy's teaching me.'

'She's very good.'

His eyes slashed through Alicia. Was that any wonder? The girl was half Spanish. The language, like many other hallmarks of his culture, ran through her veins. He noted the way Alicia wouldn't meet his eyes a second before he noticed the red rash across the base of her jaw, caused by his stubble. It was a confusing reminder, a white flag of surrender in the midst of his anger.

He ignored it.

'Do you like football, Annie?'

'It's one of my favourite things.'

'Are you any good?'

She laughed. 'I don't know. I like it a lot.'

'Annie's very—'

He threw Alicia a fulminating glare and she fell silent. He felt like a jackass, even when *he* was the one who'd been lied to.

'Okay.' The doctor snapped her rubber gloves off and stood, smiling. 'You're all done. Mind if I speak to you outside?' She addressed the question to Alicia, who hesitated a moment.

He ground his teeth together. Would she really not leave him alone with their daughter for even a few minutes? Dutifully, to avoid the same scene Alicia wanted to avoid, he moved through the door before she did, standing a little way down the corridor with his feet planted and arms crossed.

He watched as the doctor spoke to Alicia, the delineation between them clear. Legally, he wasn't her parent. He had no claim here, no business pushing into the conversation or demanding to know what was going on, but hell, morally, he did. That was his child. His family. All his life, he'd known that blood was thicker than water, yet Alicia had deprived him of Annie.

'She seems okay to me. Di wants her held overnight, for observation, and I'm happy to do that. It's sensible after a hit like she had, but so far, all the signs are good. She certainly didn't have any trouble remembering song lyrics, and could sing without slurring. Her focus is good and her eyes followed me as I spoke. Can you sit with her for a while longer?'

'I'll stay all night.'

The doctor smiled. 'There's a call button on the side of the bed. Just press it if you need anything.'

'What about her arm?'

'I'll put some notes in with her discharge file. She'll have to wear the cast for ten days, then get another X-ray to see how it's healing. Hopefully she can have it off at that point, but otherwise, she might need it to be set for another month or so.'

'She'll hate that,' Alicia remarked wryly, looking beyond the doctor to Graciano, then wishing she hadn't when the bottom fell out of her world again. 'Thank you for everything.'

'It's no problem. I'm here until three. I'll come by and see you again soon.'

'Thank you.'

What else was there to say?

She cast a glance over her shoulder into Annie's room; she was playing Tetris one-handed on Di's phone. Alicia took a step away from her daughter's—their daughter's—room, towards Graciano. His face was a sheer thundercloud.

'That's my daughter,' he said, so quietly she barely heard. But she understood. Learning you have a child is one thing—seeing them was quite another, and particularly when they looked as Annie did. She was the spitting image of him, and his family.

'Yes,' she whispered. 'I'm sorry—'

'For God's sake, no more apologies.' His nostrils flared. 'They are useless. I'm not interested in having you say sorry.'

She flinched. His voice was low, and yet the words cut deep.

'Then what are you interested in?'

'The next step.'

Her heart skipped a beat.

'Meaning?'

'Meaning, right now, I want to go in there and take my child away from this goddamned place, away from you, to raise her with me.' He glared at Alicia, who couldn't conceal her terror at that suggestion, but he didn't—couldn't—stop. 'I want to hire the best damned lawyers in the country and sue for full custody. I want to get judicial approval to move her to Spain. I want to make you feel what I'm feeling now, to know you have a child who you've missed out on so much of their life.'

She startled at his vehemence, pressing her back against the wall.

'That's not fair,' she whispered.

'Do not speak to me of *fair*.'

She lifted a shaking hand to her forehead, pressing it there as she stared up at him. An hour ago, they'd been making passionate, senseless love; now it was quite clear that he hated her.

'Write your address and phone number into my phone.' He handed it to her, then turned his back, breathing hard.

She did as he'd asked—there was no point keeping her details from him now. He knew about Annie. The game was up, not that it was ever anything like a game.

'I cannot believe you kept this from me,' he muttered, taking the phone and slamming it into his pocket. She was too shocked to refute that, to remind him she'd tried to tell him. 'I'll call you tomorrow to arrange a time to discuss this. And I'll expect you to keep me informed of her progress here.'

'Okay.' She couldn't think straight, but she knew his request was hardly unreasonable. She opened her mouth to say something—though what, she wasn't sure—but he spoke first.

'I will never forgive you for this.'

He left, and she felt as though the light in her life had been switched off completely.

CHAPTER ELEVEN

ALICIA WAS AT serious risk of pacing a hole in the carpet, but she couldn't stop moving. As the minutes ticked by and the time of Graciano's arrival drew closer, her body simply wouldn't stay still. She was like a live wire, incapable of anything but jerking and shifting.

She flicked another glance at her watch, groaning audibly to see how slowly time was moving. Anxiety was running through her. She'd been waiting for the executioner's blade to drop ever since the hospital two nights earlier, and now, Sunday afternoon, with Annie and a school friend seeing a movie together, she had this small window of time in which she could try to make some order from the wreckage of her life.

Of course, that depended entirely on Graciano, and how reasonable he was prepared to be. It depended on if he'd even give her a chance to explain.

But she sucked in a breath and reminded herself of her new favourite expression: *Que cada palo aguante su vela.*

He might be angry with her, and rightfully so, but that didn't change the facts. It didn't mean she'd been wrong, only that he didn't understand yet. It was her job to make him see things from her perspective. He might continue to feel furious with her, for what he'd lost. That would be his right. But at least if she'd told him the full story, she'd know she'd done the best she could.

The doorbell rang and she moved to it, knowing that her future depended on the next thirty or so minutes of her life.

Anxiety was a raging fire in her belly as she unlocked it and drew the door inwards, her nerves flaming at the sight of Graciano. Today he was all that was dark, dangerous and sinfully delicious, from his black jeans and dark grey T-shirt to the expression he bore— a scowl crossed with a look of white-hot accusation.

None of it helped her nerves.

'Hi,' she murmured under her breath, then cleared her throat. 'Come in.'

He stepped into the hall behind her, his eyes scanning the walls as he took in the mishmash of photos— Alicia and Annie, photos of the many moments that made up their day-to-day life.

His scowl deepened.

'I've made a pot of coffee. It's not quite as fancy as your espresso, of course.' She was nervous—over-talking. She grimaced and moved into the living room, a happy space that caught the afternoon sun and invited one to sit down and settle in. She gestured to the sofas, covered in bright cushions and blankets, and moved to the tray on the coffee table.

'Can I get you a cup?'

He put his hands on his hips, his nostrils flaring as he expelled a slow breath, then dipped his head once. Glad for something to do, she poured a cup from the French press, then moved towards him, holding it out. His eyes seared hers for a moment before he took it, their fingers brushing so her stomach catapulted through her body.

'I want to explain—'

Breath hissed from between his teeth, so she faltered. 'It's important,' she finished softly.

He took a drink from the coffee cup, then moved away from her to place it on a side table. He crossed his arms, feet planted wide apart— hardly a gesture of welcome invitation, but she had to get through this.

'When I found out I was pregnant —'

'How did you find out?' he interrupted, but dispassionately, as though it were a fact-finding mission.

'I did a test.'

'Why?'

She frowned, remembering that weekend. 'It was in the middle of a bracing heat spell. I'd gone down to the lake to swim, and as I floated on my back, I just realised that my cycle was late—that I'd been swimming almost every day since you left.' She didn't add that it was one of the mechanisms she'd used to cope, that swimming reminded her of him, of being immersed in Graciano in the same way the water wrapped around her. 'I wasn't well informed,' she said wryly. 'But I'd watched enough TV shows to know that your period being late generally meant one thing.'

'So what did you do?'

'I skipped school one day,' she said, plunging herself back into the past. 'And went to a free clinic. I used a fake name, because my dad seemed to know everyone and I was terrified of him finding out.' She toyed with the necklace she wore. 'They gave me a pregnancy test and told me to come back if it was positive. They also gave me a handful of condoms,' she added with a tight smile, an attempt to lighten the mood, but Graciano's face was like a storm cloud.

'The test was positive,' she said with a lift of her shoulders.

'And then?' His eyes were locked to her face, holding her still. She stared at him, but she was sixteen again, uncertain, terrified and also giddy with excitement at the life growing inside of her.

'I didn't know what to do,' she admitted. 'My father was barely speaking to me and I had no other family except his mother, whom I hadn't seen in years. I hadn't been allowed to see friends since you left, to speak to anyone. I was living in a prison.'

His eyes narrowed for the briefest flash of time before his face resumed a mask of unbreakable control.

He didn't speak. She moved to the coffee, pouring herself a cup even though she wasn't sure her nerves needed any extra ammunition.

'There was no one I could turn to. No one who could help me make sense of any of it.' She lifted a hand to her hair, tucking it behind her ear. His eyes followed the gesture and her stomach kicked, a confusing array of feelings rioting through her slim frame.

'The first time I called you was a brutal experience,' she whispered, turning her back on him, then moving towards a picture of Annie that hung across the room. It had been taken just before her fourth birthday. Alicia still saw this smiling face in her mind when she closed her eyes. 'I was so in love with you.' She shook her head slowly.

'That wasn't love,' he responded acerbically. 'It was teenage hormones.'

The pain she felt was as real as if she'd been stabbed in the belly.

'For me, it was love,' she said. There was no point in denying it, but nor did she need to wax lyrical about all the ways in which Graciano had brought her soul to life. 'I missed you like I'd lost a limb.'

She kept her back to him so didn't see his expression, didn't see the way he closed his eyes and inhaled.

'I didn't come here to talk about us. I want to know about my daughter.'

'Aren't the two inseparable?' she wondered aloud, her throat dry and sore, then pushed on, ignoring his interjections. There was a story to tell, and she couldn't skip ahead, but she could truncate it. 'I was devastated by what had happened between us, traumatised by the way my father had been. I didn't know you'd gone so far away. I called, the first time, because I wanted to come to you. I wanted to run away and be with you.' She lifted a hand to her heart, pressing it there in an attempt to stop the twisting pain. 'But your feelings had changed.' A divot formed between her brows as she recalled his repeated insistence that it had just been sex, not love. 'Or maybe they hadn't. Maybe I'd mistaken your feelings all along. That would make sense, given how easy you found it to shut me down.'

She sipped her coffee, eyes on Annie's face in the picture, not seeing the pallor of Graciano's.

'So when I found out I was pregnant, I was scared to tell you. Even you. I was totally alone, Graciano. No family, no friends, and no you.'

Silence, while she brought herself together, and she waited for him to speak. Eventually, he did.

'I used a condom.'

Her eyes swept shut. He was determinedly focused on Annie's conception. Nothing more. The difficulties Alicia had faced meant nothing to him. *Because he doesn't love you.* Realising that she loved Graciano changed nothing about his feelings.

'Regardless of the fact you'd made your feelings clear to me, you were still the one person I thought I could turn to. This was *our* baby,' she said bitterly. 'And in spite of what you'd said on the phone that afternoon, I knew you'd help me.'

He didn't speak, but now sadness and hurt were turning to anger.

'Do you remember that call?'

His eyes bore into hers and then he nodded, once. 'I was angry.'

'Yes. You were. My world was falling apart and I turned to you, needing you, needing help—' She left the words suspended in midair. 'I wanted to tell you, Graciano. I never intended to do this on my own.'

'So why didn't you?'

'Come on. How? How could I?' She moved to him instinctively, needing him to understand. 'I was still in love with you, heartbroken over what had happened, and you told me none of it meant anything to you. You told me to stop calling you—that you never wanted to hear from me again. You were awful.'

'Yes,' he said after a beat. 'I was.' He shoved a hand in his pocket, his eyes moving to the picture of Annie. 'But you were pregnant. No matter what I said, you should have found a way to tell me.'

'In theory, sure, but I was a scared, rejected sixteen-year-old. It's very easy to say that now, to see with clarity how I should have behaved, but back then, I was completely shut down by that call. I was destroyed.'

His mask slipped for just a moment, and she saw the anguish on his features. She wanted to weep for how their lives had unravelled.

'So what did you do next?'

'What could I do? I told my father.' She winced. 'It didn't go down well.'

Graciano's lips compressed, forming a tight, white line in his face.

'He called me every name under the sun, then slapped me.' She lifted a hand to her cheek, remembering the sting of that assault, aware of the way Graciano's bigger body startled now at the admission. 'Within an hour, he'd dropped me at the airport. We haven't seen each other since.'

'*Bastardo.*'

'Yes. Apparently I made a mockery of all his teachings.'

'He made a mockery of his teachings,' Graciano corrected.

'I came to live with my grandmother. She was… helpful,' Alicia said with a frown. 'Not loving, not even kind, really, but she did enable me to go back to school, and she helped with Annie when she was little.'

'Did you try to contact me at any other point?' he asked, again, focusing solely on the matter of Annie.

She bit down on her lower lip. 'I have thought about it every day.'

His eyes bore into hers and she felt as though so much was riding on her next few statements. 'When Annie took her first steps, I tried to contact you. I was overwhelmed with a need for you to know.' She shook her head slowly. 'Do you have any idea how hard you are to contact?'

He closed his eyes for a moment; his face was impossible to read.

'I tried,' she said softly. 'But I gave up quickly.' Only the truth would do. 'I was still just a kid.'

'Yes.' It was an admission she hadn't expected. 'And since then?'

She lifted her fingers and ran them over the ends of

her hair. 'You've become even harder to contact,' she said frankly. 'Your success made you untouchable. I tried two more times. Around her fourth birthday, and again on her fifth.' She swallowed. 'She was growing so fast. Your assistants refused to put me through.'

Something moved on Graciano's face, an emotion she couldn't comprehend. Did he believe her?

'It's the truth,' she said flatly, something like defiance strengthening her in that moment. 'But don't forget, Graciano, you had turned your back on me a long time ago. Not once did you check on me after that morning. Putting aside the question of pregnancy for a moment,' she said firmly, 'you knew my father was furious. You didn't wonder how that anger might move from you to me? You didn't wonder how he was treating me?'

His mask slipped completely, and she saw that she'd hit a nerve. His eyes swept her face and a muscle jerked at the base of his jaw. 'I presumed with me out of the picture, your life would return to normal.'

'You were wrong.'

'His anger was completely directed at me. I disappeared so his anger would no longer have a target. I was the bad guy who'd taken advantage of his precious daughter...'

'Until I told him the truth,' she said. 'Until I defended you, and then his anger moved to me.'

'I had no idea you'd do that. I don't know *why* you did. What did you stand to gain?'

'How could I not? I didn't want to live in a world where anyone, especially my father, thought those things of you. I *loved* you, Graciano. I couldn't betray you like that. All these years you've thought the worst of me, but you were wrong.'

'Careful, *querida*. We are here discussing a nine-year-old child I knew nothing about. I don't think you can claim the moral high ground just yet.'

'Are you even listening to me?' she asked, infuriated. 'I'm trying to tell you what happened. I'm saying I tried to tell you. *You* were the one who made that impossible.'

'You should have taken out a damned ad in the newspaper,' he muttered. 'I deserved to know about her.'

'Yes,' she agreed. 'And she deserved to know you. But what if you hurt her? What if you rejected her like you did me? Like my father rejected me? All I have ever done is try to protect Annie, to pour all of my love into her so she had what I never did.'

'You cannot have it both ways. Either you tried to tell me, or you didn't. Which is it?'

'How can you think I'd lie about something like that?'

He made a snorting noise. 'Look at where we're standing, what we're discussing.'

'Damn it, Graciano!' Anger burst through Alicia. 'I never wanted this!' She sucked in a deep breath, trying to calm her nerves. 'Let me show you something,' she said through gritted teeth, moving away from Graciano and into a narrow hallway, then up the stairs and into her room. She knew he was right behind her; she felt his presence.

She crouched down and pulled a plastic crate out from under her bed, then unclipped the lid. There were two folders inside. She thrust one at him, too angry to meet his eyes.

He took it, flipping over the cover with the same anger she felt, until he became very still, his eyes devouring the first page, inserted into a plastic slip. It was a newspaper article about him from nine and a half years ago—a small clipping about an award he'd won as a realtor.

His expression shifted, but she couldn't interpret it as he flicked to the next page. Another article, another award, another accolade. Then the articles shifted a little, to speak of his business deals, and the photos changed, too. Now Graciano was rarely snapped without a glamorous woman on his arm. He flicked again, and again, until he reached the end of the folder, the most recent article taken only three months earlier, about the acquisition of a chain of supermarkets in the UK.

'What is it?' he asked, finally, his voice raw.

'It's for Annie.' She wrapped her arms around her torso. 'I tried to tell you about her, but when I couldn't, I started to do this. I wanted the two of you to be connected one day. Or for her to know that I'd tried. I don't know. It just felt…important somehow.' Tears filmed her eyes. 'But in collecting those clippings, I came to understand how much you'd moved on, how your life was in a completely different sphere to mine. I told myself I was glad. I was raising Annie alone, but at least you had what you'd always wanted.'

He stared at the folder, his face ashen.

'And that one?'

Now her fingers really trembled as she crouched down and lifted the second folder. But she held it close to her chest, anxious for some reason to pass it over.

'It's about Annie,' she whispered. 'I wasn't sure if you'd ever want to be a part of her life, but I kept everything, just in case.'

'Show me.' It was a demand. She had saved these things for him, and yet she hesitated a moment, before passing the folder across.

He opened it to the first page—a tiny birth announcement, a hospital bracelet and a snip of hair sticky taped against an aging slip of cardboard. The next page showed a handprint and footprint.

'She was tiny.'

'She was a month premature,' Alicia said, memories slamming into her.

'Why?'

'I went into labour early.' She didn't meet his eyes; her gaze remained on the folder. Her fingers trembled a little as she lifted the next sheet to turn it. 'This was her first Christmas. Wasn't she adorable? I made that dress.' She ran a finger over the photo, remembering the austerity of that day, the loneliness. Her father hadn't called. He hadn't sent a card, nor a gift. In fact, there'd been no presents whatsoever, but Alicia had had Annie, the love of her life. She was so young in the photo, her face that of a child's.

He turned the page quickly—artwork of Annie's, from when she started nursery. Silly splashes of paint and blobs of colour on cardboard. A student report card. On and on it went, all the small things from her life— piano recital programs, photos of the milestone moments like first lost tooth, riding a bike, and sometimes, Alicia had included a handwritten note about a memory so she wouldn't forget, and wouldn't forget to tell Graciano. All of it had seemed important at the time, but she wondered if he'd understand that.

He came to halfway through the folder, then stopped, lifting his face to hers. 'Can I take this with me?'

She hesitated. 'I made it for you,' she said slowly.

'I won't lose it.'

'I know.' She pressed a finger into the page, strangely sentimental about the memory folder, but it wasn't hers.

She'd had Annie, the real thing. This was just a memento. 'Of course.' She stepped back, blinking away the tears, her heart heavy, her soul exhausted.

'I never wanted her to be separated from you.'

'And yet, if I hadn't been at that charity auction, I still wouldn't know about her.'

Alicia grimaced, because that was true.

'I understand why as a sixteen-year-old you couldn't tell me. I take responsibility for my part in that,' he admitted after a beat. 'And even for being almost impossible to contact since. I accept the truth of your explanation.'

'How magnanimous,' she muttered, even as her heart soared with relief.

'But what about on the island, when you had my full attention?'

Her heart dropped to her toes.

'It's very easy to stand here now and say that you were planning to tell me, when everything has fallen down to circumstance. I happened to be at the charity auction. I happened to be with you when you got the call about Annie's injury. I have to wonder—if those things hadn't happened, would I know about her yet?'

'Yes,' she promised. 'I went to you last night intending to tell you. The truth has been eating me alive. On the island, I couldn't stop thinking about it—'

'Yet you said nothing.'

'It was hardly a straightforward situation,' she said pointedly. 'Sleeping together—'

He moved closer, eyes holding hers, body so close, so large, everything inside her sparked, and she almost cried because she wanted to collapse against him.

'Sleeping together is the only thing that's ever made sense with us,' he muttered.

'At the time, yes, but it always makes things worse afterwards.'

'Does it?' He lifted a hand, catching her cheek. 'Maybe if we never left bed, we'd never fight.'

Her eyes widened, her lips parted, and then he was kissing her, his mouth claiming hers, and it was just as he said: everything made sense. This was exactly what she needed, what made her feel right and complete and as though everything was going to be all right. Her mouth filled with salt as tears rolled down her cheeks—not sad tears so much as tears of acceptance, because he was right. Theirs was a relationship of contradictions, of dependence and need, even when that need terrified them both.

'This doesn't solve anything,' she groaned, even as she pulled him down to the floor.

'No.' His agreement sealed some part of her. She kissed him back with every fibre of her being, even as her heart was turning frozen, made frigid by the impossibility of this.

Their mutual explosion was as powerful as ever, robbing him of sight, sense and the ability to think while it racked his body, and then as he came down on top of her, his weight something she welcomed with a soft groan, he felt as though he'd done something monumentally stupid. Sleeping with Alicia might feel great in the moment, but it just complicated the issue.

They had a daughter. He couldn't seduce his way out of that.

A tidal wave of emotions worked through him, anger at the forefront. But it wasn't just anger at Alicia. It was so much more complicated than that.

He'd fought with her because he hadn't been willing

to give any ground, but her words had worked their way into his soul, and now, he saw her as the sixteen-year-old she'd been, pregnant and terrified, then a seventeen-year-old single mother, and he felt his own failings every step of the way.

Why hadn't he called to check on her?

Why hadn't he at least made sure her father hadn't taken his anger out on Alicia once Graciano had left?

Because she was quicksand. Because a conversation could so easily turn into something more, and he hadn't been willing to let her hurt him again. He hadn't wanted to let her in.

And now?

'I need to think,' he said, shifting away from her and standing, frowning as he dressed. Alicia stayed where she was, staring at the ceiling. It was only when he was fully clothed and he looked at her again that she realised she was shaking.

He crouched beside her, unable to keep the concern from his face.

'Shock,' she said in explanation, her face pale. 'I'm fine.'

And he saw her strength then, the strength she'd needed as Edward Griffiths' daughter, the strength she'd needed as a teenage mother, and every day since.

She was quicksand.

He wanted to draw her into his arms, to hold her close, but there were several issues at play here. Being parents to a nine-year-old didn't mean he was willing to open himself up to Alicia and the risks that came with being near her.

'I need to think,' he repeated, and now, she nodded. His eyes shifted to the book she'd made, on the edge of the bed. 'Do you mind if I take that?'

She shook her head. 'I made it for you.' Her eyes stared right through him. 'I wanted—what I wanted wasn't possible, Graciano. But I always intended for you to know.' She bit down on her lip.

He wanted to believe her. Hell, he *did* believe her. But that just made everything worse. He leaned forward, pressing a kiss to her forehead, then standing.

'And eventually, I convinced myself that you'd have wanted it this way. Your life was so…much. It was huge. You were so successful, so far away from us. I told myself you'd want it this way. I meant nothing to you— why should you have to pay for a mistake you made ten years ago?'

That just made it so much worse—that she could even think that of him. A deep, shearing sadness broke him in two. 'I'll be in touch.'

He didn't see the look of concern that crossed her features, but at the door, he turned back to face her and something inside of him shattered. He'd fallen in love with Alicia when she was just a teenager, and she looked so heartbreakingly young now. He stared at her for a moment and then left quickly, before he realised that the thing he wanted most of all was to stay.

CHAPTER TWELVE

GRACIANO CRADLED THE Scotch in the palm of his hand, staring at the collection of memories with an ache low in his gut. He was only four pages in. He couldn't get past Alicia's handwritten note.

Annie is walking. At ten months. All the doctors said she'd be delayed in her milestones because she was born early, but so far that's definitely not the case. She's so sturdy on her feet, so strong and stubborn. She's so like you.

He closed his eyes on a wave of emotion, drinking Scotch simply to clear the knot in his throat. Alicia had written this for him. She'd used the only means possible to share Annie with him. She'd thought of him—with every milestone Annie had achieved. Carefully, he flipped to the back, to a photo of Annie reading a comic book. Closer inspection showed it to be Spanish.

Annie is officially more competent in Spanish than I am. She's beginning to slip between both languages effortlessly. I've worked hard to teach her what I could, but she took it in her stride and

has been watching shows in Spanish and read-
ing books, too. She's very bright, but it's more
than that. She has Spanish blood, and her tongue
knows it. One day, I want to take her there.

He could almost feel her hesitating, feel her emotion.

I want her to see the places I love.

He shut the book at the same time he closed his
eyes. These memories were important, but reading
about them like this wasn't right. He wanted to hear
Alicia's voice recounting the memories to him, describing them in greater depth. He wanted to be able to ask
questions, to hear her voice as she answered them. He
wanted more.

But what exactly?

His brow beaded in perspiration as he stood, then
moved to the window to stare out.

Ten years ago, he'd believed the worst in Alicia. Why
hadn't he realised that she'd speak the truth? That of
course she would defend him? She had been a teenager,
sheltered and adored, and until that morning, had idolised her father. Naturally she hadn't been able to defy
him in the moment.

But she'd loved Graciano, too.

He made a growling noise, because she *had* loved
him—yet he'd been so quick to judge her. To *hate* her.
And up until two nights ago, he'd been willing to make
that same mistake.

To prejudge her. To see the worst in her actions.

To fail to listen to her.

To fail her, point-blank.

His shoulders dropped, because the more he looked at their situation, the more he realised he'd messed up.

Alicia stared at the text message for several seconds.

Do you have a minute?

It was so like Graciano, so short and to the point. So unclear, too. Two days earlier, he'd walked out of her home and ever since she'd been tormenting herself with wondering.

What had he meant? What did he need to think about?

In the back of her mind, all she could think of was his reaction in the hospital, his threat that he'd take Annie away to punish her. But then she remembered the way they'd made love, and the way he'd been afterwards—surely he couldn't be so cruel? She gripped her phone more tightly.

Yes. I can talk.

It was almost ten o'clock, but she was nowhere near ready for bed. She'd barely been sleeping. She held her phone, waiting for it to ring, but a moment later, a knock at the front door sounded. Heart leaping into her throat, Alicia stood, moving quickly to the door, fingers shaking a little as she slid the chain in place and opened it an inch. Graciano stood there against the inky black sky, his dark eyes unsettling her, burning her, probing her, his face a mask of intense concentration so she was startled.

'I presumed you meant to call me,' she said quietly.

'No.' Then, with a grimace, 'Would you prefer that?'

She frowned, the question unexpected. 'You're here now,' she said, casting a glance over her shoulder. 'Annie's asleep.'

'I presumed she would be—this is a conversation between you and me, not our daughter.'

Our daughter. She shivered, her heart spasming at that simple statement.

Alicia closed the door so she could release the chain lock, then opened it wider, waving for him to come in. He held Annie's book in his hand, and Alicia felt a tug of sentiment towards that item.

'Through here?' he prompted, nodding towards the living room. It took her a moment to galvanise her limbs into action.

'Right, yes. That way.' They moved through to the lounge and Alicia's eyes fell on her glass of wine. 'Would you like a drink?'

'Thanks.' He dipped his head. She weaved away from him into the kitchen, careful to give Graciano a wide berth or risk igniting with him all over again. But oh, how she craved his touch! The reassurance and familiarity of his arms wrapping around her... 'Wine? Beer? Whisky?'

'Whatever you're having.'

She poured another measure of wine, then passed it over the counter, watching as his long-fingered hand curved around the glass, carrying it back to the sofa. He didn't sit, though.

Alicia reached for her own glass on the coffee table and lifted it to her lips.

'You wanted to talk?'

His eyes bore into hers. 'I think we must, don't you?'

Her throat was dry. This was excruciating. Agony pummelled her. Slowly she nodded, taking another sip of wine before sitting on the edge of the sofa, perched in an almost crouch, ready to spring up if needed. Defensive. Uncertain. Wary.

Graciano placed the folder on the coffee table, staring at it a moment before looking to her. He read her body language like a book, and knowing him to be the cause of those emotions fractured something deep inside of him, causing a fault line he doubted he'd ever be able to repair.

'I have no intention of taking Annie away from you.' The thread he'd made had loomed large in his mind for days.

Her eyes widened and there was some satisfaction in the look of relief that immediately crossed her face.

'It was beneath me to imply it. I'm very, very sorry.'

Her lips parted and her pale, pinched face angled to his. 'It wasn't—' She shook her head in consternation. 'I don't understand. What does that mean?'

'I haven't seen you interact with our daughter for more than a cursory amount,' he said, careful to keep any hint of reproach from the words. 'But I know you. I know who you are, and the kind of mother you would be. I've seen this.' He gestured to the folder. 'You have given her so much.'

Alicia's eyes filled with tears and something rolled in his gut. He hated seeing her upset. He'd always hated it. So much had clarified for him in the last twenty-four hours and now he wondered how he'd ever been such a stranger to himself, his feelings—how he'd let time and success change him so completely.

'Are you saying—' She looked up at him carefully, then blinked away, her lips pressed together. 'You're leaving?'

He furrowed his brow, not following her logic. 'What?'

'You don't want to be in her life after all?'

He swore in Spanish, then moved towards her, crouching in front of her so their eyes were closer to level. 'That's absolutely *not* what I mean.'

Her gaze roamed his face, trying to understand. 'Then what?'

'I have to explain something to you,' he said after a beat, knowing how important it was to go right back to the beginning. 'You know I told you that leaving you, that first time, was like having the rug pulled from under me? I didn't recognise myself, *querida*. Without you, nothing made sense. Somehow, without me realising it, you became a part of me that summer. I breathed you in, and you weaved through my DNA, so that even when I left Seville, you stayed in me. I hated that. I fought it. Every day, I pushed you away from me. I pushed you out of my mind—my dreams. I willed you away from me with everything I had. I had to. I had to be strong, because if I was weak, I'd go back to you. I'd do whatever it took to be with you, even risk prison.'

'I would *never* have let that happen.'

'Your first instinct was right. You were powerless against your father.'

'He was wrong.'

'Yes,' Graciano agreed. 'But so was I.'

She blinked up at him, then sipped her wine, too fast so she coughed a little. He eased back on his haunches, waiting. 'Why?' she asked, eventually.

'Your father's words were a test of my honour, and I failed it. I ran when I should have stayed and fought. I ran, and in that way, I failed you. I failed the faith you had in me, the love you had given me. I'm sorry.'

She made no effort to disguise her tears now as her lower lip trembled. 'It was a lifetime ago.'

'Was it? Because it feels very much like that failure haunts us both, to this very day.'

She didn't meet his gaze.

'Tell me something, Alicia.'

She blinked at him, her features taut.

'Have you been with anyone since me?'

Alicia's eyes widened and he saw the struggle in them. A moment later, she shook her head slowly. 'But you have. Lots of women.'

'Yes.'

She flinched, and now he could take absolutely no pleasure from her response. Guilt flamed him. 'Physically yes. But I have never become emotionally close with another woman. Not since you.'

Frustration was obvious on her features and then she stood, almost tumbling him backwards, but he gained his balance and stood also. 'So? Nor have I. I haven't been with anyone else since you, Graciano. And before you get ahead of yourself, I don't mean that to stoke your ego. It wasn't about you,' she said. Then, wavering a little, 'Not directly. You broke my heart. You broke it so completely. How could I ever give it to someone else? It wouldn't work. I could never trust another man. I could never let myself believe…in happy endings and roses and romance and promises.' She shook her head angrily. 'Every day with Annie was both a privilege and a torment. I have loved her so much, from the moment I learned I was pregnant, but she has been a constant reminder of you, too.'

'I haven't forgotten about you either, Alicia,' he said urgently. 'You are the only woman I've ever loved, the only woman I've ever truly given myself to. If I broke your heart, you stole mine, and when I left you, I failed to bring it with me.'

She spun away from him, his words not changing her countenance one iota. She was still angry.

'Stop. Just stop. I'm not an idiot, Graciano.'

'I know that.'

She turned back to him. 'Then don't treat me like one.'

'How am I doing that?'

'I know you've taken your time to get your ducks in a row. Did your lawyers advise you you'd never get sole custody? Is that it? So now you're trying to ingratiate yourself with me to be a part of Annie's life?'

He shouldn't have been surprised that she believed something so low of him, but still, it cut deep. It showed him just how far he had to go in earning back her trust.

'You don't need to do that,' she said, grinding her teeth. 'I never intended to keep you from her. If you want to see her, that's fine, so long as we come up with a way that works for Annie. That's all I care about.'

'Actually, my lawyers advised me—' he saw her face tighten and quickly edited what he'd been about to say '—that it would not necessarily go as you imagine.'

Her eyes swept shut and he felt the fear radiating off her. He swore internally, moving towards her until she flinched.

He hated himself in that moment.

He had done this to her.

He was pulling at the threads of her life, after she'd fought so hard to piece it together. He couldn't do this to her.

He sought for the best way to explain what he'd come to say and in the end settled on the simplest. 'I love you.'

Her face squeezed up.

'Ten years ago, you became a part of me, and you still are. I want Annie in my life and I want you in my life. That's what I came here to say.'

He waited, his nerves pulling taut as he stared at her, until she shook her head sadly.

'No, you don't.'

He frowned.

'The other night, at your place in Knightsbridge, you told me you wanted to hang out for as long as it took to get this out of our system. Before you knew about Annie, you were prepared to allow me only a very limited space in your life.'

He swore aloud this time. 'What I said does not accord with how I felt. I was just too much of a fool to understand that then.'

For a moment, he thought he might have got through to her, but after a beat, she pulled a sad face. 'Do you have any idea what it's like to be a single parent?'

He shook his head slowly.

'It's hard,' she said on a sob. 'Every day. And it's rewarding and wonderful and I know I shouldn't complain, because you've missed so much, but you have to understand: I have fought to be here, to give her this.' She waved a hand around. 'I love our daughter, and I would always, always choose the life I have over what you're offering.'

The rejection dug into him, making it difficult to breathe for a moment. But he wasn't getting through to her. She didn't believe him.

'Tell me this,' he said quietly, sipping his wine, then replacing it on the coffee table. 'Do you love me?'

She jerked her head back as though he'd struck her and he waited, knowing Alicia wouldn't lie. It was a trap—unfair, but necessary.

'I—' She rolled her lips together. 'I'm a realist,' she said after a beat. 'I understand the limitations of our circumstances.'

'Do you? Because when I look inside at my own heart and feelings, I see only possibilities. For ten years I have run away from you, and I have hated every day. Even my biggest successes have been overshadowed by personal misery. There is one perfect person on this planet, designed to be my other half, and I have been fighting that knowledge to the point I have been barely myself. So to imagine a future not only with you but with our daughter—this is not a limitation, but a world we could inhabit, if we were brave enough to step into it together.'

'Don't talk to me about brave,' she said on a shiver. 'I've been brave. I was brave when I found out about our baby, when I tried to tell you, again and again, when you said those awful things, when you started dating anyone with a vagina in Spain, when you went from strength to strength and all my professional ambitions withered and died. Do you have any idea what it was like when I had my baby, alone in hospital, no one with me except a midwife? And then Di came into my life as my saviour. I have been brave for a long time,' she said stoically, lifting her chin, then fixing him with a defiant expression and wobbling lips.

'I hate that you went through that,' he groaned, the truth wrenched from him. 'What can I say or do, Alicia? I stuffed up. Again and again. Every day that I fought my need for you I have hurt you. I see that. I acknowledge it, and I want to fix it. I have ruined the last ten years, but surely our future is still worth fighting for?'

Her chest shuddered as she inhaled. 'I can't do it,' she said with a small shake of her head. 'I'm so scared,

Graciano. After you left, I changed. Trusting people doesn't come easily and you—'

'I know.' He couldn't bear to hear another description of his shortcomings. 'I'm not asking you to trust me all at once,' he said slowly, moving towards her.

'Then what are you asking me for?'

'A date,' he said, his eyes holding a challenge. He lifted a finger between them. 'One date. If you enjoy it, if you enjoy spending time with me, I will ask you for another. And another. And another. And as many dates as it takes for you to understand that my love for you is as real now as it was ten years ago. For as long as it takes for you to understand that I'm sorry. I will never disappoint you again, *querida*.'

'And Annie?'

'For now, she'll know me only as your friend,' he said, knowing he couldn't afford to alienate Alicia on this score. 'I would like to meet her,' he said, cautiously, eyeing her, wondering if that was too much. 'If you're comfortable with that.'

She nodded unevenly, her eyes moving to the folder. He could feel her uncertainty, and he took a step towards the door. 'You let me know when you're free,' he said quietly. 'And I'll arrange something. Okay?'

She bit down on her lower lip. 'I—okay.' Then, taking a step towards the coffee table, she gestured to the book. 'Would you like to look at her folder together?'

Something inside his chest leaped. Hope. Desperate, aching hope. 'Are you sure?'

She nodded. 'I want to share it with you.'

By the time they reached the pages surrounding Annie's sixth birthday, it was almost midnight, and Graciano's words had been going around and around in Alicia's head for a long time.

She closed the folder, lifting her face to his. They were so close it was almost impossible to fight the urge to kiss him.

'The thing is,' she said, eyes on his lips. 'I do love you, you know.'

It was relief that marked his features, not the triumph she'd expected.

'That is very good news.'

'But I can't…risk feeling like I did back then.'

'And you don't trust me?'

She tilted her lips to the side, considering that. 'Honestly? I don't know. But… I haven't dated anyone, ever, really. It sounds kind of fun.'

'You, my darling, deserve to be dated until your feet spin off the earth. It would be my pleasure.' He moved closer then, brushing his lips over hers in a chaste kiss. 'Thank you.'

'What for?'

'A second chance I'm pretty sure I don't deserve.'

'Everyone deserves a second chance.'

EPILOGUE

'YOU KNOW, I thought you meant the movies, or dinner. Maybe a walk afterwards.'

'We can definitely walk if you'd prefer,' he grinned, leaning back a little so it was the most natural thing in the world for Alicia to lean back into Graciano's chest, to rest her head on his shoulder and sigh as she looked overhead. It was only their third date, but she already knew that her heart belonged to him, just as his did to her.

'Maybe,' she said, happy right where she was. 'We'll see.'

Stars shimmered overhead, more visible here in the Spanish countryside than London. She looked up at them, remembering a long-ago version of herself and the stars that had blanketed the sky the night they made love.

He'd recreated so much of that evening, from the strawberries to the birthday cupcakes to the weather—though she suspected that wasn't in Graciano's control. He'd added a bottle of delightful champagne to the mix, and some Belgian chocolates.

Plus, the property they were on was his—all his. They'd spent the afternoon touring it, from the grand old house to the farm surrounds, seeing the chickens and llamas, the goats, meeting his manager.

'I had no idea you were into all this,' she said, shaking her head.

'As a child, I loved animals,' he said. 'I wanted to be a vet.'

'You're kidding?'

'No.' His eyes roamed her face. 'We had a dog, Brisa. She never stopped—hence the name.'

'Breeze?'

'Yes.' He kissed the tip of her nose. 'We could not contain her, no matter how hard we tried. One day, she got out. A car hit her.'

Alicia turned to face him, sadness softening her features.

'I found her first. I was powerless to save her. I wanted to. Only six months later, there came the accident. I watched my parents die. All I could think of was that I wanted to grow up to be strong, to be knowledgeable.' He shook his head. 'A child's whim.'

'I don't know,' she said, shaking her head. 'The money you donated to McGiven House has saved a lot of people from fates worse than death.'

He squeezed her hand. 'It is a worthy charity.'

She lifted her shoulders. 'They help people who need it most.'

'People like you were, at one time?'

She nodded slowly. 'I don't know what I would have done without my grandmother's generosity.'

It was a sore point and she felt Graciano flinch. She understood. She lifted up, kissing him gently. He wrapped his arms around her, holding her tight.

'I know what I would like to do, for our next date.'

'Oh? What's that?'

'It's a surprise.'

Three days later, during Annie's school hours, Graciano flew Alicia back to Spain—this time, to his charity headquarters.

'I had no idea you did all this,' she said, shocked.

'By design. I don't need people to see this side of me.'

'The secret philanthropist?'

'Money is a burden,' he said after a pause. 'I have more than I could ever spend. More than I could spend in a thousand lifetimes, in fact. There are some people who cannot afford to feed their children.'

Alicia sighed. 'Your heart is big.'

'My heart is yours.'

'I know.'

For their fifth date, Graciano arrived at Alicia's early, while she was still getting ready. He'd planned it that way, and for a man like Graciano, things almost always went according to plan.

Diane was in the kitchen, finishing dinner for herself and Annie, who was still upstairs doing her homework.

'I wanted to speak to you,' Graciano said, walking into the kitchen but keeping a respectful distance. Here, this was Diane's domain, and where the older woman had been polite to him, Graciano knew he had a long way to go with her yet. She'd seen Alicia broken; she'd picked up the pieces. If anything, Graciano loved that she was still protecting Alicia, even when Graciano would make sure no one ever hurt a hair on her or Annie's head, ever again.

'Yes, Graciano?' Diane's voice was cool but polite. He had to hide his smile.

'You know how I feel about her.'

Diane lifted a brow. 'Do I?'

'Si.'

Diane lifted a single brow. 'The important thing is, does she?'

'I think so. And tonight, I'm going to be sure of it.'

He reached into his pocket and pulled out the ring box, sliding it across the counter. Nerves assailed him.

Diane eyed the box, hesitated a moment and then lifted it. She cracked the lid, making a low, whistling sound.

'Goodness, I think I'm blind.'

Graciano dragged a hand over his stubble. 'Too much?'

Diane laughed—the first time he'd heard the noise from the older woman. 'I mean, it'll be visible from the moon…'

Graciano stared at it. Maybe he'd gone too far?

'Perhaps I should change it.'

Diane reached over, putting a hand on his. 'Pish, it's perfect. I'm only messing with you—I think you deserve a little of that, don't you? She'll love it.'

'I just wanted her to know…to really understand…'

'She will,' Di assured him.

Graciano cleared his throat, taking the ring back from Diane's outstretched hand. 'So, do I have your approval?'

'Are you asking me if you can propose?'

Graciano shrugged, feeling completely stupid now. None of these were familiar emotions, but then, everything about life since he'd confided his feelings in Alicia had been new and scary, but also absolutely wonderful.

Diane laughed properly then at Alicia's faraway voice calling down, asking what was going on. Graciano threw Di a warning look and she covered her mouth.

'Sorry,' she replied, *sotto voce*. 'It is certainly not my place to give you permission. She's her own woman and always has been.' A sheen of tears moistened Diane's eyes, and there was rich affection in her features. 'But if you're asking if I approve, the answer is yes.'

Graciano expelled a slow breath.

'I've seen how happy you make her. I've always cared for her, you know, but it's only in the last few weeks I've realised that I knew a very small part of her. She's been waiting for you. Don't make her wait any longer.'

The helicopter came in over his island and Alicia, blind-folded beside him, jiggled her fingers in her lap. He couldn't stop smiling.

They loved each other. It was mutual and absolute. And tonight, he intended to formalise that.

Only he hoped and prayed she'd say yes, that it wasn't too soon—that she wasn't still weighing up her future.

But if she was, that was okay. He'd wait. He'd be here, enjoying her, loving her, for as long as she let him.

'Where are we?' she said on a smile, her lips so full and curved that he couldn't help himself. He leaned forward and kissed her gently, so she smiled against him.

'Wherever it is, I'm happy.'

'Good.'

The helicopter thudded down and a moment later the door was opened.

'Ready?'

'You betcha.'

He removed the blindfold as the golf buggy pulled up beside the helicopter. It took her a moment to realise what was happening.

'Your island?'

'Someone organised a very elaborate party. I didn't want it to go to waste.'

She frowned, confused. 'You want me to come to the party as your date?'

'You are the party,' he said.

She stared at him, shocked. 'That's… You can't be serious.'

But he was. Every element she'd organised had been scaled back to suit two guests. There was food, dancing, champagne, and when the barge just out from the island began to release the fireworks, Graciano went down on one knee, squeezing her hand to draw her attention to him.

'There is no one on this earth I love like I do you. In every way, for all time, since we first met, you have been my other half. I was foolish and arrogant and I will never be able to change our past, but you are my future, Alicia. You and Annie are the meaning to my world. I know it's soon, but having wasted ten years, I can't wait another night. Will you marry me?'

She stared first at his face and then at the ring he'd opened a box to reveal, and tears sparkled on her lashes—tears of such happiness. 'I never thought this would be our ending,' she said. 'All those nights spent missing you, wondering where you were, worrying for you, loving you without purpose and hope…'

'There is always hope,' he corrected, standing so he could draw her into an embrace. 'With a heart so full as yours, there is always hope.'

He slid the ring onto her finger and she stared down at it, mesmerised by the enormous, sparkling gem, but also by the future they were stepping towards. Everything about this moment, his proposal, felt absolutely perfect.

One year later, Mrs Alicia Cortéz had the pleasure of telling her husband of six months that they were to be parents again—and this time, together. Their journey would be a shared one, every step of the way. Their time was split between Spain and London. Both would have preferred to relocate to Spain full-time, but Annie had a life in London, and there was Diane to consider, now as dear a friend to Graciano as she always had been to Alicia. When their baby boy was born, it was Diane who oversaw his medical needs, and a month later, Diane who was named their son's godmother.

Graciano could only look at his family with gratitude for the second chance he'd been given. A third baby would someday bless them, but before she was born, Graciano received a call that would change his life for ever.

He answered his phone on the third ring, watching his wife and daughter play with his little boy, his heart stretched to a wonderful breaking point.

'Cortéz?'

'Speaking.'

'It's Caleb James.'

Graciano, momentarily, drew a blank. 'Yes?'

'The investigator, from Washington.'

It had been so long since he'd engaged the man—of course he'd forgotten. He'd seen a bill from time to time, and had been content to let the matter tick along in the background on the basis that maybe, one day, he'd get lucky and something about his brother would turn up.

'Can I help you?'

'I think I've got something.'

Graciano stood straighter. 'You think, or you know?'

Out of the corner of his eye, he saw Alicia shift, her face turning to his, curiosity on her features. They were so in tune it was predictable that she'd hear his voice and worry.

'I'm ninety-nine percent sure.'

'What is it?'

'I believe your brother is in Savisia.'

'The Middle East? Why?'

'I'm still looking into that, but the theory holds together.'

'I don't want "holds together",' Graciano said, shaking his head. 'I want watertight.'

'Let me tell you what I've got.' He proceeded to outline the working theory. When the accident occurred, the sheikh of Savisia was touring Spain with his young wife. We don't know much, but they donated a large sum to the hospital to keep everything off the books and your brother seems to have gone home with them. This all checks out—the dates, their visit, the two-million-pound donation.'

Graciano closed his eyes. 'My brother disappeared off the radar. It explains why no adoption agency has ever heard of him. Why I couldn't find him.'

'What about the American connection?'

'Best I can guess, they used an American senator's private jet to fly him out—a diplomatic favour.'

Graciano swore.

'I have a photo of him.'

'Send it to me.'

The investigator paused. 'I will. But before you open it, there are two things you should know.'

'Yes?'

'Your brother was very young.'

'I'm aware of that.'

'He suffered a lot of trauma in the accident. Preliminary reports suggest his memory may have been affected by his injuries. That would explain why they were able to take him.'

'And why my visit was upsetting to him,' Graciano said, piecing it together.

'Yes.'

'You said there were two things I should know?'

'Your brother is now the ruling sheikh of Savisia. He may not welcome a voice from his past, challenging his right to the throne.'

Graciano gripped the phone tight, staring at his family with all the love in his heart. 'He will,' he said, nodding confidently.

'How can you be so sure?'

'Because I've recently become a believer in second chances.'

* * * * *

THE PRINCE'S FORBIDDEN CINDERELLA

KIM LAWRENCE

MILLS & BOON

For Sally, who dedicated her birthday to raising money for a cause close to my heart. Thank you!

CHAPTER ONE

RENZOI WAS OFTEN referred to as a jewel, and it was rare for those enjoying their first glimpse of the island kingdom from the air to disagree.

There was one airport on the island, and the coastal route from the international airport hub to the walled city capital of Fort St Boniface was considered by many to be one of the most beautiful stretches of road in the world, beloved by film crews over the years, and by those with a head for heights, the nerves for hairpin bends, and a love of dramatic seascapes.

Many travellers who arrived on the island took the less dizzying option of a transfer on one of the water taxis that ferried their passengers across the glittering waters of the grand harbour.

You could no longer gawp at the luxury yachts moored in the deep water as they were now floating, with their billionaire occupants, in a brand-new purpose-built marina on the opposite side of the island, contributing to the island's thriving economy and reputation as a haunt for the rich and famous.

These days the only obstacles to negotiate on the short crossing were a few sailing and fishing boats. Part of the charm of St Boniface was that it remained a working harbour.

The short crossing offered the best view of the walled capital with its towers and domes. Dramatic though the capital's architecture was, it was the royal palace centrepiece, rising like the top tier of a wedding cake above the medieval sprawl of picturesque narrow streets and cobbled squares, that everyone wanted to be snapped outside.

In daylight hours the sparkling stretch of water swarmed with brightly painted speedboats. Even as the sun was replaced by stars and a full moon, several continued to work the stretch, ferrying groups of eager tourists staring with wonder at the illuminated fairytale castle with its dramatic dome and myriad towers.

One such vessel held no tourists, it was not draped with colourful bunting, instead, it carried a solitary passenger and, for the observant, a discreet royal logo illuminated by the strings of twinkling fairy lights reflecting off the water as it reversed towards a pontoon that was set a little away from the main landing area where the tourist fleet was moored.

Seemingly not having the patience to wait for the final manoeuvre, the passenger leapt casually out over the several feet of water and landed with athletic jungle-cat grace on the gently swaying pontoon.

A figure who had been standing on the dock lifted a hand in greeting, pausing as the tall, loose-limbed, suited figure negotiated his way over the pontoon towards him.

'I wasn't expecting a reception party—' the arrival began, only to pause as the phone in his pocket began to vibrate. He raised an apologetic hand. 'One moment, Rafe.'

The waiting figure, who might have been considered tall himself had he not been standing beside the Prince, who stood six four in his bare feet, watched as a spasm of irritated comprehension moved like a slow ripple across the contours of the handsome carved features of the heir to the throne of Renzoi, before the silver-grey eyes lifted to make contact with his.

'I was about to ask if there was a problem, but...' Marco glanced at the screen of his phone one last time before he slid it back into his pocket. 'The airport is closed...?'

The other man gave a rueful nod. 'Everything is grounded. This storm is heading straight for us.'

'You're heading out there now?'

'It kind of comes with the job description.'

'There is a job description for Minister for Transport and Tourism?' Marco drawled, his darkly delineated brows lifting.

The other man gave a self-conscious shrug. 'When someone says "Minister" I keep looking over my shoulder.'

'Not such a bad idea, palace politics being what they are,' Marco observed sardonically. 'Though luckily the knives are *mostly* metaphorical these days. So, how many times have you been told you have big shoes to fill so far?'

'Everyone seems shocked. The minister's death was—'

'Shocked? The man was ninety,' Marco cut in. 'Drank like a fish and the *big* shoes he died in were golf shoes. As his assistant you've already been doing his job for the last five years while he took the accolades.'

Rafe permitted himself a grin, which faded as he added earnestly, 'You putting your neck on the line for me...it meant a lot to me.'

'Neck?' Marco rotated the part of his anatomy under

discussion, releasing some of the tension that he hadn't been aware was there. 'Hardly that. You have nothing to prove to me, Rafe.'

His neck was safe but when he had used his veto to override the Council of Ministers' choice to fill the senior vacancy, Marco had known that any mistakes on Rafe's part would be eagerly pounced on as evidence of Marco's meddling in matters he did not understand by the palace mandarins, who preferred he should emulate his much more compliant father.

Nepotism in the palace was an accepted route of promotion. Just five families held virtually every position of power on the island, and they had no intention of ceding that power without a struggle. This was fine, Marco could be patient, and he had his father's backing, even though the King was too easy-going and, yes, it was true, *lazy*, Marco acknowledged, one corner of his mouth lifting in an affectionate grin as he thought of his father, who, as the courtiers pointed out, was much loved by his people.

The hardly subtle shorthand being that if Marco took up golf or beekeeping or taking afternoon tea with his long-term mistress, and left the mandarins to run the country, he too would one day be loved by his people.

Marco, whose marriage had ended with the death of his wife, did not have a long-term mistress, nor a short-term one. He wasn't a monk. One-night or occasionally discreet two-night stands seemed a much less demanding way to satisfy his natural physical needs. Also the old adage that there was safety in numbers held true.

One day he would marry again, but he intended to delay that day for as long as possible.

'At least you made it home before the closures, Highness…'

'*Highness...?* Rafe...*really*?' Marco's expressive lips twitched.

The other man grinned and pushed his wire-framed glasses up his nose. 'All right, Marco, but...'

'*But* there is no one around to hear. You can grovel as much as you like in company, but being called *Highness* by a man I once saw dance on a table after half a cider—you really are a lightweight—and a man I used to thrash at rugby doesn't sit right.' Not that friendship, or even the pleasure of winding up the cabal of blue bloods that took their power for granted, was the reason that Marco had given his old university friend and son of his chauffeur the lynchpin role. It was for the simple reason that Rafe was the best man for the job.

'Rugby... I think recollections may vary on that one, but as you're my boss I'll let it pass. I take it the flight in was...*interesting*?'

Marco's grin flashed. 'You could say that. I think I have had my week's adrenaline rush.' Had he not known the service history of the decorated pilot at the controls he might have been worried at their third attempt at landing. His grin faded as he observed Rafe's glance drifting to the waiting boat.

'You need to be off?'

Rafe nodded and, excusing himself, climbed into the boat with more caution than Marco had exited it. Marco watched the boat speed away before striding towards the waiting car. As he reached the long, low, armour-plated limo with the blacked-out windows a power surge caused the lights, including those dancing on the water, to flicker.

The door was opened by a suited figure who had emerged from the driver's seat. 'Did you see Rafe, Tomas?'

'My son, the minister,' he self-corrected, 'is work-ing.' Despite the stony expression Marco could hear the pride in the older man's voice.

'Of course.' Marco's finger traced the white scar on his cheek. Tomas had been Marco's personal childhood bodyguard before an injury acquired rescuing Marco after he tested out his youthful theory that a waterfall was made for leaping into and sliding down had put Tomas on desk duty.

The thin white line on his cheek was Marco's only lasting reminder. Tomas's reminder was the bleep of metal detectors when he walked through them, and a limp that had negated his role as a personal security guard.

Desk duty had not suited him, nor had early retire-ment. He had jumped at the chance to enter service as Marco's personal driver.

'He is grateful for the chance you have given him, Highness.'

'He deserves it.'

'Yes,' the older man agreed factually, adding, 'The storm has followed you home, I think, Highness.'

Marco made a non-committal sound in his throat. He did not assign human characteristics to forces of nature, he simply respected them. The door closed behind him. The air-conditioned interior of the car was pleasant after the sultry pre-storm heaviness outside. Marco loosened his tie and shrugged off his jacket, dislodging the small gift-wrapped package in his breast pocket. It was hard to know what to get a five-year-old girl who had pretty much everything. In the end he'd opted for a delicate necklace, a silver hand-beaten shell on a silver chain.

Would Freya like it?

He had no idea; he dodged the acknowledgment of

his ignorance but not before he experienced a stab of something that felt like loss…what five-year-old was *not* a mystery?

Freya would smile and say thank you. His daughter was a very polite child…her old-fashioned manners were a credit to Nanny Maeve, his own nanny back in the day, who was reluctantly retiring due to crippling arthritis, but she had insisted she was well enough to stay on another month and ensure a smooth transition before she moved to the luxurious surroundings of an upmarket retirement village in her native Ireland.

Opening his laptop, he began scrolling through emails as the car drew away from the dock. They had driven through the gate cut into the sixteenth-century walls of the capital before the dark outside was briefly illuminated by a sodium-silver flash that for a brief moment blinded the passenger to the iconic image of the castle. A moment later the much-replicated image of the illuminated honeyed walls that inevitably drew gasps of amazement reappeared.

Marco didn't gasp. He was focusing on the laptop in front of him. He had grown up inside those fortified walls and was more interested in the results of the latest opinion poll he had recently set in motion.

A quick scan of the table of figures twitched the corners of his wide sensual mouth upwards into a satisfied smile. This information would be useful ammunition at tomorrow's scheduled meeting. It was just what he needed to pull the rug from under the expensively shod feet of the cabal of palace officials who held strong to the belief that any change was a bad one.

There were days, in fact entire weeks, when it felt to Marco he was banging his head against a brick wall when he tried to convince the courtiers who felt it was their job to keep the status quo that stagnation was not a good thing, and that the subjects of the admittedly prosperous island state were a lot more open-minded than the courtiers believed.

And the figures he was looking at backed up this view. A representative cross section of the island kingdom's population, when asked their views on a fictional scenario equivalent to the real one he had in mind, were not so closed-minded.

As he closed the laptop the time in the corner of the screen caught his eye, causing him to self-correct the thought. It actually already was tomorrow.

Ahead the gilded gates silently swung open. There was no visible security presence beyond the sentinel figures in traditional dress who stood at intervals along the battlements, but it was there. Marco had signed off on the new improved security measures six months ago in direct response to the *incident* that had involved a tourist armed with nothing more sinister than a camera who had somehow wandered into Freya's fifth birthday party.

A guest speaker at a European climate-change conference, Marco had learnt of the incident second-hand from his mother, who had told it as an amusing anecdote, which was possibly to be expected of a monarch who regularly rode around the island on a bicycle with her security detail trying to keep up.

His mother refused to accept that there were bad people out there…just misunderstood souls. He was surprised her good nature was not taken advantage of more.

Marco had *not* been amused and had instigated a full-scale overhaul of the palace security arrangements. He had not kept her mother safe but the child she had died giving life to would be protected.

Marco pushed away the image of his late wife's pale

sweat-slicked face as, utterly exhausted by the traumatic birth, she had refused to look at her newborn child, before the image could shift, as it inevitably did, to the next scene.

The scene that culminated in him standing in front of an empty bed covered in crumpled blood-stained sheets. He always remembered the weight and warmth of the baby in his arms, her big accusing blue eyes looking up at him, before she was whisked away and the doctor appeared, the news he was there to break written in his compassionate eyes.

The weight of the crushing guilt Marco felt at that moment had never lessened. It was always with him. He wore it like a second skin. It was no more than he deserved.

Like his own father, he had failed as a husband. It seemed inevitable that, like his own father, one day he would also fail as a father. To be on the receiving end of his daughter's love would make him feel like the fraud that he was, not the grieving loving husband the world thought of him as.

Was he even capable of loving?

The self-contemptuous curl of his lip flattened as his assistant appeared. 'Luca.'

The young man, knowing his boss's impatience with small talk, fell into step with him and launched straight into the requested update without preamble as the two men walked together towards the entrance of Marco's personal apartments.

They reached the pillared doorway. 'So, the new nanny has arrived?' It was an afterthought.

There was the faintest of pauses before the younger man responded. Marco noted and filed away the information. 'Her flight was delayed, but yes, she's here.'

'But?'

'But I'm afraid the anticipated handover won't be happening. Miss Fitzgerald's sister has been admitted to hospital back home.'

'So where is nanny now?'

'Which one…? Oh, I see… Miss Fitzgerald is in Cork. I put her on a private jet…arranged for someone to meet her on the other end and escort her. Oh, and I sent some flowers to the hospital for her sister… I assumed that you would want…?'

'Of course.' Marco dismissed the unnecessary question with a flick of the long fingers of his left hand, light catching the gold wedding ring he still wore.

So the new nanny would be thrown in at the deep end. He shrugged. He hadn't interviewed her personally but on paper she'd been the best candidate by far—an experienced teacher who had been deputy head in a school of five hundred could look after one small five-year-old. And if she didn't make the grade, the solution was not a difficult one.

Her six-month trial could be terminated at any point and there was a small army of nursery nurses who had learned their trade under nanny Fitzgerald who could fill the gap. He did not foresee a problem, so he moved on to the next issue.

'Luca, could you send over the details of the eco-friendly start-ups who applied for the new sponsorship fund?' Before becoming a father, investing in firms that were intended to address some of the world's environmental challenges would not have been on Marco's radar, but now he was passionate about making the planet's future a safe one for his daughter.

'I already have. There has been quite a response, even after the business team filtered them for obvious duds, though I shouldn't really be surprised. The kudos of having your name and "royal" associated does bring the sort of brand awareness that any start-up—sorry,' he tacked on, stifling a yawn.

Marco felt his guilt stir. *He had to be hell to work for.* Just because he could not manage more than four hours' sleep it didn't mean his staff couldn't have a life outside the office.

'Take tomorrow off.'

The younger man looked startled. 'Oh, but the—'

Marco shook his head, the smile staying in his grey eyes and not altering the sensual line of his firm lips as he reiterated firmly, 'Go home, Luca, and thanks.'

The startled look again and Marco made a note to self to express gratitude where it was due more often. Luca was a really excellent aide and he would be sad to let him go, but the young man had outgrown his position long ago. He deserved some autonomy. The post Marco had in mind for him would give him that.

His own rooms were on the ground floor, his bedroom opening directly to a private quadrangle. Two floors above him was the tower room that he had had equipped as a private gym. Very useful for an insomniac. Choosing between his bed and the treadmill, he selected neither. Instead, he entered the hallway where the stairs led up to the nursery wing.

The need to see his daughter was a physical ache. She would be sleeping but she often was when he chose to visit her. It was easier than when she was awake. Pain flickered across the strong contours of his face. Her eyes were so like her mother's, the woman he had not loved.

Her eyes accustomed to the dark now, Kate looked around the unfamiliar room and the unfamiliar objects from her position in the high canopied four-poster.

She was really here, and in the process of getting here she had burnt all her bridges. Her stomach tightened as she was seized by a deep visceral longing for all things familiar: her tiny home snuggled between an antique shop and a tea room, her classroom... *Stop it, Kate,* she told herself sternly, *look forward not back!*

Her thoughts were slow to react to the reprimand and lingered on the image of her parents' hurt, guilty faces when she had confronted them...

'You lied to me, all my life you lied, my entire life has been a lie. I need to get away.'

They thought she'd been talking about a holiday. Good idea, they'd said, suggesting a week somewhere warm.

Then she'd seen the online ad.

A new job, a new life.

'It's so far away, Kate,' her dad had said.

'We will miss you,' her mum had said.

Kate fought free of the memories. Just because she had stepped off the path she'd been on did not mean, as her brother had claimed, she was punishing Mum and Dad. It was good to get out of your comfort zone, especially if you were trying to get to grips with your life when everything that made you feel safe and who you were had vanished.

Comfort zone, she mused with a wry twist of her lips as she looked around her surroundings, thinking, *And then some.*

The post had been advertised as live-in and though she hadn't been expecting a room in the attic, given who her employer was, she had been taken aback, pleasantly, when she had arrived at the palace to be shown to a self-contained luxury apartment. Self-contained up to the point there was an adjoining door to the nursery occupied by her new charge, Princess Freya, a shy five-year-old with big blue eyes who she had met very briefly when she had arrived.

Raising herself on one elbow, she reached for her phone and groaned when she saw the time. Every cell in her body was aching from exhaustion but her brain was buzzing. Flopping back down, her flame red hair spread across the silk pillow, she swept back with the crook of her elbow a tangled shiny strand of long golden auburn that was tickling her nose, and sighed before levering herself upright once more and shaking her head to free the fiery strands that were sticking to the dampness of her skin.

Renzoi, she had read during her fact-finding Internet frenzy after she had got the job, enjoyed an enviable temperate climate.

This didn't feel temperate, it felt clammy and stiflingly hot. Pushing back the covers, she swung her legs out of bed and padded barefoot across to the window and, pulling aside the heavy curtains, she stood on tiptoe to unfasten the window latch and settled back on her heels as the warm air rushed in. At least the light breeze was welcome. She pulled at the neck of her loose cotton nightgown and, head back, she breathed, lifting her hair from her neck to give the breeze access to her hot sticky skin. Her nostrils flared as the room was filled with the strong night-time scents redolent of mint and rosemary. Her reading matter had told her that both grew wild on the hills of the island.

She wandered out of the bedroom and through the pretty living room, into the fitted kitchen with its stone worktops. In the morning she would tackle the coffee machine, which looked impossibly complicated. She opened the fridge, which was stocked with an assortment of essentials, and enjoyed the cool as she filled her glass with iced water from the dispenser.

As she gulped down the water she caught sight of her reflection in one of the shiny cupboards. She looked like a pale wraith, a ghostly vision in need of a comb, some concealer for the dark shadows under her eyes and a good meal. Not that the meal part would matter—no matter *what* she ate her collarbones stood out, leaving delicate hollows above. She envied other women their lush curves, not that her lack of them kept her awake nights.

She was firmly of the mind that you worked with what you had. From nowhere the tears welled in her eyes, emotion kept locked inside spilling out in the form of salty liquid that slid down her cheeks.

She gave a loud sniff. 'Oh, God, Kate, what are you doing?'

Running away? Trying to find herself?

Her lips twisted in a grimace of self-mockery. A few weeks earlier she would have poured scorn on both options. She was proud that she never avoided reality even when it was not palatable.

Take her early obsession with ballet, not in itself so unusual for a young girl, but what set her apart was the fact she didn't drift away like most of her friends and become distracted by the latest craze or boys. The only thing that had made her walk away from her dream was the realisation that she lacked the indefinable *something* that a top-class dancer needed. She would only ever be competent.

Competent wasn't good enough, the brutal truth was her best wasn't good enough, so she had diverted her passion into something that she didn't have to be second-best at: her schoolwork. And then, after she won a scholarship to a top university, gaining a degree in teaching.

Kate knew she was a good teacher. Her natural aptitude for engaging children's interest and her work ethic had been recognised.

The youngest deputy head at the prestigious primary school, being groomed, everyone knew, to take over when the head retired in two years. Not that she'd necessarily intended to take the post—she'd had a tentative approach from a failing inner-city school in a deprived area. They needed someone with an innovative approach to turn the school around, someone who thrived on a challenge.

She was no longer the person who had been excited by the idea, the person who had known who she was and where she was going. Now, shaking her head and brushing the last cooling tear from her face, she closed the fridge door.

Bed, she decided, calculating that if she fell asleep in the next thirty minutes she could still get five hours' sleep in before she had to get up again.

She had barely taken a couple of steps when a sound made her pause. Head tilted to one side, she listened, straining to make it out. *Music?* Her brow furrowed. Or a *voice*?

There was nothing but silence. She shrugged. She had imagined it. A few moments later, her hand reaching for the handle of her bedroom door, she stopped. This time there was no doubt: another noise, a thump and even a muffled curse, emanating from the speaker on the wall that, as had been explained to her earlier, was wired into the nursery. It was one piece of the massive amount of information she had received that her time-zone-whacked brain had retained.

It was not the sort of sound a child made…it was…

There was someone in Freya's room and the only way to find out who was to go in. She stared, her thoughts racing, at the wall that separated the room from the nursery, seeing the layout in her head, rows of books, their spines colour-coordinated, educational toys and… well, actually it looked like a very expensive toy store glossy advert. Everything looked pristine, brand new, neatly arranged on shelves and in labelled boxes. A world away from her own childhood bedroom or, for that matter, her brother's.

Thinking of her brother brought a half-smile to her face. It lasted a split second before she remembered the row they'd had before she left. *Like she would ever forget?* The spark left her eyes as the sense of betrayal resurfaced.

It had been enough of a life-changing blow to learn that her parents, who had always taught her the importance of truth and honesty in life, had been lying to her, but discovering that her brother had been party to the conspiracy of deceit had been worse somehow.

She would never forget the expression she'd seen in his eyes when she had broken it to him, but before he'd said a word she'd known that this was not news to him.

He'd known they were adopted, that he wasn't even her brother.

They had argued before but nothing like the argument that had followed. Jake, she'd discovered, had found out by accident too, but years ago and he couldn't see why she had a problem.

'It doesn't change anything.'

For Kate it changed *everything*. She really couldn't understand *how* he could feel that way. Jake told her that this reaction was exactly why he hadn't told her.

She dashed away a stray tear angrily as the conversation ran through her head.

'You're the best friend, or sister, a person could have. You'd fight to the death for the people you love.'

'And that is a bad thing?'

'You don't just love Mum and Dad, you put them on a pedestal, Kate. You're tough on yourself and the rest of us, you expect too much. Can't you see that Mum and Dad were protecting you, I was protecting you?'

'You don't protect someone from the truth.'

He had not even come to say goodbye.

Kate gave her head an angry little shake to dislodge the memories and thought, *Stop dithering.* Straightening her narrow shoulders, she pulled the connecting door open. Whatever was on the other side could not be more disturbing than the company of her own thoughts.

Or maybe not?

CHAPTER TWO

DESPITE HER THUDDING HEART, Kate did not actually expect to discover anything sinister on the other side of the door and she was fully prepared to feel stupid.

In her head she was inventing crazy scenarios she'd discover, the room filled with people disinfecting the toys, or sweeping for bugs, the snooping kind, or maybe both...? The nursery did not remain showroom pristine without a lot of work.

So, it took Kate several frozen seconds before the adrenaline rush kicked into life. By this point the large figure on the opposite side of the room had put a toy doll back on a shelf that was, her racing brain noted irrelevantly, out of reach to a five-year-old. For that matter it was out of reach for someone her own height, which was a diminutive five three.

It was definitely *not* out of reach for the intruder, whose back view was revealed by the light shining from the room behind her as tall and also powerful. She took in the stretch of fabric across his shoulders, making her aware of the muscles beneath the tailoring. This was one well-dressed and very fit intruder!

If good tailoring was an indicator of character, she had nothing to worry about, but it wasn't, and she did.

Better to assume the worst and laugh when the innocent truth was revealed, but laughter would be premature. The main thing was to stay calm and not panic...

Oh, God, the panic button beside her bed!

Five minutes ago was the time to remember that. When the red button had been pointed out to her it had seemed a massive overkill because you'd need to be some sort of ninja warrior or possess superpowers to get past the armed guards that had seemed to be lurking around every corner during her whirlwind tour of the nursery wing.

The point was someone had, and the button was not within reach. She weighed the option of retreating but realised the chances of doing so without alerting this man to her presence were zero. He was going to turn around any second, at which point she might discover there was a perfectly reasonable explanation for him being there, but she wasn't about to give him the benefit of the doubt. Caution was called for and there was a five-year-old child to think about.

He'd have to go through her to get to her new charge... *Which probably wouldn't take more than a few seconds.* She pushed the unhelpful thought away and, her bare feet silent on the polished boards—not so her heart, which was throwing itself against her ribcage—she edged towards the little princess's bedroom door. The intruder remained oblivious to her presence.

She reached the door, took her position and cleared her throat, trying to project her inner Amazonian kickboxer, while aware that on the outside what he would see made any threat she made laughable.

'Security is on its way.' Pleased her voice did not even wobble, she pushed ahead with her warning. 'I suggest you—'

'Hold on a moment, will you?' Marco pushed out between gritted teeth, irritated that the entire elaborate toy display was about to slide once more, domino fashion, off the shelf. On the plus side, the new nanny possessed not only a pleasant speaking voice but excellent hearing, which was one up on her predecessor, who'd refused to wear the hearing aids she really had needed in her advancing years. It could make for some interesting conversations, especially as she took offence if you raised your voice.

She squeaked when one of the dolls let out a horribly realistic crying sound. Marco's response was to swear, proving he had mastered three languages or at least he knew how to swear multilingually.

'Right, sorry about that.' Marco turned, transferring his attention towards the waiting new nanny…only to discover that the person standing there was *not* the new nanny!

He refused to accept this possibility as for a few stark mind-freezing seconds his brain shut down. Not so his primal functions. Hormones pumped through his bloodstream, leaving heat that pooled hot and heavy in his groin and making a mockery of both the control he prided himself on and his much-admired lightning wits.

In two startled blinks he took in the cause of the blip in his self-control, his glance sweeping her from head to toe—not a long journey. She was petite.

He knew about female nightwear. He'd removed quite a bit of it over the years, but none that looked like the thing the woman standing there was wearing. Not intended to titillate or light the sort of fire it had in him and therein lay the irony. The white cotton shapeless thing covered quite a lot and heavily hinted at a hell of a lot more, courtesy of the directional beam of the wall light in the adjoining flat making it one shade short of transparent. It revealed the dark tips of her small high breasts, the dip and flare at her waist and hip and the shadow at the juncture of the slim, sinuous length of her thighs.

Her skin was the next pale on the colour spectrum to her nightdress but, unlike the fabric, had a pearly, almost opalescent quality. Again, probably courtesy of the lighting. She possessed the most extraordinary hair he'd ever seen; the lustrous waves and heavy coils didn't need any lighting effects to reveal the gold highlight interwoven with the deep titian waves that fell untidily around her small oval face and tumbled down her back.

As their glances connected her luminous amber eyes widened and her mouth fell, not unattractively, open. As he stared at the pink, slightly quivering outline any number of inappropriate thoughts slithered through his mind. Inappropriate when thought in connection with his daughter's nanny and they made it hard to retain his mental image of the anticipated sensible female in his head. In essence she would be a slightly younger version of Nanny Maeve, all no-nonsense common sense and even more sensible shoes. His glance ran to her bare narrow feet and glittery painted toenails.

Clearing his throat, he dragged his gaze upwards.

'If you're not going to use that…?' He nodded at the porcelain vase she held in a white-knuckled grip.

He watched her eyes travel to the ugly thing in her hand, a look of surprise widening the eyes she took off him for one split second. Her elbow dropped but not all the way, similarly her defences as she retained a grip of both.

'Your only chance of braining me was utilising the element of surprise and you've lost that now, so you might as well put it down.'

Tomorrow, he decided grimly, he was going to find out which proxy had decided at interview that this woman represented a suitably *mature* candidate. And it wouldn't have been one person; the vetting procedure would have been as detailed as the background check.

Deep velvet with an edge of gravel to the dark chocolate flavour, his sardonic drawl shook Kate free of the thrall that had held her staring transfixed, mouth open, drooling… She closed her mouth with a snap.

Drooling…? God, I really hope not.

'You could drop it if you like. It'll be insured and it is extremely ugly.'

With elaborate care she placed the vase she didn't actually recall picking up in a space beside a row of colour-coded books that she already had marked out as one of her first changes.

As first impressions went it was hard to imagine one worse than this. 'S-Sorry…' she stuttered and stopped.

What was she meant to call him?

'I didn't realise it was Your…' *Highness? Majesty?*

Obviously, she knew *who* he was. Crown Prince Marco—then a lot of other names followed—Zanetti, her new boss. His every utterance was picked up across the media spectrum, analysed to the nth degree and imbued with hidden, deep meaning.

His height and his superb athletic body meant that a photo of him shirtless, all golden skin and sculpted muscle, was worth mega bucks. Even an image of him conservatively dressed in a suit could send social media wild, especially as they were relatively rare. His face with its razor-sharp cheekbones, silver-grey stare and sinfully sexy mouth had been called perfect, though now she was seeing it in the flesh she decided she agreed with one jaundiced critic who had called it *too* perfect!

For the first twelve months after his beautiful wife's tragic death in childbirth, he'd vanished, fallen off the edge of the earth. One or two snaps of him looking brooding and beautiful in a hollow-eyed, gaunt-faced way had been the only visuals to feed the appetite for news about the iconic tragic figure he had become in the eyes of the world.

Does a man ever recover from the loss of his first love?

Learning to love again...will Marco?

Advice from someone who has been there and come out the other side.

Is Marco putting his child ahead of his happiness?

Hypnosis and a carb-free diet helped me recover from PTSD after my boyfriend left me, it could help the lonely Prince too.

The headlines, from the inane to the academic, all had a similar theme, and who knew? Maybe the man under discussion read them, because the tragic prince did move on.

A year after his wife's death Marco Zanetti re-emerged, affording an interested public discreet glimpses of his private life. His name started to be linked with a succession of beautiful women. The longevity of his associations with the women he escorted varied, one night or a week—this was presumably his version of long-term.

No matter how discreet or short-lived the liaisons were, inevitably every beautiful woman his name was linked with was viewed as a prospective future queen and mother, her privacy invaded, her past love life scrutinised. Despite this price, which to Kate, whose blood ran cold at the thought, seemed a high one, there was no shortage of candidates, which had seemed inexplicable, though less so now when she was standing in the same room as him.

Luckily he was a million miles from the sort of man she found attractive—her type was good-looking, but not too good-looking, kind and sensitive. Shaking her head slightly to clear it, she tried to kick-start her brain for the correct form of address.

It was so damned frustrating. She'd made a point of knowing, and the knowledge had simply fled. Maybe because worrying about titles offended her egalitarian nature?

She had already decided that she would not be curtseying to anyone.

She finally settled for a slightly breathless, 'Freya's dad, that is you, or… I heard a noise and—'

Marco cut across her before she ran out of steam. 'And you are…?'

The Prince sounded haughty and looked…well, he looked like something out of a fantasy—or a nightmare, depending on your preferences, and her fantasies were *not* of men with hauteur stamped into their too handsome features, even if he really was several billion times more dramatically gorgeous in the flesh than in print or video.

The camera made him look good, it accurately captured his patrician features, all hard angles and intriguing carved hollows, the tummy-quivering gleam in his heavy-lidded silver-grey eyes with the famous long lashes, his masterful nose and the much-raved-about sexy mouth.

Kate had always privately suspected that the real in-the-flesh man would be a bit of a let-down. She'd been prepared for it. What she hadn't been ready for was the fact that no photo could do him justice. It did not even hint at the skin-peelingly raw masculinity he exuded or his physical presence so strong it seemed to suck the oxygen from the room, or at least her lungs.

Her chin lifted as she tried to regain a little dignity.

As first impressions went…maybe he had a sense of humour but, looking at his fallen-angel dark face, she decided it was doubtful.

'I'm Kate Armstrong, the new nanny.'

She took a step forward and held out her hand, dropping it a couple of humiliating moments later when he showed no sign of taking it.

God, perhaps it was against the law to touch his royal personage.

'Should I curtsey?' The words were out before she could stop them.

Marco's eyes slid to the high but loose neckline of her nightdress. His eyes darkened a shade to steel.

'Probably not.'

The way his eyes slid downwards made Kate remember for the first time that she was just in her nightdress. The knowledge that it was the sort of nightdress your grandmother would approve of eased her flurry of sink-through-the-floor horror.

'I appreciate your efforts to protect Freya, but the next time maybe just press the panic button…?' The sardonic suggestion sent the heat flying back to her cheeks. She resented the fact he could make her feel a total idiot just by lifting one of his eyebrows.

'Oh, gosh, yes, definitely,' she agreed, nodding her agreement and vowing there would not be a next time. She wouldn't give the sarcastic superior devil the satisfaction to patronise her. 'But I wasn't in bed. I couldn't sleep, it's so hot.'

She pulled at the neck of her nightdress, seemingly oblivious to the provocativeness of the action.

'A storm is coming,' Marco said, feeling the prickles of attraction like a rash across his overheated flesh as he dragged his glance upwards, only to have it fall on her soft sensual mouth with the promise of… He brought his line of speculation to an abrupt control-claiming halt.

This was crazy. There were any number of attractive women working at the palace, which proudly proclaimed itself an equal opportunities employer, but it was irrelevant to Marco. There was a code—which his father had never quite got his head around—which meant that there were things a man in his position did not do, and that was sleep with a woman who called him Highness, or sir, or, in this case, *Freya's dad.*

The fact was his annoyance was not about her uncontrollable flamelike hair or her sensual mouth, or the sledgehammer attraction hit her appearance had delivered. It was the fact that she was wrong for the job, too young, too much of a temptation for staff less controlled than he was. He wanted a calming, stable influence for his daughter, he told himself, choosing to forget the occasions recently when his daughter's lack of spontaneity and mischief had caused him the occasional passing concern, enough concern for him to ask his mother's opinion.

'Freya is a sweet little thing. We have lovely cosy chats. She is not the least bit like you. I never had a moment's peace worrying about what you'd do next.'

Her response had eased his concerns, even though his mother had not to his knowledge ever worried about his welfare. That arduous task had been delegated to nanny. Pretty well nothing disturbed his parent's serenity, which as far as he could tell was achieved by deciding that she simply wouldn't see or hear anything that wasn't *nice*, including her husband's in-house mistress.

Kate shivered. She had never liked storms much, though she wondered if the electricity she felt in the air was entirely to do with atmospheric conditions and was not connected in some small way to the gleam in his slitted sliver eyes.

'How long is your trial for, Miss Armstrong?' he asked.

Kate, who had been surreptitiously edging towards the door, froze at the abrupt question. *'Trial?'* She looked at him, her nose wrinkling as she focused, or tried to. This had been a long day that had been topped by making a total fool of herself in front of her new boss. She expelled a slow steadying breath. She'd seen the clause in her contract but had not really paid it much notice.

'Six months…oh…' Comprehension dawned. 'I do know how important continuity is for a child,' she told him earnestly. 'I would never leave you in the lurch,' she went on to assure him, sounding shocked at the idea of such dereliction of duty. 'I'm yours until Freya starts school formally.' Seven seemed late to Kate, but, as the educational system on the island was envied around the world, she was willing to learn. In fact, she was eager.

'You are mine,' Marco mocked and was punished for his cruelty, or rewarded, depending on your viewpoint, by a rush of hormonal heat. This was more than slightly insane. He had gone too long without.

It was an obvious explanation for this explosion of unprecedented lust. His recent work-pleasure balance had of late been pretty heavily skewed in favour of work. He needed to make the effort, though that was part of the problem. There was no effort.

He knew most women he was attracted to would be available, not because of his irresistible charm, but because of who he was, and if he was honest the entire *effort* involved in the mating ritual had become… tiresome. Boredom had set in. It was all so predictable, as was the inevitable post-coital guilt that followed those moments of mind-blanking pleasure when he forgot, when he lost himself in sex. No matter how mind-blowing the sex was, he paid the price in guilt, the *empty* feeling.

Kate watched the Prince rub the gold marriage band on his finger with his thumb, a reminder of what he'd lost, but it didn't make his mockery any more palatable or this situation any more comfortable.

'I'm your employee and I'd frankly feel more comfortable discussing my role here during office hours and when I'm not jet-lagged and likely to say something I'll regret.' She registered from the look of astonishment that washed over his face that she probably already had. She was too tired and stressed by the situation to care much. 'Goodnight, and sorry to disturb you… Your…'

There was a sudden loud rumble of thunder, the vibration continuing long after the sound died. It wasn't the only vibration. The sudden shock had made her flinch and drawn a soft cry of shock from her lips. It also affected her centre of gravity. She had the oddest feeling of being drawn towards his mid-section, which looked as solid as iron. Her delicate fingers flexed as she made a conscious effort to redress the balance, quite literally.

She'd heard about male magnetism before, but she'd never actually felt the tug personally.

She was shaking. Marco could see the fine tremors running through her body. Sympathy overrode the justified irritation he felt towards her having been dropped into his neatly managed life, a small piece that didn't fit and skewed the neat symmetry of the whole.

'You're afraid of storms?' he said, thinking quite weirdly of her soft warm body burrowing into him for comfort. *Burrowing* was a thing he discouraged in women, or he would have if any had shown the desire to do so.

He'd grown to be a good judge of women who wanted sex without the window dressing, which was useful because there were a lot of women who wanted the window dressing, especially a crown. Marco was under no illusions he was the optional extra; it was the status he represented they wanted.

The women he shared a bed with had one thing in common: they were all happy with sex on equal terms. They were discreet and if their lives and careers got a little boost from the media speculation of being seen with him, that seemed fair.

Kate reacted to his sympathy as though he'd just insulted her. 'I am fine with storms,' she lied, accompanying her words with a chin-jutting glare.

At that moment she'd have chopped off a finger and not admitted it hurt. She would not admit to any weakness because she had just discovered a weakness she had not seen coming.

It wasn't on a par with discovering you were adopted, but it still came as bad news to realise that she was susceptible to the waves of hot male magnetism he oozed.

But she was, and the discovery made her feel horribly self-aware, and, yes, vulnerable too. More vulnerable than meeting your boss in a granny nightie could explain away.

This was far worse, far deeper, an awareness of vulnerability of the body that the acres of cotton concealed. She was more aware of her body than she had ever been. She shifted her weight from one foot to the other, conscious of the feeling of congestion low in her pelvis.

It rocked her to her core to have a fresh set of preconceptions challenged, to realise that it actually was possible to lust after someone you really didn't instinctively like. *Liking* was not necessary in an employer-employee relationship and luckily that was the only relationship there was ever going to be here.

'Goodnight.'

Looking at the closed door, he pondered the extraordinary fact that he had just been reprimanded by an employee, but employee didn't seem the right description—this woman clearly had no concept of hierarchy.

CHAPTER THREE

MARCO HAD HOPED his father could be coaxed into showing some interest, but so far his response had been vague at best. Marco pretended not to notice the multiple hints the conversation was over and continued to push his theme.

'You'll agree that primogeniture is outdated...?' he asked, throwing the question over his shoulder as he walked towards the window. 'That a male taking precedence over an older sister is wrong.'

'I'd offer you tea, but—'

'It's fine. I don't want tea.' He resisted the temptation to point out he didn't like tea and had never drunk the stuff in his thirty-two years.

The King sighed and regarded his son with an attitude of resignation. His only child never had been able to take a hint and once he got an idea into his head he was exhaustingly relentless. 'I hear what you are saying, Marco, but is it worth upsetting people?'

'Upsetting?'

His father sighed again. 'The council, you know they won't like it, Marco. They have strong opinions on tradition.'

Marco smiled, biting his tongue to prevent himself saying of how little interest the *council's* opinion was to him and where he would have loved to suggest, politely of course, they could shove their opinions in anatomical detail.

'The opinion poll I put out there shows quite clearly that the public at large won't have a problem with this. The figures—'

The King held out a hand to halt the flow of information. 'If you say so.'

'So you agree in principle, Father, that Freya should be given precedence over any son I might have?'

'Of course. Are you thinking of getting married again, then? That's good…a king *should* be married. Without your mother's support…' The King caught his son's eyes and his voice trailed away.

'I won't be King for many years,' Marco pointed out swiftly. This at least was one decision he could push down the road. 'And when I am you can be sure I will fulfil all my obligations.' He might be considered a maverick by the palace courtiers who worshipped tradition basically because it was good for them, but Marco had been brought up to respect the role he had been born into. He loved and had pride in his country, and he accepted that one day marriage would be necessary.

And when it came there would be no tragic rerun. The next time, his bride would know that while respect, liking and hopefully great sex would be part of their contract, love would not be.

Unless of course he fell in love… A gleam of self-contempt filtered into his heavy-lidded stare as he contemplated this very unlikely possibility.

If that had been going to happen it would have by now. If he were capable of falling in love it would have been with Belle. The guilt hit him as it always did, clutching like an icy fist in his belly when he thought of his dead wife. The woman who had died before she had lived—and the life she'd shared with him had been some sort of half-life.

If she hadn't married him, she would still be alive.

It *should* have worked. They had been friends long before they had become engaged. He'd *liked* her, and surely liking and respect, two people who had similar viewpoints on the important subjects on life, were a more solid basis for marriage than some unrealistic fantasy based on a temporary hormonal reaction.

He remembered when Belle was in her early teens, her own parents had divorced. Both had been members of one of *the* families in Renzoi. It had created a stir in the general populace, and misery for all involved. His own parents had been together but they had fallen out of love and he and Belle had bonded as unhappy teens over the shared experience of parental mess-ups!

She'd been the first to say it… *'When we grow up let's never fall in love, Marco.'*

If you'd never fallen in love, you couldn't fall out of it. The logic of the plan had stayed with him, but Belle had grown up and she had fallen in love—with him. She'd hoped that he would learn to love her, and it had killed her.

It had always been there, the elephant in the room that he had dealt with by ignoring. But that had become impossible when he had found her weeping. Her tearful, 'It's a girl,' had left him bewildered. His awkward attempt to soothe her had resulted in the truth spilling out of her, the hopes she had kept hidden.

She had believed that giving him a male heir would make him love her back. He had told her in all honesty that he didn't care what sex the child was, and that he would always love her as his dearest friend and the mother of his child.

'But you'll never be in love with me, will you, Marco?'

It was the moment that the truth killed something inside her… *Why the hell couldn't he have lied?*

Experiencing an ice-water rush of the toxic shame the memories brought with them, Marco claimed the present, letting his father's voice drag him back to the moment.

'Rosa has been telling me about the new nanny.'

The changes were micro—Marco's lashes veiled his eyes, his shoulders tensed—subtle, but they were there.

Lady Rosa. Her official title was Master of the Royal Household, but her unofficial title was the King's mistress.

The widow of a minor royal, she was responsible for overseeing the domestic and social calendars across the royal residences, a job she carried out with unflappable calm and efficiency. Marco had hated her very existence once, back when he had thought his parents were a happy couple. Now his attitude was far more pragmatic.

'Don't worry about it, I'll sort it,' he cut in, only too easily able to imagine what Rosa had said about the would-be red-headed usurper to the old favourite Nanny Maeve's role.

'Sort…?' The King looked confused. 'Rosa said you have chosen well. That the woman is a breath of fresh air who knows her mind—those were her words, and coming from Rosa that is quite a compliment.'

Marco compressed his lips over a biting retort. Easygoing to a fault, his father was *not* easy when it came to defending his mistress from criticism.

Marco's restraint did not come easily. It had been

years in the making. For a large part of his life the mention of his father's mistress had been enough to trigger one of the monumental arguments he'd had with his father during his teens.

The way he had discovered the affair had not helped. Walking in on his father in bed with his mistress, or in this instance on a sofa with her, was one image he really wished even now that he could un-see. Almost more infuriating was the fact his mother tolerated the situation, which she said made her husband *happy*.

The entire set-up encapsulated for him the utter hypocrisy of marriage, the damage that people did in the name of true love and the fact that if he had never been born three people would have been happier.

Nowadays there was a truce. Marco accepted that it was their life. They had found themselves in an imperfect situation and they had made the best of it. If it hadn't been for his unexpected appearance after years of trying for a child, his parents would have quietly divorced with the blessing of the council, who were anti-divorce but could get very flexible when it came to maintaining the continuity of the throne.

It would be small wonder if Rosa resented him. Without him she'd probably be Queen now. Trying to conceive him had put his parents' marriage under strain. *Well, that's life for you*, he thought with an internal shrug as he gathered up the printouts he'd brought for his father knowing the King would not look at them. Glancing at the wafer-thin metallic watch on his wrist, Marco made his excuses, pretending not to notice that his father looked relieved.

After depositing the papers in his own office and responding to a couple of emails, he looked around for

Luca and remembered he'd given him the day off in a moment of uncharacteristic generosity.

His movements around the room woke the dog in his basket but he went back to sleep after Marco had found the magic spot behind his ears. He was not as young as he once had been, but then who was? Marco mused, stretching, his expression growing thoughtful as he recalled the *look* he'd noticed from Luca the previous night when the nanny situation had come up. There were two explanations for that: either his assistant didn't want to be the messenger that got shot or he had a thing about the newest employee.

It seemed about time he took charge of the nanny situation personally because so far delegation had gone so well...*not*!

Was he the *only* person in the place who could see the stark staring obviousness? An image of the flame-haired woman drifted across his vision. The woman, despite her impeccable qualifications, was totally unsuitable.

Because you can't stop thinking about how very *suitable she would feel under you*, Marco mocked the voice in his head.

Reviewing the previous night, Kate filed her part in it under *Could have handled things better.*

She might well have already lost her job before it had started. Not a good look on a CV, but if she was ready to pretend last night had never happened maybe her employer might be also. In her opinion he hadn't come out of it very well either.

Whatever the reality was, she was going to do what she was being paid for, which was not to become obsessed with her boss. Sure, he was good to look at, but didn't he just know it? The uncharitable thought was immediately followed by a slug of shame as she realised she was making this nasty assessment purely on his spectacular looks and the debilitating effect he had on her nervous system.

He might be vain, he might be humble—a *big* if there—but she had no intention of allowing herself to be sucked into the entire tragic past situation, or the length of his crazy eyelashes, or his mouth. *Do not even go there, Kate.* Though in her defence there was no harm in looking, was there?

Good to establish that just in case it turned out she couldn't *not* look.

There was a table in an alcove in the nursery, which Freya had solemnly explained was the quiet reading area. Her husky tones suggested this rule had been quite rigid.

'I cleared my own place after breakfast,' she added proudly.

'So do you always have breakfast here?'

The little girl nodded.

Kate's throat ached with the emotion lodged there, and nostalgia for her own different breakfasts when she had been five, the good-natured and occasionally not so good-natured bickering. Quiet was one thing they had not been.

Of course, things had changed as she and Jake had got older. Breakfast had become less of a social start to the day and more self-service, with her mum putting the toast in her hand and packed lunch in her school bag as she left to catch the bus, her mother yelling after her that breakfast was the most important meal of the day.

The wistful wave of sadness and loss was, for a split second, so intense that she couldn't breathe.

They might often have been short of cash but compared to this rich little princess she had been wealthy.

And you threw it all away on a stupid stiff-necked principle!

Pinning on a smile, she turned a deaf ear to the troublemaking voice in her head, and reminded herself that *she* was the one in the right. They'd all lied to her and then made out she was the unreasonable one! Well, Jake had, at least.

'Did you have a nice breakfast?'

'I did,' said Kate, who had located the rather uppercrust staff dining room with some difficulty.

Her entrance had drawn a lot of curious looks, some friendly, some less so. There had been a faint buzz when she had selected a table, after recognising one of the nursery maids she had seen the previous day.

The reason for the buzz became clear when the young girl looked surprised and explained that Kate was allowed on one of the other tables. It didn't immediately click, but when she examined the people sitting on the other table, the significance of the lack of uniforms and the preponderance of suits hit her. The tables, she realised, were actually arranged in order of hierarchy and apparently in the scheme of things she was several tables above a mere nursery maid.

She had laughed and pronounced herself quite happy where she was. The food might be Michelin-star stuff but the entire set-up belonged, in her opinion, in the Dark Ages.

But then a child eating in the nursery alone was in itself a brutal Dark Ages throwback.

'Do you eat all your meals here?' Kate asked, nodding as one of the maids appeared carrying the tray she had requested earlier. 'Oh, thank you…just put it down there.'

'Oh, no, Granny has me over to lunch quite often.' The little girl looked at the tray and its contents. 'It's too early for my milk and apple,' she observed anxiously.

Kate responded to the five-going-on-forty-five comment with professional discretion, even though she just wanted to hug the child. 'This is a "saying hello" break to get to know one another. Granny sounds fun.'

'Oh, she is…and Grandpa too. We have picnics, though I get my knees dirty and nanny…the old nanny looked sad. Grandpa says it doesn't matter, he gets messy loads, but he's King so nobody tells him what to do. Papa will be King after him and then my brother, when I have one. He paints, you know, Grandpa.' She lifted a conspiratorial hand to half cover her mouth. 'He's not very good, but Granny says I have to be kind so I say I like them.'

As she listened to the artless confidences it seemed to Kate that the Prince could take some lessons from this interesting-sounding monarch.

'And Daddy…do you eat with him sometimes?'

'Daddy is a very busy man.'

Kate could almost see the invisible quote marks around the sentence. The man, she brooded, was actually even more of an idiot than she had decided he was.

'Nanny says he has very important things on his mind and I shouldn't bother him.'

This extra information sent Kate's temper into double digits. She imagined that Prince Marco's mind was most often focused on which six-foot model to bed next, if his reputation was to be believed! Keeping her opinion of a man who was *far too busy* for his own daughter to herself, she managed a smile despite wanting to hit something or, more accurately, *someone.*

'Well, I have our special early elevenses on my mind so do you think someone could fetch me a chair so I can join you?'

'All you have to do is ring and you can have anything you want.'

That had to be the saddest sentence she had ever heard, Kate reflected as she sat on her requested chair, which had magically appeared in seconds. What this child needed no *ring* was going to give her. What she needed was a daddy who cared!

The second chair was identical to the one that was the perfect size for Freya. The fit on her was comical enough to make the child giggle before she put her hand over her mouth to smother the sound, as if she expected to be reprimanded.

'Do you think I'll break it?' Kate asked as she balanced on the seat, feeling glad for the sake of her modesty she had opted to wear a pair of pale blue linen culottes with a darker blue sleeveless silk blouse that she wore tucked into the plaited belt. She hoped the outfit gave the professional but practical look she had been aiming for.

Her stint with an infant class had taught her that you needed to stay flexible and not just physically. A young mind not weighed down by preconceptions could seriously challenge you. She had always liked that part of working with young children.

The smile crept back on the little girl's face. 'Don't worry if you do, I'll say I did it. No one will shout at me, they'll just be disappointed.'

This heartbreaking statement did not give Kate a good opinion of her predecessor or, for that matter, the child's father. In her mind he already had a set of horns, now he had added the forked tail to match.

It had always made sense to her that the devil would be handsome—how else would he make sin look tempting? She could imagine that Marco Zanetti could make sin look *very* attractive.

'Are you hot?' Freya asked innocently.

Taking control of her wilful imagination, Kate called a halt to the speculative stream of steamy images sliding through her head under the title of sin and Marco and willed the guilty colour in her cheeks to fade.

'No, not really, and I won't break the chair, Freya, so don't worry. I'm actually quite skinny. My brother says my hair weighs more than I do.' Her smile faded and her hair came in handy as a distraction as she tossed her ponytail over her shoulder as she swallowed past the lump in her throat. 'How about you pull up your chair and we have some cake to celebrate?' she suggested brightly.

The worried look that should not be a factory setting for a five-year-old reappeared. 'Cake is bad for your teeth.' The child raised her eyes from the plate of pastries on the table. 'I have very good teeth.'

'I can see that.'

A smile of pride appeared.

'You also have a lovely smile. Sorry about the cakes. I just thought for a treat…as it's a special occasion—our first morning—we might be naughty?'

The child's eyes grew round as she shook her head. 'I'm not naughty or I try not to be. Nanny Maeve says Papa was never naughty.'

Marco, who distinctly recalled his Irish nanny calling him a *limb of the devil* on more than one occasion, repressed a laugh, and closed the door behind him. The sound was drowned out by the new nanny, who showed less restraint in response to his daughter's claim. Her laugh was low and husky.

From where he stood, Marco got a good view of the puzzled expression on Freya's face but only the back of the redhead's burnished head as she turned the laugh into a cough.

'Does your papa have good teeth?' Kate asked, even though she already knew the answer to that one—his royal *perfectness* could have given an alpha wolf a run for his money.

Actually, now she thought about it, the wolf analogy was not such a terrible one, she decided, a little shiver slithering down her spine as she remembered his heavy-lidded steely grey eyes.

Shaking her head a little to dispel the image, she decided she had to be tolerant, which, despite her brother's accusations, she was. An only-child prince told he was perfect from birth—no wonder the man was so up himself!

She was nothing if not tolerant.

You could almost feel sorry for him, not that she did, but his daughter had clearly been raised to put her father on a pedestal and Kate knew well how that ended, when you inevitably realised the people you'd idolised had feet of clay. So, her sympathy was saved for the child's future disillusionment and her present isolated loneliness.

The former she couldn't do anything about, the latter she intended to. Her mind was buzzing with innovations to help this child discover fun.

'Papa never eats sweet things.' The little girl's voice

halted. 'At least, I don't think he does. He doesn't like them.'

'Good for *Papa*,' Kate murmured under her breath, oblivious to the fact the words had reached the object of her sarcastic undertone.

Out of her line of sight the Prince moved into the room, as Kate dwelt contemptuously on the things that Papa, if the reports were to be believed, *did* like. Fast cars and tall, elegant, enigmatic, classy women, blondes, brunettes, redheads... Kate tucked behind her ear a strand of auburn hair that had escaped the fat pony-tail that fell down her slender back, and diverted her thoughts before her imagination gave the redhead in a clinch with the Prince features or an extra six inches.

She could not imagine a scenario where the tag of *irresistible* attached to a man's name did not make her wince and it was used overtime when Marco Zanetti's name came up.

Still, she could forgive him for being far too good-looking if he'd just give a little of his apparently precious time to his daughter.

Kate felt an ache of sympathy for the child, anticipating the day when Freya realised that the figure she appeared to idolise was several light years away from perfect.

'Do *you* like sweet things? Cakes or sweets...chocolate...?' She ticked the treats off on her fingers.

'I don't know.'

It took Kate a few moments to realise that the child was speaking literally. Her professional scruples about respecting parental wishes slid away. 'Well, it's very important to look after your teeth.' She displayed her own, which were pearly white and even, barring a slight gap between her front ones. 'I like chocolate, but I wouldn't eat it for breakfast…unless, obviously, it was my birthday.'

The little girl stared at her with the expression of someone encountering a foreign life form.

'You eat chocolate for your breakfast?' She regarded Kate with a mixture of awe and horror.

'Well, birthdays are special and a little treat occasionally is nice.'

CHAPTER FOUR

FREYA WATCHED AS Kate popped one of the pastries into her mouth whole.

'Mmm…that was lovely.' Kate sighed, smacking her lips and leaving buttery crumbs around her mouth.

The little girl gave a giggle. 'You have sugar on your nose!'

It was the smothered giggle that stopped Marco, who was about to reveal himself to the oblivious pair, in his tracks. He couldn't remember the last time he'd heard his daughter *giggle*. Her solemnity and her slightly accusing stare, or so it always seemed to him, had been something else that had reminded him of her mother.

One of the many *somethings* that had made him limit his contact with his daughter. Better by far to be a distant father than a terrible one, one not deserving or capable of returning her love. He had no idea if it was genetic, but he did remember the day that he had discovered his father was not a hero. He would spare Freya that disillusion.

Who are you protecting, Marco, asked the unsympathetic voice in his head, *her or yourself?*

Now able to see Kate Armstrong's face, he watched as, head tilted back, his daughter's new nanny went cross-eyed pretending to try and reach her nose with her tongue, while her charge fell off her chair onto the floor, laughing helplessly.

Kate wrinkled her nose. 'Have I got it?'

'No, let me…'

Kate turned her head literally as he spoke. A split second previously she had spotted him in the periphery of her vision. Shock nailed her to the spot as he planted himself beside her chair and leaned down.

It felt far too close and far too personal, close enough for her to feel the warmth of his body, and see the faint white scar on his lean cheek, white against the bronze.

Her nostrils flared and her stomach quivered in response to the clean male scent of him. He leaned in and touched the pad of one thumb to the sugar crumbs on the side of her nose.

The eye contact was infinitesimal but long enough to send her pulse rate into the stratosphere and her stomach into a deep dive.

He didn't straighten up fast enough and the nerve-shredding interval necessitated several deep breaths before she could respond.

Oh, hell, what a time for her hormones to come out of hibernation!

'Thanks.' She didn't make the mistake of eye contact a second time. Instead she focused on the little girl who was trying to get his attention. It made her want to kick him for not noticing.

Even surfacing from her semi-catatonic state Kate recognised that the child wanted to fling herself at her father—had his arms opened even a little she'd have been in there, but they didn't and slowly Freya's little smile wobbled.

Kate's heart broke, her empathy swiftly followed by

a rush of anger that freed her from the last lingering wisps of brain fog. *Oh, God, you stupid man!*

For a split second as his head turned and her eyes were once more captured by his cold hard gaze she really thought for a horror-struck moment that she had voiced her thoughts out loud.

'Hello there, Freya, are you being a good girl?'

Too good, Kate wanted to yell as she watched the stilted exchange between father and daughter.

'Good morning, Ms Armstrong. I would ask you if you slept well but I suspect you didn't.'

Kate hoped he was rudely referring to the bags under her eyes and that he had no insight into the dreams she had fought her way out of every time she had dozed off, leaving her guilty and exhausted. A situation she blamed on the flight.

'I slept very well, thank you.' She lifted a hand to her left eye to still the contradictory flutter of her left eyelid.

Marco watched as she rose from the awkward position on the chair in one fluid graceful motion—any clumsiness on her part had obviously been feigned for comic effect.

The sinuous action grabbed him below the belt, reinforcing the artistic analogy that had occurred to him in the early hours when his brain would not switch off. She looked as if she had stepped right out of a Degas painting—a warm, breathing version of one of those slim supple ballerina figures, all graceful, slender, boneless limbs and big eyes.

There were a handful of people in his life who gave it to Marco straight and none of them were female—his mother thought the best of everyone—but even his critics had never displayed the open angry contempt that was sparkling in this woman's tawny eyes.

Kate was on her feet but had not gained any advantage, because the Prince still towered over her. She refused to acknowledge the physical or, for that matter, every other advantage in life this man had over her.

She wasn't impressed by an accident of birth or by the fact that fate had given him perfect everything and then an added extra wow factor ingredient...that was just luck. It would have been different if he were something she could admire—like a good, caring father.

Even if he hadn't been the breed of male who took it for granted that he ruined a woman's sleep—admittedly there were probably more than a few women who would have paid good money to have him disturb their sleep—his attitude to his daughter would have made her despise him.

She had already decided her strategy on the next official meeting was to be cool and totally professional. That was the best way to deal with men like this in her experience—not that men like this were in her experience.

Unfortunately the professional, cool message hadn't reached her eyes, which slid of their own volition to the moulded contours of the Prince's sinfully sexy mouth. The sculpted cruelty of the thinner upper lip contracting with the sensual fullness of the lower.

She moistened her own lips and congratulated herself on the fact he wouldn't be wasting his empty charm on her. She didn't feel lucky though, as his mobile mouth lifted in one corner and her stomach gave an elevator lurch. She felt fascinated.

Watching him could, if a person was not careful, become compulsive viewing. The way he moved made her think of some feral creature you recognised the beauty of but that beauty hid danger. Not to her though—that much had been made clear during a conversation at breakfast.

The conversation had turned to men after a handsome, bold-eyed young man, whose strut had made it clear he would have agreed with the description, had walked past and paused to smile at Kate.

'I dated him,' one of the other women at the table had told her. 'Good for fun,' she admitted to a chorus of giggles. 'But if you were looking for anything serious…?'

Kate said thanks for the tip, but she wasn't looking for anything serious or, for that matter, *fun*—not that sort anyway. Nobody believed her and supplied a list of men who might make her change her mind.

'Of course, Luisa has already got the best-looking guy in the place.' The woman in question looked smug and extended a finger with a sparkling ring on it for Kate to admire. 'Obviously he doesn't hold a candle to the Prince.'

'Oh, has anyone dated him?'

The comment turned all eyes on Kate.

'We should be so lucky. But the Prince is a gentleman. He doesn't mess with employees.'

'Understandable,' someone said behind their hand and others on the table exchanged significant looks.

Kate missed the significant looks. She had been too busy choking on her cereal after hearing Marco Zanetti, with his devilish grin, described as a gentleman.

'The…the storm last night didn't disturb you?'

Determined not to give him the satisfaction of reacting to the gleam of mockery Kate decided was shining in the Prince's eyes, she was still choosing her words carefully when her charge diverted his attention.

'She has ear things, Papa.' The child put her fingers in her ears.

'How do you know?'

'I had to shake her, just a little bit, to wake her up.'

Marco watched as Kate blew a strand of her hair from her face. She wrinkled her nose, frowning in concentration as she pinned the hair behind her ear. It was mundane but, watching her, he experienced a rush of excited anticipation in his veins unlike anything he had felt in a long time.

'Was I snoring?' Kate teased, shaking her head and creating a ripple in the waving heavy ropes of gleaming coils that lay down her narrow back.

She hadn't been asleep but the touch had made her leap a foot or so off the bed. She must have looked almost as shocked as the kid who had stood at the bedside looking at her with big terrified eyes as she introduced herself, in case, presumably, Kate had forgotten who she was, with a formal little curtsey in her cotton teddy-bear-printed pyjamas, insisting with shaky bravado when the room was illuminated by a flash of lightning that she was not scared of storms because storms were just science, and anyhow they had very good security.

Kate had replied that she was right, only Kate herself was a little bit scared so would Freya mind awfully keeping her company for a while?

Looking relieved, the little girl had crawled under the duvet at the bottom of the bed and into Kate's heart at the same time. She had fallen asleep about an hour later and had stayed sound asleep when Kate had scooped her up and tucked her back into her own bed when the sun appeared.

'Girls don't snore, it's science,' the little girl announced, her confidence slipping slightly as she looked to her father for reassurance. 'Do they, Papa?'

Kate turned her head and got a little shock as she encountered his enigmatic metallic stare. The insidious desire she was uneasily conscious of flared up hot. She wanted to look away, but she couldn't.

'Papa…?'

The spell broke and Kate shook her head, feeling stupid and also wary.

It took Marco a couple of seconds to focus on his daughter, for the thud of blood in his ears to grow quiet enough for him to respond.

'I've never heard a lady snore.' It was the literal truth. He had also never seen a woman without full make-up, which was why he had only just realised that the new nanny was not wearing any. His fingers flexed involuntarily as the thought of touching that skin embedded itself firmly in his head.

It was not his habit to spend the night with a woman. Love-making did not leave him feeling relaxed. He had never seen the appeal of pillow talk or the illusion of post-coital intimacy and during his marriage he and Belle had had separate rooms. He liked his own space and she had not questioned the arrangement, but then she wouldn't have, he thought bleakly.

'I do snore.' He returned his focus to Kate, who was biting her lip.

'Who told you that?'

Kate responded to the taunt with a thin smile. 'My

brother always said he could hear me through the wall.' Though the walls in their three-bed semi were a lot thinner than the several feet of stone here, and neither of them lived at home any more.

'You have a brother?'

Even without the flinch, the way her face closed down, he could tell he'd hit a nerve. Even if he had made the effort to locate this nerve he wasn't sure he could have. This woman seemed to have almost as many shields as she did prickles.

He watched her notice he was staring at her hair— it was hard to miss it—and found himself saying, even though he didn't need to explain himself, 'Are you alike? I mean...' he nodded to her shiny head, imagining the silky threads running through his fingers like liquid fire '...red hair runs in families.'

'No, I...he...we...we were adopted.' They were words she had never said out loud before and the effort it had taken to push them out did not receive a corresponding momentous response, just a shrug and the impression he'd tune her out the moment he left the room.

She might have suspected he was making conversation just to be polite, except he didn't seem the type to feel the need, especially with a staff member, even if she was allowed to sit on the next-to-the-top table.

She was sure if she had accepted her place on her designated table she would have heard a much better class of gossip. As it was, she had gleaned some very interesting facts, like the guest list at the ball that was due to be held to celebrate the King and Queen's golden jubilee. A model whose name had been linked to the

Prince had been invited, which was creating a lot of speculation.

Kate had looked suitably interested, even though it seemed to her that this didn't make the woman that special. The women the Prince dated might be a select club but the membership was not small.

She would have loved to be able to dismiss him as a playboy prince, but the general consensus was that he worked as hard as he played and was considered to bring with him a wind of welcome changes. So, she was going to reserve judgment.

'I wish I had a brother,' the little girl said wistfully. 'But I need a mummy first.'

Kate turned her head but before her glance reached the child her eyes got enmeshed in the smoky silver stare of the father. The raw emotion written there only lasted a moment before his mask slid into place but the knowledge that the bleakness and pain existed came as a shock to Kate.

It had loosed something inside her that she didn't want to feel...she didn't want to name... Sympathy.

He held her gaze for a further uncomfortable moment, the laser-steel stare seeming to dare her to feel what she was feeling.

Which was fine by her. For once they were on the same page. *I don't want to feel anything around him*, she thought fiercely... Well, mild contempt, she could live with that.

It wouldn't be *mild* though, that was the problem. Nothing she felt about him was mild, it was extreme. And not just over the top, but liable to swing from one extreme to the other.

She didn't actually break free from the stare until he

released her. She took a deep breath to compensate for the fact she had been holding her breath and hid behind her thick straight eyelashes.

Marco had been waiting for the pity to die, and it did, but in its place... Analysing those last few moments, he decided that chemistry covered it, but whatever the name you used she was hiding from it. He controlled it ruthlessly, because it wasn't going anywhere. She was off limits.

'I'm sorry...' she muttered.

'For what?' His voice was hard as iron filings.

She lifted her head, feeling as awkward as hell. 'Your wife... I...sorry,' she ended feebly.

Can you ever just say nothing, Kate, or at least not the first stupid thing that pops into your head?

During breakfast she had barely been able to stop reacting with an eye roll when the table discussion had briefly drifted to the Crown Prince's tragically short marriage. 'Never a voice raised in anger,' someone had said to a murmur of agreement.

But that look she caught...the real pain... Her cynicism had taken a serious hit. Just because he was an arrogant pain didn't mean he hadn't loved and lost the woman he had intended to spend the rest of his life with.

Her glance was drawn to the wide gold band on his finger. Whoever came along to fulfil the advertised role of mother and lover would have quite an act to follow—it was hard to compete with a ghost.

Good luck to her, Kate thought, trying to conjure some sympathy for the future bride and failing—maybe it wasn't very sisterly but surely any woman who married this man would know exactly what she was getting.

'I just came to—'

'See Freya,' said Kate, who knew full well he had come to check up on her.

He responded to the smooth interruption after a short, startled silence with a tip of his head.

'Well, it's great timing. I was just going to order some outdoor play equipment. Freya and I are going to start on a collage this afternoon. Perhaps your papa would like to help you collect some things outside—leaves…twigs… And I wonder where Nanny keeps her glitter.'

'*Glitter!*' the little girl echoed, round-eyed.

'Don't worry, I'll find some,' Kate tossed over her shoulder with airy confidence.

Marco watched her go, a reluctant, admiring gleam in his eyes, well aware that he had just been ruthlessly manipulated. She had balls, he would give her that, but that did not mean he was going let it pass.

The other side of the door, Kate took a step into the sitting room and, backing into the wall, leaned weakly against it, the adrenaline rush making her knees shake, but before she could nurse the triumph the door opened with no warning.

Marco Zanetti stood in the open doorway saying loudly, 'I have an idea about the glitter.' Before he added, 'Be right back with you, Freya!'

'*Glitter?*'

Marco closed the door and got straight to the point. 'Save your child psychology for the five-year-olds. I think you're a little out of your depth with the grown-ups.'

Kate levered herself off the wall. She had never liked confrontations but she was not going to back down from this one. 'I don't know what you mean.'

'The playing-dumb thing will not work with me. I *mean*, I will not be played. Certainly not by a woman whose sole role is to provide a safe, stimulating and educational environment for Freya. You will not designate me little tasks. I am not a five-year-old. Nothing else outside the nursery concerns you,' he outlined with biting emphasis.

Her apprehension was swallowed by a wave of anger. 'Well, that's me in my place,' she snapped out sarcastically. As if she were ever likely to forget what her place was in an environment where you were judged on which table you sat on. 'You say that Freya is my only concern, and I agree. Quite frankly, I don't give a damn about you except in the way it influences your daughter...she is *aching* for you to notice her. She is hungry for your attention.'

It was the verbal equivalent of having the rug pulled out from under his feet. In his head Marco was stretched out on the floor with her small foot on his chest.

'I do notice her,' he pushed out dangerously quietly, but she seemed oblivious to the danger, the warning.

'It's not her fault her mother died. What would your wife think if she knew that—?'

The slow-burn fuse finally reached the blue touchpaper and all Marco's hard-fought-for control snapped. He took a step towards her, his fury only increasing when she took an involuntary step back, seemingly intimidated by his sheer physicality and the waves of emotion rolling off him.

'That I am a cruel, unnatural father?'

Kate shook her head, desperately trying to backpedal.

'I know you have other calls on your time, but this

time with Freya at this age—it is such a small window, and before you know it it's gone, and Freya is lonely.'

He met her appeal with cold silence and an expression that would have made a stone wall look warm and yielding.

'If you can't, then she at least needs more social contact with children her own age, she needs…'

What he could not give.

'She is so isolated. Are there no other children in the palace her age?'

'It is a bit late to go into professional mode,' Marco bit back, seeing her flinch and telling himself her white face meant nothing whatsoever to him. Why would it? 'You may disapprove of me but I'm the only parent Freya has ever had, her mother's not here.' The words slipped under, around and through every steel impenetrable barrier he had ever erected.

Kate froze, her eyes sliding from the visible pulse in his temple to his grey metallic *hurting* stare. 'S-sorry?'

'Her mother never even got a chance to hold her!'

'I'm sorry.'

'So you keep saying. You ask about children—there are cousins. My wife had three brothers.'

'So…' she began eagerly.

'I have little contact.'

He responded to her wide-eyed look of enquiry with an impatient explanation. 'My wife's parents, both members of two of the prominent families on the island who run the show, or would like to, are divorced. That happened fifteen years ago now and the families are still at one another's throats. There is only one person they hate more than each other.'

'They don't like you!' she exclaimed and then

blushed under his ironic stare. 'Obviously I don't need to know why…'

'You have no idea how relieved that makes me feel,' he drawled with a sarcastic smile.

Kate's lips clamped tight. He really was the most arrogant son of a…king and queen. *And your boss to boot*, supplied the cautionary voice in her head.

'So you knew your wife—?'

'Before she was my wife. Yes, for many years she was my best friend.'

The information was delivered in a matter-of-fact manner that somehow made the statement all the more heartbreaking.

As he watched Kate's jewel bright eyes fill, he wondered just how someone who empathised to this extent survived in the real world.

'Perhaps we could make this about *Freya*?'

Kate's chin lifted; she was insane to feel sorry for this man. She should save her sympathy for the woman he did eventually marry because he was obviously still in love with his dead wife.

'Fine, let's do that. So perhaps you could put your feelings to one side and approach your in-laws, this being about Freya and not your feelings.'

His nostrils flared as the insult hit home. 'It is always about Freya,' he ground out. 'Protecting her is always my priority.'

'Good,' she said with a display of brisk false bravado as she brought her lashes down in an ineffective shield against the silver glitter of outrage in his eyes. When angry he was really daunting. 'What ages are the cousins…their names…?'

'I have not the faintest idea.' Her face presumably reflected her shocked horror, as a sighing sound of exasperation escaped his lips. 'I will discover this information, but after B... Freya's mother died, her grandfather blamed Freya. He will *not* repeat those words. I have made that clear to him.' The emphasis in his bleak eyes made her shiver.

'I'm sure he doesn't think that way now. No one could. People say things in grief that they don't mean.'

'You excuse him...?'

'No, of course not, I...' She bit her lip, aware she had blundered into territory where she didn't have a clue what was going on.

'Not black and white...not binary.' Her brother's voice was so loud in her head it sounded as though he were standing behind her.

'I'm sorry...'

'So you keep saying.'

'I tend to say things without...'

'Yes, this I have noticed. You have strong opinions. I will listen to what you have to say about Freya's welfare, but only if your comments are professional and evidence-based.'

And then he was gone. His reaction was more than she could have hoped for, given the absolute mess she had just made of that. *Professional.* He was right. A professional distance was something she never normally struggled with and yet with this father and daughter her objectivity had vanished.

Her emotions all over the place, she followed him back into the nursery in time to see him press a kiss to his daughter's head.

'Sorry I have to go...' Marco suddenly felt so weary it didn't really matter what excuse he gave. The endless list of duties meant nothing to his daughter, who could not filter out the bull... He could feel the amber gaze upon him and kissed Freya again.

Damn the woman, even if her only sin was to point out the obvious. The obvious that no one else had ever had the guts to voice: that he was a poor, pathetic excuse for a father, just as he'd been a poor excuse for a husband.

Maybe it was Kate's courage that had pushed him to say the things he had, share the things he had. It was as good a reason as any other to explain what had made him tell her private details he had never revealed to anyone.

Breathing in the scent of his daughter's hair for a final second, aware of the hard knot of loneliness in his chest he rarely acknowledged, he lifted his eyes, his gaze drawn as if under the control of some invisible force to where the slim figure stood watching them. Kate looked shocked. Strangely, considering he was not a man inclined to trust, he knew at some deep unfathomable level that had nothing to do with proof or logic that the secret, that any secret, was safe with her.

'Be good for...' his eyes slid to the petite figure watching him with big golden eyes and the word *nanny* just wouldn't come '... Ms Armstrong.'

He tipped his head towards Kate and the next second he was gone, leaving trails of energy that seemed almost visible in his wake.

'Right, what shall we do now? Would you like to play?'

'Read. I always read after snack time. I'm a very good reader.'

A few minutes into the reading session Kate was assailed by a suspicion. She tested her theory and her suspicions were proved correct. The little girl with the seemingly advanced reading age couldn't read a word. She had simply memorised it all.

CHAPTER FIVE

KATE PRIORITISED THE changes she intended to make, always supposing she had the opportunity, and high on her list was the abolition of the strict adherence to a timetable, which was fine when it gave a sense of security but destructive when it became stifling and inflexible.

Testing the water, she had casually floated the idea of a slight diversion from routine, which had resulted in confusion among the staff and her charge. She knew she would require some tact, diplomacy and determination.

After yesterday she could not claim that tact and diplomacy were her strong points. Her strong point was that she possessed the determination that would see her through. There were some advantages to being consider *mule-stubborn*.

On her second evening she made her first move. Kate waited for the two nursery maids who were on duty to appear after Freya had gone to bed.

When they did, she suggested that they might leave the collage-making messiness spread out on the table.

They had looked longingly at the pile of fabric scraps, leaves and gluey mess on the table, but they had worriedly gone along with her request, so Kate considered it a win, considering they had almost fallen down in a heap when she had asked them to call her Kate. They were baby steps but she would get there!

Returning to her own flat, she was contemplating a walk to orientate herself to the grounds. So far, she had only seen the area set out as an outdoor play area for Freya. The only piece of equipment that gave any hint of play was a swing. Kate intended to change that.

Her exit was delayed by the unexpected arrival of a visitor. The tap on the door made her heart thump. It would be just like Marco Zanetti not to recognise her off-duty time, but it would be very unlike him to tap. He was definitely not a tapping man—more a bang-and-demand or just-ignore-the-door man.

So by the time she had opened the door she was not surprised to find, not a six-four challenging figure, instead the plumply pretty figure of Lady Rosa with her head of dark, wiry grey-streaked hair.

The woman who had been Kate's reception committee the previous night had an impressive-sounding job title, but then so did every other person in the place, but by this point they had all blurred into one, so she stuck to Lady Rosa.

The older woman didn't stay long. She had just dropped by to see if there was anything Kate needed, any problems…?

There were, of course, but the problem in question was one that Kate knew she needed to discuss with Freya's absentee father before anyone else. When, of course, he decided to put in another appearance.

The fact he hadn't did not improve her opinion of him. Her slight thawing hardened into solid ice. Could he really not know that he had a child who was hungry for his attention? It made her want to shake some sense into him, though the effort would be wasted—the man was built like… Stomach muscles quivering, she sharply veered away from Marco Zanetti's build.

His no-show was frustrating professionally. Personally she could have done without seeing him ever again! But she wasn't going to allow personal feelings to get in the way of her doing her job well.

Her suspicions had not gone away and she had done her research. She was ready to present the facts demanded when he did decide to honour them with his presence. The lack of surprise at his no-show spoke volumes: no one was shocked. Everyone was so *understanding*. He was a busy man. Well, the photos in an old online article she'd seen had shown that he wasn't too busy to escort beautiful women with interesting back stories!

She popped back into the nursery to tell the young women where they could find her if she was needed.

'I've got my phone on me.'

'It's fine,' one assured her cheerfully. 'Nanny always used to have…' She paused to straighten her apron and a wicked voice in Kate's head filled in the gap with inappropriate suggestions… *A gin and tonic… Afternoon sex.*

She choked off a laugh and turned it into a cough.

'She had a nap,' the girl supplied. 'Are you all right… Kate?'

'Fine,' Kate said cheerily. She didn't need a nap or, for that matter, afternoon sex. With anyone, she added to herself, as a possible playmate for the latter option bounded lithely into her head unbidden.

She attempted to walk off her anger and general frustration in not being able to discuss Freya with her father. Since the storm had passed over, the weather on the island had reclaimed its reputation as a temperate paradise on earth.

She had explored only a fraction of the grounds, which, once you got beyond the formal gardens around the palace itself, were divided into a series of separate rooms. They were designed in such a way that you would be surprised by a sudden breath-catching view out over the city to the sea beyond and you could walk from a bog garden complete with dribbling fountains, springs and moss-covered statuary into a wild flowers meadow and then a walled kitchen garden smelling of herbs and greenhouses full of produce used in the palace kitchens.

She walked out of this area, eating a ripe nectarine she had picked, feeling more settled because she had made a decision. If the arrogant prince wouldn't come to the nursery, she'd take it to him...or rather, she'd take herself to him.

She frowned at the tortuous grammar of the thought, her feet crunching on the gravel path of an intricately designed parterre she had passed through as she'd left the nursery playground, which meant there should be... She looked for the gap in the high hedge and realised as she did so that this was not the same piece of formal garden.

The hedge was lower and... She stopped. It was low enough to see a dark head above it.

She yelled out and hit the ground running.

Jogging along the grassy path between two rows of tall sentinel horse—the trees in full blossom made her think, between breathless huffs, of the one at the bottom of their drive where, as kids, she and Jake had fought over the best conkers. She pushed through the feeling of intense loss.

She had managed to keep the dark head in sight but she was already red-faced and breathless, her desperate *hey!* came out a wheezy croak.

She paused a moment, hands braced on her thighs as she fought to catch her breath. Jake would have seen the hilarity of this situation… He would never have let her live it down.

The wave of loss this time was even more painful. It made her forget the stitch in her side. She and Jake shared no blood link but they shared more important links, a lifetime of links, which was why his betrayal hurt so much.

Should she make the first move? Call him?

Before she could get sucked any deeper into the circuitous internal argument in her head, the dark head disappeared and she set off in pursuit again, heading for an archway in the wall, relief flooding her as the dark head came back into sight.

'Wait! Hold on!' she yelled out, breathless as she made it through the arch at a sprint.

The tall figure remained oblivious. He wasn't running but due to his superiority in leg length and the fact she was out of breath the gap wasn't getting any smaller, and she had the mother of all stitches in her side.

Then, just when she thought she might have to admit defeat or at least lie down, he paused and bent over as though he'd dropped something. She took her chance and yelled.

'Wait!'

His head lifted and he straightened up. She was too far away to see his face, which was a blur, but she could make out his bare arms, dark against the white of a tee shirt. Her gaze didn't get any lower than the black shorts. One minute there was only the thumping of her heart and the sound of birdsong, the next it was chaos, yells and waving guns all around her.

The sinister black-clad men had appeared from nowhere. It felt like dozens but, in reality, there were three. One relaying staccato information into a mouthpiece, while they all carried guns.

They were yelling at her in Italian. Actually, it could have been anything—her faculties had frozen in shock and icy, sense-numbing fear.

She said something back to proclaim her innocence and assure them that she was harmless. It was a waste of breath as they continued to bellow over her and indicated she should lie on the ground.

It was beyond disorientating and surreal to find yourself in the scene of an action movie, cast as one of the bad guys. A push in her back she didn't see coming sent her onto her knees. It was at that point that all the yelling stopped as though it had been switched off.

There was just one voice now. Deeper, clipped, anger vibrating in every commanding syllable.

Relief so intense that tears came to her eyes washed over Kate. Slowly she lifted her head from her chest, where it had sunk. She saw the men in black had melted away, though she could hear the buzz of radio voices in the distance, and the man she had been pursuing was standing there.

She had caught him.

What was she going to do with him?

Her imagination, assisted by her hormones, supplied a stream of suggestions. It was shock, she told herself by way of an excuse, and she tried to think cooler thoughts.

One day she'd laugh about this with friends around

a dinner table, but that day was a long way off. Right now, she'd settle for not having him guess her thoughts. Getting up would be good too. She took a deep breath and pressed her hands into the ground to help lever herself to her feet, but nothing worked. Everything shook, confirming her previous diagnosis of shock.

As she waited, their eyes met and she saw the anger in his face slide into another expression. Something that made her internal tremors worse.

'I think… I think I might be sick…' she warned.

As her head went down the last thing in the world she would have anticipated was Marco lifting the heavy ropes of hair from her face. She could feel his fingers cool on the back of her neck. He didn't say a word.

'I'm not going to,' she said finally as the waves of nausea passed.

The hand on the nape of her neck vanished and he stepped away, waiting silently as she sat back on her heels, her hands on her thighs visibly shaking.

'Please do not be nice to me or I will cry,' she begged between her chattering teeth, as if this weren't a humiliating enough position to be in.

'I have no intention of being nice to you,' he promised grimly, reliving the moment that he had seen the security guards move to contain her.

They had been doing their job and his fear had been they would do it too well. They had not deserved his reprimand or the curt dismissal. She, on the other hand… His jaw clenched, and the muscles quivered as he ground his teeth.

Left with nothing to do but wait to regain control of her body, she took in his outfit, what there was of it.

As distraction went it was a good one. Her covetous glance moved up from his bare feet shoved in a pair of leather sliders up strong, lightly hair-roughened brown calves and deeply muscled bronzed thighs. His wet black shorts were the mid-thigh, low-on-the-hip variety and a sleeveless white vest revealed his muscular shoulders and biceps.

He had the sort of body that you saw on men who leapt off a diving board and arched through the air, throwing impossible shapes before they hit the water without a ripple. Sleek, streamlined, powerful—there wasn't an ounce of excess flesh to hide the taut, perfectly formed muscle beneath oiled smooth skin.

Marco dragged a hand through his hair and some of the excess water that came away with it splashed icy droplets on Kate's face, breaking her free of the sexual thrall that had gripped her.

Lust, mindless attraction, chemistry, she listed them in her head in the hope that facing her monsters would make them vanish…aware that the exercise did smack of something horribly close to desperation.

'You can't wander around at will. Did you not see the signs saying private?' he ground out, the fury etched on his face emphasising each plane and hollow. 'This area—' his expansive gesture took in the lush green they stood in and caused a sequence of fluid contractions of muscle beneath the listening golden skin of his torso '—is,' he spelt out, gouging out each syllable for biting emphasis, 'off limits to—'

'No one told me. Those men—' She stopped and looked around, half expecting to see them lurking, but there was no sign of them. 'Those men could have…' Conscious of the whiney note in her voice, she bit her lip. What was she making excuses for anyhow? She'd done nothing wrong.

'Those *men* were doing their jobs.' Pausing as she continued to crouch there looking like some sort of bewildered supplicant, he held out his open-palmed hands in a gesture of impatience. When she didn't respond to encouragement he snapped out, 'Get up!'

'Do not order me around...' Her angry defiance vanished in the blink of an eye. She bit her lip harder this time and admitted, 'I don't think I can.'

It was the ruefully reluctant admission itself that hit him in a spot he didn't want to acknowledge. He knew that it had hurt her to have to admit she needed help. Taking a step towards her, he bent forward and held out a hand. 'Come on!'

Shifting her weight to one side, she reached for the hand but before her fingers had made contact his had curled around her wrist. He casually hauled her to her feet and immediately let go, but Kate had not got her land legs yet and she staggered, grabbing for anything to stop herself falling.

The anything was his vest.

Both hands clutching the white fabric, damp from his body, she fell against him, experiencing an immediate thousand-volt shock that stopped her breathing. It was only the large hand that moved to the small of her back that stopped her sliding back down to her knees.

It was sensory overload, the heat of his body, the hardness, the warm male scent of him... Her nostrils flared, her eyes closed, as she dug deep to break free of the mind-numbing tsunami as she leaned, weak-kneed, literally plastered to his front. The tremors that had been shaking her took on a different quality, no longer fuelled by shock but by the breath-catching, illicit excitement swirling through her veins like champagne bubbles.

She could hear him swearing above her head, feel his breath in her hair on the side of her face as the hand in the small of her back slid around her waist. The other curved around her jaw, turning her face up to him.

'You are not going to faint.'

She wanted to tell him she never fainted, but her throat felt too thick and scratchy.

He studied her face. The dilated pupils leaving only gold rims. 'Take some deep breaths…not *that* deep…'

Reacting to his *give-me-strength* tone, she rallied slightly and rebutted shakily, 'I do not need you to tell me how…' *How to stay standing?*

Fighting the mindless hunger clawing in his gut striving to get a firmer hold, Marco swore and stepped back. 'Fine, you do not need me.'

Arms folded, he watched as she wobbled before, with another curse of defeat, he grabbed for her, but she backed away like a drunken tightrope walker, strangely graceful.

He huffed out a sigh of defeat and reached for her. She wheeled backwards, muscle memory co-ordination keeping her upright, and instead of his hands landing on her shoulders they came to rest either side of her face.

A face minus make-up and its usual fiery halo, the purity of her features washed pale by shock making her look even younger. Even though he knew this was an illusion—he had made a point of checking her age and knew she was twenty-seven—it did serve as a timely reminder of the very real but invisible barrier they stood on opposite sides of.

The barrier wavered as her heavy eyelids lifted and she looked at him with eyes that were so *hungry* it took his breath away. The promise of passion sending a thudding stream of neat hormonal heat through his body.

Still, he rose above his baser instincts, though fingernails were involved this time. 'Next time,' he promised, reliving the blood-freezing moment that he'd recognised the figure surrounded by the men, crack marksmen all, whose jobs it was to protect him and his family, 'I'll cut out the middleman and shoot you myself. Do not,' he added with grim warning, 'say *anything*. Not a word!'

She blinked, a belligerent glitter cutting through the shocked glaze in her eyes. She didn't respond well to ultimatums and that went double when the person issuing them was this man. She didn't care how many titles he had, she was not going to be silenced.

'I...they could have shot me; I could have died!'

'Do not dramatise!'

The response struck her as not only unfeeling but hypocritical. 'But you said...' She lost what little colour she had. 'Oh, God, I really could have died,' she repeated in a barely audible whisper. Less drama and more acknowledgment of her mortality as she saw the image in her head of her parents when there was the knock on the door to break the news...seeing all the things she had never done that she wanted to.

Kate, head full of missed opportunities and regrets, felt her lips respond to some invisible tug and land on his mouth. All the things...said the voice in her head.

She had no more control over the impulse than she would have had over the self-protective reflex that would have had her jerking her hand from a hot surface, except in this instance she was moving towards the danger, the *heat*.

Her hands were in his damp vest to give her enough purchase to stretch up her body. 'Thank you for saving me—' Her lips brushed his.

Danger, yes, she could feel the danger in the pit of her belly, not repelling but attracting, and cool.

Her lashes lifted off her smooth, flushed cheeks and her eyes met his. He grabbed for her, hauling her into his body, all mindless need and no logic.

The rest of her words were lost in the kiss that started out hard and angry and changed to something else, something deep, slow, seductive. Some previously un-tapped place in her core that had nothing to do with logic and self-preservation took over and she melted into the warm, explorative, heart-stoppingly exciting intimacy of his tongue and mouth, his taste, his scent.

With a small mewling cry vibrating in the back of her throat, she strained upwards to deepen the pressure, tangling her fingers in the dark hair at the back of his head and pushing her breasts against his hard chest.

A moment later, or it might have been an hour, she was standing on her own feet separated from all that warmth and hardness with several inches of cool air be-tween them feeling *bereft*, her nostrils still full of the musky male scent of him.

Then stupid.

Marco stood there, dragging air into his lungs as he pulled back from the heat that had surged through all the barriers that had never failed him before. All it had taken was the touch of her warm lips.

The loss of control was all the more serious, dan-gerous, because the woman who had instigated this meltdown was in his employ. She worked for him. He'd crossed a line and he didn't even bother rationalising it, instead he went into damage-control mode. It wouldn't happen again, he told himself, regaining by painful increments his habitual emotional distance. The few extra feet of physical distance seemed a sensible back-up plan.

When she spoke, he registered she sounded dazed, appalled even. 'Did I start that?'

Could her action have been construed as an invitation to what followed? She had no words to describe the kiss. She hadn't known a kiss could feel like that, that you could feel *want* and need in your bones, in your skin, in the soles of your feet.

'Yes, but I finished it, and it is…' his steely eyes sought and found hers '…finished,' he said, for his benefit as much as hers.

She felt the heat run up under her skin, leaving it washed with soft rose. Oh, yes, she was getting the message loud and clear. Did the man think that she was going to pin him down and… *Given half the chance, Kate, who wouldn't?*

'I was in shock,' she said, observing with growing resentment that he had recovered his cool with remarkable ease. The idea that anyone could be that *hot* one minute and then be so *clinical* the next—warning her off. It was mortifying.

'You kissed me back.'

He could hardly deny it. He said nothing.

'What are *you* even doing here?' *Other than the fact he lives here, Kate, this is all his, you're just the nanny.* 'At least I have clothes on!' The shrill addition put a dangerous glow in his eyes that made the pit of her stomach dissolve.

'I've been known to wear less when swimming.'

Kate immediately saw him wearing less.

'Relax, *cara mia*.'

Kate was too busy staring at her clasped hands and no doubt resenting the languid advice to register that he looked less than relaxed himself, the nerve beside his mouth throbbing extra time.

'Sexual attraction is not something that can be rationalised so stop trying.' He had, simply because there was no logical rationale that could explain away the fact, *wanted* the taste of her. From the first moment he had set eyes on her he had been ravenous for it.

Now he had tasted her and he could move on. Been there, done that.

He almost laughed aloud at this piece of pathetic self-delusion. As he was mocking himself her lashes lifted, revealing layers of emotion in her golden eyes. Something in her gaze made him feel stripped bare of his normal protective layer.

'I'm not—' Kate stopped, her chest growing tight. Was he? The idea excited and frightened her in equal measure.

'It is, however,' Marco continued, more to remind himself of the fact that she was off limits, 'something that can be controlled, so stop worrying. I will save you from yourself.' He would also do something about the recent imbalance in his work-sex life, which had a way of messing with a healthy man's head and his control.

Control that showed a danger of slipping every time he thought about how she had tasted, how she had felt...

No, he would *not* remember, because this would be a complication too far.

He was not his father. Thinking of his father was the sense cooling reminder he needed.

The implication that she would be the one making the move brought a flush of outraged anger to Kate's face and helped clear the remaining sensual fog of confusion in her head.

'I can assure you that you are safe from me, Your...' Oh, God, she came up against the same stubborn mental block that she seemed to have with his title and stopped.

'It is Highness, but you can call me Marco.'

'Well, Your *Highness*...' she said, adopting an attitude of mocking disdain and thinking, *You are just too stupid, Kate, you kissed him, you* wanted *to kiss him, you lost the moral high ground at that moment.* 'Forget it,' she suggested to him magnanimously.

The *I have* stayed silent, but was very much there, hanging in the air between them.

'Heightened emotions...' She managed a pretty credible shrug. 'I nearly got shot.' It got her off the hook, technically at least.

'Shot...a slight exaggeration.'

Her lips compressed and she swore softly under her breath. '*What* did my predecessor call you?' Not caring if the change of subject was not really subtle, she didn't want this conversation to move to a place that blurred any lines she had drawn in the sand.

His lips quivered slightly. 'Nanny Maeve knew me when I was seven.' *I never kissed Nanny Maeve*, he added silently.

Once was enough, he thought, looking at her mouth

and thinking once was too much, a taste had made him hungry for more. As recreational drugs went, this woman's mouth had addiction written all over it.

'Well, I hope you'll be able to afford me the same professional courtesy you did her. I didn't intend to intrude but I spotted you and, as I was hoping to speak to you about Freya, I just—'

'Chased me.'

'Sorry if I interrupted your…swim…?' Not that she could see any sign of a pool.

'I was retracing my steps looking for my phone.' The recollection brought a frown to his brow.

Losing his phone made him seem almost normal but he wasn't, he really wasn't, he lived in a different world from the one she inhabited.

'I had assumed,' she continued frigidly, 'that I'd be able to make contact when you came to see Freya.'

He scanned her face with narrowed eyes. 'Do I detect a note of disapproval in your voice?'

'It's not my place to disapprove, as I'm sure you'd be the first to tell me, but I'm not sure how this works. Do I make an appointment?' She allowed her chilled question to hang there a moment before adding with barely disguised sarcasm, 'Or do I need to relay the information through some intermediary?'

If she had been hoping to elicit some guilty response, she failed, but the permanent groove between his brows deepened. 'Firstly, what you do *not* do is create a security incident, and if you have any information concerning my daughter there are no intermediaries, you contact me directly.'

'I was trying to.'

'Well, go ahead.'

Her eyes slid up and down his tall, angry, half-dressed frame. 'Here?'

'Why not?'

'I would prefer a more formal setting,' she announced stuffily, thinking, *With no ripped body clouding my judgment.*

He looked inclined to argue the point but shrugged. 'Fair enough. I can give you half an hour in my office. Is that *formal* enough for you?'

She ignored the mockery and nodded, following him across the green expanse of grass to the stone wall of a tower.

'It's a short cut.' He nodded towards a flight of steps cut into the stone. He paused at the foot and turned to her. 'You going to be all right with the steps?'

Her lips tightened. 'So long as there are no gun-toting ninja warriors hiding around the next bend, I'll be fine…'

'Right, then, after you.'

She stepped out smartly, not slowing even when her thigh muscles began to complain and burn. That was about the same time that she realised this arrangement gave him a very good view of her bottom. He was probably comparing it unfavourably with the innumerable curvaceous bottoms he knew intimately.

She glanced suspiciously over her shoulder and he smiled back innocently.

'You'd be insulted if I wasn't.'

Turning back, she stomped her way up the rest of the steps at a breakneck speed that reduced her legs to jelly by the time she reached the top, where she promptly forgot her aching legs.

'Oh, my goodness, this is…' She looked around, too enchanted to maintain her icy distance as she smiled.

The swimming pool they were standing beside was built into the section of roof and surrounded by a terrace filled with lush greenery. It was stunning in itself, but it was the most spectacular view across the capital and out to sea that was truly breathtaking.

'This is your office?' she asked, thinking, *Nice work if you can get it.*

His lips twitched. 'No, but it does have access to my office. This way.' He opened a door that was partially concealed behind a classical statue of a bare-chested woman being ravished by someone Marco was probably distantly related to.

This time she followed him down the internal staircase and proved her moral superiority by not looking at his bottom, or not much.

'Take a seat.'

She looked around. There were options aside from the modern-looking chair behind the massive desk that was empty bar from a few monitor screens, an Anglepoise lamp and a photo, of what or who she couldn't see from where she was standing, but if the gallery of snaps on the wall of exposed stone were any indication they were of Freya. Or maybe his late wife. There were none of her on the wall, which seemed... *None of your business, Kate.*

The other two walls were covered floor to ceiling in bookshelves where the books were *not* colour coordinated, and a surreptitious glance at the spines suggested the collection was eclectic. The last wall was taken up by open leaded windows set in a deep stone embrasure that offered a view almost as good as the one from the pool.

She stood there for a moment feeling awkward before she selected one of the leather chesterfields and sat down.

'I'm just going to change into something less comfortable.' He flashed her one of his enigmatic smiles and vanished.

If he'd returned thirty seconds earlier, he would have found Kate studying the gallery of framed photos that covered one wall, trying to work out why a man who had this amount of photos was so physically absent from his daughter's life, but when he did emerge she had retaken her seat and was sitting with her hands primly folded in her lap.

His quick change had obviously included a shower. She could smell soap and shampoo mingled with his clean, inimitable personal scent as he walked past her to the desk.

His hair, wet and slicked back, curling on his neck, caught the light shining in from the window as he propped his denim-clad rear on the desk top and stretched his long legs out in front of him. His attitude was a match for the navy shirt, the sleeves of which he'd rolled up to reveal his sinewed bronzed forearms. He wore a pair of faded jeans that clung to his thighs in a way that made her tummy muscles quiver. All the laidback designer casual contrasted starkly with the steely gaze he pinned her with—no casual there.

The moment stretched beyond what was polite, but then he clearly didn't think the normal social rules applied to him. He made his own rules.

'You look guilty. What have you been up to...?' Then, ignoring his own question, he spread his hands, palms up. 'So, what was so important?'

CHAPTER SIX

KATE TOOK A deep breath and tried to organise her thoughts into some sort of coherence.

One long finger had started tapping the polished surface of his desk. 'You have my attention.'

Which was part of the problem. His unblinking regard was unsettling. It was those eyes; she shook away the crazy idea that he could read her mind and cleared her throat, wondering if he had a timer going and any minute he'd look at his watch and say, *That's it for today.*

Or was that a therapist?

'It's about Freya.'

He did the brow thing again, his growing impatience communicating itself across the intervening space.

'Did my…?' Hesitating, she lifted her eyes from her contemplation of her interwoven fingers. 'Did the previous nanny ever mention Freya's reading?'

'She did say that it is very advanced for her age.'

'Ah…right. Well, her language is certainly extremely advanced for her age, and I can see how it might have looked to someone that her reading was too,' she said tactfully.

'*Looked* that way?' He shook his head and rose to his feet, towering over her, his eyes watchful and not friendly.

She'd seen defensive parents before but not as beautiful as him, none that made her tummy muscles quiver. None that had kissed her.

It was hard, looking at the compressed line of his lips and knowing that only minutes ago they had moved skilfully, sensuously, over her own, to think that this was the same man.

She tuned out the memory and painted on a professional smile, a bit frayed at the edges but it gave her the confidence to push on. 'Freya was eager to show off her skills. She is very eager to please.'

'Now why do I think you don't think that's a good thing?' he drawled.

Kate ignored his dry insertion. She couldn't afford to drift from the point. 'She appeared very fluent with her reading. In fact, streets ahead of the curve for her age.'

'Then what is the problem?' he asked, wondering if she was inventing some issue to make herself look important. He discarded the idea almost immediately. He had experience of women who would do any number of things to gain his attention but Kate Armstrong had not come across like that at all.

'The thing is she can't read, which would not make her unusual for a five-year-old, but there are some indications that there might be a problem.' It was blunt but sometimes blunt was the best way.

'That is ridiculous you just said yourself—'

'She isn't *reading*. She has memorised the texts of her favourite books. She has an extremely good memory, really very good, but that is often the way with people with dyslexia.'

'*Dyslexia!* You are saying my daughter is dyslexic, and

you have picked this up within hours and Nanny Maeve didn't and she's been with Freya all her life.' His lips curled in expressive contempt as he hooked his thumbs into the belt loops of his jeans, his body language challenging her.

She nodded and stayed calm. The 'shoot the messenger' thing was not exactly unexpected.

'I know how it must seem but sometimes a fresh pair of eyes…' She swallowed a sigh, unable to detect any thaw in his hostile manner. This was not going to be easy. 'This is no reflection on…anybody… People with dyslexia are very good at disguising the fact,' she told him with diplomatic restraint. Privately she thought her predecessor had a lot to answer for. 'It's easy to miss.'

'Or invent,' he threw out. 'Some people will do anything to hog the limelight.'

In response to the insult, he received a compassionate little smile that was all teeth-clenching understanding. He had never encountered a woman who grated on him more. Kiss her, throttle her—his reactions to her breathing were way beyond what was reasonable.

'I know this is a shock, but—'

Marco dragged a hand through his sleek wet hair, his jaw clenched and quivering. He found himself unable to keep the doubt from edging into his voice. 'I *would* have noticed…'

Sure, Marco, because you hear your daughter read such a lot. The recognition added a fresh slug of toxic guilt to the burden he already carried.

For a second Kate's compassion warred with her disapproval of his parenting style. Compassion won. It was not the first time she'd seen parents angry and in denial when they were told there was an issue with their child. This situation felt a lot… This was not like any job she had experienced. It wasn't as if ordinarily she forgot about work the moment she went home, there was always preparation, but she was able to switch off. Here, she felt immersed, and she was fast losing her professional distance, which, along with compassion, was in her view essential for a good teacher, or one that wanted to stay sane, at least.

'Look, I don't expect you to take my word for it,' she said, keeping her voice calm and unemotional. 'And I'm not suggesting for one moment that I'm an expert, but there are tests that would confirm the issue and I strongly advise that Freya have them. The earlier these things are picked up, the better.'

She hesitated a moment, worried she was throwing out too much information, before continuing. When people were shocked there was a saturation limit of how much they could retain.

'I have looked it up and your psychology department here at the university have just completed a world-class study.'

He looked down at her in silence, then, twisting away, walked around the desk before lowering his long lean frame into the leather chair behind it.

'How did we…how did I not pick it up?'

Kate didn't say anything. She suspected he already knew.

She watched, her heart squeezing in her chest as he picked up the photo from his desk and stared at it. Only a parent who loved their child could feel that sort of pain she saw written on his face: pain and guilt.

He put the photo down and, resting his elbows on the desk, looked up. 'Is there a cure?'

He already knew the answer. He remembered the boy at school who had been singled out by teachers and pupils alike as lazy and stupid. The fact that boy was now a man whose entrepreneurial skill had made his name world-famous did not alter the fact his schooldays must have been hell.

He would not let that happen to Freya.

'Is home schooling an option?'

It was, but not a good one as far as Kate was concerned. 'I think you're jumping ahead of yourself, and it's really not useful to think in terms of a cure. Freya is not ill. People with dyslexia, their brains are just wired differently but the earlier a diagnosis is made, the easier it is to formulate strategies which make life easier. But first I think you should get it confirmed...'

His curling lashes lifted off his razor-sharp cheekbones. 'You were sure enough to come here and...' His voice trailed away. He could have done without the insight that told him he was looking for someone to blame but himself.

Kate was really missing her professional distance. Her heart ached painfully with sympathy. If she had thought he was an uncaring parent, she was ready to admit she had jumped to conclusions.

'I told the truth.'

'As *you* see it.'

She nodded. 'I know you didn't want to hear this and I...' She lowered her gaze, not willing to acknowledge the level of her empathy for him, an empathy that went way beyond what she would normally feel. 'It's always best to tell the truth.'

The frown still stamped on his face, curiosity filtered into his silver eyes as he looked at her. '*Always? Do you really believe that?*'

Her delicate jaw quivered at the incredulity in his voice. 'Of course.'

'No exceptions?'

'No.'

'You have no doubts, do you? I almost envy your ability to see everything in black and white.'

His comment came so close to one of Jake's accusations that she flinched. A moment later she lifted her chin. 'Actions are right or wrong, they are either a lie or the truth.' She got to her feet. 'Finding out your life is a lie, that you are not —' She broke off, dodging his eyes.

It would be too much to hope that he'd miss the open goal she had just presented to him.

He didn't.

'Who lied to you?' he asked, probably imagining a cheating lover.

The sly question made her stiffen defensively. Even if it was a slightly off-target shot in the dark, it showed he possessed a spooky perspicacity, which made her deeply uneasy. She really did not want this man wandering around in her head.

Either he was way too sharp or those eyes really were X-ray and not just X-rated.

'I think we have rather drifted from the point.'

Which was that he was one hell of a father! Guilt curdled sourly in the pit of his stomach as he considered his arresting style. He'd farmed out his daughter to an elderly woman and then blamed her successor rather than place the blame where it lay, on his own shoulders.

'I actually find it kind of reassuring that little Miss Goody Two-Shoes is as messed up as the rest of us,' he drawled.

She compressed her lips over a retort. It took all her willpower not to respond, and focus instead on the cool professional advice she was meant to be delivering.

'Look, I know I've given you a lot to think about and it's hard to take in.'

She had no idea.

'I've made a list of articles, books that you might find helpful, but, as I say, I'm not an expert. Fortunately you have access to as many experts as you need.'

Freya would not be at the back of any queue, sad that she had the best of everything but all she wanted was her dad.

'I'll send you my personal email. Could we keep this between ourselves for the next few days?'

'As you wish,' Kate responded stiltedly. She had no idea why she felt so disappointed by this response. 'Dyslexia is nothing to be ashamed of,' she added, struggling not to show her contempt and, if his expression was any indicator, failing pretty miserably.

The heel of one hand pressed to his forehead, he looked at her for a moment and then appeared to come to a decision. 'I am not ashamed, not of Freya at any rate.' Her lips, compressed in a disapproving line, parted. 'I am going to share some information with you.'

Not obviously, because he cared one way or the other what her opinion of him was. It was simply that he didn't want her saying something that would come to the ears of the council.

'Do I have to sign the Official Secrets Act?' she asked, her flippancy masking her confusion, which turned to disquiet when he didn't smile.

'That will not be necessary.'

'I wasn't being serious.'

'At the ball next week I intend—' He paused and angled a questioning glance at her face. 'You have heard about the—?'

'Yes.'

He nodded and sketched a smile without humour. 'It is hard to keep a secret in this place.'

'The ball is a secret?'

'The announcement I am to make at it is.'

'You're getting married and you think your fiancée might have a problem with Freya's—?' Her hand went to her mouth. Had she really just said that our loud?

His deep bellow of laughter cut her off before she could dig herself a bigger hole.

'That is quite an imagination you have there!' he said. His mild scorn made it worse somehow, making her face burn. It would have burned hotter had she known he was wondering if that fertile imagination extended to the bedroom.

Marco took a deep breath. He wanted to have sex with her, and he couldn't have it. It was not a complicated concept to grasp and yet his brain was still swerving around it, creating imaginary steamy scenes that were never going to happen.

'I am not getting married, and when I do it is Freya who will be the one giving *her* approval, not the other way around. When she's older she'll need a female role model...'

Kate noted the revealing fact that love didn't feature at all and felt a stab of sympathy. 'Poor woman!' she exclaimed without thinking.

His dark brows shot up as he slumped with elegant negligence into his chair, spinning it back a couple of feet across the wooden floor to see her better. She knew the pose of lazy grace touched by decadence was an illusion. No man had a body like his without some pretty stern self-discipline.

'You think being my wife, the future Queen, makes someone an object of pity?' He posed the question, anticipating her discomfort. 'I wish you'd tell that to the women queuing around the block to interview for the vacancy.'

Kate's jaw literally dropped at this addition—outrageous even for him. The knot of incredulity in her chest bubbled to the surface and she laughed.

'You have my sympathy. It must be *so hard* being catnip to the opposite sex.'

When they were handing out ego he really had stood in the line several times, but then if you looked at that face in the mirror every day who wouldn't be arrogant? Her glance drifted to his sensual mouth. Where kissing was concerned he had the right to be arrogant, and if his skill at love-making was even a fraction as skilled... Unable to cling to her mockery and painfully aware of the ache between her legs, she found herself staring helplessly at the fascinating symmetry of his face. It was a face that in all its moods exerted a troubling fascination for Kate, a fascination that exposure didn't diminish, but fed.

Head dug deep into the leather head rest and tilted to one side, in a what she was recognising as a characteristic gesture, he made some elegant adjustments to his posture and swirled the chair from side to side.

He laughed, the deep sound warm and uninhibited. Kate felt the rumble under her skin as a tingling warmth.

Helpless not to, she found herself smiling back.

God, what could he do if he put some effort into being charming?

She dodged the worrying answer to that one.

'Oh, I'm under no illusions. I know it's the crown that is the attraction. I will not expect any future bride to pretend otherwise.'

'Oh, I don't know about that.' The unwise words were out there before she could stop them.

He tipped his head in acknowledgment and she blushed. His smile faded into a sombre, introspective look.

'I would not expect a future bride to pretend to be in love.'

'But what if she is?'

'Then I would not be marrying her.'

Because he thought he'd never love anyone the way he loved his first wife?

'I think that is sad.' She felt her cheeks flare again as she gnawed on her full lower lip. 'I spoke out of turn.'

'It's not stopped you so far,' he inserted drily as he pulled himself upright in one smooth, graceful motion. 'So please enlighten me as to what is *sad*.' He managed to keep his voice totally neutral, but still imbue his words with cheek-stinging sarcasm. It was a neat trick that had probably taken years of practice.

She took a deep breath. It was hard to be sympathetic to someone who gave a new meaning to unpleasant.

'Freya's mother, it was tragic, but some people do fall in love again, you know.'

Her interpretation of his comment stopped him dead in his tracks. He wondered how fast that idealistic glow of compassion would fade from her eyes if she knew the truth—that he'd killed Freya's mother.

The doctors could talk about her ruptured uterus and massive blood loss, but he knew differently.

'Is that your experience?' he countered softly, and watched her eyes flare in alarm before the barriers were raised.

'Oh, I've never—' she began, stopping as she heard the echo of her brother's accusations in her head.

Jake would have said no man ever reached her high standards, but it wasn't that at all. She was what some people might call a closet romantic. She really believed in soulmates, that there was someone who completed you out there.

She didn't think everyone was lucky enough to find theirs, but she didn't want to settle, which didn't mean she hadn't dipped her toe in the dating waters, it was just that she'd never really gone any farther, which had led her to the conclusion that she really wasn't that highly sexed.

A conclusion that had just been thrown into doubt by a kiss. Not just the kiss, the fact she had not wanted it to stop. The inconvenient possibility that the wrong... *very* wrong man, and not the man who was her perfect match, would awaken her dormant sexuality had never even crossed her mind.

She had always felt confident about her choices, but her right-and-wrong, black-and-white world view was taking some serious hits and the problem was that once you started questioning *one* certainty you started questioning everything!

'I have been very busy with my work, career.' Able to hear the defensive note in her voice, she brought her lashes down in a protective sweep.

'Climbing the greasy ladder,' he drawled, recognising the lie but letting it go. 'And then you leapt off,' he added, miming a diving gesture with his long fingers. 'Curious?'

She compressed her lips and clung to her defiance. 'I have always wanted to travel.'

'You really are a very bad liar, but shall we get back to my announcement? As things stand at the moment, when I die Freya is first in line to the throne, but should she have a male sibling he would take precedence.'

This man was so vitally alive, the most alive person she had ever met, to think of him not *being* around set off a discordant note of denial in her head.

'Freya does talk a lot about a brother.'

'You're telling me I should hurry up? I think I have a few years left in me yet.'

His mercurial mood shifts made Kate feel constantly on edge, and his lazy mockery made her teeth clench. Ego was not an attractive thing even when justified, and his was. His sexual potency entered a room before he did!

'The point is,' Marco continued, picking up his original thread, 'as things stand a younger brother would be heir.'

'Primogeniture.'

'Exactly, well, I have dragged the royal council kicking and screaming to the point where they are willing to sign off on the change. If they learned that Freya has anything *they* consider a handicap...' he emphasised, forestalling her protest, 'keeping in mind,' he added drily, 'that most of them have not changed their minds about anything since birth...they are so risk averse that some might consider that something as simple as red hair...' his eyes came to rest on a rope of curls that lay against her neck 'might set a dangerous precedent. You get my drift?' he said, thinking of those ropes of russet gold against his skin as she sat above him.

She nodded. 'Does Freya know?'

'Not yet.' Marco was unwilling to acknowledge he had not thought that far ahead. Had he worked so hard to gift his daughter something that he hadn't considered her rejecting the gift? Maybe she wouldn't want equality if equality meant her future was mapped out as his was.

'Will she be at the ball when you do the big reveal?'

'Freya!' he exclaimed. 'I don't think that would be—'

'Oh, she'd love it,' Kate cut in, seeing the smile on her charge's face if she could walk out beside her father. 'She'd be so proud to walk in there with you. She should just put in an appearance, of course,' she added hastily. 'It's not like she'd be there until the small hours...?' Head tilted to one side, she looked at him appealingly.

'Am I being manipulated, Kate?'

She shook her head, genuinely confused by the accusation. 'Of course not. I just thought, if she hates the idea she can sit somewhere and watch with me.'

'Sit and watch...' he said slowly. 'A delightful, if slightly Victorian image. I shall invite my daughter to the ball, but you will of course need to accompany her and whisk her away like a mini-Cinderella before the guests start misbehaving.' *If only*, he thought. The formal occasions were suffocating not scandalous.

Kate could not hide her horror at the prospect. 'But I couldn't. I don't...'

'Consult with my mother on clothes, accessories and such—despite appearances she has a very good sense of fashion.'

'The Queen? I couldn't possibly…maybe Lady Rosa. She seemed…'

'Charming? Oh, she is,' he said with an edge to his voice. 'But do *not* go to Lady Rosa.'

Despite the dismissal, Kate felt inclined to argue the prohibition. As mental images of the woman flashed into her head, she conceded that the woman was possibly not very stylish, certainly not as elegant as the pictures she'd seen of the Queen. Still, Lady Rosa was less regal but much more approachable than the actual monarch.

Kate was already dismissed, his fingers moving across one of the keyboards on his desk. 'And do not use her as an intermediary to my mother,' he added without looking up.

She shook her head in bewilderment even though he couldn't see her. 'But why not?'

He looked up then. 'Because, Kate, Lady Rosa is my father's mistress and there is a limit to *civilised*.' At least for him there was.

CHAPTER SEVEN

'OH, YES, THAT ONE is perfect... Oh, but the bra will definitely have to go.' The Queen turned to her granddaughter, who was dancing around in a pink ballerina dress. 'Don't you think so, Freya?'

The child paused to consider the subject, her expression so like her grandmother's that for a moment Kate forgot she was stressed as hell by the whole process and laughed.

'I think you're right, Grandma...no bra. Oh, I think I'm beautiful,' she added, swirling in front of the mirrors that covered one entire wall.

'Oh, you are!' both women exclaimed in unison and exchanged a smiling glance.

The Queen, despite her patrician looks, was possibly the least regal person Kate had ever met. She exuded a warmth, professed herself to be *quite lazy* and didn't appear to be tuned into the palace gossip machine at all. She was definitely not Kate's image of a wronged wife. She didn't seem angry, bitter or downtrodden. She seemed a woman who was very comfortable in her own skin.

But behind the *lazy* facade she could be relentless when she made up her mind, which was why Kate was standing there in the most fantastic dress she had ever worn being told her bra would have to go.

She was not going to accept the dress. She was just humouring her royal companion.

'I really don't think... It's beautiful but I don't *need* a dress and I couldn't possibly afford...' Her voice trailed off as she glanced at her reflection in the wall of mirrors in the body-hugging, deceptively simple bias-cut slip of blue silk, and she sighed, admitting, 'It is lovely.'

'It is perfect, and the matter is settled. As for the cost, Marco is picking up the bill. This is a work-related expense.'

Kate's husky laugh rang out. 'He'll be furious,' she added, sobering.

'This is his instruction, my dear,' the Queen inserted gently.

Kate looked doubtful. He might have said dress, but he could not have meant a dress like this.

'Now,' the Queen added briskly. 'Shoes. You have tiny feet,' she observed, looking at the trainer-clad feet exposed as Kate lifted the hem of blue silk.

Half an hour later, the items wrapped in layers of tissue were packaged up and stacked, waiting to be carried to the waiting car.

'We must do this more often,' the older woman said, turning to Kate with her warm smile. 'I can't remember the last time I had such fun.'

Kate, who could not imagine another occasion when her role would involve picking out a designer evening dress and accessories, gave a non-committal cover-all grunt and smiled. She had, despite all her misgivings, enjoyed the day.

Outside on the wide tree-lined street, which housed

a row of high-end designer shops to rival any capital city, the air was warm but not unpleasantly so. Kate inhaled the smell of the horse-chestnut blossoms and sneezed violently.

The allergy coming back to haunt her.

'Are you all right?'

'Fine,' Kate assured the older woman. It seemed incomprehensible to her that the King should humiliate her the way he did by keeping a mistress that it transpired everyone knew about.

'Freya is happy. I think that is down to you, so thank you.'

'Not at all, it is my—'

'Ah, duty… I know about duty, my dear.' She touched Kate's face, her expression wistful, or was Kate just imagining that because she felt sympathy for the woman's position? She wasn't sure. 'I admit I cannot get excited about babies, but Freya is just becoming *interesting*, don't you think? Marco, of course, was always interesting but so very…self-sufficient, even as a child.'

Kate, who didn't have a clue how to respond to the information, just nodded.

'Now we will take afternoon tea, unless you share Nanny Maeve's disapproval of such indulgences…?'

'I don't.'

'It's fine,' piped up Freya. 'Kate has lovely teeth and it's a celebration, we can have chocolate.'

'Well, that is settled, then,' her grandmother said, looking amused.

It was just left to Kate to follow meekly behind. The parcels were piled into a waiting car and the Queen announced they were going to walk to the tea shop.

The information that they were walking had created a flurry of activity as the security detail adapted, clearly not thrown by the Queen's mercurial change of timetable.

The Queen watched with a benevolent smile as her security team swung into action. 'This…they are Marco's doing. I used to cycle around the city with no issues, but he is so overprotective, especially where Freya is concerned.' Her glance went to the little girl, who was skipping along happily. 'Understandable, but he means well. I was so happy, we all were, when he had someone to share his life with, and Belle always adored him. Such a tragedy and he never talks about it. But that is Marco's way, strong and silent. Here we are.'

One of the security guards emerged from the café, his nod presumably conformation that it was safe for them to enter.

There was a perimeter of empty tables around the table they were led to.

'I want a chocolate milkshake.'

'It is always good to know what you want and go for it,' the Queen said, requesting iced tea for herself. When asked Kate said iced tea would be nice.

'Freya is the image of her mother. Belle was always a pretty child. It was such a wicked loss.' She sighed. 'For a long time after her death I feared for Marco. He shut himself off and…' She shook her head. 'He was in a dark place.'

'I can't begin to imagine what it would feel like,' Kate reflected, watching Freya, who was slurping a milkshake noisily through a straw. 'To make a new life with someone you love and then at the perfect moment everything falls apart…'

Did you ever recover from something like that? Or did you just go through the motions…functioning compared to living?

Recalling his comments about his future wife, she didn't think that Marco had; his scars might be the invisible variety but the past was still impacting his life.

'Everyone was distraught. Belle's family—' The Queen cleared her throat. 'It was understandable, I suppose, people in pain hit out.'

'Yes, Marco… Prince Marco,' Kate corrected with a self-conscious blush, 'did mention what happened.'

The Queen's feathery brows lifted in surprise. *'Did he?'* she said, an alert look sliding into her eyes. 'My son is not known for sharing…and a *lot* falls on his shoulders. It has done from an early age. His marriage may have ended but I think that Marco is married to this land, this country… It makes me sad that he has no one to share the burden with now.'

Before Kate could think of how to respond to this flow of confidences, the Queen rose to her feet displaying an energy a woman half her age would envy as she announced it was time to leave.

As the security detail rose from the tables they occupied she pitched her voice loudly. 'Actually, the cycling is good for these men. I have actually improved their stamina.'

Kate laughed, more confused than ever that a man who had a wife like this would choose to keep a mistress who, by any conventional standard, was far less attractive. And how did the Queen cope with the humiliation of everyone knowing about his mistress? The arrangement seemed crazier than ever to Kate.

She thought her own family was odd, but by comparison…

His mother had reported in her own inimitable way that she liked the new nanny. 'So easy to talk to…don't you think so, Marco?'

It was a given his mother would love Kate. His mother would have seen the good side in a serial killer, it was just the way she was, but her insistence was particularly vehement when she spoke of the English nanny.

'Do not hurt her though, Marco. I think she is very empathic. It makes her vulnerable.'

Marco had no intention of hurting her, and he was here to see his daughter, not her disapproving nanny, who, when he'd entered, had been standing in the middle of the room, dancing with his daughter in something that was vaguely recognisable as a waltz.

'Papa, I have a beautiful dress and I had chocolate milkshake with cream on top. I had a moustache! And I am learning to dance, see?' Freya gave a wobbly twirl to illustrate the fact.

Watching, Kate found there was something endearing about the awkward way he ruffled the child's hair. The fact he was making the effort made her throat ache with emotion.

'It sounds like I missed a lot of fun,' Marco observed, his eyes sliding to Kate, who had not moved since he'd entered. 'Are you going to show me your dress, Freya?'

'You want to see my dress?'

Her astonishment sent a slug of guilt through Marco, who found himself remembering the way he had sought his own father's approval, how much an 'Excellent' or a pat on the head had meant to him.

'Yes, I would.'

Freya's eyes went to Kate, who nodded, and the child rushed off.

Kate walked over to her phone and switched off the music that had been playing in the background.

'So you are a dance teacher too?'

She shrugged. 'I took lessons for a while.'

'Are you good?'

'Not good enough.'

'Are you going to show me your dress too?'

Kate flushed. 'Your mother insisted. She thought—'

'My mother thought right.'

'She was very kind; she is so beautiful…'

'And you are struggling with her unorthodox relationship with my father.'

'I wouldn't dream of—'

'Everyone else does. My parents' marriage had effectively ended years ago. The pressure to provide an heir took its toll. I suspect they were drifting and probably behind the scenes being *encouraged* towards separation.'

'But they stayed together.'

'Because then *I* happened, after they had given up hope. The only reason divorce would have been sanctioned was the need for an heir, but here I am. Do not look so sad. It is not an unhappy marriage, just different. He does love her, you know, but, as he is fond of saying, what the heart wants…'

'Do you believe that?'

He looked at her before dropping into an armchair in an elegant heap. 'I believe that love is used as an excuse for selfishness among other things. It's been a long day. I could do with a drink.'

'This is a nursery, so there is no bar, but all you have to do is click your fingers and you can have whatever you want, so I'm told.'

'Is that a fact?' he purred, looking at her mouth.

The moment of crackling, stomach-quivering tension stretched until he broke it, rising with restless grace to his feet and dragging a hand across his dark hair. 'Sorry, Nanny.'

Kate didn't know what he was apologising for, but she was glad she was no longer subjected to that soul-stripping, truth-drug stare that made her want to tell him what a good kisser he was.

'It doesn't really matter what I believe, does it?'

She didn't say anything even though he glanced her way as though expecting her to argue the point, making her think it was a point he had argued with himself over the years.

'My *mother* believes that Rosa makes my father happy. Their relationship preceded that of my parents but there was never any question of him marrying Rosa. She came from the wrong sort of family. Back then those sorts of things mattered.'

'And they don't now?'

'I don't know what the world's coming to. Non-virgins have even been known to marry into the family.

'The bottom line is my parents are both lovely people and they have a relationship that works for them, but I don't even pretend to understand.'

Freya came in at that moment, an explosion in pink, and as she glowed in response to her father's suggestion she give him a twirl, feeling surplus, Kate made a tactful exit, leaving father and daughter together.

She was in her kitchen making a coffee when the door opened.

'You should lock this. You need your privacy. You're not on duty twenty-four-seven.'

Kate looked at the man whose six-feet-plus frame

made the room suddenly very small and arched a brow. 'Most people knock,' she said pointedly. 'And I have been told several times that my predecessor was a saint who hadn't taken a holiday in ten years.'

'Nanny Maeve was pretty much a fixture. People will get used to you. I think they have noticed you already.'

He was looking at her hair and Kate, who was used to people commenting on it, shrugged, thinking that noticing was not the same as accepting.

'Look, I have read the literature and research you sent me and... I've spoken to the professor who has produced the research in the psychology department, and he has arranged an appointment in the education department at the university tomorrow for an assessment for Freya. There is apparently an ongoing research programme and he seemed keen to have Freya take part in it.'

'And how do you feel about that?'

'My daughter is not a guinea pig.'

She studied his rigid jaw and nodded without comment at this understandable response. 'Oh, that's great, well, I mean good that you are taking some action so quickly.'

'And you can't wait to be proved right.'

'That is unfair!' she exclaimed.

His lips compressed as he dragged a hand through his dark hair, creating attractive spikes. Damn her, but she was right, it wasn't. 'Life is not fair, Miss Armstrong. The professor asked me if there was any history of reading problems in the family.'

'Is there?'

'If there was it would have been hidden, to avoid

any suggestion of a taint in the royal bloodline,' he explained with a cynical grimace. 'And Belle's family... I have no idea. The lines of communication, as you are aware, are not open.'

'Couldn't you make the first move?'

'Freya's grandfather lost his right for access when he said that she killed her mother.'

'I'm sure he regrets it...?'

Marco sketched a hard grin. 'I do not regret cutting that bastard out of our lives.'

Kate looked at his flinty eyes and nodded, deciding it was not the moment to push the idea of reconciliation. It would seem that the Prince was not big on forgiveness.

'So tomorrow if you could have Freya ready for ten, under the pretext we will be going...to the beach?'

'Then you will have to go to the beach. You can't promise a child the beach and then change your mind.'

She half expected some push-back but to her surprise none came, just an admonition to remember sunscreen because she was fair-skinned.

The brush of his eyes as he left made her aware of every inch of her pale skin.

'Would you like to take Freya to the playroom while the professor speaks to her father?' The young woman in jeans threw a smile that was several thousand more volts than was appropriate towards Marco, who was shaking hands with the professor who had arrived after his team had completed their tests.

She turned to Freya. 'Would you guys like to go to the playroom while we chat with your daddy, Freya?'

'And then we can go to the beach?' Freya asked Kate.

'Then we can go to the beach,' Kate confirmed.

'I wish I could go too,' the assistant said, only she wasn't looking at Kate and Freya but at Marco, who appeared deep in conversation with the older man.

The young woman might have been showing an unprofessional interest in Marco but her directions were good. They soon found themselves in a sunny playroom.

Freya looked surprised when she saw the other children. She held back for a while, staying close to Kate until a little boy wearing a hearing aid came across and held out a wooden puzzle to her.

'Can I?'

Kate nodded and watched, her heart aching as the solitary little girl responded with growing confidence to the approaches of the other children there.

She didn't really register Marco's presence until he was at her elbow. She rose to her feet, a question in her eyes.

'Well, you will be pleased to hear you have been proved right, they concur with your diagnosis.'

Kate frowned at the direct attack. 'I would have been happy to be proved wrong.'

He pressed the heel of his hand to his forehead and cursed. 'I know, that was…extremely unfair. I should be thanking you. They were very impressed that you had picked up the markers so quickly,' he admitted.

'Apology accepted. Ready to go, Freya,' she yelled.

'Wait a minute!' Marco and Kate watched as she hugged the little boy standing beside her.

'What is she doing?' Marco asked, watching as his daughter waved her hands.

'Signing,' Kate said with a watery smile. 'There is

an audiology clinic going on this morning. I think sign language should be taught in all schools; children pick it up so easily.'

'Do you sign?'

'I have the basics.'

Freya reached them, smiling. 'That's my friend, Simon. He's teaching me how to talk with my hands. Can he come to play some day?'

'I don't see why not, if your papa…?'

'Don't ask me, I'm just the driver,' Marco said drily as they walked to the waiting car, flanked by two cars containing the inevitable security detail.

On the beach, empty but for them, which Kate suspected was not accidental, Kate supervised Freya's application of suncream before she slogged up the slope to a stall selling ice cream. He was not doing much business, so he looked happy when she ordered twenty and he put them in a box for her.

Kate ferried them up to the waiting parked cars and tapped on a blacked-out bulletproof window.

'Thought you might like some ice cream,' she shouted as the window rolled down.

Juggling the three remaining rapidly melting ice creams in her hands, she went back down to the spot where she had left Marco and Freya spreading a blanket on the sand. 'One for you…' Freya snatched the proffered ice cream out of her hand.

'And one…' She switched one ice cream to her free hand.

'That,' Marco observed, nodding to the cars, 'was straight out of my mother's playbook. You trying to win friends?'

Kate flashed him a look. 'Eat it quickly, Freya. It's

melting.' She went to hand over one to Marco, holding it at an angle as she licked the melting ice cream off her wrist. 'Oh, my… I'm so sorry.' She giggled as the melting ice cream landed on his immaculate trousers.

From where she stood Freya let out a loud guffaw, Kate's lips quivered, then flattened in shock as her own ice cream made a similar bellyflop and landed in a greasy smear down her front. The child fell about laughing.

'Not so funny now,' Marco said, his mocking voice against her ear sending a shudder through her body.

She dabbed ineffectually at the melting blob, alarm flaring in her eyes as Marco produced a large tissue and approached her. She felt a tiny beat of heat as she visualised his hand against her breast and reacted in panic to stop it happening, snatching it out of his hand with a prim thank you.

'Spoilsport!' he whispered under cover of kneeling down to retrieve a towel. 'Are we going for a swim, Freya?'

'You and me?'

The astonishment in her voice could have been laughable but it wasn't. Marco felt a surge of emotion he could not put a name to, or was too ashamed to.

He could face down a room of critics in dark suits willing him to fall flat on his face and not stumble, not put a foot wrong. His confidence was impregnable, but here on a sandy beach with his own child the things he wanted to say he could find no words for.

And the fact he wanted to say them was all down to Kate. His eyes were sliding to the slim, silent figure when Freya spoke.

Hands set on her skinny hips, his daughter gained his attention as she looked him up and down. 'Papa, you have clothes on.'

His grin made Kate's heart flip.

'Not for long.'

As he stripped off his linen suit and shirt to reveal the pair of black swim-shorts he was wearing underneath Freya was clapping.

Kate's reaction was less enthusiastic, more *visceral*. Her internal temperature had risen several uncomfortable degrees as a shock wave of reaction hit her.

His body was…well, *perfect*. An overused term but in this instance… Long and lean, broad of shoulder and narrow of hips, his legs long and muscular, built for speed and not brute strength. There was not an ounce of excess flesh to disguise the corrugated muscles of his belly or the slabs on his chest.

He made her think of an anatomical diagram of perfect musculature brought to warm, golden, gorgeous, sense-sapping, carnal life.

'Coming, Kate?'

She sat there frozen and shook her head. 'I didn't think, so I forgot my swimsuit,' she improvised, even though it was actually in her bag, and she didn't care if he knew it, there was no way in the world she was changing into it here, in front of him. She felt vulnerable enough as it was without exposing her imperfect body to someone with the most perfect body that ever existed. 'You go and enjoy yourselves.'

'Swim in your pants, Kate. I did when I forgot my swimsuit.'

'Yes, Kate, swim in your pants.'

Her eyes narrowed on his beautiful mocking face. 'Have fun, Freya. I brought a book. Go for your swim and then we should go back. The midday sun is very strong, lethal.'

It wasn't the only thing, she decided, watching as Marco took his daughter's hand and they ran down to the water's edge.

In the car on the way back Freya fell asleep. 'I have a meeting with the educational people next week. Will you come?'

'Of course.'

'They said pretty much what you did. I have let things slide with Freya. I have…that is going to change…she just…'

Kate waited.

'She looks very like her mother.' The guilt tightened its grip on his shoulders. It felt as if he were wearing a lead suit.

The woman he had loved. Kate's heart ached for him. 'That must be hard, not that I know but… I'm sure she has both of you in her, but Freya is her own person.'

'Seeing her today in the playroom…' At her fifth birthday there were no children.'

'You were there.'

'No, actually, no, I wasn't. The only reason I remember at all is because there was an intruder that night and I upped security.'

'You could be there for her sixth birthday.'

'I don't like making promises I can't keep, even though I want to. Freya deserves a hands-on father, a loving father,' he said fiercely.

Kate found herself staring at his beautiful hands,

her eyes settling on the gold ring. The symbol of what he had lost.

'I think Freya just wants you. And if anyone told me you don't love her, I'd call them an idiot. My dad...' She stopped, an image of her dad appearing in her head, the dad who loved her.

The dad she couldn't forgive. Oh, God, she was an idiot!

'I have sand in my knickers!'

The complaint from the back seat broke the tension in the air and Kate laughed. 'Straight in the bath when we get back, then.'

Marco struggled to focus on the road. Only the image of Kate, in a shower with the water streaming off her lily-pale skin, made him glad to turn into the driveway.

CHAPTER EIGHT

KATE LEANED IN as she applied the finishing touch to her make-up, which was a generous skim of soft pink lip gloss applied with far more precision than she would normally have used.

'Too much?' she asked her reflection of the stranger in the mirror. Some people did this every day but in her view life was too short. She was strictly a flick of mascara, smudge of shadow and smear of gloss kind of girl.

But for special occasions, and she was pretty sure that a ball in a royal palace counted as special, it was good to make the effort. And yes, she was pleased with the results, she decided, turning her face from side to side. She'd skipped a few steps in the online guide to the perfect but subtle party face but the results were pretty good. She quite liked the way the eyeliner emphasised the almond shape of her eyes, and on the third attempt she had nailed the blusher.

As Freya would have said, it was science...or maybe art?

She twirled around on her stool as a small serious voice responded, 'No, not too much. You look...you look shiny.'

'Thank you, Freya.' Kate smiled at the little girl, whose eyes were bright with suppressed excitement.

'Can I put on my dress now, please? I won't spill anything on it again…promise.'

Kate smiled. 'I know you won't, and it was only lemonade, it should be dry now. Ask Julia.'

Her pink robe, adorned with cartoon cats, flapping around her, Freya ran from the room.

Kate slipped off her own robe and laid it on her bed. Her underclothes, which had been bought at a ridiculous price to match her dress, did not cover much. She had passed on the braless option, but the strapless silky bra afforded only a token stab at modesty. And the matching silk knickers cut low across her hips and virtually non-existent on her bottom were held together with bits of silk ribbon. They had been designed to incentivise their removal.

Not tonight though, she told herself before her imagination could enter forbidden territory as she shook out the dress and slid down the neatly hidden zip. She ran a hand over the buttery ice-blue fabric and let it slide through her fingers. The other hand remained pressed to her stomach to ease the quivering sensation low in her belly where there was a pack of butterflies running riot.

Kate had smiled at the child's antics, but the truth was she was probably just as excited and apprehensive as Freya, which was stupid. This was just a party. She'd been to parties before. This one was just bigger and involved the odd orchestra and film star. She wasn't even a guest…she was just there as a glorified babysitter.

Admittedly the dress didn't look like one your average babysitter would wear. Reverently she stared at the dress before she wriggled into it. As she reached for the zip she wondered how many times you had to tell yourself you were totally cool before you actually were.

Tomorrow morning, probably, when it was all over.

She practised her cool nanny expression in the mirror and held it about four seconds longer than the last time, before, her heart racing with a mixture of anxiety, excitement took control.

Hardly surprising. Tension was contagious and the palace had been buzzing with it for days, culminating in a general organised mass hysteria today as the final preparations kicked in.

She pushed away the suspicion that the presence of one tall handsome prince might be an extra contributing factor for her. More than the presence of news crews nabbing their spots and doing their soundchecks, or having an entire orchestra stream past her in full evening dress, or hearing the constant buzz of helicopters ferrying guests landing on the lawn.

Looking in the mirror, she adjusted her dress, being assailed by the possibility of a wardrobe malfunction as she visualised the shoestring straps going south and leaving her standing in a pool of silk.

Blinking away the waking-nightmare image, she enjoyed the feel of the silk fabric that hugged her body in all the right places, making the most of her slender curves. She relished the sensuous swish of silk against her legs as she moved, the discreet split in the folds down one side revealing a flash of pale thigh.

Her only jewellery was a pair of amber drop earrings that had been an eighteenth-birthday present from her parents. They'd said the stone was the same colour as her eyes.

Remembering the day brought a fleeting shadow to her eyes, a sadness that a sudden stab of pain offered her an escape from. Tongue between her teeth, she carefully freed the curl that had snagged in one of

KIM LAWRENCE 119

the butterfly clips behind her ear, carefully untangling it without ruining her hair.

She had weighed up the option between loose or an up-do and in the end settled on a compromise—a *half* up-do, that left her hair long and flowing but showed the delicacy of her facial features and emphasised the slender length of her neck.

Kate was slipping her feet into a pair of satiny high-heeled mules when Freya reappeared, her dimples on show as she tried not to grin. When she saw Kate she clapped.

'Wow, you really will be the belle of the ball!' The maid behind Freya clamped a hand to her mouth. 'Sorry.'

'Julia is right. I'm a princess but you look like a princess tonight.'

'But you are a *real* princess.'

'I have something for you, for your hair.'

Kate was fully anticipating that she'd be offered some plastic hair ornament that she would be obliged to wear, and her smile faded when she saw what Freya was holding.

In the shape of a starburst, the gold hair clip was encrusted with diamonds.

'Oh, Freya, it's beautiful but I couldn't. It's too precious, too valuable.'

'Granny gave it to me for Christmas, it's mine, so I can give it you…or lend it, if you like, for the ball… please, please.'

Responding to the pleading blue eyes, Kate sighed, unable to disappoint the little girl, though the idea of walking around with the princess's jewellery in her hair made her very nervous. 'All right, just for tonight.'

'Julia will put it in for you…sit still,' Freya added.

'Princess bossy,' Kate observed, doing as she was instructed.

'It looks perfect. Come on, Papa is waiting.'

'He is?' Kate's stomach did a double flip. This hadn't been the arrangement as had been relayed to her. 'I thought I was taking you to meet—'

'He's here to escort us.'

Escort you, Kate thought, following the child from the bedroom.

Marco made an unnecessary adjustment to his spotless cuff and continued to pace the room impatiently, unable to control this uncharacteristic restlessness.

The evening would go smoothly. Whatever else Rosa was, she was faultless when it came to organising the big events. She had an eye for detail and delegation.

He did not suffer from stage fright, and the ability to hold his audience was not something he had to work at, but being good at something didn't mean you necessarily liked it. Marco hated working a room and being nice to people that your instinct told you to cross the street to avoid. He'd been smiling for the cameras since he was younger than Freya, wheeled out, hair slicked down for a photo op. There was nothing like the snapshot of a cute kid to distract people from a political scandal or a financial crisis.

Normally he would get through these mind-numbing but necessary social events—necessary in the loosest sense of the word—by anticipating the reward he allowed himself afterwards. The last reward had been a weekend on the Caribbean island that had been a wedding gift for his parents, which they had never to his knowledge visited, in the company of a beautiful corporate lawyer who had a delightfully uninhibited and unemotional attitude to sex.

But there was no naked swimming with a beautiful companion or sundowner cocktails to look forward to this time. He had nothing planned. This oversight likely explained in part the restless tension that he was suffering, that and the fact he had serious doubts about allowing himself to be persuaded to include Freya. His protective instincts were telling him to keep her away from this sort of circus for as long as possible.

Kate Armstrong could give a masterclass in soft power. She'd manipulated him and the hell of it was he had enjoyed it, or at least enjoyed the illicit pain/pleasure of the forbidden desire he experienced in her company. If it were only in her company, he reflected with a bitter laugh of self-contempt, he might be getting more sleep than he was.

He was starting to think the entire illicit situation was part of the problem—it was the pull of the forbidden pleasure. If he'd slept with her, taking into account his normal game plan, the interlude would by now just be a pleasant memory.

The line was still there, and he was not about to step over it, even if it was slowly driving him mad. It would still be an abuse of a position of power.

A swirl of pink in the periphery of his vision made him turn.

Marco let out a silent whistle, a smile on his lips he picked Freya up and looked beyond her to the figure who had materialised in the doorway. A tremor went through his body, his smile froze. Everything froze. Brain-numbing desire engulfed every cell in his body. If he hadn't been holding his daughter he was sure he would have lunged for her, the need to crush her beautiful mouth under his was so primal, so utterly over-whelming.

That dress… Thinking about the body it covered would cause him serious pain on top of the serious pain he was already enduring. He was starting think he had regressed to his hormonal teens.

'Papa, too tight!'

'Sorry.' Putting his daughter down gave him a chance to claw back some of his self-control. He had not felt this out of control since the day he had jumped into a waterfall head first and been carried down to the rocks below.

People had said it was a miracle he had survived with only a scratch to show for it.

There was no miracle to ground him now, only rigid, hard-fought-for restraint.

He straightened up and the silence stretched and so did Kate's nerves. 'You look very…' She stopped, swallowed and fished around for a description that was not *sublime*.

Which he was.

Tall and commandingly exclusive in perfectly tailored formal attire, his dress shirt creaseless and perfect, the brilliant white emphasising the golden olive of his skin. And with the dark suit hanging off his broad shoulders and emphasising the muscular strength of his long legs, he looked lean and lethal.

'Nice,' she finished lamely.

'Beautiful dress.'

'You paid for it.'

His brows shot up. 'Did I?'

'It was very expensive.'

The confession brought an enigmatic smile. 'Money well spent, I would say. Are we ready, ladies?'

He held out a hand to Freya, who took it, and held out a crooked elbow to Kate, an invitation presumably for her to lay her arm on it.

An innocent enough gesture, and part of her wanted to accept it graciously, but that part of her wanted way too much. Best to avoid physical contact, especially when proximity affected her ability to think coherently.

She made a point of not noticing the invitation instead, moving around to Freya's other side and taking the little girl's other hand in her own.

Mockery shone in his eyes as they challenged her, but Kate tuned him out and turned to Freya.

'A lovely necklace,' she said, touching the delicate silver shell suspended from a chain around the child's neck.

'Papa bought it me.'

Kate looked at *Papa* and immediately regretted it. It took another few moments for her to get her galloping self-control on a leash. This was crazy, and it was going nowhere. He made every woman he looked at feel she was the only woman on the planet. That was the secret of his success. She couldn't allow herself to think otherwise.

'Very pretty.'

'You haven't got a necklace.'

The childish comment brought Marco's eyes to Kate's pearlescent creamy skin. The slender column of her body was immediately under attack from streaks of heat. 'She doesn't need one.'

'I have the lovely hair clip you let me use,' Kate said, struggling with the after-effects of a brief brush with Marco's predatory stare to the extent that it didn't even cross her mind that to the casual observer there might be anything misread in the little procession.

It wasn't until after they had encountered a few uniformed staff that Kate realised that the picture they presented could be easily misinterpreted by someone who didn't know her position in the palace.

This was about the last thing she needed. The way the gossip mill in this place worked, she could only imagine what stories would be circulating by the end of the evening.

They had reached an open area, the stone walls banked with elaborate flower arrangements, when the guests clustered there, awaiting their entrance, parted like a well-dressed sea. The reason soon became obvious. Up ahead she and presumably everyone else could see the King and Queen flanked by a number of high-ranking officials in ceremonial dress heading their way.

She let go of Freya's hand and stepped back, not wanting any part of the prearranged ceremonial procession.

Marco frowningly looked over his shoulder. 'What are you doing?'

She shook her head and said quietly, 'The optics wouldn't look good.' Then, giving Freya a thumbs-up sign, added, 'Have fun and save me a dance.'

Marco nodded, his eyes gleaming dangerously. 'I will.'

Continuing to walk backwards, she blushed. 'I was talking to Freya.'

'*I* was talking to you.' The least he could reward himself with was a chance to hold her in his arms and feel her body against his.

Not in the way he wanted to and it would be a kind

of torture probably immediately regretted, but his defiant determination was set in stone.

Kate gave a small, tense smile as his eyes burnt her up. She pressed a hand to the flutter at the base of her throat, almost weeping with relief when she heard a familiar voice at her elbow.

'Going my way?'

It took her a few moments to identify Marco's assistant, who she had met on several occasions now. 'Luca…my, you look smart.'

He looked pleased and twiddled his bow tie, pulling what appeared to be a spare duplicate out of his pocket and admitting with a humorous grin, 'Couldn't tie it. Someone lent me a clip-on.'

'I couldn't tell,' she promised.

'God, I could do with sunglasses,' Kate murmured as they slipped into the ballroom through one of the side entrances. Between the chandeliers suspended from the high vaulted ceiling covered in frescoes and the jewellery the female guests were wearing it was a real bling fest. 'I suddenly feel quite underdressed,' she admitted, taking a glass of champagne from a passing waiter.

'You look fabulous,' the young man said with such sincerity that she might have been flattered if she hadn't been able to see he was checking out the crowd for someone. She watched him with a smile for a moment, wondering if he'd been tasked to look after her, before taking pity on him.

'I suppose we should mingle. See you later.'

He vanished so fast that she almost laughed. Instead, she exchanged her empty glass for a second one, which would usually be her last. She knew her limit but, seized by uncharacteristic recklessness, she found herself wishing that she were in a position to go over it…a long way… However, drunk in charge of a child would not look good on her résumé.

Kate was nursing the second glass when a hush of expectation fell over the room, the lights dimmed, all but the ones on the grand sweeping staircase as the orchestra began to play the national anthem.

The King and Queen appeared at the top of the stairs and began their ascent with suitably regal majesty, the Queen wearing a tiara that put any other jewel in the place in the shade. But it was the couple behind that Kate was watching as the camera bulbs flashed.

Her heart twisted in her chest as she watched Freya, in her pretty pink frothy dress, pick her way down the steps in her embroidered pink slippers, glancing up after every other step up for reassurance from the tall man who held her hand.

That Marco looked simply magnificent was a given. He made every man in the room look like a pale imitation, but it was the fact the world could see the pride on his face and the words of encouragement he was mouthing to Freya that brought tears to Kate's eyes.

She wasn't the only one who was moved, she suspected.

The photos would be guaranteed international front-page coverage.

If she'd seen the photos without having any insight, she might have viewed any photo spread with a degree of cynicism and she'd have been wrong. Wrong about how much else? she wondered.

She was in a position now to know that first impressions would be wrong. This was no PR stunt.

Instincts were not always right. There was sometimes a back story that changed the narrative. Had she even considered her parents' narrative…?

She had not given her parents a chance to offer their viewpoint. She had made no effort to see things from where they had been standing. She'd been too hurt, too eager to condemn without question. Kate felt her grip on the high ground slip as the infectious germ of doubt took up residence in her head while the orchestra struck up the chords of a Strauss waltz. With her inside information Kate had known they would.

She had walked through the steps with Freya all week and the little girl had them nailed, so long as nerves didn't get in the way.

Kate watched, willing Freya on as the couples circled the floor, the King and Queen giving a practised performance. But all eyes were on the little girl and her father.

As if he sensed her gaze across the room, Marco's eyes found hers. Tension slid down her spine, the people, the music all seemed to fade and grew fuzzy until Kate's entire world narrowed to his bold silver stare. She didn't even register the music stopping. It was the applause from the guests around her that shook Kate free of the spell that gripped her.

Real or imagined, she was shaken by the effect of the silent communication across the room. She watched as Marco took Freya to stand with his parents and walked back to the raised dais where there was a microphone.

It was clear immediately that Marco was as adept at public speaking as he seemed to be at everything else. Of course, it helped that his deep vibrant voice could have made a grocery list sound interesting.

He had his audience from the first introduction line as he issued the anticipated congratulations to his parents on their special day and spoke of duty and the unity that was the strength of the country and its people.

The real news he couched as an afterthought wrapped

inside his deep gratitude to the forward-thinking royal council for their wisdom in proposing a change to the outdated rule that gave males precedence over females, thus altering the royal line of succession in a way that made it fairer.

At least she wasn't the only one who found his voice hypnotic, Kate thought as the room exploded into applause that was not polite but spontaneous. It lasted while Marco, after producing a charming smile of thanks, walked across to join the rest of his family.

Kate watched Freya, who was clapping non-stop as her father reached them. A smile tugged at her lips. It was amazing how the child's confidence had grown in such a short space of time. She was as easy to love as her rather less huggable father was to... As her eyes drifted to the tall dynamic figure, Kate's thoughts skittered to a halt. She sensed that if she allowed them to run free for another moment there was something *looming*, an answer to a question she had not even asked herself yet.

The thought of the question panicked her so thoroughly that when a man who addressed his invitation to her cleavage, not her face, asked her to dance, she couldn't think of a plausible reason to say no.

'I have just been telling Freya that one day she will be Queen, but she is more interested in teaching your mother how to salsa...' The King lowered his voice. 'Is salsa an appropriate dance to be teaching a child of Freya's age, Marco? This new nanny...is she working out, do you think?'

Marco opened his mouth and closed it again as he caught sight of the top of a red head on the dance floor, his eyes narrowing as he struggled to identify her partner. The tension in his features relaxing when he recognised a married courtier whose wife was rumoured to keep him on a short leash.

'She is well qualified. I doubt if we could keep her even if we wanted to.' And he wanted, he wanted Kate Armstrong. His mind knew it was a bad idea, but his body didn't care, his body wanted Kate Armstrong, and wanted to find the oblivion he craved deep in her warm body.

'Oh, well, Freya seems…less tongue-tied at least, which is a good thing. And you must be pleased with yourself. There's no backing out now, is there?' the King observed with a chuckle. 'I must say tonight is a great success, thanks in large part to Rosa… I always enjoy these occasions.' He looked at his tall son curiously. 'Unlike you?'

'Does it show?' Marco asked, flicking an invisible speck from his lapel as he watched Kate circle the floor.

'Not at all. You're very good at the diplomacy, you could always leave early…?'

Marco laughed at the suggestion. 'Your concern is appreciated but what do you suggest, Father, I get a headache…?' Marco excused himself and walked across to where an animated Freya was chattering to her grandmother.

'Having fun?'

'Yes, Papa, I think that lady over there is waving to you.'

Marco turned his head to follow her finger and identified the tall blonde who was waving to catch his attention. It took him a moment longer to recall her name.

Kate's polite smile was wearing thin. Her dance partner had stepped on her toes again.

'Did I mention my wife couldn't come tonight? Her sister is ill. I'm fending for myself.'

No, she thought, you were too busy telling me what an important person you are.

'Oh, what a shame,' she said, matching his sincerity while watching as a tall blonde on the other side of the room, in a dress that she just had to have been sewn into, placed a proprietorial hand on Marco's arm as he leaned in to hear what she was saying.

Kate knew who she was because she had looked her up in relation to the gossip. Out of curiosity, she had told herself, as she was telling herself now that the shaft of pain that felt like a knife sliding between her ribs was because she'd skipped lunch.

The leaning in, the dark head next to the blonde head—the imaginary knife twisted. Kate stumbled and saw her partner wince.

'You trod on my foot!' he exclaimed, sounding outraged.

After the trampling her poor toes had suffered she thought this hardly redressed the balance, but she settled for a meek and diplomatic apology. 'So...sorry.'

'My wife is a very good dancer.'

There was a plus side. His clammy hand no longer strayed down to her bottom. Things got even better when he developed a limp and excused himself.

'Jackie, you're looking good.'

'Don't worry, darling, I'm not stalking you. I'm here as a plus one.'

The guest list was not something that Marco took a personal interest in. Any specific requests would have come from his office.

Too tired to respond to her flirtatious laughter, Marco

found himself wondering how he had ever thought the fake sounded amusing.

'I can see you're sceptical.'

He wasn't interested enough in the conversation to be sceptical, but he could definitely feel boredom setting in.

'But seriously,' he heard her say. 'Lawrence… I'm his plus one…was hoping you could take a meeting…? There are rumours of an airport expansion and you know he is—'

'I know who Lawrence Milton is, but the answer is no because there will be no airport expansion, so I can save you the softening-up process.'

The model's smile was tight. 'Oh, I told him you don't "soften up" *and* my influence was only ever limited.'

Non-existent would have been more accurate but Marco let it pass.

'But I thought I'd give it a try…?'

'No expansion.' Aside from the green issues, bringing in more tourists would despoil the very things that attracted visitors.

It was all about balance.

'Oh, well, thank you for the heads-up…' A half wistful expression crossed the model's beautifully made-up face. 'We had fun didn't we…?'

Marco raised a brow. 'Sentimental? That's not like you.'

She shrugged. 'We all change. You have.'

Marco bent in to kiss her cheek, barely registering the comment as he moved away, his eyes scanning the crowd for a distinctive redhead.

In her search for Freya, Kate noticed the dance floor had emptied. She soon discovered why. Her shy charge, who had discovered her inner diva, was there, taking centre stage, partnered by her grandfather.

As the last chords played Freya curtsied to the King before clapping herself.

Guests' cameras were banned and the palace censored any releases from the official photographers and film crews present, but if that image got out it would capture the hearts of millions. Kate, who knew that despite his multiple faults Marco was all about the best interests of his child, suspected it wouldn't.

An ebullient Freya spotted Kate and came running over, pushing her way through the crowds and effectively putting all curious eyes on her nanny, an identity that she heard pronounced on all sides as Freya pulled her onto the floor for their dance.

Kate recognised the child was over-wound and over-tired, *over* being the operative word at the moment the normally sweetly biddable child showed a marked inclination to pout when thwarted. Kate knew that she just as easily become tearful.

I've created a monster, Kate thought with fond amusement. There was definitely more of Freya's father in her than she had realised, watching as the little girl imperiously demanded a *'salsa if you know one'* from the indulgent conductor.

A ripple of laughter went around the room as the salsa beat, backed by a full orchestra, pumped out.

'You promised,' Freya reminded Kate. The bright cheeks and glitter in her eyes had all the hallmarks of exhaustion as she held out her hands and showed a strong inclination to sulk.

'One dance and then you say goodnight.'

Freya looked inclined to argue but after a moment, much to Kate's relief, she nodded and sighed. The last thing Kate wanted to cope with was a childish melt-down in front of the several hundred VIP pairs of eyes.

'OK.'

As couples joined them on the dance floor and she gently pushed the child through the series of moves they had been practising as a pre-bedtime treat, Kate's eyes were drawn to a laughing young couple sealed at the hip, moving in unison as they swayed sinuously to the music with practised show-stopper ease.

What would it feel like to dance this one with Marco? To move to the beat with their bodies sealed? She pushed the image away but not before her body reacted feverishly to the imaginary scenario.

After the dance ended and before Freya could make the inevitable plea for just one more, Kate scanned the room but failed to locate Marco. It wasn't as if he blended in with the crowd. Nor could she see the beautiful blonde model. *What a coincidence*, she thought sourly.

She looked at Freya's too bright, overtired eyes and pale face and made a unilateral decision, which was what she was being paid for.

'Let's go and say goodnight,' she said, placing a hand on the child's shoulders and guiding Freya across to where the King and Queen were watching the proceedings in the company of a select few.

Rosa, who had organised the entire event, was not one of them. At least the King did not rub his wife's nose in it publicly.

Marco struggled and failed to hide his frustrated response to the interruption.

'Yes?' Like all his team, the head of security was dressed to blend in. He didn't, but then that was not necessarily a bad thing.

'Can you not deal with it?' Whatever the 'it' was, he already knew the answer. The man had ten years' special forces experience. If he couldn't deal with it, Marco wouldn't stand an earthly chance.

'I could, as I told His Majesty, but the message came back and he has requested that you personally...'

Marco sighed. 'What is it?' he asked with forced calm. You didn't question a royal command, at least not in public.

'A helicopter has strayed into the no-fly zone... It's not an issue, our intel suggests just an opportunist film crew, and we have two of our choppers escorting them into the airport as we speak.'

'It sounds like you are on top of it. So what does my father expect me to do?'

'As to that, Highness, I have no idea, but the message I received was that he wanted you to—'

Across the room the King caught Marco's eye, tipped his head and tapped the side of his nose in a secret-shared attitude.

Marco heaved out a sigh of understanding. Now it made sense! His father had decided to don the mantle of an unlikely fairy godmother, in a 'you will *leave* the ball early' sense.

The request was his legitimate headache, get-out-of-jail excuse; the irony was that on any previous occasion he wouldn't have needed asking twice.

'Fine,' he sighed out, clinging by the skin of his teeth to his sense of irony. With a well-meaning father like his, who needed anarchists to spoil your plans? 'A royal command? What can you say? Lead the way.'

Despite her previous vow not to curtsey, Kate found herself doing just that, or at least a modified version, when she came face to face with the King. Did size matter, curtsey-wise?

Kate had been prepared to dislike him but, like his wife, he actually came across as very approachable, a lot less daunting in reality than his son, though she suspected that Freya's presence helped. It was hard to be standoffish when a five-year-old was declaring herself bored, but at least she managed to get through the ordeal of introduction without saying anything controversial.

'Where's Papa?' Freya sulked as she got into bed, protesting she wasn't even slightly tired.

'I don't know.' Kate had her dark suspicions, though, and all of them involved a blonde with endless legs. 'How about you just close your eyes and if you're still awake in a bit you can have a story?' she suggested, switching on the night light before she switched off the main light in the room.

'I won't fall asleep,' the child asserted confidently.

Kate smiled and brushed the hair off her warm forehead before quietly moving around the room, picking up the clothes that had been dropped on the floor. By the time she left Freya was sleeping deeply.

Moving back to her own apartment, switching off the lights behind her as she went, Kate was pretty sure that she wouldn't be able to follow suit. Her thoughts were still racing, the sights and sounds of the glittering evening a confusing blur, but most disturbing was the imprint scorched into her brain of Marco's face as he had stared at her. The fierce, scorching intensity still making her stomach flutter now, and feeding her restlessness.

The party would still be going on, though Marco, his

duty done, might have taken his party somewhere more private by now, she thought, feeding her misery with the masochistic imagined scene of seduction. Which was ridiculous because she already knew what his lifestyle was, it was just that seeing him in action tonight had brought it home.

She'd seen him at work and he was good, very good. Was he as good at play? wondered that little voice in her head—the one that enjoyed picking at an unhealed wound.

Except she wasn't wounded, she was just thinking of someone having meaningless sex with her boss. She didn't envy her one bit. She had decided a long time ago that she didn't want meaningless sex, she wanted something deeper, more meaningful.

'And Kate never changes her mind about anything.'

Her delicate jaw quivered and her eyes filled with tears as she heard her brother's voice in her head.

The accusation might have been true once, but in the short time she'd been here Kate knew she had changed. Her preconceptions had been challenged, not just by Marco, but by the feelings he had shaken loose in her.

She considered her options. A long relaxing soak in the bath, or slipping between crisp sheets and falling into a deep sleep? Both excellent options had she not known that there was zero chance of relaxation or sleep, deep or otherwise.

The evening scent of flowers blowing in through the open window suggested another option. Sliding her feet back into her shoes, she winced, the pressure on the balls of her feet burning.

She sat down and checked out her feet, relieved to see they were not blistered, but she definitely wouldn't be squeezing into any heels for the next few days. In fact, why bother at all? she asked herself rebelliously. The idea of damp grass on her bare feet was actually rather appealing.

CHAPTER NINE

ALTHOUGH MARCO WAS ninety-nine per cent sure that his father's command that he accompany the security detail to the airport was a ruse to provide him with an excuse to absent himself from the ball, there had been the one per cent possibility there was a legitimate reason for his presence.

This possibility quickly vanished; his royal presence was actually a hindrance to the men who knew their jobs. Marco only stayed long enough to have his suspicions confirmed, before bagging a car to drive himself back from the airport.

He'd learnt to drive in a similar open-sided soft-top Jeep. He smiled to himself as he negotiated the white-knuckle bends of the coastal road, remembering the days when being grounded for taking the off-roader onto a road, and practising his behind-the-wheel skills on this very stretch, had got him grounded.

Grounded, the worst thing in the world that, to his resentful teenage mind, could happen. *Dio*, he felt quite nostalgic for those lost days as he accelerated smoothly out of a bend in a way that only someone who knew the road like the back of his hand could.

How did life get so damned complicated?

Complications, he mused, thinking of Kate Armstrong dressed in that blue dress looking… The woman had taken up residence in his head. His had not been the only eyes following her, the only eyes admiring her fresh beauty, her glorious hair.

He didn't want her in his head. He wanted her in his bed—you couldn't get much more simple than that. He was actually creating complications where there weren't any.

And any rules he'd be breaking were of his own making. Couldn't he *unmake* them?

The party was still in full swing when he slipped back into the palace through the kitchen. He got as far as one of the corridors leading off it. This corridor was lined with cool rooms, tonight acting as a rat-run for wait staff, who stared at him and, when he stopped dead, diverted around him.

They were probably wondering what he was doing, and now Marco was asking the same question of himself. What *was* he doing? He'd been gifted his get-out-of-jail-free card by his father. Only a masochist, a madman or someone who actually enjoyed small talk, which was the same thing, would walk back into his cell and lock the door behind him.

So instead he retraced his steps, on impulse snatching a bottle of champagne from a cooler containing dozens, and headed out into the night.

He knew where he was heading but he didn't acknowledge it even to himself. Only when he reached his destination did he admit that it was not by accident.

It was by *need*.

He allowed himself to relive that sizzling moment of eye contact when all the pretence had been peeled away. He had to do something about it… Two people who wanted sex should be a straightforward thing, and to hell with the consequences, mocked the voice in his head. *Very mature.*

The simple pleasures, Kate thought with a sigh as she enjoyed the squish of the cool grass between her toes, were underrated. She rubbed her upper arms as a cooling breeze all the way from the ocean made her shiver. She found herself at one of the viewpoints scattered around the grounds. This one the nearest to the nursery wing. Eyes trained on the ocean, a dark strip beyond the glitter of the illuminated walled city of St Boniface.

A dark strip that represented miles and miles of emptiness…vast. And…she slowed her breathing, trying to emulate that emptiness, conscious of the tension loosening its grip on her body.

When she closed her eyes could she hear music or was it simply the gentle breeze in the trees? She didn't care as she let herself sway to an invisible rhythm, her dress floating around her as she dipped and whirled, head back, eyes closed. At the end of the silent melody she paused and curtsied to the invisible audience until she realised it wasn't invisible, at which point she pulled herself upright in a jerky motion, and, heart pounding, faced her audience of one.

'What are you doing here?' she snapped spikily, thinking goodbye relaxation, goodbye common sense.

'I live here. That was very pretty.' But she was not pretty. She was *beautiful*, and never more so than at that moment. He ate up the visual, committing to memory her eyes, enormous in the pale oval of her face, as she stood there looking like some sort of sexy sacrificial virgin in that dress.

Then he saw her feet and a slow smile spread across his lean face.

'To lose one shoe, Cinders, could be considered a misfortune, but to lose two…?'

She responded to his taunt with a defensive, 'I haven't lost them. I know exactly where they are.'

Pity the same could not be said of my mind, Kate mused despairingly as she struggled to remove her hungry stare from his mouth. *When was the last time I actually felt in control of my life…?* At least when she had arrived she had still had the security of knowing what was right and wrong. Now exposure to this man had blown that out of the water.

It was wrong to want him, but she did. Did that mean she was wrong about other things too?

Feelings she hadn't known she possessed had been awoken and they hurt. The constant confusion, the constant questioning, the constant yearning that made her *feel*… Feel as if she were walking on the edge of a cliff. She glanced towards a very real cliff in the distance. It didn't seem nearly as precarious as the one she was balancing on.

No wonder her nerves were shredded.

'Have you come to say goodnight to Freya?' she asked, thinking, *Have you come straight from the blonde's bed?* A question that came straight from her newly discovered jealous streak.

She silently listed the reasons she shouldn't feel jealous: firstly she had no right, and secondly… Actually, firstly was enough.

'I'm afraid she's asleep.'

'As all good girls should be at this hour…' he drawled, his voice dropping a seductive octave as he delivered a skin-tingling, 'Are you a good girl, Cinders...?'

Kate moistened her lips and swallowed, fighting the childish impulse to cover her ears to cut out the insidious sound of his beautiful voice, all honey warmth and sinful suggestion.

'I am not a *girl*, I'm a woman, and it will be a cold day in hell...' She paused, discarding the analogy. No analogy was strong enough to convey how much she *didn't* need a prince to save her. A miracle...now that was different. If there were one of those on offer she'd definitely be a taker!

Shaking her head, she walked over to a gentle mound in the grassy expanse some feet away from where he stood and sat down, her eyes directed at the distant sea view. Regaining that little window of peace she had enjoyed was, she suspected, a non-starter, but at least it was breathing space.

After a pause, Marco came over to where she sat. 'Can I join you?'

'It's a free country,' she retorted childishly, and then sighed because it was *his* country. Lucky his shoulders were broad because the idea of that much responsibility was daunting in theory, but for him it was a reality.

She stared ahead, resisting the temptation to turn her head when her tingling senses told her he had come to sit beside her, not close enough to shift her defences into the red-alert zone, but enough to make her...twitchy.

'I was just getting some fresh air,' she said when the silence became unbearable.

'Me too.' He held up the bottle he carried, tilting the tip before, with an expert twist and a gentle pop, he released the fizz.

'You've done that before.'

'Like to join me in a toast?'

'To what?' she asked, feeling as though this conversation of nothing was just a prelude... *Or foreplay*, suggested the voice in her head.

What she knew about foreplay could be written on a postage stamp.

'To fresh air?' he suggested, his eyes going from the bottle to her face. Confessing with a lopsided smile, 'I haven't got two glasses. In fact, I haven't got one.'

Something about him, the reckless combustible quality in his attitude, made her wonder if this was his first bottle.

'No, I haven't even had a sip,' he said, responding to her unspoken question. 'There we go!' He held the bottle like a trophy, before lifting it to his lips and taking two deep gulps. 'Waste not want not, is that not what you say?'

She responded to the challenge in his eyes by snatching the bottle off him and taking a large swallow, rather spoiling the effect when she choked.

'Not your first...?' he suggested, taking it back.

'I had two glasses, my limit,' she admitted.

Their eyes connected. 'So, you are playing dangerously tonight?'

A little shiver went down her spine as she veiled her eyes with her lashes. 'I'm not the type.' But there were times when she wished she were.

He took another swallow. 'Who told you that, *cara*...?' he drawled.

'I was always the sensible one at home. Jake was the emotional, reckless one.' She laughed, suddenly realising that the roles had been reversed.

'What's the joke?'

'Me?'

He arched a brow but didn't say anything as he lifted the bottle to his lips. Kate watched his brown throat work as he swallowed and felt a stab of pure lust. He put the bottle on the ground and turned his head. Caught looking, she lifted her chin, refusing to lower her gaze.

She managed to maintain eye contact for seconds until the heat in his gaze, the quickening in her blood, got too frightening. She had never felt this way, never imagined feeling this way.

For a while they sat side by side not saying anything. She'd heard of companionable silence, but this one was not. It was *dangerous* silence. It made Kate think of a pile of dry tinder waiting for a spark, and yet, despite the tension in the darkness and silence, she felt a strange connection to the man beside her.

Kate shook her head, swallowing to alleviate the dryness in her throat before she skimmed her lips quickly with the tip of her tongue.

'Tonight went well…you must be pleased.' Her voice sounded high and forced even to her own ears.

'Have I done the right thing…?' he wondered out loud. 'Or will one day my daughter curse me? You know, I never even considered that possibility. That she might not *want* to be Queen. That it is more a curse than a gift. It was a battle and I won…' The last self-condemnatory insight was muttered half to himself.

'Freya could always walk away. You could have walked away if you had wanted to.'

He turned and looked at her, a series of expressions drifting across his face. 'I suppose I could have but it never occurred to me. Duty is not an optional extra. I never fought against it, it's more like I filtered it out. Like the bodyguards, you stop noticing them.'

Kate, who felt hideously conscious of the men with guns, could not imagine that ever being true.

He saw her expression and grinned. 'It's different for me. I've always lived under a microscope. My actions always judged. I don't want to make it sound like I'm a victim. I'm not. I lead a very privileged life. I have freedom.'

'There was no pressure for an arranged marriage like your parents.'

'My parents' marriage was not arranged.'

'Oh, sorry. I just assumed…'

'Because my father keeps a mistress and my mother pretends not to notice? Yeah, I can see how you would… But no, my parents were a *love* match.' The sneer in his voice was overt. 'It was quite a scandal at the time. They were both being *encouraged* to marry other people, but people fall out of love.'

And he had thought, in his arrogance, that he had avoided the trap his parents had fallen into. If you were never in love you couldn't fall out of love. There was a lot less pain and humiliation involved in a loveless marriage. The destructive power of love had had the last laugh.

'Your father…the King…he was very polite when…'

'He is always polite. If there is anything that appears unpleasant, my mother ignores it. On paper they are the perfect couple.' On paper he and Belle had been the perfect couple.

'He looks just like his photos, very *noble*. Did you have a mistress when you…?' Her hand went to her mouth as she looked at him, her eyes wide and horrified. 'I am so sorry, that was…'

'No, it's a legitimate question, but no, I didn't. That is

not to say I wouldn't have at some stage,' he observed, self-contempt in his voice. 'Not much like your parents' marriage, I suppose.'

She gave an odd little laugh. 'My parents' marriage? I don't even know if they had one…a marriage, that is. I don't know who my parents were…are…but my mum and dad love one another. Well, I always thought they did, but then I always thought that they were my parents. I always thought I knew…' Her voice cracked.

'I don't know why I'm telling you this. Oh, God, it's so embarrassing. I really hate crying,' she gritted as she dropped her head to her chest, hiding behind the veil of flaming hair, chest heaving as she fought to contain the emotions that were leaking out of her.

Marco had been an objective observer to many tears, the majority of these calculated displays aimed at eliciting a reaction in him. The only thing they left was a nasty taste in his mouth. He dealt with these types of situations by removing himself from the scene.

Watching Kate declare her utter contempt for her tears of genuine emotion, he felt no urge to walk away, he felt an alien urge to comfort her, but his utter cluelessness of how to go about this left him feeling unaccustomedly helpless.

Lust was normally a lot simpler than this. Walking away from uncomfortable situations a lot easier too.

Placing a thumb under her chin, he tipped her face up to his and he looked into her swimming eyes. How could a person be so tough and self-sufficient and so vulnerable at the same time? A vulnerability he could see she hated owning.

'I can see why you hate it; you look terrible.' She actually looked breathtakingly beautiful.

Kate looked at him for a moment, her amber eyes

shining with indignation before she laughed at herself. 'I can be so ridiculous sometimes.'

He grinned back. 'That's better, and you're telling me because I asked.' Which was not keeping things simple. His motivation remained something of a mystery to him, unless the answer was as simple as that he simply wanted to know.

'So you discovered you were adopted recently?'

She nodded. 'My gran died.' As she began to explain the sequence of events, she realised that it was a relief. After all the weeks of bottling it up, sharing her story was cathartic, even though the recipient of her confidences was the last person she would have expected to choose. 'At least, I *thought* she was my gran. I was helping go through her papers, and I discovered our adoption papers. Discovered my entire life has been a lie. Everything changed.'

'So you and your brother—older or younger?'

'A year older.'

'You're both adopted. How did he take it?'

'He already knew.' Hurt quivered in her voice. 'He's known for years, and he didn't tell me. I thought we were so close and *he* was angry with *me*. Jake thinks I was punishing our mum and dad.'

'Are you?'

She opened her mouth to angrily deny it, and then closed it, shaking her head. 'Maybe a little,' she confessed. 'But I suddenly didn't know how to act around them. It felt surreal. Why didn't I sense it? Don't people sense these sorts of things? I think Jake did. He went looking for proof of his suspicions…went looking for his birth parents. But his mother is dead and his father has another family and didn't want to know him.'

'Poor guy. Maybe your brother wanted to save you from that.'

'I don't need saving or protecting!' she flared. 'I am more than capable of looking after myself.'

'All right, maybe they, your mum and dad, were the ones who were afraid? Maybe they were uncomfortable about telling you, and every day they didn't just compounded their guilt? I don't know, why don't you ask them?'

'I can't even talk to them. They lied.' Even she could hear the doubt in her voice.

'They messed up, but people do that every day of the week. Do you want to know who your birth parents were?'

'No. They didn't want me, why would I look for them?' She shook her head and angled a confused look at his face. 'I really don't know why I'm telling *you* this.'

'Maybe because of my warm, understanding personality…no…? Ah, well, maybe I just happened to be there when you had, what do they call it, a trigger moment?' He picked up the empty bottle, his lips quirking as he shook it and looked at her with eyes dark enough to get lost in. 'Or possibly…?' he mocked.

'If that were the case *you* would be telling *me* your deepest darkest secrets. I only had a mouthful.'

'Oh, the night is young yet, *cara*,' he teased. 'You might unlock my secrets yet.'

'It isn't…young, that is, the night,' she realised, catching sight of the face of the thin-banded watch he was wearing.

'Hold on, Cinders,' he said, catching her arm as she went to get to her feet. 'I haven't had my promised dance yet.'

Kate subsided again, her skin tingling not just where

his fingers had lain but all over. She felt the dark scratch under every inch of her body.

'Be serious,' she said, trying to sound exasperated and missing by a mile.

'I am deadly serious. Always,' he said, straight-faced, the gleam in his dark eyes making her stomach flip.

'When you've just drunk a bottle of champagne?'

He grinned and, rising in one fluid motion, dragged her with him. 'It might have taken the edge off, but no, I am not drunk. Dance with me.' He took hold of both of her hands and performed an artistic flamenco stamp.

'There is no music,' she countered, struggling to inject some sanity into this increasingly surreal conversation.

'A mere technicality.' He put one of her hands on his shoulder, then the second, before placing his on her waist.

'Are you off your meds?' she pushed out, drawing a deep growl of laughter from him. There was no corresponding laughter in his eyes. They were darkly focused...relentless.

Kate's chest heaved as she fought to compensate for the fact she'd forgotten to breathe. What she really needed was air between them, space. His proximity was doing terrible things to her nervous system. As for professional distance...the ache at the damp apex of her legs was not professional.

'You are quite beautiful.'

She wrinkled her nose, her eyes sliding from his. 'I'll take that as a yes, then.'

'You are the strangest woman I have ever met, full of contradictions.'

'Sure, I'm a real enigma,' she muttered, fighting the urge to follow him and losing as he began to move. He was actually a good dancer, but then he was one of those tedious people who were good at everything, she told herself, trying to feel scorn or even resentment but it wouldn't come. Instead her thoughts moved dangerously on to all the *other* things he might be good at.

He'd had very good reviews and even allowing for exaggeration… *Did she want to find out?*

'There, you can hear it now too.'

'No,' she said, fighting hard to retain a grip. But, as if pre-programmed, her body had started to follow his lead.

One hand placed, long fingers spread, in the small of her back, his hooded eyes darkened as she responded to the slightest of increases in pressure. Stepping into him until they were so close there was no oxygen between them.

Kate made a conscious effort to breathe, focus, afraid she might forget and fall in a dead faint at his feet. He was all warmth and solid slabs of muscle.

Her skin prickled, her insides dissolved, her heart climbed into her throat, the spreading tingle of excitement igniting and spreading across the surface of her skin, the sensation as though she had woken up from a dream to discover it wasn't a dream, it was real.

Desire pumping through his body in a steady logic-destroying stream, he held her eyes with his bold black hypnotic stare. Watching her face as he ground the bold imprint of his erection against the softness of her belly, watching with a smile of predatory pleasure her pupils eat up the gold.

His action drew a shocked gasp from Kate as she felt the heat between them reach scalding point. The air around them seemed to shimmer with the combustion they were creating. Shimmer with the passion that burned away any sense of self-preservation she might have retained. She was deep, *deep*, and lost inside to-hell-with-the-consequences territory.

She watched, her eyelids heavy, the ache between her legs throbbing, and as his sensuous mouth came down she stretched up, greedy for the contact. When it came, the slow, sensuous, skilled seduction of his mouth just fed the urgency building inside her. She wanted more. The passion was like nothing she had ever experienced, nothing she had ever dreamed existed.

He bit into the lush softness of her lower lip, sliding his tongue into her mouth, as they continued to drift around. Moving in slow, lazy, ever-decreasing circles until they were not moving at all.

Her curves had automatically acclimated themselves into his hard angles, their bodies sealed. Her entire body quivered with the expectation of what happened next. They were standing still, Kate's head tilted, her hands cushioned between them, pressed flat against the hard barrier of his chest. Everything locked, including their eyes.

He traced the angle of her jaw and ran his fingers down the extended column of her creamy neck, brushing his lips against the blue-veined pulse point before he kissed her as though he wanted to drain her. Fine tremors ran through his powerful body, as if the effort to contain the need and hunger driving him was making him shake.

'I want to take your clothes off,' he purred throatily. 'I want to see you, touch you… I want to be inside you, *cara*, I want to have you hold me there all night.'

His teasing words made her whimper, made the wet core of her sex ache as she rubbed her body against him, while she struggled to get any words past the occlusion in her throat.

'Not here…'

He looked at her face, the driven need in his drawing the golden skin tight against his marvellous bones, and nodded, then, without a word, scooped her up into his arms and strode off towards the building.

To the victor goes the spoils.

The words drifted through her head, except this was not a war and there was not some unwilling prize…victim. She was an eager partner in this seduction.

They encountered no one on their way to her flat. She was past caring if they had. She kissed him, their hot breaths mingling, as he collided with the wall and items of furniture along the way.

Marco put her on her feet beside her bed and as she stood there shivering, not with cold but with the need that was sweeping through her, he left her side to turn the big key in the lock, turning at the last moment.

'I have no discovery fantasies…unless you do?'

The lines fanning out from his eyes deepened as he watched her eyes go round with horror at the idea of someone walking in on them.

'I've always thought if you were doing it properly you wouldn't notice. Don't worry. I have other fantasies though, always happy to share,' he rasped wickedly as he came back to join her. Then, leaning in close to kiss her, he whispered against her lips, 'Do you have fantasies, Kate?'

She responded with the simple truth. 'You're my fantasy.'

He said something in Italian, the stark hissed meaning pretty clear as, holding her eyes, he reached for the zip on her dress, sliding it all the way down. She shivered as his fingers, cool against her own, moved over heated skin, brushed the flesh in the small of her back, spreading out across the curve of her tight bottom.

His eyes only left hers when he slid the thin straps over the curve of her smooth shoulders and watched the dress fall to the ground at her feet in a silken heap.

Standing there in the strapless bra and pants, she felt a flurry of uncertainty. Her toes curled and her hands clenched as the silence stretched. Was he shocked by her skinniness, the jutting bones, the lack of curves, not at all what he had been used to?

'You are even more beautiful than I imagined and I've been imagining since the first moment I saw you. These are very pretty,' he purred, sliding a teasing clever finger under the silk of her bra, causing her nipples to instantly pucker and harden painfully.

The intensity of his stare made things shift deep inside and fed the increasingly urgent signals zinging between her nerve endings.

'You are so sensitive,' he observed with gloating approval. 'I *need* your skin,' he growled throatily as he trailed a kiss over the gentle curve of her cleavage before peeling back the bra cups and allowing his eyes to feast on the perfect oval mounds of coral-tipped flesh. While he was unclipping her bra he bent his head to suckle and tease the hardened peak into even more aching prominence, sending shards of pleasure through Kate's body as she arched her back, her fingers sliding into his thick pelt of hair to hold him against her as she squirmed against him and began to pull at his clothes, frustrated beyond reason by the layers separating them.

He absorbed the softness of her body like a man finding water in the desert.

Her eager hands were clutching everywhere, not

slickly, but desperate and clumsy, tearing a button, clutching at his behind, digging in, her breath coming in a series of uneven gasps and sighs.

Marco felt as if he were in an inferno. He had never wanted a woman the way he wanted Kate, never experienced this elemental level of need, a need that involved every nerve ending, every fibre.

She finally found some skin and pressed her lips to the golden section of chest, finding his pebble-hard nipple, his deep, almost animal groan shocking and exciting her, filling her with a sense of glorious female power she had never experienced before.

The primal emotions ripping through her made her knees shake and then it didn't matter because she was on her back on the bed and he was peeling the silk knickers down her thighs.

He stared at her body, the pale skin, the tight apple-sized perfect breasts, the fuzz of red between her legs. He was utterly transfixed, freed only when he encountered the silent plea in her eyes.

CHAPTER TEN

KATE'S BREASTS QUIVERED with each shallow breath as she watched Marco rip off his clothes, revealing his bronzed chest but taking longer to release his erection from his shorts.

She stared, the fist low in her belly tightening. She was utterly consumed by a primitive hunger, a need she had no words to express. He was quite simply beautiful. A perfect classical statue brought to warm, wonderful glowing life, each muscle perfectly defined under a warm wonderful skin.

He joined her then, arranging his long length beside her before pulling her to him. The first skin-to-skin contact drew a low keening cry from her throat.

Her back arched as his tongue slid between her parted lips while one hand moved in delicate arabesques down her back along the ridges of her spine, the other kneading the tender flesh of one breast before his mouth replaced it.

She touched him, no science or finesse to her actions, just feverish hunger for his body and an endless fascination as her hands lowered.

He pulled in a hard breath as her fingers curled around his erection, tightening around him. He stroked her arms, a feather-light touch all the way up to her chin as he found her lips. The whispered words against her mouth, forbidden exciting words, the more so because they were in a language she didn't understand, but she didn't need to.

Throbbing, he pulled away from her touch and slid his fingers into the soft wet curls at the apex of her legs, which parted to allow him to deepen the exploration as he slid one finger into her.

'You're so tight,' he murmured as her back arched to deepen his penetration. His hand still between her legs, he reached for his trousers, digging a foil package out of the slim leather clip inside before returning to her.

His nostrils flared as he stared down into her sex-flushed face, her pleasure-glazed eyes.

'Please,' she begged.

Face taut with need, he slid on the condom with a shaking hand and parted her legs, wrapping them around him as he bent over her. She felt suspended in time as she waited and then he entered her. Her body resisted just for a fraction of a second and then it expanded to accommodate him.

Kate's eyes closed as she sank deep into herself, awareness of her own body heightened in a way she had never experienced, each nerve ending quivering as he continued to stroke to reach places she had not known existed.

The words in her ear sounded like praise and encouragement as she arched into him, her fingers sliding over the sweat-slicked muscles of his back and shoulders. He was sliding over her, her skin was as hot and damp as his with the exertion of maintaining the increasingly frantic rhythm, then everything went crazy mad, and she got whisked away by a series of deep contractions that reached her toes.

Her cry of astonished pleasure was lost in his mouth.

He lay on top of her while they both fought for breath. She missed the weight when he rolled away and lay there, one hand above his head, breathing hard.

Waiting, he rubbed the ring on his finger, knowing there was always a price to pay for the pleasure of sex. The escape from his demons was only ever temporary, guilt always found him.

When nothing happened to disturb a feeling that was as close to peace as he had experienced in a long time, he turned his head. Kate smiled at him with lips swollen from his kisses, her eyes still languid and sparkling with an uncomplicated happiness that under normal circumstances he would have thought fake, but hers wasn't.

'You look very pleased with yourself.' If some major hang-ups had kept her a virgin, she was displaying no signs of them.

'I'm very pleased with you… That was… Thank you. I really didn't know it could be like that.'

'You gave yourself to me… I was your first.' It was a precious gift that he was not deserving of, but had he been offered it again, knowing what a mind-blowing experience it would be, he doubted he would have refused it.

'Mm, I suppose that does seem a bit weird. I didn't set out to stay a virgin, it's not some life choice,' she promised him earnestly. 'It just never happened, and I always thought I wasn't very…you know, I was a bit of a cold fish.'

If she had met Marco when she was eighteen there would have been no waiting.

'I have a very low opinion of the men in your life, *cara*,' he said, sounding justifiably smug.

'Not them, me,' she said, her face serious. 'I have had a…' Her nose wrinkled. 'A *tick-box* attitude to life. That probably sounds stupid, but I never realised that you can't score everything safe or unsafe, right or wrong. Some things are wrong on so many levels but yet they are marvellously, gloriously right!' Her face melted into a smile. 'I feel quite liberated.' *Also sad.* Not that she would let it spoil this moment, but she knew Marco's modus operandi, so she knew that it wasn't the start of anything marvellous, more a glimpse into what she could have had.

'I am wrong on so many levels?'

'Too many to count but you are so right…that was so right.'

'You know that this is just sex, Kate?'

She ignored the stab of hurt and rolled her eyes. 'You mean you're not going to marry me? Oh, I'm devastated,' she drawled, her eyes sparking with anger. Why did he have to ruin her perfect moment? 'But don't worry, I'll get my revenge by bad-mouthing you online.'

'I've annoyed you.' She really did look magnificent angry. Despite the fact the sweat of exertion had not dried on his skin, he felt a kick of lust.

'Why would that be? It's only fair, given there's only one of you, that you share your *magnificence* around, and I'm not greedy.'

A low rumble of laughter vibrated in the barrel of his chest as he went to grab for her, but she pulled away, sitting up in one energetic bound, her glorious hair falling in a fiery cloak over her shoulders, allowing a tempting peek of one tight nipple.

'Granted it's awkward, given my position here. But do you really think I need it spelling out that this was a one-night stand?'

'We could get around awkward.'

She stared down at him. 'You want to do this—' her gesture took in the tumbled bedclothes '—again?'

'You're blushing.'

'I'm not,' she denied crossly. 'You want to have sex again? I didn't know you did again.'

His eyes glowed wickedly. 'Five minutes, maybe two, and I'll disprove that theory.'

It took a couple of seconds for his meaning to crystallise. 'Oh! You know what I mean…how many times?'

He turned his head and laughed. 'You intend keeping count with bedpost notches?'

'I meant—'

'I know what you meant and I know these things generally have a natural life span…they're self-limiting.'

'So, you want to sleep with me until *I* lose interest.'

He took the *I* on board and his eyes glittered with amusement. 'All right, my ego has been known to get ahead of me…until *you* lose interest?' For the first time it crossed his mind that she might say no.

'I'd love to do that again, but only—'

'You have conditions,' he said, sounding astonished at the role reversal.

'I don't want anyone to know. I don't want people to look at me and think the things they do about Rosa.'

'People respect—'

'To her face,' she interrupted, 'they show respect. I know what people think because,' she admitted, shame-faced, 'I did, a bit anyhow.'

He shrugged. 'So, you want to sneak around? That could work, in fact it might add a frisson.'

'I don't need a frisson. I just need you, and if *you* need a frisson, I don't want you.'

'Come here,' he growled. 'And I'll show how much I don't need a frisson.'

A bike ride with the Queen, a woman forty years her senior? Kate had assumed she could take it in her stride. It was actually a relief to fall off and be excused the rest of the ride.

Kate dabbed some antiseptic on the graze and flopped down on the sofa, happy to enjoy a little downtime. Freya was on a play date with her new little friend and she had the afternoon to herself.

In theory.

She had enjoyed about three minutes' alone time when Marco appeared, or, more correctly, exploded into the room.

'You have had an accident!' he accused, seemingly annoyed to find her with all her limbs intact and a chunk of chocolate halfway to her mouth.

'No…well, not really. I came off my bike before I actually expired from exhaustion. Your mother is a very fit lady. A few scratches is all.'

'Oh,' he said, losing some of the high-energy tension that had accompanied him into the room and looking almost self-conscious.

'I thought you had meetings all afternoon.'

'I did, I cancelled. Where is Freya?'

'A play date.'

'So, we are all alone.' He looked at her curled up like a kitten and felt the need rise up in him, the need to lose himself in her. The craving was like a flood tide rising.

The moments when it was possible to satisfy the hunger she evoked in him were infrequent enough to frustrate him. Without realising it, he had fallen into a pattern of planning his weeks and days around moments like this, scheming, plotting to have time alone… The subterfuge had lost its appeal.

The knowledge that she was ashamed to have anyone know of their affair, that she was in some way ashamed of him, was really eating away at him.

It wasn't as if he wanted to take out a full-page ad to announce they were having sex, or shout it from the rooftops. Her obsession with secrecy was making a big thing out of something that wasn't… It was just sex.

Just sex. He recognised his rationalisation was becoming increasingly difficult to make, because this *just sex* had nothing in common with any *just sex* he had ever experienced before. With Kate he was feeling things he had never experienced before, that he had never allowed himself to feel before.

This should have been the ideal situation. Great sex, a beautiful woman who made no demands, but he wanted more. He didn't have a clue what more he wanted, but he did. There was a secret corner in his heart that craved something he refused to name, something that he felt he was close to when he was in her warm tight body, when he felt whole for the first time in his life.

He pushed away the thoughts. Need for her overwhelmed his disquiet that this was dangerous territory, an emotional minefield.

He bent over, kissing her as he slid a hand under her shirt and up over the warmth of her stomach until he found a breast. He weighed it in his palm, and stroked the peak with his thumb. It fitted perfectly in his hand.

'Did you lock the door?' she whispered, pushing her fingers into his dark hair but holding back as he bent in to claim her mouth.

They had been very careful but if she was honest the appeal of the illicit-thrill thing had worn off very quickly. Not so the great mind-blowing sex. Fear of when he would get tired of that lurked in the edges of her mind, unacknowledged but revealing itself more and more often of late.

She had taken great pains not to be seen as a royal mistress, but wasn't that what she was?

She was tired of the physical hiding, but more than that she was tired of pretending that she hadn't fallen deeply in love with Marco. She knew that the truth would end it all and she wasn't ready for that.

'What if I didn't?'

'You're angry?'

'I'm tired of this creeping around,' he flared without warning as he began prowling across the room with the leashed power of a big sleek jungle cat he made her think of.

Kate felt a nervous flutter in her stomach. Was this where it ended? She'd told herself she was ready for this moment and now it was here, she knew she wasn't. She knew she never would be. She loved him and when she lost him her life would be scarily empty.

He stopped, exhausted from fighting feelings he couldn't bring himself to acknowledge. 'Oh, hell, I'm sorry, it's been a foul day and... *Dio*, Kate, take me to bed.'

They took each other, stumbling across the sitting room, shedding clothes as they went, ending in her bed.

He watched her slide sinuously down his body, allowing her mouth and hands to drive him to the brink before he twisted her under and reversed their positions, entering her in one swift hard thrust, her body arched up under him to meet him.

A while later they lay in a tangle of sweat-slicked limbs.

I love you, she whispered in her head. Sad beyond measure because she knew that if she spoke those words out loud, the words she ached to say, she would lose him.

Marco entered the apartment, his dark hair ruffled from the five-minute energetic kick-around with his daughter, and called out Kate's name.

There was no reply.

He knew she was here; the nursery nurse supervising Freya's play session had given out the information readily enough when he had casually asked her whereabouts.

She had complied, but behind the respectful smile he had been left with the distinct impression that the *casual* wasn't working. His brow furrowed. He knew how much Kate hated the idea of gossip but he had thought of a possible solution. He was working out the best way to sell it to Kate, who was not always taken by logic.

In fact, for someone who considered herself practically minded she positively embraced illogic, which was fine so long as she carried on embracing him.

Marco found himself in the unique position of having nothing to compare to the sex he enjoyed with Kate, because it wasn't like any sex he'd had, and he'd thought he'd seen it all, done it all, short of falling in love.

Love was a no-go area that he had spent his entire adult life staying clear of, and now…he wasn't in *love* with Kate?

How would you know?

He laughed at the question in his head, swerving

away sharply from that line of thought. The fact was he couldn't be in love because if he had been he'd be running in the opposite direction, and he wasn't. So why not enjoy what they had, explore it and not worry about labels while it lasted?

A furrow formed in his wide brow. It was lasting—was that significant? Boredom should have set in by now, but it hadn't. On the contrary, his *need*, his *appetite* for her had only increased over the weeks.

Some days he was…*counting the minutes*?

He made himself wait. Masochism or just to prove he *could*? Luckily, he was not into self-analysis, and he didn't need deprivation to up his libido. All that took was the thought of touching her glorious skin, of kissing her mouth when it tasted of him, of hearing that guttural little lost whimper in the back of her throat, of seeing the glazed heat in her eyes when she came.

The list of what turned him on was endless.

Walking towards the bedroom, shedding his jacket, he called her name again and pushed open the door. His smile immediately faded. He felt icy fingers in his belly.

'What are you doing?'

'Oh, I'm so glad you're here!' she exclaimed.

Some of the tension left his shoulders, then she turned and he saw she had been crying, before she literally hurled herself at his chest. His arms came around her as her head tucked under his chin.

'What has happened? Tell me,' he said, struggling with the surge of protectiveness that was too strong for him to deny ownership of.

She wanted to stay there for ever…feel his arms around her even if the safety was an illusion… She took a breath and eased herself free, struggling for composure as she tilted her head up to look at him. As their glances locked his hands slid down her arms before dropping away.

'I had a phone call from Jake,' she revealed quietly.

A dangerous scowl settled on his lean features. 'Your brother has upset you!'

Kate saw his dark expression and added quickly, 'No, not in that way. We have actually sort of made up. But he rang to give me bad news. Mum had a stroke, not serious apparently, transient something…but…well, it is considered a warning. I must have caused it, the worry about me and—'

'It is not *your* fault.'

Her slender shoulders lifted, and her lips twisted in anxiety. 'That's what Jake says, he said the doctor had suggested lifestyle changes because of her high blood pressure, a year ago or more, but she just laughed it off. The doctor also prescribed her medication, for her blood pressure and cholesterol, but she didn't tell anyone and she hasn't been taking them.'

'So *not* your fault, then.'

'If I'd been there, she might have told me, and I would have persuaded her.'

'Your mother is an adult, as stubborn, it seems, as her daughter, and she made a choice. Now hopefully she will make a better choice. It sounds like she has a second chance. Not everyone does.'

She gave a sniff and, tucking her hair behind her ears, stepped back, glancing towards the bed and the pile of clothes she'd been bundling into her case. 'I suppose you're right.'

'I am *always* right,' he corrected, hoping to make her laugh, or hit him… She managed a watery smile.

'So you are going home?' He was prepared for it,

which didn't mean he had to like the idea. Freya would miss her, he told himself, not willing to make any further admission even to himself—especially to himself.

She nodded. 'Of course. They need me.'

It was the right thing to do, and he would not have expected otherwise of her, but there was a selfish part of him that wanted to say, *What about me? What about what I need?*

It's always about you, Marco, mocked the voice in his head.

'I will arrange—'

'Oh, it's all right. I explained the situation to Luca so that he could make arrangements for someone to stand in for me with Freya. My flight is all in hand apparently.'

He watched as she began to methodically fold items of clothing and stack them in her case. 'I wonder what the weight limit is—'

'There is no weight limit. Luca will be arranging for you to fly in one of our private jets.'

She wheeled round, astonishment written on her oval face. 'But—'

'Why did you tell Luca and not me?' That she had reached out to his assistant, albeit a very superior assistant about to be promoted to the post of their ambassador in the UK, troubled him more than he was prepared to admit.

Kate had too much on her mind to register his accusatory tone. She was trying not to think of saying goodbye to Freya. She had grown to love that child. Her eyes slid to the man she also loved… *Love crept up while I wasn't looking.* The words that had been going through her head while she packed shouted in her head. 'I didn't want to bother you.'

'Did it occur to you I'd want to be bothered?'

His tone made her turn, with a folded skirt pressed to her chest, a puzzled frown pleating her brow. 'Honestly, no, it didn't, Marco,' she said quietly, before turning back to her packing.

Presenting him her back was not accidental. She didn't want him to see or even suspect the tears pressing to be released, the emotions narrowing her throat.

She was a woman who had always prided herself on being self-sufficient and able to stand on her own feet. To admit the weakness was totally unacceptable and, besides, not an option.

Turning to Marco in moments of need was not the relationship they had. He had made no secret of the fact that he wanted sex with no complications. That involved no hand-holding, so his apparent indignation now was hard to stomach, she decided angrily. As if it weren't hard enough as it was, hiding the extent of her feelings, without him blurring the lines he himself had drawn.

She had worked hard at acceptance. It hadn't been easy for her. It would have been easy if she had allowed herself to read something that wasn't there into their intimacy—taking the shared laughter for tenderness, the mind-bending lust for love—and drift into a world where princes fell for the nanny. But in the real world the Prince was in love with his lost one true love.

Kate intended to live in the real world too, the one where you enjoyed it while it lasted and then felt sad, maybe even bereft, who knew? But it was her decision to take what was on offer and accept the consequences.

She needed his attitude like a… Her lips compressed. She didn't need it full stop!

'How long do you think you'll be gone?'

She paused. 'I'm not sure. It depends.'

She finished her packing methodically, aware of him moving around the room until she could bear it no more. 'Will you please stop pacing?'

'Will you stop messing with those clothes?' he retorted, grabbing a silk shirt out of her hand and dropping it to the floor. It landed on his foot.

'That was childish,' she said when he ground it into the floor.

He looked at her for a long moment, his chest lifting as if the effort of forming the words were an effort akin to running a marathon.

'Are you coming back?'

The silence stretched. She could feel the pressure of it pounding in her ears. 'I don't know,' she admitted quietly.

'So you've thought about it!'

'Don't take that tone with me. I'm not one of your minions,' she snapped back, ignoring the fact she had never heard him be less than scrupulously polite to people who couldn't answer back.

'Of course I've thought about it.'

'I thought so!'

'You sound like you've caught me stealing the silver. Obviously, I've thought about it. I'm going and I don't know for how long. It's a natural break, a clean break.'

The thought of returning only to discover that he had moved on with someone else or just no longer wanted her was too horrifying to contemplate.

To simply slide back into the nanny role was not an option.

'Freya…'

'No!' She shoved her clenched hands in the pockets

of her already snug-fitting jeans simply to stop herself hitting him as she advanced on him, making Marco think of a stalking feral cat, elegant and hissing. Even at that moment he could not but help appreciate the tight rounded curves of her bottom.

'Do not dare use Freya,' she hissed.

His head reared at the suggestion he would use his daughter, then he saw the tears standing out in her golden eyes and his antagonism fled, leaving behind an aching, a *bewildering* need to hold her, kiss away the tears.

'And do not try and guilt me out!' she snapped back.

'I wasn't. I was simply going to say that we both will miss you,' he said, not quite meeting her eyes. 'But if you want to go nobody is stopping you.'

She moistened her lips. How much, she wanted to yell, how much will *you* miss me?

The depressing answer was probably not much and not for long, whereas she would miss him for ever. Even thinking of it made the world lose its colour. The thought of her Marco-free sepia-tinged future.

'Well, it was going to happen some time, you said so yourself.'

'Did I?'

'Self-limiting? Natural lifespan? Should I go on?' She might have been flattered by his sudden desire to keep her with him had she not been fully aware the thing he objected to was not her going, but her going at a time that wasn't one of his choosing. When he was done with her there would be no long goodbye. She knew that Marco didn't do sentiment. He could be utterly ruthless.

'I will miss Freya too,' she said, her voice thick with emotion and unshed tears. 'I love her.'

She saw something flare in his eyes but a moment later they were shielded by his long, extravagant lashes. 'I know you do.'

'But we both know that when you…we…move on, my position here would be untenable. People know… the little looks. I walk into a room and they stop talking. They know, so it's going to happen some time.' Her shoulders lifted in a fake philosophical shrug. 'So why not now? I don't want to turn into Rosa.'

'I have no desire to move on, as you so euphemistically put it.' His slate-hard eyes held hers. 'Do you?' he challenged. 'You showed no desire to move on last night or—'

'Fine, point taken and no,' she admitted. 'But I don't want to drift into a situation where…' Frustration welled up inside her and the words burst out of her. 'I do want to move on to something…*more*…but you won't, Marco, you *can't*, not while you are in love with a ghost!' she finished breathlessly.

The breath hissed through his teeth as his jaw clenched. 'You know nothing about my wife or my marriage.' His voice, low and quivering with emotion, held more anger than a bellow of fury.

She bit hard into her quivering lower lip. 'I do not need it spelling out that I can't compete, and I don't want to!' She looked at the ring on his finger. 'I just pity the woman you do marry one day because she won't stand a chance, will she?'

He didn't deny it, why would he? He never had. He'd offered her no-strings sex and she had accepted the terms. This was always going to happen. There had always been a moment when she was going to find herself standing there saying goodbye to the man she loved. Leaving her heart behind and putting on a happy face.

To hell with happy faces, she decided, feeding her growing resentment.

'True, which is part of the reason I think…'

She looked at him blankly, jolted free of her dark self-pitying thoughts. 'You think?'

'I think why wait, to get married?'

She went quite pale with reaction as his meaning sank in. 'You're getting married—should I ask who the lucky lady is?'

'There is no one,' he said, sounding impatient. 'It will take me months to vet a candidate.'

She let out a whistling sound of mockery. 'And they say romance is dead!'

His lips thinned with annoyance at her flippancy. 'People search for love, but love causes more pain than anything else in a marriage. My mother and father were in love and look how that ended. Belle loved me and…'

'What happened to you was tragic,' she said quietly, her empathy for his pain almost unbearable. 'But you can't blame love.'

'It *happened* to Belle, not me.'

'This fixation you have on a loveless marriage to stay faithful to Belle… I don't see how it will work. What are you going to do? Get your bride to pass a lie-detector test? That was irony, by the way, not a suggestion.'

'I have no fixation. Marriage is a contract. I can get sex anywhere!' She winced and he grimaced. 'I did not mean you.'

'You didn't mean that I'm easy? You know, Marco, not everyone in the world conflates love and sex.'

'They do, you have no idea how rare your attitude is.'

Kate could only stare. To think she had worried that he would see through her facade. 'My attitude, really?'

'Absolutely, a healthy attitude. Why look for a woman who won't fall in love when she is standing here?'

Kate resisted the temptation to look over her shoulder.

'You must see the pluses. It would be the ideal solution,' he added, warming to his theme. 'Freya loves you, we have great sex, you probably know me better than anyone…' He paused, the furrow between his dark brows deepening. Sometimes it felt as if they had known one another for years not weeks. 'And there would never be the worry that you have unrealistic expectations.'

'Like love you mean?' He acted as if he were offering her some perfect solution, not a nightmare life of lies.

Her tone made him frown. 'Don't make up your mind now. Think about it.'

'Have you any idea how much I hate your *reasonable* tone?' she asked him, delivering a rot-in-hell glare. 'I don't need time. The answer is a big fat no. I resent being considered the marriage equivalent of convenience food. What about what I want from life? I don't think love is fiction. I think it is a real, breathing reality!

'Your parents married for love. And,' she added, cutting off his interruption with a wave of her hand, 'it turned out badly. *You* married for love and it turned out tragically, but you think I should be denied that opportunity and settle—for what? *You?*'

His jaw quivered as he fought to make allowances for her attitude, her irrational response. She had just had bad news so it was probably not the best timing.

'So let's bring this spectacularly awful proposal to an end. I've made up my mind. I'm not coming back.'

His features froze over. 'If you think I'm going to beg you to stay…'

The idea had genuinely never crossed her mind. 'I

think you will have forgotten I even existed before I walk, or actually *run*, through that door.'

He didn't say no so she took it as given.

'You know something, Marco, the next time you think your analytical brain is so bloody brilliant that you are tempted to believe your own PR machine, remember this—you just proposed to a woman who loves you...' She pressed her clenched fists against her chest and pushed out passionately. 'I love you, you stupid man, now get lost and think what a lucky escape you've had.'

'I don't want to go and see Grandpa, I want Kate. I miss Kate...' Freya wailed as she released her father's hand.

'I have explained that Kate has her own family and she has gone to see them.'

'Kate is my family...she is mine. Get her back for me. Has Kate gone to heaven like Mummy?'

Marco dropped to his knees beside the weeping child, his heart in bits. 'Oh, baby, no, she hasn't...she's in England.'

'You swear?' The little girl sniffed. 'Cross your heart?'

Marco solemnly did just that. 'Kate has other people in her life. We have to share the people we love sometimes.'

'I don't want to share her. I miss her! It's not the same without Kate here.'

A thousand images of Kate slid through his head. The feelings rose up in him so strongly that he forgot to breathe.

'I miss her too.' The admission came from some place deep inside him where a secret corner of his heart had always longed for all the things he had denied himself over the years. The things that Kate had given him: love and a family.

All the things he had denied himself out of fear of failing, of being hurt…like he wasn't hurting now!

'You do? Then will you bring her back, Papa?'

He nodded slowly. 'I will try.' *If I haven't left it too late?* He shook his head. He wouldn't, he couldn't, let himself believe that their moment had gone, that he had thrown away his one hope of happiness.

The thought of being alone again terrified him.

'Now you go to see Grandpa while I…' he began, his thoughts already moving ahead.

'You're going to get Kate, Papa. You won't forget?'

'I won't forget.'

Marco put his head around the door of his assistant's office where two young women and a man seated in a semi-circle around Luca were hanging on Luca's every word.

'Luca, a word.'

His assistant followed him back into the adjoining room.

'I am going to England, the Dorset house, I think. Oh, and I'm taking Freya with me, so her things will need to be packed.'

'There is a skeleton staff, but it will be… The security will need to be…' The younger man began thinking out loud, breaking off when he realised what he was doing. 'So when are you thinking of making the trip?'

'Tomorrow morning.'

The young man swallowed, but he had been working too long for the Crown Prince to make the error of saying anything along the lines of *impossible*.

'I need some information. I'll email the details over.'

'Fine, sir,' he said, walking into his office and addressing the heads that lifted at his entrance. 'Anyone with any plans for tonight, cancel.'

CHAPTER ELEVEN

KATE AND HER mum crossed the finish line hand in hand for the five-kilometre park run.

Kate, hands clenched against her thighs, fought for breath.

'I let you win,' her mum, in a similar position, claimed as she slugged down the contents of her water bottle before regressing to her maternal nagging role. 'Hydrate, Kate.'

'Whose idea was this?' Kate asked as she arranged her broken, or at least seriously bruised, body down on the grass.

'Yours.'

Kate propped her head on one arm and closed her eyes. 'And the doctor really signed off on this?'

'He *encouraged* this,' her mum retorted. 'It's important to stretch during cool down, Kate.'

Kate rolled her eyes and groaned.

'Now, where are your dad and Jake?'

'I don't care.' Despite the contention, Kate raised herself on one elbow. 'They were…'

'Kate, what's wrong?'

Kate said nothing. Either hallucination was a common by-product of Lycra and over-exertion, or the Crown Prince of Renzoi was standing there in conversation with her brother and dad. Did hallucinations laugh? Because hers were.

It didn't feel like much of a joke to Kate.

Her mum was shading her eyes and squinting. 'Who is that extraordinarily good-looking man talking to your dad and Jake?'

'That's Marco,' Kate said, in a flat, expressionless voice.

'Marco?'

'He was my…boss.'

'The Prince! My, what a coincidence. It really is a small world.'

Kate envied her mum her innocence. It was *not* a small world. It was a big, massive, diverse world, and no coincidence had brought Marco here today.

Speculating what had sent her thoughts in a dizzying spin. 'I feel sick,' she said faintly.

'I told you to take on more fluids.'

Kate gave a weak laugh.

Her mum looked stern as she stretched her quads. 'Seriously, Kate.'

'Your mother is right…it is science.'

Kate felt her eyes fill with tears. 'How is Freya?' she asked huskily.

'She is going to join us for supper.'

She stared at him and thought, *Back up there, mate.* 'I am not having supper with you.' She struggled rather inelegantly to pull herself up from her prone position. Once sitting, she drew her knees up to her chest and she glared up at him.

'Go away!'

'Kate!' Her mum sounded outraged.

'Mrs Armstrong, I am delighted to meet you.'

'Well, she's not delighted to meet you, so why don't you just push off?'

'Katherine! My daughter has not been herself, Your…'

Marco nodded. 'Actually, I have not been myself either, and it is not a bad thing.'

Her mother gave a wary smile. 'Well, I will leave you young people to…' She broke off as a person wearing a mini telephone box on his head, who appeared not to have read the *fun* part of the race, huffed past, yelling, 'Obstruction!'

'I really am not sure if that is totally in the spirit of the thing at all. Your father has my energy drink. I'll save you some.'

'God, let me die now.'

'Your mother looks well, you look less…'

'She trained. I didn't.' She gave a tremulous little sigh, hating that part of her wanting to beg him to stay, beg him never to leave her again.

But *she* had left and it was the right thing to do. The right thing felt absolutely mind-bogglingly miserable.

'What are you doing here, Marco?' she asked, rising to her full and not very impressive height. What she lacked in aches she made up for in imperious disdain, and Lycra made her feel taller.

He was impressive though, another scale of impressive—his sheer physicality made her stomach muscles lurch. She felt like a recovering addict coming face to face with her drug of choice.

'Your mother is well?'

Kate nodded.

Her mother had taken the warning to heart. She had turned into a health zealot. Kate had her every mouthful critiqued for nutritional value. She knew more about ketogenic deficit, good fats and the benefits of a Mediterranean diet, the last being the only fun part of the whole re-education process.

There had been a lot of education going on. For the first time, Kate had pushed through her hurt and asked questions about her adoption, and then listened to the answers.

They had *intended* to tell her, they'd explained, but the perfect moment had never arrived and they had been afraid that she would feel rejected and different. Kate found she could accept they had been trying to protect her. How could she stay angry with people who loved her so much? Nobody made the right choices all the time. She had made some massive wrong choices of her own.

'Very well, thank you.' Aware that her face had to be shiny with sweat, she surreptitiously dabbed her upper lip with her sleeve and drank him in. The vibrancy of his skin, the razor-blade sharpness of his cheekbones, the silver grey of his eyes and the beautiful sexy outline of his sensual lips.

'Why are you here, Marco?'

He looked around. 'Is there somewhere a little more private we can talk?'

'No.' The last thing in the world she wanted was to be alone with Marco. It was also the thing she wanted most in the world as well.

The guarded expression in her beautiful eyes made him realise how much he had hurt her; his levels of self-disgust rose. 'Fair enough, but…' He glanced around and saw a bench set under a large horse-chestnut tree. 'Can we sit?'

He waited for her to step ahead of him and they walked across to the shady bench and sat down.

'Is Freya all right? Nothing is…'

'She misses you, but she is well. You and your parents, your brother…?'

'We have talked and it is…*better*. It's not an overnight process but we are working through it…'

And Kate had realised that to save Freya a moment's pain, a child who she had not given birth to, she would have lied her head off, that had been the game changer.

'Why are you here, Marco?' she asked, studying his face with hungry eyes, seeing the lines bracketing his mouth that seemed deeper and the dark smudges under his eyes.

'I missed you.'

She blinked. 'You did?' she said cautiously, damping down her ridiculous optimism. The last awful two weeks ought, if she had a brain cell in her head, to have killed her optimism stone dead.

'I want… Well, first I want to correct a few misconceptions. Firstly…'

'That is not necessary.' The last thing she needed was to be told how he was right and she was wrong. 'I know you like the last word, but—'

'Stop talking!'

'What?'

'I… My marriage to Belle, it was not a great love match and I am not a tragic hero. Belle and I were… We watched our respective parents' marriages go down the drain. We made a youthful vow never to fall in love.' He shook his head at the memory. 'We were friends. I cared for her, valued her as a friend.'

'How is that possible? Everyone says that…?'

He saw her shiver and slid off the jacket he was wearing, draping it over her shoulders. 'You need to keep your muscles warm.'

She wasn't cold, but she liked the second-hand warmth of his skin in the fabric and the smell of his signature fragrance. 'But I thought—People say—'

'I know what people say,' he cut in with a cynical smile. 'We had the perfect marriage, never a cross word...?'

She nodded.

'No expectations, no disappointments, that was what our marriage was meant to be about, but Belle did love me. I think there were clues, but I didn't see them, didn't want to.

'I loved her, but I was not *in* love with her. And I hurt her, she was my dearest friend, the mother of my child and I hurt her.'

'Oh, Marco!'

'Belle married me, believing she could make me love her. She got pregnant because she thought a baby, an heir would... But I couldn't love her. I didn't think I could love anyone.

'At the end, she was too ill to even hold Freya. There was... It was chaos.' He closed his eyes to blank the images playing in his head. 'She would have grown to love Freya so much. I know she would.'

Kate caught his hand, took it between both of hers and raised it to her lips. 'Of course she would.'

'One day Freya will know that I killed her mother and—'

'No!' Kate shuffled along the bench, moving in close so that his free arm automatically went around her, pulling her into his side.

'You didn't kill her, Marco.' She turned and caught

his beloved face between her hands. 'Or you would be banged up in jail,' she told him bluntly. 'What happened was a tragic accident.'

He shook his head, hugging her so close that she struggled to breathe and not even seeming to be aware of it. 'She got pregnant because she thought that's what I wanted. If she hadn't…well, she'd still be here. I was the catalyst and if I had paused to see that being what was convenient for me, I… None of this would have happened if I had noticed she was unhappy.'

The self-loathing in his voice made her heart ache.

'It's crazy to blame yourself, as crazy as your father-in-law blaming Freya. Bad things happen. You can't spend the rest of your life wearing a hair shirt, you're alive,' she said, pressing a hand to his chest, feeling his heart beat beneath her fingertips. 'And Freya is alive.'

'I love Freya.'

'I know you do,' she said, her eyes warm and loving on his face. She caught his hand between her own and froze as she let it go. 'You're not wearing your ring?'

He shook his head. 'I wore it to remind me that I didn't deserve to be happy, that I didn't deserve Freya's love, and then you…' He framed her face between his big hands and took a deep breath, looking like a man who was building himself up to take a leap into the unknown… Kate watched him, her heart thudding hard against her ribcage.

'A word not spoken can change the course of your life. There is a word I have not allowed myself to speak or hear or even believe existed… Has my moment gone?'

The agonised expression on his face bewildered and alarmed her. 'It depends on what the word is.'

'Love. You are exasperating, beautiful, you swept

into my life, changing it…me…for ever… I love you, Kate,' he said, giving voice finally to the words that he'd held in his heart. 'I cannot believe that I let you go because I was too much of a coward to speak. Is there any possibility that you still feel something for me…?'

A slow smile spread across her face. For Marco it was like the sun coming out.

She gave a crooked little smile the tears streaming down her face. 'I love you, Marco!' she cried joyously. 'You have no idea. I've missed you so much and…is this real?'

The kiss that went on and on proved that it was very real indeed.

'Coming up for air any time soon?'

Kate pulled away, though not too far, clinging to Marco as if she were afraid he'd vanish. 'Oh, Jake—this is Jake, my brother. Jake, this is Marco, my—'

'Future husband,' Marco inserted, nodding to Kate's brother. 'We have met.'

'Future husband…married? Should you not ask me first?'

'I'm asking you now.'

'In that case, yes, please.'

'Shall I go away?' Jake asked, and did, but the couple wrapped in each other's arms didn't notice.

EPILOGUE

KATE TWISTED TO get a look and see if the stand-up pearl-encrusted collar that framed her face was lying properly, high in the front, the contrasting low vee neckline at the back revealing the delicacy of her shoulder blades.

She had requested nothing that resembled a meringue and no train. The first wish had been granted—her dress was a column that spilled like a pool of warm ice at her feet.

The clever design made her feel taller and the ivory silk, one shade up on the colour chart than her skin tones, made her skin glow like a pearl.

Allowing for artistic over statement, Kate was happy with the results. She had a train, but it was short, and encrusted with pearls and finely embroidered wrens, which were the symbol of Renzoi.

'You look beautiful.'

She turned to find Marco looking gorgeous in black denim and an open-necked shirt, standing watching her, a half-smile on his face.

'It's unlucky to see the bride in her dress before the wedding,' she reproached sternly.

'We're already married, *cara*, and I'm happy to break tradition.'

Her expression softened into goofy adoration. 'Not technically.'

There had been no celebrant, but the vows they had exchanged in front of their family, Kate carrying a posy of daisies, and a few close friends in Dorset the previous week had been for them a special thing. It might have no legal standing that would come with the pomp and circumstance of the full bells-and-whistles royal wedding tomorrow, but they had considered themselves bonded for life from that moment.

'Thank you for doing that for me.' The royal wedding had not been optional, but Marco had known how much she was dreading it and had arranged, with the help of her mum, something that was just for her. The wild flowers in jam jars decorating the tables had been the thoughtful contribution of Lady Rosa, and the tandem with the big shiny bell was the Queen's gift, along with a new bicycle for the bridesmaid, their daughter.

'I was checking it still fits.' She pressed a hand to her stomach.

'And does it?'

She nodded. 'I won't show for ages yet.'

'Our secret. I like that. Keep the world out for as long as possible, or as long as Kate cannot blurt it out to everyone.'

'It still doesn't feel real. I don't know how it happened.'

His lips twitched. 'I think you should consider a planned caesarean.'

She pressed a finger to his lips. 'Let's just relax and enjoy this, take one step at a time and take medical advice…?'

He forced a smile. 'You're right.' His glance shifted to the box on the bed. 'Have you decided?'

Her mum had given her the box that contained everything she knew about Kate's birth parents she possessed.

She had handed a similar one to Jake and his search had not ended happily. Kate knew the same might happen to her.

'I'll open it now. Will you stay?'

'Of course, *cara*.'

He watched as Kate in her silk dress opened the lid as if all Pandora's secrets were about to rush out.

'There's not much here,' she said, picking up the few papers that were in it. A photo fluttered out from between the brown-edged papers.

Kate lifted it up, her eyes wide as she studied it.

'What is it? What is wrong?'

She handed him the photo of two babies.

'I think I have a twin, Marco, an identical twin.'

'Do you want to find her?'

'I don't know. I really don't know.'

'Well, when you decide I will be here for you, supporting you, you know that.'

Kate smiled and as always it took his breath away. 'I know that, and I hope my sister, wherever she is, has been as lucky as I am. Hold me, Marco.'

He did, and Kate knew that whatever happened, whatever decision she made, she was safe and loved.

* * * * *

COMING SOON!

MILLS & BOON®

Coming next month

RETURNING FOR HIS RUTHLESS REVENGE
Louise Fuller

As the door closed, the room fell silent, and just like that they were alone.

His heart was suddenly hammering inside his chest. So, this was it. He had imagined this moment so many times inside his head. Had thought of all the clever, caustic things to say, only now his mind was blank.

Not that it mattered, he thought, anger pulsing over his skin. Sooner or later, she was going to realize that he wasn't going to disappear this time.

Not until he'd got what he came for.

Her eyes locked with his. He felt his heart tighten around the shard of ice that had been lodged there ever since Dove had cast him into the wilderness.

She was staring at him in silence, and he waited just as he had waited in that hotel bar. Only this time, she was the one who didn't know what was happening. Didn't know that she was about to be chewed up and spat out. But she would, soon enough.

"What are you doing here, Gabriel?" Her voice was husky but it was hearing her say his name again that made his breathing jerk.

Continue reading
RETURNING FOR HIS RUTHLESS REVENGE
Louise Fuller

Available next month
www.millsandboon.co.uk

MILLS & BOON

THE HEART OF ROMANCE

A ROMANCE FOR EVERY READER

MODERN
Prepare to be swept off your feet by sophisticated, sexy and seductive heroes, in some of the world's most glamourous and romantic locations, where power and passion collide.

HISTORICAL
Escape with historical heroes from time gone by. Whether your passion is for wicked Regency Rakes, muscled Vikings or rugged Highlanders, awaken the romance of the past.

MEDICAL
Set your pulse racing with dedicated, delectable doctors in the high-pressure world of medicine, where emotions run high and passion, comfort and love are the best medicine.

True Love
Celebrate true love with tender stories of heartfelt romance, from the rush of falling in love to the joy a new baby can bring, and a focus on the emotional heart of a relationship.

Desire
Indulge in secrets and scandal, intense drama and plenty of sizzling hot action with powerful and passionate heroes who have it all: wealth, status, good looks…everything but the right woman.

HEROES
Experience all the excitement of a gripping thriller, with an intense romance at its heart. Resourceful, true-to-life women and strong, fearless men face danger and desire - a killer combination!

To see which titles are coming soon, please visit

millsandboon.co.uk/nextmonth

JOIN US ON SOCIAL MEDIA!

Stay up to date with our latest releases, author news and gossip, special offers and discounts, and all the behind-the-scenes action from Mills & Boon...

 @millsandboon

 @millsandboonuk

 facebook.com/millsandboon

 @millsandboonuk

It might just be true love...